D0560333

THE
AMETHYST ROAD

THE
AMETHYST ROAD

Louise Spiegler

CLARION BOOKS
New York

Clarion Books
a Houghton Mifflin Company imprint
215 Park Avenue South, New York, NY 10003
Copyright © 2005 by Louise Spiegler

The author acknowledges that some of the song lyrics at the opening of each chapter
are based on traditional songs and ballads that exist in the public domain.

The text was set in 12-point Minion Condensed.

www.houghtonmifflinbooks.com

Printed in the U.S.A.

Library of Congress Cataloging-in-Publication Data

Spiegler, Louise.
The amethyst road / by Louise Spiegler.
p. cm.
Summary: Having fled the city of Oestia after attacking an official, sixteen-year-old Serena—
an outcast as well as a mixed-race child of a Gorgio father and Yulang mother—
seeks to reunite her family and regain her honor.
ISBN 0-618-48572-4
[1. Self-realization—Fiction. 2. Family—Fiction. 3. Prejudices—Fiction. 4. Fantasy.] I. Title.
PZ7.S75434Ame 2005
[Fic]—dc22   2005004014

ISBN-13: 978-0-618-48572-7
ISBN-10: 0-618-48572-4

QUM 10 9 8 7 6 5 4 3 2 1

Dedicated, with love, to both my clans: the Spieglers and the Moores
and
In memory of Ora Lee Page Franklin

Even if the house falls down,
You're still the sweetest baby in town.
Say, darling, say . . .

—Paria lullaby

We are collectors.

Magpies, the Gorgios call us. They find their silver hidden away in our nests.

All my life I've heard that. To the Gorgios, all the Yulang are the same, from my mother's prosperous Kereskedo tribe, who amass great fortunes in trade, to the miserable Paria outcasts, among whom my sister and I were forced to live. All alike and all thieves, kidnappers, and worse.

It was hard not to believe it as I walked home through the Paria enclave, past collision shops and pawnbrokers, backroom psychics and overflowing trash bins. A gang of boys on the corner was digging a battery out of a long black sedan. When Willow and I first moved to this neighborhood, I would have assumed they were fixing the engine. But I quickly learned.

I crossed the street to our apartment building and rounded the corner to the front. Four flights of outdoor steps. It wasn't the climb so much as the people that made it a chore. I adjusted my book bag and started up. As always, on the landings and along the balconies I had to squeeze past Paria girls rocking their babies in packing-box cradles and boys gambling with peanut shells. No one sent a glance my way. I could always feel them not looking at me. One of the middle-aged women hanging laundry over the balcony rails threw me a curt greeting, and that was as much notice as I ever got.

Our front door was unlocked again. When would Willow learn to be more careful? When there was another break-in?

I pushed the door open and immediately tripped over a bag of beer bottles and lost my balance. Books spilled out of my school satchel as I crashed to the floor. My Romanae text slid into a puddle of blackberry jam.

My two-year-old niece, Zara, toddled over and burst into delighted laughter, as if I'd staged the performance just for her. She tried to clap but couldn't manage it, since she was clutching something in her fist. I held out my hand to her.

"What's in your paw, monster-girl? Show Auntie Reena."

It was an electric plug. Attached to a cord. Attached to a toaster.

"Who— What idiot let you play with this?"

I snatched the plug out of her blackberry-smeared fingers and carried the toaster to the kitchen counter. Zara howled with outrage.

"Willow!" I bellowed.

My sister was nowhere in sight, but two of her Gorgio friends were sprawled on our kitchen floor, fast asleep. I knew Alex, the one with the red hair and the wispy goatee. He was always here. The other I couldn't distinguish from any of Willow's other layabout friends. The two of them snored amid cups of cold coffee and plates littered with blackened crusts. That explained the floor-level toaster. An open bottle of hangover tablets lay at their feet. I picked it up and got down on my hands and knees to search for spilled pills.

While I was looking, I kept shouting, "Willow! Get out here! You need to clean up this mess!" She was probably in the bathroom, plucking her eyebrows or plaiting her hair.

The Gorgios snoozed on. They'd still been up drinking and reciting bad poetry to Willow when I left for school that morning, so it didn't surprise me that they were sleeping like the dead far into the afternoon.

I'd just found the last loose pill and shoved the cotton back in the bottle when Willow dragged herself to the doorway, wearing a lacy bathrobe. She yawned until I could see her molars and mumbled drowsily, "Give us mercy, Serena. What are you screaming for?"

Even with shadows under her eyes and curlers in her hair, my big sister looked like the lead dancer in a ballet troupe. It was that delicate, cat-shaped face of hers and the graceful way she moved. Usually I was proud of Willow's looks. Now all her fragile beauty just annoyed me.

I thrust the bottle of pills into her left hand and pointed at the toaster.

"That's what your baby's been playing with while you get your beauty sleep."

"Beauty sleep? You must be joking. She was wailing all morning, little beast." Willow placidly put the pills away in the cupboard over the sink, bent down, and poked her fingers into Zara's round belly. "Yes, you! You're a beast, aren't you?" She jerked her head toward the boys passed out on the floor. "It's Jet and Alex's fault, anyway. They promised they'd watch her while I napped."

"And they broke their promise? What a shock!" I glared at Willow. "They're here for the parties and the free crash pad, Willow. Not to babysit. I don't know why that confuses you so much."

Willow made a face and started spooning coffee into our dented brass coffeepot. "Spare me the lecture, Serena! Why are you always such a bear?"

"Why do you think? It was too loud last night, Willow! I had a Romanae test first thing this morning, and I could barely sleep. Someone could have strangled a cat in here and you'd never have heard it!"

3

"So? The louder the better." Willow placed the coffeepot on the burner and added softly, "I want to drown out those marchers. I don't want Zara to hear them."

"There weren't any White Shirts last night, Willow."

"There could have been. You never know when they'll come." Willow shuddered. "They frighten me—twirling those lightsticks, tossing bricks, chanting for us to get out!"

They scared me, too, the White Shirts bands who marched through our neighborhoods every once in a while, breaking windows and beating up anyone unlucky enough to be found out on the streets. But if I told Willow that I was frightened, too, the next thing I knew, we would have a full-time bodyguard of her admirers, and we would never rid the house of Gorgio boys. To me, that was worse than a few crazed fanatics in the street.

"That's just like you, Willow," I said airily. "You'll deal with the White Shirts by having more parties? Good thinking. They'll be shaking in their boots."

Zara had followed me into the kitchen and was leaning her head against my leg. I crouched down, cuddled her in my arms, and realized her diaper needed changing. As usual, Willow hadn't noticed. I went to the storage cupboard, pulled out the little ribbed blanket I had bleached until it was thin as tissue paper, and laid it down on the cracked linoleum by the diaper pail.

Willow was busy unrolling a pink curler from her hair. "When did you became so sarky, Serena? It must be that snotty school of yours."

"It's not snotty," I said, more to contradict Willow than anything. The Lyceum is the best school in Oestia. And it certainly *is* snotty. Who knew that better than me? I was the only Yulang student in the whole place, and I'd only been allowed to enroll because my Gorgio grandmother pulled some strings a long time ago.

"It is so snotty," Willow snapped back. "I don't know what's happened to you. You didn't used to study all the time. And you used to love parties."

That was true. I did. When our dad was alive, we had loads of people in and out of our home. Mother followed the Yulang traditions of hospitality, and Daddy, though a Gorgio, had taken to her easygoing ways. There had always been music, and games and food to share, and lots of other kids to play with.

But things were different after Daddy died. We were on our own. Mother left, and even our Gorgio grandmother, who had kept us on sufferance after Daddy's funeral, kicked us out once Willow's waist began to bulge—not that we'd brought friends to Grandmother's house, anyway. And now that Willow's unwed motherhood had set us outside any decent Yulang society, parties meant this gang of Gorgio boys sleeping off their beer on our mother's hooked rug and styling themselves the rebel poets. Rebelling against what? I had never been sure about that. Maybe against the burden of having a trust fund.

Willow was looking thoughtfully at the red-haired boy, who lay with his head flung back and his mouth hanging open. "Whatever you say, my friends aren't just here for the parties. And I think Alex sort of likes Zara. You know? He's really good with her."

I rolled my eyes. I'd never noticed him being good with Zara, aside from not offering her sips of his beer—a pastime that convulsed the others. It was just another of Willow's daydreams. She imagined that one of these boys who hung about drinking and swooning over the sound of his own voice was going to find life so unbearable without her and the baby that he would swoop them off to a life of luxury.

Willow caught my dubious look and added, "His family's very rich, you know. Alex's."

"And just dying for a Yulang daughter-in-law."

"Why not?" Willow held up her arm as if examining it for a rash. "I'm pretty fair. Not like you, Serena. I could pass. And just look at Zara."

I couldn't help looking at Zara, since I was trying to wrestle her wriggling bottom into a diaper. Zara was a china doll, all blue eyes and floating gold elf locks. The Gorgio boys teased Willow that we had kidnapped Zara and were bringing her up as our own. Sidesplitting, that was.

"Besides," Willow mooned, "Alex *likes* Yulang girls. He says we have more soul. Why else would he spend so much time here?"

Lately, it took about ten minutes of conversation with Willow for me to feel like smacking her, and my inner timer was just about to ring.

With Zara cleaned up and the old diaper disposed of, I went and changed out of my school uniform into a pair of charcoal gray trousers I wore for cleaning the apartment, and a long-sleeved shirt.

"I'm going to take Zara to the playground at Plaza Ridizio," I told Willow.

"Yay!" Zara squealed.

Willow was staring out the window, lost in thought, with Mother's blue moon cup in her hands.

"Did you at least pick up our money?" I asked her, spotting my old red sweater in a pile of clothes and pulling it over my head.

Willow broke out of her reverie. "I got it when I met the new social worker. Did I tell you? She's the mother of one of the girls in your class. The classy one, with the clothes. What's her name?"

"Janet Palmer?"

"That's it."

My heart sank. Janet's mother was our social worker. That meant she could quiz Willow about what cut of meat we were eating and what kind of underwear we bought and where we got Zara's diapers. She could come around any time she liked to examine Zara, like a judge inspecting a piglet at a county fair. They all did that. This time, though, because it was Mrs. Palmer, word would get around my school. And I was a freak of nature there already. . . .

"Well, hand over the money, Willow, and I'll pick up some groceries on the way."

I stuffed the banknotes into my pocket, gloomily.

For Zara's sake I tried to shake my bad mood as we set off along the balcony and back down the stairs. The Yulang believe that children Zara's age are purifying, like horses and beautifully wrought gold. You have to do your best by them, my mother always told me, no matter how you're feeling.

My heart squeezed, as it always did when I thought of Mother. She'd been gone almost three years. What would she say if she knew she had a two-year-old granddaughter?

Zara and I crossed the square in front of our building, heading north.

At least I knew Mother would say I was right to take Zara to a better playground than this little tramped-down square of grass in the Paria neighborhood, where the seesaw was broken and the sandpit was full of cigarette butts and the leavings of neighborhood cats. I wanted Zara to play where the sandbox was clean and the swings were new and the street cleaners and city gardeners took away the rubbish and planted flowers. But those places were almost always Gorgio places.

Except for Plaza Ridizio.

Plaza Ridizio is the dividing line here in Oestia between Yulang and Gorgio—who still don't live together, except in those rare cases like my parents', where love dissolves the boundaries.

From Plaza Ridizio, the Yulang neighborhoods run south to the industrial docks, broken up into tribal enclaves: the metalworkers and

mechanics, the traders, the musicians, the acrobats and animal train-
ers, and those, like the Parias, who catch as they can. As we walked past
the different neighborhoods, Zara pointed at the tribal amulets hanging from lampposts at the intersections, signs for the different dis-
tricts: King David's harp dangling from the lamps on the streets of
the Zimbali musicians, Hephaestus's hammer and anvil on the Ha'ari
metalworkers' streets, Fortuna's wheel for the Ammorine acrobats, and
the unblinking owls for the sharp-eyed Kereskedo merchants. Those
last I could never see without a pang, for the Kereskedo council had
confiscated all the owl amulets Mother had left us, and I'd never felt
our home was quite safe without them.

The Gorgio neighborhoods run north from the plaza. Instead of the
noisy docks, they have waterfront promenades, and instead of the
smell of the canneries, they have fresh salmon dinners on outdoor pa-
tios with views of the sun going down over the sound. My Gorgio
grandmother lives in a mansion on the north side of the city. Not that
we had been allowed to set foot there these past few years.

Despite these rigid divisions, at Plaza Ridizio everyone comes together. The Gorgio come to the outdoor market to buy the wares of
the Kereskedo Yulang and the crafts of the Jersain people, who are
neither Yulang nor Gorgio. And the Yulang come to window-shop at
the Gorgio emporiums that line the square and to spread their bright
picnic cloths on the grass. Children shriek on the carousel, students
argue on the edge of the fountain, and old men play chess at the tables under the trees. Yulang acrobats of the Ammorine tribe perform
in the open spaces and musicians of the Zimbali tribe play violins,
cymbaloms, and calliopes on the bandstand while the Kereskedo
merchants offer everything from mushrooms to gold at their stalls in
the open market.

As Zara and I threaded our way through the market, I saw a
Kereskedo woman smiling to herself as she measured out grams of yel-

low spice for a customer. My mother ran a stall once, and I remembered her smiling to herself just like that on a good selling day.

The memory quickly turned sour. If Mother ever returned, I thought, she would hardly smile at seeing what Willow and I had made of ourselves. More likely, she'd die of shame when she learned that a ritual court, under the hand of Nico Brassi, bora chan of the Kereskedo tribe, had declared Willow outcast—*ma'hane*—once her baby started to swell her belly. And that I also fell outcast, by association.

I turned quickly away from the Kereskedo stalls and took Zara to the fountain, where we knelt to cast in good-luck pennies.

Someone was watching us.

I turned and saw a tight-skinned Gorgio woman standing behind us, regarding us with narrow, unfriendly eyes. Quickly, I rose to my feet.

"What a beautiful child," the woman said. The words were all right, but her voice curdled as she spoke them.

"Thank you."

Zara was still squatting by the fountain. I pulled her up to stand next to me. She had to know, even from babyhood, to be on her feet when they approached her like this. She had to know to face them.

"Is she yours?" the woman pursued.

"She's my niece," I said, hating that I answered the woman at all. Hating that I didn't tell her to stick her skinny nose into a light socket and flip the switch.

The woman's pale eyes caught mine, wishing me twice whatever I wished her.

"Funny. She doesn't look like you."

She knelt down beside Zara and held out something to her. It was a stick of lacquered sugar that glistened green and red and shiny as the paint on the carousel horses.

Zara hesitated a moment. Then her plump little hand reached out.

9

"A darling like you should have treats and pretty clothes all the time," the woman cooed. "Poor little thing. You need someone to take care of you."

"She *has* someone to take care of her!" I snapped.

The woman was squatting and I was standing. How easy it would have been to kick her right in the teeth! Instead, I scooped Zara up in my arms and bore her away. My little niece squawked in protest, and then, in toddler fashion, forgot about it and wrapped her arms about my neck.

They steal our children, I'd heard the Gorgio women twittering as they waited to pick up their kids at the gates of my school. *They steal our golden-haired angels and trek them out of town in their filthy Yulang caravans. You can't be too careful.*

I led Zara to the carousel and held her on the back of a chestnut mare with a mane the color of cooked sugar. The horse rose and fell as though swimming across a calm river, and Zara crowed with glee. As the carousel revolved, I scanned the plaza for the woman who'd given her the candy.

"Serr-rena! Auntie Reena! Na Na!" Zara sang. I gave her a quick smile and kept searching.

If the woman was still around, we would have to leave. They are not unheard of, these "rescues." The Gorgios see a child they don't believe belongs in a Yulang family, and next thing you know, they've snatched her away and taken her to a Prevention of Cruelty to Children office. Then the child is gone for good, and soon some Gorgio woman who can't have a child of her own kindly adopts the poor, underprivileged little wight. And the real family never sees their child again.

The woman seemed to be gone. But I couldn't rest easy. It isn't safe for Zara here, I thought. We should leave.

But why? I thought angrily. Why should we have to? It was only four o'clock. Willow's foolish suitors (if only they were suitors!) would still be lounging about the apartment. Wasn't there somewhere else we could go?

I looked longingly across the road at Bardoff's Music Store. If I hadn't had Zara with me, I could have gone there to watch old Ren Bardoff, the master carver, shape the stem of a viola. His daughter, Lemon, might show me a tune on the violin. We'd share a cup of that odd, fragrant tea they drank.

But I couldn't go in a place like that with Zara—a place full of finely carved instruments she could break, and sheet music she could shred to confetti! Not that the Bardoffs would object to her. They were sharp businesspeople, but kind. And Lemon had a way with children. Still, I liked this family of Jersain craftsmen too much to put them to the trouble.

Why couldn't Willow take Zara out more? I fumed. Zara would be safer with her. Anyone could see Willow was her mother. Why should I have to do everything? I wasn't the one who'd had a fatherless baby! I wasn't the one up all night partying! It wasn't fair.

"Of course it isn't fair. But you're tough, Serena."

I whirled around. Beneath the hurdy-gurdy music of the carousel, it was my father's voice I heard. He was there and not there, as he had been several times before.

"So I'm tough," I grumbled (but under my breath, not wanting anyone to hear me conversing with a ghost). "So what? What about Willow? Why can't she be tough sometimes?"

My father laughed that gentle laugh of his. "Willow was well named."

Willow. Graceful tree. Weeping tree. Tree that bends in the slightest wind. Tree of the loving touch, the easy persuasion.

"And what about me, Daddy?" I shot back. "Serena, the serene and peaceful. Was I well named, too?"

For an instant, I could actually see him standing next to Zara on her chestnut mount. His much-loved, freckled Gorgio face was as clear to me as the strip of sunlight that fell across the brass pole. He threw back his head and laughed. And was gone.

The carousel slowed to a stop. We stepped down and I let Zara pull me over to the sandbox. She grabbed the nearest plastic shovel and started digging a hole, her brow furrowed in a look of serious endeavor. Her blue sweater set off her blond hair like bluebells next to buttercups.

Across the square, I watched afternoon strollers settling at the outdoor café tables like flocks of gorgeous birds. Women in skirts of sea green and sunset gold lit gracefully on wrought-iron chairs. A smell of roasted peppers and smoked fish drifted toward us from the servers' trays. Up on the bandstand, I could see a trio of Zimbali Yulang musicians setting up their instruments.

Suddenly, Zara gave a sharp cry.

I leapt off the bench, heart pounding.

It was nothing. A little girl in a lacy dress had pinched her because Zara was using her shovel. The girl's mother wagged her finger in Zara's face. "That's not yours," she scolded. And then, noticing me, "Do they teach you to steal before you're out of the cradle?"

"Don't tell me your little girl never took another kid's toy," I exclaimed indignantly.

Without waiting for her response, I took the shovel from Zara and threw it to the ground, then dragged Zara to the other side of the sandbox.

"Well, look who's here! Serena Wallace—babysitting again."

Janet Palmer stood on the little path that wound around the playground, watching us critically. She was wearing a slim black dress ornamented with white leaf patterns. Bootsy, her dachshund, barked and

12

wriggled at the end of a black suede leash. Mother Lillith! Had she seen that humiliating exchange?

It depressed me, in my charity-shop sweater, to see Janet in that elegant dress, with nothing to concern her but her yapping dog.

"What are you doing here?" I asked, less than politely.

Janet raised a plucked eyebrow. "Declining Romanae verbs, of course. I make a point of promenading around the plaza when I've got a batch of them to decline."

"Really?" I smiled faintly, despite myself. "I declined them already. They must have come to you looking for a second chance."

Janet was the only student from the Lyceum I ever made jokes with. We were friends of a sort, even though I knew she would never ask me to her house, and if her other friends showed up, our jokes would evaporate and I'd find myself left out once again.

"What about you, Serena? Toting mewling infants in your golden teenage years?"

"It's better than yanking that silly beast around," I said, pointing at her dachshund.

"I've got a word game," Janet said. "What's the collective noun for dachshunds? A herd? A kennel?"

I looked at Bootsy, who was yapping fit to snap his little vocal chords. "A dissonance?" I suggested. "Or maybe a dribble? At least Zara will grow up someday. You'll be pulling Bootsy out to piddle until the day he dies."

Janet eyed her dog dispassionately. "You're right. It's loathsome when you think about it. And your niece *is* fairly cute, when you consider the common run of humanity." Her gray eyes rested on me with slight compassion. "Poor Serena, you get lumbered with her a lot, don't you? What's wrong with Willow? She's not bedridden or anything."

Poor Serena! No wonder Janet's friends didn't invite me to their skating parties and dances. Who wanted a baby tagging along? And no wonder none of the neighborhood Yulang kids wanted me, either. Yulang teenagers love babies. They even love little half-Gorgio babies, if there's a proper marriage. But a little play-child, as the Yulang say, like Zara? Never.

I hugged Zara close, then let her go, thinking of Willow with a bitterness as raw as horseradish. "Willow's too busy partying with those stupid poet boys," I burst out. "Keeping herself lovely for them while I cart Zara around. Stupid thing! She can't see how useless they are. All they do is guzzle beer and impress themselves. Do you know I found Zara—"

"Where? In the laundry machine?" Janet drawled, regarding Zara with a mock serious expression. "Your mama should take better care of you, baby."

I should take better care. That was the trouble with Janet. I started talking to her and I forgot things. Such as, Janet's mother was our new social worker. And the less you told a social worker, the better.

"Poetical boys laying siege to Willow and Serena all night every night," Janet continued. "What a bohemian life you lead! I had no idea. . . ."

"It's not 'all night every night'!" I said quickly. "Just once in a while, when there's a party. Don't tell me that never happens at your house."

Janet jerked Bootsy into a walk. Zara and I drifted along with her. "Only when dear Mama and Papa go away on business. More's the pity." Envy blazed in her eyes as clear as the sun. "It must be *heaven* not to be on anyone's leash. Mother tells me Willow is your guardian, but we all know what a joke that is!"

I fell back, my face burning. *Mother tells me.* What did Janet and her mother think of us? Were we a fascinating case? Quaint? Or just pathetic?

Still, a warm pulse beat within me. Janet envied me. Envied my freedom.

She walked along ahead of us, sinuous in her black dress, her hair so pale as to verge on white. I felt shabby beside her. Janet didn't look a bit like a schoolgirl, but then she never had—not even in her school uniform. Men reading newspapers on the benches glanced up as she passed. No one scolded her to scoop up the offerings Bootsy dropped on the sidewalk.

Zara was flagging. She was even limping a little. I knew she was tired, but I didn't want to go home yet, especially now that I had someone to talk to, so I lifted her up into my arms.

But in a moment, I regretted that I'd stayed, for Janet had led us across the square, nearly to the outdoor café by the bandstand. What if she chose a table and sat down, expecting us to sit with her? I panicked. It would never cross Janet's mind that I couldn't afford a place like this. Servers would descend with clinking crystal and clanking silver—and Zara and I would never escape without becoming the butt of one of Janet's witty stories!

I half turned, as if to actually run away. But, to my relief, Janet only leaned against a lamppost near the bandstand, watching the musicians with a remote, calculating look on her face.

I drew a breath and loosened my clenched grip on Zara. How ridiculous I was! So what if Janet had sat down at a table in the café? Couldn't I have just told her I had to get Zara home? And why did I get so paranoid when I let slip that stuff about Willow and her all-night parties? What did I think? That Janet would take my words back to her mother and convince her we were unfit to care for Zara? Not likely. That required passion. I couldn't see Janet ruffling herself on our account.

I relaxed. The sunlight was dazzling through the leaves and bouncing off the shards of colored glass embedded in the asphalt. The first dusting of autumn bronze had just touched the trees. I watched as women vied with each other in elegant walking dresses, hats, and gloves. Waiters carried trays of aperitifs and carafes of sparkling wine from the little café under the clock tower. Everyone chatted and drank, rated each other's outfits, and waited for the first strains of the Zimbali band.

I edged closer to the bandstand. There wasn't a single Yulang tribe that didn't play music of some sort, but the Zimbali did it for a living. They were true artists, and much admired. Whenever my mother had wanted to compliment someone's playing, she told them they were "cora-Zimbali": just like a real musician.

As I watched the musicians, I felt Zara slip her hand into the collar of my sweater and pull out my necklace. As she often did, she began turning it, the better to examine the twenty finely worked charms that hung from the chain. Each one was a different animal, each a wonder of metalworking.

I loved that necklace. It was all I had of sparkle and glamour, and all I had of my mother any longer. She had given it to me when Daddy was still alive and there was still laughter in her, and delight in lovely things. I thought of her as she was then. She would have reveled in this golden autumn afternoon, and wanted me to show off my ornaments like any other girl at Plaza Ridizio.

Zara counted off the charms until she found her favorite.

"Cat!" she crowed.

I hugged her with pleasure. "Do you hear what the musicians are playing, love?"

It was "The Rising Road," a song my mother used to sing when we went berry picking in the mountains. *Yulang road songs are always happy,* she'd say, laughing, *and the love songs are always sad. See why the Gorgios think we're crazy?*

I started to tell this to Janet, but she cut me off.

"Do you know that violinist?"

Like most Gorgios, Janet assumed the Yulang all knew each other. They never understood the different tribes. Janet had no idea that I was Kereskedo and wouldn't be familiar with people from the musician tribe. Although, when my family still traveled, we'd once shared a campfire with a Zimbali band. It was a Zimbali boy who first taught me to play the violin. But we'd moved to the city and begun to live among the Gorgios, and I'd encountered hardly any Zimbali folk since.

I squinted at the trio. The musicians wore felt hats with small feathers and good-luck coins in the brims, and vests over their shirts, as most Zimbali did. The violinist Janet asked about was a tall boy, maybe eighteen years old, with big, uncertain hands and a look of diffidence about him. He kept glancing nervously at the other musicians as he scraped his bow.

It almost made me laugh to see how clearly—how desperately!—he wished he were somewhere else.

Soon I wished he were somewhere else, too. He was a terrible musician! I squinted at him in displeasure. How could this be? The melody of "The Rising Road" is lovely and bright, and as simple as you please. I could play it on my old violin with my eyes shut, standing on one foot. To have a Zimbali fiddler mangle it was downright embarrassing!

Maybe you don't think the Gorgios can tell, I thought, but *I* hear you, Jal. You should go home and practice!

"Well?" Janet jabbed her thumb into my ribs. "Do you?"

"Do I what? Know him? I've never seen him before. Why?"

"Because I want to know him, of course. I want to be introduced."

Zara was getting heavier by the minute, but when I tried to put her down, she whimpered. So I jostled her higher in my arms.

"Why would you want that?" I glanced at the two older men in the band and caught their grimaces as the violinist hit a false note. "I'm sure those two up there must wish they had never met him!"

"Oh, Serena, don't be an idiot," Janet drawled. "Don't you see how good-looking he is?"

I gave the boy another glance. Tall. Nice eyes. Nice face. So what?

"He's handsome, and good luck to him," I allowed. "But what a rotten musician!"

"Who cares about music?" Janet said, in such a deadpan way that I broke up laughing.

"You'd never be a Yulang girl," I told her. "If a man can't turn his hand to what he's supposed to do, we don't bother with him, no matter what his face looks like."

"I'm not interested in what Yulang girls do. Yulang boys are another matter."

"He won't talk to you." I was surprised to find myself stung.

"Sure he will." Janet was unperturbed. "Here. Let me hold Zara for a minute."

Zara was breaking my arm at this point, so I passed her to Janet without thinking twice.

"Okay," Janet whispered to Zara. "Do something cute."

"You aren't going to sink that low!"

Bootsy gave a jealous yelp as Janet plopped Zara on the ground next to him. "That's right, Zara! Play with Bootsy. . . . Bootsy, look at Zara's cute little shoes. Show Serena how you can pull them off."

Janet's dog nipped the toe of Zara's shoe between his teeth and began to pull.

Zara shrieked with laughter as the little dog worried the shoe and yanked to get it off her foot. I was embarrassed at the commotion. But no one else seemed to mind. People turned and smiled at the tiny dog playing with the tiny girl. Janet knelt down beside them and in two minutes she'd achieved her purpose. She'd distracted the violinist. His playing got so bad that the old man on the double bass looked as if he was ready to bash him with his bow.

Janet kept laughing at Bootsy's antics, like a doting young mother, while I watched her with a mixture of admiration and disgust.

By now, Bootsy had both of Zara's shoes off and was working on her mismatched socks. The green sock came off in no time flat. But the purple one stuck.

Then Bootsy really started tugging, and suddenly Zara's laughter turned into a high-pitched scream of pain.

"Your stupid dog bit her!" I grabbed Bootsy by the collar and flung him across the pavement.

"Hey!" Janet shrieked. "You can't do that to my dog!"

But I didn't care about Janet or her dog now that I'd seen what had made Zara scream. A large white bandage was taped to the bottom of her foot, and part of the tape had attached itself to the sock. When Bootsy yanked the sock off, he had ripped off the bandage as well. I sat down on the pavement and pulled Zara into my lap, turning her foot to examine it.

On the delicate little instep a proud, puffed-up circle of flesh surrounded a reddish crater. Zara curled her toes and struggled to get her foot out of my hands.

I felt sick and stupid as I looked at the wound.

But it was Janet who named it.

"Isn't that a cigarette burn, Serena? Who's been putting out their smokes on Zara?"

Two sisters walked by the river's brim,
And the older, she pushed the younger in.
—Gorgio ballad

I've never known anything like the rage I felt as I barreled home with Zara clutched in my arms. It was as though I were running through a tunnel of fire. The flames licked closer and the world shrank as they closed in.

Zara was the only reason the flames didn't burn me up altogether. For her sake, I managed to look where I was going, to cross with the lights, and to steer myself around oncoming strangers.

I avoided the broad boulevards. There were more police patrolling there, and in the state I was in, they would certainly look twice at me and Zara. They might even stop us. Instead, I cut off into the teeming Yulang neighborhoods. We complained that the cops were never there when we needed them, but now it was a relief to enter the tangle of old streets knowing that no policeman was walking the beat.

It wasn't long, however, before I remembered why I usually avoided this particular neighborhood.

I'd entered the Kereskedo district, home base for my mother's tribe. Trucks blocked the narrow alleys, loading and unloading. Boxes and crates cluttered the sidewalks. The Kereskedo were usually out on the road, so these houses existed mostly to show off their wealth. They gleamed with cut glass and refracting aluminum, as showy as the gold coins our women weave into their hair and the embroidered vests our men wear. Our! The Kereskedo were supposed to be our people. But in one of these proud houses their men had met in solemn counsel and cast us out: a formal tribunal under the hand of Nico Brassi, the bora chan, the big man, of the Kereskedo tribe.

And there he was, sitting on his stoop in that studied attitude of laziness affected by the really successful Kereskedo traders. They like to give out that they are so rich they don't have to lift a finger all day long, no matter how hard they really work.

He was cracking pistachios between his teeth and spitting the shells on the sidewalk, for the women of his household to clean up later. In my hurry to pass him, I skidded on the shells and nearly pitched over.

"Take care, Jalla!" he said pleasantly. "No need to crush the wee'n."

But when I met his eyes, his smile evaporated like mist in the sun.

The tribunal had met fully two years before. No one had paid me much heed during the proceedings, sitting in the shadows holding Willow's infant while the men grilled her, and I knew I had changed since I was fourteen. But the blankness that settled over Nico Brassi's features told me that he remembered me. I was the sister of one who had brought shame on the Kereskedo.

Looking straight at me, he popped a pistachio into his mouth. The shell he spat whizzed past my cheek.

I swallowed the curse ready to fly from my lips and bury itself in his ear.

Always treat our tribe with respect, Mother had often told me. *You never know when you'll need their protection.*

It wasn't respect that stopped me from cursing Nico Brassi. It was self-preservation.

With all the dignity I could muster, I slowed my gait and rounded the next corner.

But once out of Brassi's sight, I ran. With Zara clinging hot to my neck, I pressed on, through streets that became more cluttered with trash, more full of blacked-out windows and condemned buildings, until finally I was in my own neighborhood.

A big white trident was chalked on the wall of the handball court. It had been there ever since the White Shirts had marched. I covered Zara's eyes with my hand. Of course she'd seen the graffiti before. And of course she was too young to know that the trident meant hatred— hatred of us. But to a little girl with a cigarette burn on her foot, isn't any hatred too much?

My mind flew back to Nico Brassi. If this were his neighborhood, the stupid trident would have been painted over already. The Kereskedo wouldn't let such a thing remain for their children to see. They threw stones at the White Shirts when they marched. Sometimes they organized people from other tribes to help drive the marchers out.

These Paria tribespeople couldn't even organize a can of paint.

It was Willow's fault! All Willow's! I thought. This squalid neighborhood. The cruddy apartment. The creeps she let into it. Who had burned Zara? When? Had Willow even been home? How could she have allowed it to happen?

I took the steps two and three at a time, so anxious to get home that I nearly broke my key in the lock. I didn't care which of the poets I got my hands on. They were all responsible, as far as I could see.

Zara was whimpering in my arms. I yanked out the key and kicked the door open. It slammed back against the wall.

But the apartment was still as the grave. Carefully, I lowered Zara into her playpen.

I tried to calm down. There was no one here to punish, desperately as I wanted to punish someone. I'd forgotten to buy groceries, and I knew Zara must be hungry. I had to put aside my anger and focus on Zara.

But when I opened the nearly bare refrigerator, the rage erupted, and nothing I could do would shove it back down inside me.

I slammed the refrigerator shut, picked up one of our spindly chairs, and hurled it against the wall. My foot crashed into the tower of beer cans constructed by one of the bone-lazy poets. I grabbed the coffee cup Willow had left on the counter and flung it against the wall, where it shattered. It was Mother's—the blue moon pattern that she collected at street fairs. The pounding of my heart was beginning to slow, but my hand was already around the neck of a half-empty beer bottle and I was aiming it at the window.

Then a high-pitched sound pierced through my crashing and cursing. Zara was standing in her playpen, howling like an injured dog, her eyes wide and flat as buttons.

With enormous effort, I put the beer bottle back onto the ledge.

"Shh, darling, shh . . ." I leaned down and hoisted Zara out of the pen, cuddling her in my arms, kissing her hair.

Closing my eyes, I breathed in the smell from the top of Zara's head. It had not changed since the very first time I had rocked her in my arms. Her smell was the pure smell of innocence: new-baked bread, cakes in the oven, vanilla, rainwater. I held her close until she cried herself quiet, letting her solid warmth calm the storm within me.

Then I took her to the bathroom and washed the wound on her foot as gently as I could. Though inflamed and tender, the burn was not infected. That was a relief. Not only for Zara's sake but because I wouldn't have to call a doctor.

I righted the furniture and found Zara an egg and some applesauce for dinner. I bathed her and put her to bed in the room I shared with my sister. Then I cleaned up the cans and took the money out of my pocket, leaving it on the counter for Willow. She could at least do the shopping tomorrow, I thought. It wasn't as if she had anything else to do—except perhaps make sure no one jammed a lighted cigarette into her daughter's foot! You'd think that wouldn't be too much to ask of her.

I tried to start my homework. The grade scribbled across the top of my Romanae test seemed hardly to belong to me. It seemed years ago that I'd been pleased to get it.

I worked for an hour or two and must have drifted off to sleep, for I was facedown in my books when I heard the click of a key in the lock. The door opened halfway and stopped. No one entered. Only my sister's giggle wafted into the apartment.

I could see her through the half-opened door. The bulb that hung over the doorway rimmed her slender body with a glow against the black sky. My sister from outer space. She wore a dress I'd never seen before; a thin, clinging emerald silk, as elegant as any in the fancy department stores. More elegant. It had the air of being one of a kind. Where in the world had she gotten it?

I squinted. Her hair was woven into a knot of braids at the back of her head, and a circlet of gold shone at her throat. For a chill moment I wondered if she was really there, or if she was a glimmer from a different reality—like one of those crazy visions that Mother used to have, and that I must have inherited to some degree, I realized, since I could have discussions, now and again, with my dead father.

Was this a Willow living a life of privilege? The Willow she might have become if she hadn't floundered into motherhood and exiled us here among the Parias?

No. My stomach growled and I knew I was flatfooted in the present moment. Willow had come by her finery in some more or less sordid way. I got up and opened the door to the pantry. A row of wizened little apples sat there unappetizingly; I picked one up and bit it.

"No, I can't! Really!" Willow's voice drifted in. "I've been away too long already. Zara might need me. And it wouldn't be fair on Serena." Then a mock horrified laugh. "Oh, you are wicked!"

A young man's voice whispered, eager and coaxing.

I took the apple back to the table and sat down, waiting impatiently for Willow's date to disappear so I could grill her about Zara. There would have to be some changes made here—that was for sure.

"All right." Willow sounded out of breath. "I promise. If it's just for a day or two . . . As long as someone can watch Zara . . . Maybe Serena, after all . . ."

Then her arms went up, reaching for the boy's neck, and the whole top of her body was eclipsed in shadow. It was a long, murmuring moment, and I watched it with clinical dislike. A true Kereskedo girl would never act like this. I remembered the obsessive modesty of the women of Mother's tribe from our traveling days: their long dresses, their downcast eyes. Maybe they had been right, that court, when they branded Willow *ma'hane*. She was so shameless, so hungry for attention all the time, like a cat rolling on the pavement, begging to be stroked. Was it because we were part Gorgio? Janet's friends at school often behaved like that. Though I couldn't imagine our dad would have tolerated it, Gorgio or not.

Finally, Willow slid back down onto her heels. She lifted a hand to wave, and I could hear the sound of the boy's boots heading off along the balcony. Then she sighed happily and stepped into the apartment.

When she looked up and saw me glaring at her, she nearly jumped out of her skin.

But a foolish smile chased away her shock. She looked like Cinderella running into a girlfriend at the prince's ball, just busting with her own good fortune. She practically pirouetted across the room.

Angry as I was, there was something unbearably fragile about the wonder in her eyes and the excited glow in her cheeks. It was as if Zara's birth and the judgment of the tribunal had left no mark on her. She clasped my wrists in her hands, and my heart softened toward her against my will.

"Where've you been?" My voice was not nearly as harsh as it should have been.

"Everywhere! You won't believe what happened, Serena! Alex said he didn't want to share me anymore. Not for one more moment! He must have been planning tonight for ages. Look at this dress!"

She let go of my wrists and twirled about. The skirt of the dress billowed splendidly, like a dancer's costume. Even under our murky light-bulbs, the silk caught an underwater shimmer. Threads of blue and turquoise flickered in its emerald sheen.

"Serena, you'll never guess where he took me. The café at Plaza Ridizio. Remember how we used to go walking there with Mama in the afternoons? Watching the ladies and deciding who was wearing the most beautiful dress? This time I was one of the ladies...."

"And wearing the most beautiful dress." I had to grant that much.

Willow ran her hands lovingly down the skirt of the gown.

"Have you ever seen anything lovelier?" Her deep blue eyes held mine. "He had it *made* for me, Serena. By his mother's seamstress. Do you realize what that means? It means he must have *asked his mother* to have it made. What does that tell you? You, who are always jibing that none of their families would welcome a Yulang daughter-in-law!"

Sometimes when Willow talks to me, I want to put rocks on my feet to anchor them, or I'll float up into the stratosphere with her. I'll tell myself she's not what the tribunal said, just weak and desperate for love—or maybe not sharp enough—any excuse I can think of.

I steeled my heart. But before I could force the conversation on to who had hurt Zara, Willow was off again at double speed.

"He wants to take me out to his family's summer cottage in the mountains. He wants to *introduce me to the family*—I'm sure of it. What do you think of that, sourpuss?" She dropped a kiss on the top of my head to undo this barb and flitted about the room, unscrewing her earrings. She was as light as a hummingbird riding the wind. Her words were moonlit moths, iridescent bubbles.

But in my mouth the bubbles turned to ball bearings. "And I suppose he'll introduce Zara to his illustrious family at the same time?"

Willow came down on the flats of her feet. "Don't be so cross about it, Serena. You know Zara would ruin everything for me! Couldn't you be an angel and look after her?" Her pansy blue eyes appealed to me, wide and innocent. At the look I shot back, she faltered. "I realize how selfish it sounds, believe me. But I wouldn't do it if I didn't think it was for Zara's good."

"How is it for her good, Willow?"

She sat down at the table with me and leaned forward on her elbows. "Of course it would be for Zara's good if Alex wanted to marry me. It would solve all our problems."

"Marry you?" I hated the horsy bray in my voice. I hated that I always had to be the one with the bad news. But more than any of that, I hated Willow's simpleminded smile and her acres of ignorance. "Whose problems would it solve if Alex married you? Not Zara's, anyway. Not if Alex is the one stubbing out his cigarettes on her feet."

"Alex didn't do that!"

I stared at her, unable to believe my ears. So she knew what had happened to Zara! Somehow, I had assumed she didn't—because surely it would have upset her? She would have told me about it? She'd have been angry? Wouldn't she?

"Who was it, then?"

"That guy who was hanging around a day or two ago." Not Alex, anyway, her impatient voice told me.

I could have throttled her. "What was the guy's name?"

"Yuri something. Does it matter? He's not likely to come back. And it wasn't intentional anyway...."

I tried to keep my voice low. "How do you know it wasn't intentional?"

"He dropped a lit cigar. It grazed Zara's foot. Just an *accident*, Serena. What's wrong with you? Why do you see the worst in everyone?"

"Did you see it happen, Willow? This little accident?"

"No!" Willow's face was flaming. She glared at me and I glared back. "Alex told me," she said, looking down at the ads from the morning paper, which littered her side of the table.

I jumped up and swept them onto the floor. "You're an idiot, Willow! Are you listening? You're worse than an idiot. You just don't want to know, do you? Zara's got a perfect round hole burned into her skin. Deep, Willow. How can that be an accident? How can that be from a cigar grazing her? Who ever heard of a cigar grazing someone's foot? Have you even bothered to look at it?"

"Of course I've looked at it!" Willow yelled back. "Zara's my baby. Don't you think I love her? I do, no matter how much you cluck at me if I so much as forget to change a diaper! I'm sick of you disapproving of me all the time. You can't expect me to give up my whole life just because I had a baby!"

I leaned closer until there wasn't a finger's breadth between our faces.

"Maybe you should have thought of that a long time ago," I whispered.

Willow recoiled as though I'd slapped her. Then she began to cry.

"How can you be so awful?" she hiccuped. "On the happiest day of my life! You're getting more Yulang every day—always judging! Just like those horrible men on the court—and their witchy wives! I wouldn't be surprised if you tried to put the Evil Eye on me!"

I had only spoken the truth, even if it was spoken in anger. But Willow is the kind of person for whom the truth is always too hard. I looked at her ruefully. If only my sister could see things for what they really were! I thought. If only she could see herself....

I sighed and reached out a hand to stroke her hair. In a moment I would have been comforting her. But then came a sudden, loud knock on the door.

Willow jumped out of her chair with a transparent look of relief. Again her prince had come.

"It's probably Alex...." She stumbled against the table leg in her eagerness. I jumped up, too, and caught her by the wrist.

"Tell him to go home. I haven't finished talking with you."

Willow tried to yank her arm away, but I was stronger. I always had been.

She brought her face up to mine. "Serena, if you don't let go, I'll scream. *Then* see if you can get rid of him."

I held fast to her arm. "Tell him to come back tomorrow. We have to talk about Zara. I haven't promised to look after her for you yet, have I?"

The knock came again, even louder. An imperious knock.

Willow gave me an angry look. But she needed me if she was going to waltz off into the sunset with her prince. "All right," she muttered. "At least let me answer the door like a civilized person."

I let her go. She turned the knob and opened the door. But Alex, with his poetic goatee and expensive ripped jeans, was not in evidence.

Mrs. Palmer stood under the naked lightbulb.

You have two fine beaten swords,
And I but a pocket-knife.
—Ammorine fighting song

She was even more elegant and icy than I remembered from school awards nights; a lot like Janet, but older, calcified. Beside her was a big man in a shiny gray suit. His face was bland, his suit was bland, and his hair, shaved close to his skull, was no particular color. He was the kind of man who would have no smell if you got close to him.

I stared at the two of them, feeling the small hairs along the nape of my neck stand up, as if someone cold and invisible, a ghost, had passed behind me and grazed my back.

I was suddenly aware of every inch of our apartment, every millimeter of our skin and clothing. Through the Gorgios' eyes, I could see the trash bags stuffed with empty beer bottles, the scattered newspapers, the brown coffee stain on the wall, the diaper boxes doubling as lamp tables. I saw me in my unraveling red sweater, with my wild, uncombed hair, long and dark and straggling. I saw my mistrustful eyes. I knew that to them I looked shifty and secretive, and even the beauty spot on my cheek, which I'd had since birth, confirmed something awful in their minds.

Worse, I knew that to them Willow was no beautiful princess with a streak of bad judgment: she was a ward of the state decked out in shameless, expensive finery, doubtless paid for from the public purse.

"May we come in?" In Mrs. Palmer's mouth, it wasn't a question.

She was wearing a camel-hair blazer with turquoise gloves and a tailored skirt. Her name was printed on a little tag pinned to her blouse. I imaged she had just left a meeting, or some kind of fundraising dinner. Funds to help the deserving poor, of course. Not government leeches like us.

"Of course," Willow said. "Come in."

My eyes flew to hers, trying to telegraph a warning. But it was too late. The Gorgios had already crossed our threshold.

Why was Willow so foolish? Didn't she know anything? *Never* invite them in! Especially not a man whose name—whose *purpose*—you don't even know! There's power in keeping them on the other side of a doorway.

But Willow can't think like that. She's a stone skipper. She'll jump from rock to slippery rock before she notices she's in the middle of a raging river.

Neither of our visitors moved to sit down. The man was taking a quick inventory with his eyes, counting the windows and doors, placing the sink and the stove.

Mrs. Palmer folded her arms. "Do you know why I'm here, Willow?"

Willow shook her head, blank and frightened.

The social worker regarded her with distaste. "Ah, the little girl lost. That plays well with men, my dear. As I'm sure you know." Her tone sharpened. "But don't waste it on me!"

Willow colored. "What brings you here so late, Mrs. Palmer?"

"Are you sure you don't know?"

Willow shook her head again.

Mrs. Palmer pursed her lips in exasperation. "Well, if you don't know why I've dragged myself over at this ridiculous hour, Willow, I can assure you your sister does!"

The brush of the ghost against my back again made me shiver.

"I can assure you I *don't*," I retorted.

Mrs. Palmer's eyes flickered over me, quick and cold as a snake's tongue. "No? But you must, Serena. Why else did you show the child's wound to Janet?"

I froze.

Willow turned to me, gaping, panic and disbelief in her eyes. In one bottomless moment, I knew what was coming. It glimmered before me, a certainty, inescapable as the drop at the edge of a waterfall.

To Willow, I was no longer her strong, reliable, cranky sister. With those words of Mrs. Palmer's, I had suddenly become something else.

Passionately, I wanted to throw my arms around Willow and beg her to believe I hadn't betrayed her. I hadn't! Really, I hadn't!

Not intentionally.

"I never showed Janet anything of the sort," I said as haughtily as I could. I recognized the cadence of my grandmother's voice leaving my mouth. My father's mother might have given me nothing resembling love, but she did give me one gift: this entitled, *offended* tone that the Gorgio never expect to hear from Yulang lips.

Mrs. Palmer measured me with her eyes. Her voice slid down an octave. "It's no use, Serena. You can deny all you want, but Janet is an unbiased witness. She said it was clearly abuse."

"An unbiased witness!" I snorted. "A Gorgio witness, you mean. I hadn't heard that one Gorgio was still worth two Yulang. There was a law passed, in case you didn't know. . . ." I groped for ammunition. "The Stanno statute." That was it. Roman Stanno, the great Yulang advocate, had finally succeeded in forcing that bill through, and now Yulang witnesses were supposedly equal to Gorgios in a court of law. If Janet could witness one thing, I could witness something else!

"Oh, don't pull that nonsense with me, Serena," Mrs. Palmer said angrily. She glanced at the man in the gray suit.

As if under instructions, he sat down in the chair beside me, so close that his shoulder brushed mine. I was wrong about the smell. He had one, and it was stale and musty, like the clothes at the charity store where we did our shopping. I tried my best to ignore him.

"Screaming discrimination isn't going to get you anywhere," Mrs. Palmer continued. "Or dragging in that Roman Stanno you people think so much of! It's irrelevant. We have to take the child into care if there's evidence of abuse. The point is moot, anyway, since I'm going to have to examine her myself." She started off toward our bedroom. "Which foot is it, Willow?"

Willow scrambled after the social worker, pushing past apologetically to reach the bedroom first.

"Please don't wake her up. I'll— Let me get her. She'll be scared if she wakes up and sees a stranger standing over her...."

"Which foot?"

"The—the right."

A moment later they emerged, with Zara fast asleep against Willow's shoulder. My heart twisted, seeing her clutching her little moss green blanket in her fist.

"It's nothing at all. Really. It's silly you had to come all this way." Willow's voice was high and tight. "It was just a guy. We don't even know him. Not that it's usual for someone to be in the house we don't know!" she added quickly. "We're very careful about who we let around Zara."

"Lay her on the couch," Mrs. Palmer ordered. "I can't examine the child while you're holding her."

"Don't let go of her, Willow!" I cried, springing out of my chair. But the man in the gray suit grabbed my arm and yanked me back.

I was so shocked, I was trembling.

So that was who he was. He was one of the enforcers that the social workers bring with them, when they get people in trouble for not enrolling their kids in school—or when they take children away from their families. The Cruelty men, the Yulang call them.

Willow looked at me in alarm. Her arms tightened around Zara.

"Come on, Willow." Mrs. Palmer sounded exasperated. "If it's nothing, we'll just go on home."

I shook my head violently at my sister.

Willow looked from me to Mrs. Palmer, in growing uncertainty.

While Willow hesitated, Mrs. Palmer simply plucked Zara out of her arms and laid her flat on the couch.

Zara murmured in her sleep and flipped over onto her stomach.

The new dressing I'd taped on showed clearly on her instep. With clean, precise movements, Mrs. Palmer pulled off the adhesive and removed the cotton. Zara stirred fretfully and yawned, stretching out a small fist.

The burn looked terrible—even worse than before, since I had smeared it with orange antibacterial cream. It took something out of me, seeing it again. It was round and deep, and Zara's skin was charred around its edges.

For the thinnest sliver of a second, my heart misgave me. Go on, Mrs. Palmer! I thought. Teach Willow a lesson! It's her fault—every bit as much as if she'd done it herself! Give her a good scare!

But that was craziness.

Zara's eyes flickered as Mrs. Palmer replaced the dressing. The woman jerked her into her arms and stood up in a great hurry. It was as if Zara were already hers, to do with as she liked.

Willow just sank into the couch with a stunned look on her face.

I got up—more slowly this time, not wanting to be slammed down again by the Cruelty man. I'd seen Zara's eyes opening, and I wanted her to see me first, not Mrs. Palmer. I went over to Mrs. Palmer, caught Zara's eyes, and gave her the big *happy happy* smile that always reassured her. I put my hands under her arms and tried to lift her up and away from Mrs. Palmer. Just as if it were perfectly natural to do so. In the marrow of my bones, I knew it was important for me to keep my hands on Zara.

But Mrs. Palmer swung away from me before I could pull Zara out of her grip. She clutched Zara tighter—as tightly as the Gorgio women clutch their handbags when they walk down our streets—and stepped back toward the door.

Zara scissored her legs and pushed herself up high on the woman's shoulder, looking from me to Willow in obvious fright.

Willow glanced nervously at the Cruelty man.

Then, cautiously, she got up from the couch and held out her arms. "Here, Mrs. Palmer. Let me hold her. I'll take her to the doctor. . . ."

Zara twisted over Mrs. Palmer's shoulder and reached out for Willow, but Mrs. Palmer caught her arms and forced them down. "That's impossible, Willow. I can't let Zara stay here. Not when she's sustained this kind of injury. We have to do what's best for the child."

"Mama?" Zara cried.

"But it's not that serious!" Willow insisted. "I can take care of her. She's my daughter, after all!"

"I'm sorry. I can't allow her to remain with you."

Zara began to cry. Willow's voice was pitched high with disbelief. "Who do you think you are? You can't take her! She's mine! You can't come in here and take her just like that!"

She started angrily toward the social worker.

But the Cruelty had her before she'd taken three steps. Almost casually, he seized Willow's arms and wrenched them behind her back, twisting the wrists till she gasped in pain.

"Let go of me!" Willow tugged away from him, trying to break free, like a dog at the end of a chain. The Cruelty held her effortlessly.

Willow swiveled her head around to face the man. "Let go!"

I watched as if I'd been turned to stone.

Zara's cries changed all of a sudden. She was no longer crying like a child shaken out of sleep. She was aware of everything: the arms that gripped her, the big man holding Willow, Willow pleading.

Mrs. Palmer turned and bore Zara out the door, and her cries turned to high-pitched shrieks of panic.

Willow screamed. She was still clamped in the Cruelty's grip.

But no one's holding me, I thought. And suddenly, springs in my legs let loose.

I sprinted out the door and along the balcony. Mrs. Palmer was halfway to the stairs when she heard me running after her and turned.

Fear flashed in her eyes and blanched her red lips. I couldn't blame her. She must have read it in my face that I would have happily killed her.

She began to run, but I was faster. I grabbed her slippery camel-hair sleeve and twisted her around so we were face to face, with Zara between us.

She tried to jerk away, but I held fast, trying to wrench Zara out of her arms. Zara threw her body forward and hooked her arms around my neck, kicking at Mrs. Palmer with all the force her small legs could muster. Her curls were in my face, smelling of milk and sleep. I had to let go of Mrs. Palmer to get a firm grip on her.

As the little girl slid into my arms, Mrs. Palmer cracked her fist against my ear. Freeing one hand, I shoved her as hard as I could into the neighbors' drying rack. It collapsed under her weight and she went down with a slap onto the cement.

Clutching Zara tightly, I jumped over her and sped off toward the stairs. I glanced over my shoulder and saw the Cruelty man burst out of our apartment. He began to run after us, but when he saw Mrs. Palmer in a heap on the landing, he bent down to help her.

I kept going. Zara's fingers dug into my neck. I knew I could have let go completely and still she would have hung on.

We made it down the first flight of stairs, practically flying. A crescent moon swung crazily in the sky, rising and falling like a scythe as we descended.

Far below, I could hear the Paria boys and their boom box. They hung out on the bottom stoop nearly every night. Although they only knew me by sight, it didn't matter. If they realized who was after me, they'd part like an honor guard to let me through.

The Cruelty's voice was in my ear so suddenly that it was as if he'd dropped from the sky.

"That's a ward of the state you've got there, girlie."

His breath was as musty as his suit. It filled my nose as he shoved me back against the stairwell.

I brought my knee up sharp and hard, but the Cruelty was too fast for me. He crushed his whole weight into me, stomping my feet with his boots until the small bones stung with pain.

"Hand her over, girl. You don't want to be charged with kidnapping."

"Get your hands off me, pig!"

When he clamped his hand over my lips, I sank my teeth into his palm without hesitation, ignoring the pollution of his skin in my mouth.

He yanked his hand away and smacked my head against the wall. Black fireworks exploded. My skull rang against the cement.

Zara was howling. I still had her in my arms. But my body was trapped.

"Now give her back," the Cruelty said, "unless you want some more of that."

I didn't relax my hold on her, though the pain in my head made me want to sob.

Instead, I did something I had no idea I could do.

I closed my eyes and looked inside myself. It was like looking into a deep, dark well. I had never known I had so much darkness inside me. With a terrifying assurance, I called all the creatures of my hate out of their hiding places. At my command, they stalked out growling and hissing, merciless birds of prey and hungry tigers. I remembered the words of the curse, which I had never heard except in old stories: *Run at my shoulders, crouch at my ears, fly out my eyes!* Attack the Cruelty man trying to steal our baby.

Then I opened my eyes and let the darkness and hatred bore a hole straight through his marbled blue eyes and into his skull.

The man's pupils flickered. Yes. He'd heard of us Yulang women. He'd heard of the Evil Eye.

I could see a spasm of fear go through him.

And then it was gone.

Mechanically, he began yanking Zara out of my arms. Her screams never stopped. I clung like death with stiffened muscles and rigid hands, ignoring even the knowledge that I was hurting her.

But I couldn't hold out against him. In a minute he had wrenched Zara away from me and flung her up on his shoulder. I threw myself at him, jabbing my fingers at his eyes. But he swiveled his head and seized the collar of my sweater, tightening it around my neck until I gasped for air.

"Bitch! I should throw you down the stairs!"

With a violent lurch, I twisted out of his grip.

The stairs poured away beneath my feet like a waterfall, the gray cement shining like silver water. My slippers slipped and scuffed. I balled up my feet for traction.

I could hear the heavy slap of the man's boots as he ran up the stairs, taking Zara back to Mrs. Palmer.

If only Willow could give them half the trouble I had! It was Zara's only hope.

But now the boots were growing louder again. He was coming back after me.

I'd reached the first-floor landing. The boys on the steps were gaping at me.

"It's the Cruelty!" I shouted. "Let me through!"

They sprang to their feet, shoving the boom box out of my way.

I'd barely reached the bottom when a man screamed and I heard a crash.

I stopped. One of the boys looked at me and tore up the stairs. A moment later he was back.

"He's fallen! The Cruelty man! He's not moving!" There was fear in his eyes. "What are you standing there for, Jalla? It's you they'll blame. Now use your feet and run."

I packed my bags and went to the king.
For weal and for woe I went,
To beg of his mercy and offer my ring,
For praise or punishment.

—Kereskedo ballad

You picked a bad night." The daughter-in-law stood in the doorway balancing a basket of laundry on her hip. "You must know his daughter is getting married tomorrow. I should think the whole city knows that!"

She squinted at me, puzzled by my ignorance. "The menfolk celebrate tonight. The guests are in the garden and nothing is the way he wants it. The food is too starchy, he says. The wine's sour, and the musicians are beyond praying for. I wouldn't get my hopes up if I were you."

I wet my lips nervously. They were dry and chapped from running all this way. The Kereskedo neighborhood was a good twenty blocks from our apartment, and the house of Nico Brassi was on its far uptown side. I hadn't let myself stop or even slow to rest. It hurt to talk with my throat so ragged from panting.

The girl had noticed that I was in my slippers, without a coat, sweaty, and out of breath. Though we were both of an age, I could see I frightened her. She held the door firmly between us.

"Is there no one I can speak to?"

I peered over her shoulder into the opulence of Brassi's front hall. The floor was green-veined marble. The wallpaper was dusky red damask. The banister of the stairwell was walnut inlaid with mother-of-pearl. And this was a hall the family used only for wiping their feet! Where my Gorgio grandmother's oyster-colored carpets and pale gold couches had whispered of money, Nico Brassi's house blared his wealth like a trumpet blast. Such a man, I thought, must have a deputy to whom I could plead my case.

His daughter-in-law was already pushing the door shut.

"Come back tomorrow," she was saying, "or the day after. If you really hope to fare well with him, wait a whole week. He'll have recovered from the wedding by then. Believe me, you'll have better luck if you wait for his mood to sweeten."

Before I knew it, the door was nearly closed. The eclipse of light from the foyer panicked me. I jammed my foot in the door. It hurt, because my thin slippers offered no protection.

"But I have to see him now! It's important."

The girl held the door firm against my foot. "Important how?"

"My family is Kereskedo. . . ."

"Surely. Or you wouldn't be here seeking favors like all the rest." Her eyes went small and unsympathetic. "Try another one, Jalla."

She was trying to push the door shut again. Gritting my teeth, I wedged my knee into the crack.

"I need protection," I said in a low voice.

"Why? Your boyfriend smacking you? Go home and make up, that's my advice. I tell you, the bora chan is too busy for this now. It'll be more than a smack for me if I take you in there."

"Real protection," I said. "I've hurt a man from the Cruelty. Maybe killed him."

The girl's mouth fell open. The pressure from the door eased. She opened it and stepped back an inch. "Little you? How?"

"He fell down a flight of stairs."

Her eyes registered fear and respect.

"It wasn't intentional," I added quickly, wincing as I remembered the curse I'd put on him just before his fall. "Please. You know what they'll do if they catch me."

She hesitated. But I was lucky. She had an imagination. Even here, kept and fed by the Kereskedo big man, trading her youth for safety, she could picture what the Gorgios would make of me.

"All right. Come in." She opened the door wide.

Weak with relief, I stepped into the foyer. The girl closed the door behind me and gestured for me to follow her.

I'd thought the house empty. But as I followed her down a long hallway, I could hear it thrum with activity. Somewhere there was a jangle of strings and the sound of a bass being tuned. Children shrieked and laughed. A woman scolded. Far off, I heard the bray of men's voices.

The girl pushed open a door to a small laundry room, and the churning of the machines filled the air. She dropped her basket inside and closed the door again. I kept close behind her, bewildered by the twists and turns of Brassi's corridors. A sweating, bald-headed man nearly bowled us over with a cask of beer. We flattened ourselves against the wall of the narrow hallway to let him through. Quietly, the girl propped open the door he had left swinging and peered inside.

Over her shoulder, I saw an enormous kitchen. Pots boiled on a black iron stove. A stringy old woman opened the oven and pulled out a big pear tart. She put it down, grabbed the nearest bottle to hand, poured its contents over the pear topping, and dropped a lit match on it. The alcohol ignited. Blue flames danced above the fruit, melding the scent of pears to the sugar and liquor with such powerful sweetness that I thought I would swoon from hunger and greed.

A younger woman was dropping spoonfuls of batter into a fiercely boiling cauldron.

The crone turned and spied us. The girl next to me froze.

"You!" the old woman cried. "Where've you been? Lolling about spangling your eyelids? I've been waiting for you! And who's this? More kitchen help? She'd better be. Here, take these to the yard." She picked up a tray piled with stuffed mushrooms, came over, and shoved it into the girl's arms. It jammed into her stomach. For the first time, I noticed she was pregnant. She was younger than Willow had been when she'd had Zara. Maybe even younger than me, and I had only just passed through the arch of my sixteenth year.

The girl making the dumplings turned her head. Her eyes met those of the pregnant girl, in an intense exchange of fellow feeling. Then we turned to go and the door swung to behind us.

"My husband's grandmother," the girl whispered. "She thinks daughter-in-law means slave, and no one dares tell her no."

"Is she the bora chan's mother?"

"Who else?"

"Then her son's the spit and stamp of her, isn't he?"

The girl looked surprised at my gall. "Yes!" she whispered. She giggled into her palm and turned bright red.

It boded ill for me. But what else did I expect? Nico Brassi was the big man, the star in the center of the solar system, the rooster in the henhouse. I was so far beneath him that he'd spat at me that very afternoon. The only way I'd get any help was by really groveling. And I'd never been much good at that.

"Come on." The girl smiled at me. "I'd better take these out back."

I followed her out the back door onto a porch that opened onto a walled garden. Underneath a large cherry tree, men were seated around a trestle table—surely the families of the couple to be married the next day. They were talking loudly, swooping firefly lines in the air with their burning cigarettes, and gobbling up plates of goat cheese and olives in brine. Gallant feathers adorned their hatbands. Their trousers were ironed into sharp pleats, and the embroidery on their vests was of a holiday brightness.

No one was paying the slightest attention to the bora chan, who stood not ten feet from us, up on the porch. It was a good thing, too. He was flaying the musicians, and it wasn't a pretty sight.

There were three of them: an old bassist with a tremendous white mustache combed into teapot spouts; a beetle-browed man; and a boy not much older than me.

Nico Brassi was half suspending the bassist off the ground by his green silk tie.

"F sharp and C sharp!" the big man screamed. "Everyone knows that! It's no Zimbali trade secret! A simple enough thing to teach even that imbecile! Or must I step in? Along with feeding five hundred people tomorrow, overseeing incompetent cooks, and supporting a gaggle of layabout relatives, must I also fiddle the tunes at my own daughter's wedding? Is it my job to teach that useless nephew of yours the key of D?"

"He is learning . . . ," the old man choked out through his constricted windpipe. Though attached to the earth only by the toes of his boots, he was making a valiant attempt to maintain his dignity.

"Put him *down*," the boy told Brassi.

He had to be the nephew in question.

Nico Brassi gave him a contemptuous glance.

"Put my uncle down. You can't treat him like that!" the boy shouted.

He was a tall, loose-limbed person, with a sharp chin and very intense brown eyes. I registered that I had seen him somewhere before, though I couldn't place where. Something about the way he was holding his violin reminded me of how Paria boys held crowbars in street fights, and I could see it took every bit of patience he could muster not to haul off and slug Brassi with it.

"I'm the imbecile you want, Bora Chan! Not my uncle! Let him alone!"

Nico Brassi considered this. Then he released the old man's tie with a flourish.

The old bassist drew a rattled breath and smoothed his clothes. Thank goodness. I hate to see people humiliated—especially people older than me. It reminds me of how my grandmother used to treat my mother.

The boy looked surprised that his words had succeeded. Hastily, he put his violin behind his back and bowed to Brassi. I hoped his next words would be a bit more conciliatory, for Brassi seemed fully capable of another assault. The last thing I needed was to try to talk to Brassi when he'd just emerged from a brawl.

"Accept my apologies, Bora Chan. It's my fault. I'm not a skillful player. But you can't deny the talents of my uncles." The boy glanced at the old man and the other, who held a cymbalom miserably in his arms. "Allow us one more chance. . . ."

Nico Brassi was wearing a pair of fine leather boots, and their heels made the floor resound as he advanced on the young musician.

"One more word and I will throttle you with those violin strings you've been tormenting!" His hawkish gaze slid to the boy's uncles. "I won't have you play at the ceremony tomorrow. Contract be deviled! If there is one thing we Yulang do not lack, it's scrapers of catgut! But tonight you will have to do. With one caveat." He jabbed a heavy index finger at the violinist. Suddenly, I realized who the boy was. He was the fiddler whose attention Janet had angled for at Plaza Ridizio. Though I disliked the way Brassi treated his family, I knew that the bora chan probably had good reason for his dissatisfaction, and I couldn't condemn him too much when he declared, "I will not have that nincompoop play one more note!"

"But, sir," the cymbalom player objected, "this music is made for violin. We cannot do without a fiddler!"

"Then find one!" Brassi snapped. "In ten minutes, or I will call my council together and declare all of you *ma'hane!* The Vadesh family will never play again!"

Even I knew that the council would never approve such tyranny. But that didn't matter. Just the rumor of Brassi's threat would dissuade others from giving this family their business. They would be ruined.

My mind whirred. Putting aside my sympathy for the family, I thought: Their trouble has been put in my way for a reason. I have to use it to my advantage.

Clearing my throat, I pushed myself forward. "I can play the violin, Bora Chan. Will you let me take the fiddler's place?"

The old bassist sighed in such relief that I could see his chest rise under his embroidered vest. The cymbalom player smiled uncertainly. I had the grace not to look at the ejected violinist. He would come off badly no matter what. If Brassi didn't get him, I was sure his uncles would.

The bora chan stared at me.

Of course he knew who I was! I could see his knowledge clicking away in those shrewd, narrow eyes. He knew me, he knew my sister, and he knew who my mother had married (though this didn't worry me as much as the other things; the Kereskedo had a good opinion of my father). He had seen me today, carrying the baby who was the badge of our shame. I struggled to keep my face bland, thanking the guiding stars that I hadn't cursed him earlier.

Instead of answering, he burst out, "I am plagued with interlopers! What are you doing in my house, girl?" He didn't even call me Jalla.

I swallowed the insult, remembering how much I needed him. If he helped me, perhaps Zara could be returned to us. Perhaps I could find a safe place to hide, waiting for the Cruelty to forget....

"I'm here by good fortune," I said, smooth as olive oil, "willing to play when you need a player."

"Nico!" one of the old men at the table called to Brassi. "Your guests are dry! Stop piffling with those strummers and join us."

"Sit down this minute, Bora Chan," a fat man with a golden watch chain chimed in, "or we'll bandy it about that Nico Brassi is a mean host who won't share the table with his new in-laws."

I held my mouth like a steel wire, quashing my urge to smile. I could tell that one of the many things Nico Brassi would not tolerate was being laughed at.

"I cannot allow my house to be polluted . . . ," Brassi muttered.

My heart sank. Of course, I polluted his house just by standing on his flagstones. Willow! I thought again. Her negligence got me into this, and her—her wantonness was going to make it impossible to get out! Brassi would never help me, knowing she was my sister. What hope for getting Zara back, then?

Rescue came from an unexpected quarter. The old bass player misunderstood the bora chan's meaning. He snatched the hat from his nephew's head and crammed it onto mine.

"In exceptional circumstances allowances can be made," he said. "None of your guests have paid the girl any heed. Tuck up her hair, put my nephew's jacket on her, and who will notice you allowed a woman to play? Fortunately she is already wearing trousers. . . ."

The big man stamped his foot. "A girl or an imbecile!"

"That's right," I agreed. "And you'd do better to choose the girl. None of your guests will know, I swear. And I promise you, I'm ten times the fiddler that boy is. I heard his atrocious playing only this afternoon. Let me play and you can enjoy your happy night."

I glanced at the young violinist. He was taking these insults with a fair bit of self-control, although he was watching me narrowly. I could see him wondering what my game was.

The bora chan threw his hands in the air. "Fine! Should I care? The big man of the Kereskedo made a fool of by a pack of catgut beggars!

47

Do your best, girl. But I warn you, a note out of place and I'll kick you into the street with my own boot."

With that he stumped off to the trestle table, where cheers greeted him.

I wasted no time getting the violinist's jacket off him, and no words of apology. To his credit, he was businesslike about it.

"Roll up the sleeves or they'll swamp your hands and you won't be able to play. Not like that." He flicked the wrists back in a neat creased fold. "Try and look professional. Don't embarrass my uncles . . . at least not any worse than I have."

"No one could do that," snarled the cymbalom player. "You'll never amount to anything, Shem Vadesh! We've always known that. But you're not going to drag us down with you!"

"I've been telling you that, Uncle Panno. Now will you let me go?"

"Go, then! It's high time we were shot of you!"

"Panno!" the old man remonstrated. "Remember your brother."

"I am remembering him! And my brother would have died a second death if he knew he had such a good-for-nothing son!"

The boy turned away, fixed his eyes on something far in the distance.

"Leave be!" the old man growled. He turned to me. "Here's our play list, Jalla." He rattled off a string of well-known drinking songs and dances, with one or two sentimental ballads thrown in. I nodded at most of the titles. He frowned severely at the one or two with which I was unfamiliar.

"Do you read?" he demanded.

"Yes."

"Shem. Find her the sheet music. Perhaps they'll be too drunk by then to notice."

Among most Yulang—and, unquestionably, among the Zimbali—it

is a tremendous disappointment if a musician needs to read his music.

"Forget it," I told the nephew. "I can fake it as well as anyone."

"You'd better," Panno growled. "Or Nico Brassi won't be the only one placing his boot on you."

I gave the cymbalom player a cold look. "You'd do better kissing my foot than trying to bully me. I'm the only reason he didn't brand your backside."

Panno's eyebrows flew up. "And you've nothing to gain yourself, I suppose?"

"That's my business."

"This won't serve anyone's purpose!" The boy turned to me in exasperation. "You, whoever you are! Treat my uncles with respect! And, Uncle Panno, don't waste time losing your temper."

"Perhaps if I'd lost it with you more often, we'd all be better off!"

The boy ignored him and handed me his fiddle and bow. I took it, resolutely keeping my mouth shut. The main thing was to impress the bora chan. My safety, and Zara's, would depend on it.

When Panno gave the signal, I fitted the violin under my chin and pulled the bow in a long, keening arpeggio. The faces around the trestle table looked up expectantly. They had paid none of us the slightest heed while Brassi yelled at us. But the music had their full attention at once. If a Yulang audience likes you, they sing along and whoop and shout, and maybe pick up instruments to join in. But they are not easily won. They won't accept mediocrity. If a musician is bad, they'll jeer and throw things, until someone from the audience takes pity on him and goes up to take his place.

I wasn't worried about that happening. I knew I could play the violin well, even though I couldn't really love it. Perhaps I would have if we'd stayed with the Zimbali clan we'd shared a campfire with when I was young. But music was a different matter when Willow and Mother and

I moved to my grandmother's household. Grandmother's harangues about practicing and the way she rapped my knuckles when I played amiss were enough to change my feelings about the violin. Playing Yulang tunes in the kitchen with Mother was the only thing that reconciled me to the fiddle. Even so, Lemon Bardoff, whose father owned the music store, told me she could hear the dutiful sound in my fiddling. She said it was like listening to a long-married couple who are no longer in love but speak to each other with impeccable politeness. A musician, Lemon told me, is great only when she speaks through her instrument with the passion of first love, no matter how long she has played.

Panno played that way. Bad-tempered though he was, I had to admit he was an artist. It seemed unjust that my violin should take the lead when he was so talented. It baffled me even more that this superb cymbalom player and the sonorous bassist would have sullied their talents with that clod of a violinist, nephew or not.

But I spared their family concerns little thought as I sawed, glided, and plucked my way through the tunes. While my fingers vibrated and my bow flashed, my mind was running along one track: how to turn this service to account with Nico Brassi so he would feel bound to help me in return.

The daughters-in-law were running across the lawn, laden with steaming pots, heavy platters, and bottles of wine and brandy. They raced from the kitchen to the table to the scullery and back again. The girl who had led me to Nico Brassi only chanced to lift her eyes to our musical trio after making her circuit five or six times. When she recognized me in my male garb, a broad smile swept across her face. The next moment she was gone.

After about ten tunes, Panno caught my eye and gave a little nod. Nothing enthusiastic. But I would do. It was enough to save his family's standing in the community.

The night wore on and the men began dancing on the table. Some danced skillfully; others weaved and stumbled. Finally, the big man himself was up and the men were tossing him the china. In fine disregard for their worth, Brassi lobbed the plates against the trees and into the sky to shatter on the ground. This brought on a storm of approval from the others. The head of the Kereskedo tribe was wealthy enough to lay waste to a whole set of china. Even I felt a thrill.

But I also began to wonder if Brassi was drunk. Would he be sober enough to help me when I sought him out? My heart sank with every flagon of wine the girls carried to the table. The dancers flopped in their chairs, exhausted.

Finally, coffee arrived, the thick black Yulang coffee that could raise a demon from the pit of hell, and my hopes revived. The talk turned boisterous, sometimes even drowning out our music.

I watched it all with my arms aching and my head throbbing from the Cruelty's blow. Where had he and Mrs. Palmer taken Zara? Was she in an office? A car? A hospital? A government nursery somewhere? I winced. Wherever she was, I could picture her. She was winding her hands into some mildewed institutional blanket and weeping inconsolably. And I knew she would cry and hiccup until she nearly made herself sick. To her mind there would be no return to Mama and Auntie Reena. We were as lost as the dead, and she would mourn and mourn. I could not bear to think of it.

A tear rolled down my nose and dropped onto the violin.

Suddenly, Nico Brassi ambled over to our trio and held up his hand.

"Enough," he said. His voice was thick with drink. "Your performance was adequate. No more tonight."

Panno and the bassist bowed low. I followed suit, hastily wiping my nose on my sleeve.

"My mother will settle your accounts. And while you are counting your cash, count yourselves lucky that a fiddler dropped out of the sky to save your skins." He laughed at his own wit, then peered earnestly at the old bass player. "Take my advice, old father. Even a fool does not help a relative who brings him a poor reputation. Let your nephew fend for himself from now on."

Pleased with delivering himself of this charitable advice, he turned and began walking back to his guests.

I watched his broad back in his dapper silk vest and saw my chance of help slipping away. With undignified haste, I trotted after him.

"Bora Chan! Wait! Please!"

He turned. His condescension toward the musicians had put him in a jovial mood. There was even a sliver of a smile on his face. "Ten Times Better Fiddler, I have advice for you as well. I am a fount of good counsel tonight. Better you may be, but you are not born to that instrument, either."

All of a sudden, he frowned. He had remembered who I was, under my man's attire. "What is it, *Ma'hane?* Speak, if you've something to say. My guests are waiting."

I took a breath. "I'm—I was honored to spare you embarrassment tonight, sir. And I am glad my playing was satisfactory—"

"Yes, yes." He glanced toward the table where the men had launched into a storytelling competition. "You're transparent enough, girl. You crave a favor and try to sound worthier than you are. I'm listening. But don't forget who and what you are. I don't."

I barely heard his warning. "Bora Chan, I came to you for protection. I've had trouble with the Cruelty. They took away my sister's baby."

Distaste flickered in the big man's eyes. I knew that mention of Zara could only work against me. But what could I do? Like any other Kereskedo, he, too, must shudder when the Gorgios steal a Yulang child. Even one like Zara.

"Forget that her mother's *ma'hane*, Bora Chan! Forget that I am! Forget our Gorgio blood, if that troubles you! Zara is the best baby in the world! Don't throw her mother's fault on her head. She's one of ours and they took her!"

I imagined I saw a flash of sympathy in his eyes and felt bolder.

"I grabbed her and ran, but the Cruelty man got her back. Then he chased me. I don't know why he fell! But he fell down the stairs of our apartment building. I don't know how badly he's hurt. You know how they are when one of the Cruelty men gets injured. . . ."

"You want my help?" The bora chan jerked his head up and his eyes flashed. "I should slap you! You wretched girl! Now there will have to be gifts, reparations. Do you have any idea what it takes to keep the peace with them?"

"Oh, yes. Yes, of course I do," I said uncertainly. "But . . . when they come and take our children . . ."

"Did you or your slut sister give them an excuse to take the child?"

I hung my head. His anger was fiercer than I expected. I saw Zara's foot, bright orange with antiseptic, and the guilt crashed over my head. If I had watched Zara more carefully, if I'd been harder on Willow, could I have prevented it? I heard my petulant voice whining to Janet, *It's not fair! I have no time to be young!* Sometimes, in my secret wicked heart, I had wished Zara away. . . .

I could not speak. Tears were streaming down my cheeks and I swiped at them angrily.

The bora chan read my silence exactly as I had feared. "You did! You gave them the rope to hang us!"

"Not me! A stranger. We didn't know—"

"If you'd watched over the child like proper Kereskedo women, you would have known!"

True, I thought miserably. It was my fault, trusting Willow, worrying about my grades at the Lyceum when I should have been worrying about the boys she trekked in and out of our apartment.

His face curdled. "Whether I wish it or not, you leave it in my lap."

"You'll help us, then?" I couldn't believe my luck.

"You!" he spat. "I do not help you! You are *ma'hane*. Your value is below dirt. But I serve the Kereskedo. I'll protect my tribe from what you've brought upon them." His voice was tight. "Leave the city, girl. That advice is all the help you'll get from me. I'll tell the Cruelty you've disappeared. Go to Anchara Pulchra's camp, if you can. Perhaps she'll give you a scrap of her wisdom. Something you and your sister clearly lack!"

"But the baby?"

"For the child, whatever serves the Kereskedo best."

A wild hope seized me. "Please help the baby. If not for me—please, for my mother."

"Your mother?" Yes. I was right to mention her. The bora chan's eyes softened. "Galeah Silvani. I remember Galeah. A beautiful woman. A spirit of sun on water, our folk used to say. Even after she married that Gorgio. Your father, was he?"

I nodded.

Then his voice was hard again. "But where is your mother? Let her return and plead with her own tongue if she cares so much for her foolish daughters. Which I doubt, or she wouldn't have left you. She knew what she was dealing with." He made a sound of disgust. "Go! Consider yourself lucky I didn't throw you out."

I just gawped, clutching at the sleeves of my sweater, as if reassuring myself that I wasn't naked. For the bora chan had stripped me of honor. To him, I was not a worthy human in the light of the moon. I was a lump of wet clay, filthy and senseless as earth.

There was hardly enough spirit left in me to lift my voice. Yet it came of necessity. "How can I leave? I have no money. I don't even have a pair of shoes! Nothing!" I lifted my foot in its flimsy slipper.

The bora chan wasn't interested in my slippers. "That's your concern. Beg your portion from the musicians. Perhaps they have softer hearts than I. They are all failures. They can afford to be softhearted."

I stood transfixed as he walked away. I'd known Willow and I were *ma'hane* before this night. But cast out to live among the Paria, we weren't reminded of it as much as we would have been among the Kereskedo. And because I still went to the fine Gorgio school Grandmother had wheedled me into, I had not felt any special sting for being outcast. It made no difference to the Gorgios that I was *ma'hane*. A Yulang was a Yulang—there were no gradations in the dishonor of that.

For the first time, here in the Kereskedo enclave, I grasped how completely we were cut off. The big man had washed his hands of me. In my deep trouble, he had turned me away. And as he did, so did all the tribe.

The cold that crept along my skin sank into my heart. I was alone. Aside from Zara and Willow, I had no one, and now they were gone, too. It was as if I had been asleep, and suddenly I was wide awake in the ugly light of day. And this despite the lovely light of that crescent moon, so soft and glowing above the cherry tree.

Brassi's daughter-in-law swept by me with a platter of dirty dishes on her head.

"Where are the musicians?" I asked leadenly.

"The musicians?" She balanced the pile on her head with a reddened hand. She was distracted, exhausted. She didn't even look at me. "The musicians have gone."

5

Riddle me ree, riddle me rye,
Tell me the truth and I'll tell you a lie.
Tell me a lie and I'll tell you the truth
We'll laugh at age, and cry at youth.

—Zimbali catch

The cough at my shoulder made me jump.

The disgraced violinist was sitting in the shadows nearby. He was leaning back on one of Brassi's wrought-iron chairs and regarding me with lively interest. I hadn't thought I could feel any lower, until it dawned on me that he had probably heard all that had just transpired between me and Nico Brassi.

"Well? What are *you* looking at?" I snapped.

"At you, of course. I should think that was pretty obvious." He sounded pretty devil-may-care for someone who had nearly sunk his family business.

"Well, stop it. Who told you to hide out there and stare at people?"

"I stare on my own initiative, Jalla. No one tells me to."

"Aren't you ambitious!" I snapped. "Too bad you never used your initiative to learn the violin! It must take effort to grow up among the Zimbali and play like you do!"

"Lucky for you, though. Wouldn't you say?"

"If I were feeling charitable!" But my ears flamed. He had figured out my game, after all.

"And are you? Because if you are"—he pulled a penknife from his pocket—"would your charity stretch to sharpening this for me? Whatever you use on your tongue would do nicely. Do you take a whetstone to it?"

I stamped my foot in exasperation—at myself, as much as at him—for I realized that I was yammering insults at the very person I needed to get my share of the money! And I didn't seem able to stop.

"Why don't you get lost?"

"Oh, I will," the violinist promised. "Once I've finished the inventory."

"Inventory? Of what?"

He ran his eyes from my head to my slippered feet and began clicking off a list on his fingers. "My dad's best felt hat. I took it from his place at the funeral feast, so I'd be obliged if you'd give it back. And my jacket. Smells of camp smoke, did you notice? Can't seem to get that out. What else? You didn't take my trews as well, did you, girl?" He stretched out a leg and pretended to inspect it. "No, you've left me my modesty! Now, what other fascinating things do I see in your possession?" He snapped his fingers. "Ah, that's it! My violin!"

I sent him a hateful look. I'd forgotten that I'd left home in nothing but my old red sweater and my housecleaning dungarees, and that the warm hat and jacket I wore belonged to him.

I laid the violin in its case and peeled off his jacket. The night air was icy and I felt the heavy fabric with regret as I handed it back to him.

He slipped his arms into the sleeves and sniffed deeply. "You must wash your hair in wildflowers," he observed. "There's a smell of them on my collar."

That didn't merit a response. "I'll have your portion of the brass, fiddler. You owe me that, at least."

The boy's grin slipped right off his face. He folded his arms and looked at me as stonily as if he'd never made a joke, or even heard one, in his life.

I caught my breath, suddenly fearful. He couldn't refuse me! Could he?

Foolishly, I'd taken Nico Brassi's evaluation of the musicians at face value. To him they were powerless, laughable little men. But I wasn't Nico Brassi. What if the musicians decided to wash their hands of me? Could they wipe their boots on me as Brassi wiped his on them?

I read my answer in the boy's face.

They could. Even this failure of a fiddler was of higher status than an outcast like me! He could enjoy making me sweat. I bit my lip, cursing myself for an idiot. Why had I been so rude to him?

Because he was insufferable, that was why! I thought. I didn't need to put up with his having fun at my expense. Or scaring me with his hard look. Why should I?

I clamped my hands together, squeezing my fingers tightly. Nico Brassi had nearly crushed the spirit out of me, and I was damned if I was going to let anyone else finish the job. At least, not without a fight. What did I have to fight with? The boy said my tongue was sharp. Well, then. My sharp tongue, my hard heart, and my fists. First one, then the other. If need be, the last.

I took a step closer to him. The fiddler's eyes were shadowed, and I noticed that his nose must have been broken not too long before, for the crooked bump in the middle of it spoiled the symmetry of his features. Troubles, then. People with troubles have the least sympathy for others.

Well, I would not ask for sympathy. When I spoke, I spoke through my teeth.

"If it weren't for me, your hopeless twanging would have ruined your family, fiddler! You'd think yourself lucky to scrape a string in the subway and hold out a hat to the Gorgios! Pay me my due or I'll spread the story to every Yulang from here to the outskirts of the city."

The boy's walnut brown eyes rested on me as if I were a stuffed grizzly in a museum—curious, but not threatening. Then a cool, sarcastic smile touched his lips.

"A mighty threat, indeed!" he jibed. "But unfortunately, you've forgotten something. You're *ma'hane*, little sister! You said so yourself. Who would give two cents for your tale? And as to holding a hat to the Gorgios—you're half Gorgio yourself! Without even a hat to call your own!" He snatched his felt hat unceremoniously off my head. "Seriously, as between you and me, Jalla: your words sound fine and you use them well. But words are just words, and threats are whistles in the wind when there's nothing behind them." He stopped himself, as if struck by his neatness of phrase. "Just like your music, friend. You wouldn't think I could tell, but I can. The notes are right, and you play them well, but there's nothing much within, is there?"

I stared.

Then I grabbed his violin case from the ground. "Are you going to pay me or not? If not, I'll hold this for security until you see reason."

The boy shrugged. "Does it seem to you that I value that fiddle? You're a strange waster of words, girl. If you want to bargain, you can't use empty words. There has to be something behind them."

He turned away. But I lurched after him.

"There's me behind the words!" I yelled. "Me! I'm hungry! And I'm cold, now that you've got your blasted jacket off me! And I'm not safe until I'm miles away from here! What else do you need behind my words?"

I expected him to ignore me and stride away. But he stopped and turned around, as if waiting for something. For what?

"And why so much of my words?" I pressed on. "There are still some words I need from you. Will you pay me—yes or no?"

He looked me straight in the eye.

"No."

My hands dropped to my side, heavy and useless. Come on! I urged myself. While he's still here, there's hope. Say something. Do something.

"But you have to—" was all I could muster.

"I don't have to do anything except walk the road and die," he shot back. It was a common Yulang saying. "You're right if you think I owe you something. I *should* pay you, Jalla. Unfortunately, it's not possible. But I wasn't going to leave you here, either." He looked at me severely. "At least, not until you started hurling threats. Empty threats are next door to lies. I can't stand lies or liars, Jalla. And from the first, half of what you've said has been lies. . . ."

That snapped me back into myself. "And it's easy to make such distinctions, fiddler, when you have the gold in your pocket!"

"But I don't have any gold in my pockets. I gave it to my uncles to buy my way out of the family business." His voice sharpened. "All right. If you don't believe me . . ." He pulled his pockets inside out, emptied them, and shoved the contents into my hands.

I was taken aback.

"Go on. Look. See if I'm telling the truth."

I looked. There was a compass. Some squashed chocolates in foil. A tin amulet in the shape of Mother Lillith's foot. A needle and a spool of thread. Some wire. A collection of pawn tickets for things like cufflinks, boots, candlestick holders. Even one for the violin—but I saw that it had been redeemed the following day.

If he'd raised a chunk of money at the pawnshop, and if his uncles had really given him any share of tonight's pay, he must have spent it all. For he was telling the truth. There was no money in his pockets.

Not a bent penny.

How could I leave the city now?

The wooden columns of Nico Brassi's porch swam in front of my eyes. I saw the men under the cherry tree slumped over their plates, the women still stumbling under their loads. I had a sick fancy that I would never leave here, that I would fling myself down on the slate tiles and give myself up to sleep until someone came and threw me out on the street. It seemed almost inviting. I felt I was sinking. . . .

The warmth of a hand on mine called me back to myself. It was the boy's. I thought he was trying to keep me from falling. But he was only collecting his possessions, which had begun to slip between my slack fingers.

"There's no call to go green like that, Jalla."

I looked up at him hopelessly. "What do you know? If you'd paid me, I would've had bus fare, at least out to the foothills. Now I'm stuck. You heard what I told Brassi! I need to get out of this city—I can't—"

"Listen," the boy interrupted. "Jalla, listen. I can't pay you. I'm sorry about that. But I can give you something much better than gold. Much better. Under one condition."

Despite the kindness of his tone, I shuddered. "What condition?"

"That you tell me three true things."

My worry melted into outrage. Who did he think he was? A judge? A fortuneteller? What right had he to know my secrets?

But what did he have to offer that was better than gold?

"What do you want to know?"

He bent down and picked up the compass, which I'd dropped. "Are you really running from the Cruelty?"

"Yes." He'd overheard as much. Did he think I'd lied to Brassi? Probably.

He stood up again. "Why is your sister *ma'hane*?"

I bristled but then thought, What a stupid boy! He'd heard me talking about Zara. I wasn't telling him anything he didn't already know!

"Because she had a baby with a Gorgio boy and he didn't marry her. Because she can't control herself or give a thought to anyone else. Because—" I bit my tongue.

The boy grinned. "You're telling the truth there, for sure. It doesn't hurt that much, does it?"

"Yes!" I snapped. "It does! And there's your last answer."

"Don't be so clever, you. You owe me one more and you know it."

"Let's see what it is."

He looked at me closely. "Are you *ma'hane* by association, or in your own right?"

Color drenched my face. No one had ever asked me this before, though I had many times wished someone would. Most likely it made no difference to anyone but me.

"By association. I was living with Willow when it all happened. The court said I'd been corrupted."

The boy dropped his stuff back into his pockets. "Do you think you were?"

"I've answered three questions," I pointed out. "In case you haven't noticed. Now it's time for your end of the bargain. What are you going to give me that's more precious than gold?"

The boy looked at me and a laughing spark lit up his eyes.

"Gas," he answered, as if it were some marvelous thing.

"Gas?"

He heard the disappointment in my voice. "No, really, Jalla. Follow me."

We went around the side of the house and out a little wooden gate.

I probably shouldn't be following him, I thought. He could be taking me to a vacant lot to beat my brains out, or to one of those night bazaars where girls are sold like summer melons. You'd think after a day like today I would be a bit more wary. But my need was so strong that I had to temper my distrust.

I followed him along the sidewalk, under the line of maples, their autumn colors now dulled by darkness. My legs felt flimsy as crepe paper. The night had stolen my substance. I was drained, flattened like a shadow against the walls of the Kereskedo houses we passed.

I did not balk or protest when we stopped next to a squashed shoe-box of a car—dark blue, and tired-looking as an old man's hat. Hitched to it was an aged caravan of middling size. It was white aluminum, except for the wooden shutters on the windows, which had been painted a glossy green, with the feet of Mother Lillith, King David's harp, and Euterpe's flute embossed in gold on the wide slats. I caught only a glimpse of the back door, but enough to see that equal care had been taken with the painting there.

A memory stabbed me like a fork of lightning. When my Yulang grandfather died, he'd left his caravan to Mother. For several years we'd traveled up and down the coast, and out to the isles, trying hard to make a living as Kereskedo traders. That was when we'd sometimes camped with the Zimbali tribesmen—their caravan had the emblem of David's harp, just as this one had. Roaming around was heaven for Willow and me but not easy for my parents. Father had no knack for trade, and we had to rely on Mother's contrivances, which were limited, as the other Kereskedos would never do business with another merchant's wife, so we had to make do trading with the Gorgios. Rags and Bones, the Gorgios called us, when they didn't say Magpie, and rags and bones we were down to by the time my parents decided to give it up. Where had that caravan gone? I wondered. I could see it now: red and yellow, so brightly painted ...

I blinked and found myself back in the present. "Is this yours?" I asked the boy warily.

"Now it is. I've just bought it off my uncles." He looked at me. "I suppose I should thank you, really. It was my portion of tonight's take that brought me up to their price—the portion that should have gone to you. And it was Brassi's threats that made them willing to sell it to get rid of me."

"Get rid of you?"

"I've been telling them to let me go for the best part of a year. Though it's one thing to tell them to do it. It's another to have it done." He shrugged. "Enough of that."

He went around to the driver's side, opened the door, and sat down. When he leaned over and pulled up the lock on the passenger's door, I hesitated a moment.

"Have you decided, Jalla? Will gas be acceptable in place of the cash?" he asked.

I nodded and climbed in.

The black plastic seat was cold and patched up with electrical tape, but it was a place to sit, and I had not rested for hours. I pulled the door shut and pulled my knees up to my chin to cradle my body heat.

The boy put the key in the ignition and the dashboard lights flashed. The old circular clock showed a little after four in the morning. The gas tank was full. I prayed that the whole tank was to be my payment.

"Gas isn't more valuable than gold," I said quietly, "unless you're taking me where I want to go."

"I am." The boy set the car in reverse. I heard the back of the caravan grate against the car parked behind.

I caught my breath. Could he be leaving the city? Oh, please, Mother Lillith. If only I could find myself far from the twisted streets of Oestia by morning light!

I struggled to keep my voice level. "How do you know where I want to go?"

He jammed the gear shift into first and this time hit the car in front. "Anchara Pulchra's camp," he said. "Isn't that what Nico Brassi told you? She was on Mount Avo, last I heard."

I'd already braced myself for the next impact when the boy backed into the car behind us a second time. He had never driven before. That was clear. But I was in no position to complain.

"Why would you take me all the way out there?" I asked.

"Because I owe you," the boy answered sharply, "and I'm seeking Anchara myself."

"Who is she? I've heard the name before, I think. . . ."

The boy looked at me incredulously. "She's the mara chan of your tribe, girl. And your last chance for help, if Brassi is actually sending you to her. How can you not know that?"

A honk came from behind us. The boy looked in the side mirror and threw his hat off his head onto the seat between us, as if it were blocking his view. Biting his lip, he hauled the steering wheel hard to the right and rattled us out of the parking space. Another angry honk jolted us.

"What—"

"Oh, shut up and go to sleep, will you, Jalla? You're probably tired, and I drive better without people jabbering at me."

Perhaps it was because I cannot take direct commands; or because I expected the boy to wrap the caravan around a lamppost; or maybe there's some sort of fate that makes sure we see what we need to see, even as some demon ensures we also see what we wish we hadn't; I don't know. At any rate, I kept my eyes open as we threaded our way through the narrow streets and out onto Trebizond Boulevard. The globe lights glowed on their columns by the side of the road. Though the boy— Shem, I suddenly remembered his name was Shem Vadesh—wasn't speeding, somehow we still lurched toward the windshield every time he hit the brakes.

The street ran into Plaza Ridizio and turned east. The plaza was dark. Houses and shops drowsed behind bolted doors and barred windows.

But I noticed that the lights were ablaze in Bardoff's Music Store. The door was gaped wide, and a long white drape kept wafting out on the light breeze.

It puzzled me. Why would Lemon and her father be working at four in the morning? I knew they lived in the apartment above the store, for I'd visited there, so I supposed that if they needed to do late-night work, it would be a simple matter. Still, it seemed strange.

Then I noticed a big white van parked in front of their shop. I saw the government insignia on it and the words TAX SERVICE.

It was not as strange as I'd thought. The Bardoffs were Jersain. The city council gave them permission to work and own property in exchange for paying taxes at double rates. I remember Daddy telling me that Roman Stanno himself, the great Yulang lawyer, had protested this in Parliament. But no one supported him. No one stands for the Jersain. They are better off than us Yulang, but fewer and more insular. In some ways, they're even more distrusted and disliked. Lemon told me that the tax collectors visited them often, wanting detailed accounts of their every transaction. The way she mimicked their nosiness made me laugh. But she had never mentioned that they visited at four in the morning!

I had nearly decided to put it out of my mind when I saw old Ren Bardoff come out of the doorway, fully dressed in his caftan and skull-cap. A uniformed officer, more like a cop than a tax inspector, stepped out behind him. He looked at the caravan and stared me full in the face.

I gave a harsh gasp. Could anyone in a uniform arrest me?

"The tax police—" I began. The caravan's undercarriage gave an agonized squeal as Shem swerved.

"Keep still when I'm driving!" he yelled.

I twisted around and saw Lemon rush out after her father, with a red blanket thrown about her shoulders, shouting and shaking her fist. The officer shoved her father toward the back of the van. Mr. Bardoff remonstrated with him, but the officer jabbed his nightstick into the old man's back. The cops were rough. I'd seen boys in the Paria neighborhood often enough, spread-eagled over the hood of a patrol car. But to use a nightstick on an old man! What could he have done?

Shem turned the caravan around the corner and they were gone. I blinked. The scene had been so sudden and unexpected that it was in me to wonder if I was already asleep.

But I knew I wasn't. I couldn't rid myself of the image of Lemon hurling defiance at the white van. Her tongue could blister. I'd heard it many a time! But her blistering words made no difference. Just as my putting the Evil Eye on the Cruelty man had made no difference when he came for Zara. Poor Lemon! I wished I could help her....

But then a cold thought came to me: the Jersains had their troubles, surely, and the Bardoffs had always been kind to me, but I couldn't add their problems to mine. It was sad to think that old Ren Bardoff, with the gout in his knee and with his gentle manner, might be heading to debtors' prison. But the Jersains had a network. They stuck together. They didn't need the Yulang to worry for them. I'd heard they had even shrugged off the great Roman Stanno's goodwill.

I needed to concentrate on my own difficulties.

I had no food, no money, no shelter, and no friends. That should be enough to worry about! I had only one resource—this brief chance to sleep while Shem drove—and I needed to take advantage of it.

But it was many minutes before I could free my mind of Lemon and her father, and many more before I could close my eyes.

Kick off, kick off your high-heeled shoes,
All made of Yulang leather.
Put on, put on these low-heeled shoes,
And we'll ride off together.

—Zimbali ballad

Sometimes you know you are dreaming and the dream is so bad, you struggle to wake, kicking your way up to consciousness like a salmon struggling up a fish ladder.

But this was different. I knew I was dreaming and tried to hold the dream inside me, like a sweet biscuit on the tongue, before it melted away.

My mother held out her hand and helped me jump a mountain brook. The water was so clear that every pebble shone in its bed like a polished gem. I was small and straight as a boy, just above the height of my mother's waist.

"For that leap, a mouthful of berries." She'd a bucket in her hand. Dusky blue orbs crammed it to the brim.

"Greedy!" Mother laughed as I scooped out an overflowing handful. The berries burst in my mouth, the sweet and the sour together. I beamed at her and knew from her laughter that my teeth were purple with juice.

We kept climbing the slope of the mountain, under the high canopy of cedar, hemlock, and fir. Beards of lichen drooped from the branches of the trees. Sometimes Mother would hold me high, next to the trunk, to draw the tangy resin of the cedars into my nose. Or she'd stop to lay a twig under the belly of a banana slug to show me how the slimy thing would curl and draw in its antennas.

From the dank, ferny mud we picked wild mushrooms with delicate fins. Mother laid them carefully in her wicker basket for market. We found scads of them in this dream forest, far more than we'd ever found in waking life.

My short legs began to flag and I pulled on my mother's skirts.

"It's not far, Serena. Not far now, darling. I'll carry you a ways."

I leaned against the curve of her back, wrapped my arms around her neck and my legs about her waist. With a heave, she stood and began to carry me up the mountain. Needles of yew and leaves of maple brushed my shoulders. Spiderwebs caught on my face as I rested my cheek against Mother's thick black hair and smelled the scent of wildflowers on her neck.

As I rode, I played with the charm necklace that had been her last gift to me. I wore it in the dream, even though I hadn't owned it as a child. *A perfect gift for a Yulang girl,* Mother had told me, *because you can give the charms away one by one. That is how we are connected to the world,* she said. *In love or in hate, we always give.*

It was still my most prized possession, in real life. But I must be mostly Gorgio, for so far I had given away none of the charms. Not the cat hunched to pounce or the dove with its head under its wing. Not the dog howling at the moon or the eagle diving. And especially not the horse, which mother had told me was the most precious.

In my dream, I tugged on her braids, the way Zara pulled on mine. "Why is the horse so special?"

"Don't you know, love? Horses are the opposite of *ma'hane.* Horses purify. They bring happiness. You give that only to one you hold as precious as a traveler holds his finest stallion."

"You mean his finest car! Who has horse caravans anymore?"

Suddenly, Mother stopped. "Look, Serena," she whispered. "Over there in the clearing."

A sunbeam had dropped through an opening in the canopy. Its light dripped like honey. In the glow stood a fawn, gold from ears to hoof, gilded with light as if worked from bronze or rose gold. And I knew, with my older dreaming mind, that it was astonishing good luck to catch a glimpse of a golden fawn. . . .

I was thrown hard to one side. A metallic whine drilled through my skull.

The small dashboard lights flickered. I was being pulled in a sickening swerve. Then the swinging stopped. The seat belt jerked me back, vengeful gravity claiming its own.

I was actually awake for a moment or two before I realized I was still in the car. Next to me, in the driver's seat, was Shem, looking blue and shaken.

"What happened?" I croaked.

"A deer ran across the road. I nearly hit her."

He threw the gear stick into neutral, yanked up the parking brake, snapped the keys out of the ignition, and tossed them in my lap. "Shove over. You're going to drive."

He opened his door and got out. The air that drifted in was cold and earthy with the smell of wet leaves.

Mechanically, I undid my seat belt, swung my door open, and stepped out. When I was last awake, we had been driving through the outskirts of the city. Now we were deep in forest land. Trees loomed dark and shadowy. Fans of needles hung over us like tarps. The underbrush was gauzed with fog, and a watery dawn light was dimming the headlights, diffusing their glare in the morning mist. I could smell burned rubber.

I hesitated before I took Shem's seat. I had never driven a car before, much less one pulling a caravan. But anything I did could only be an improvement. From what I had seen, Shem was even less equipped to drive than he was to play a violin.

When I slid into the driver's seat, he was already beside me, with his head tipped back and his eyes shut.

I jabbed his arm. "Wake up. You have to tell me how to drive this thing."

"I thought you were Kereskedo," he muttered sleepily. "Don't your people travel?"

"Not since I was ten." Though Mother had traveled, all right, I thought. She just hadn't taken us with her. Crabbily, I poked Shem's shoulder again. "Just tell me how and I'll do it. *Your* people travel, but you drive like you're from a place where people ride elephants."

The boy gave a sleepy laugh. "It's not one of my talents."

I couldn't imagine what his talents might be. At least he admitted what they weren't.

He showed me the clutch and the gearshift and what you were supposed to do with them. I had him go through it four times, which he did patiently enough. That's the way I learn. I don't mind running through something again and again, so long as at the end I know it.

It worked pretty well for Romanae declensions. And to my surprise, it worked for driving, too. After one false start, when I jerked the car forward and then sent us slamming back against our seats, I managed to move it pretty smoothly into first and then second gear.

"Not bad," Shem told me. "But do you feel the way it's lagging? That tells you it wants to go into third gear. You probably can't go much faster on an unpaved road like this."

"This car wants things? You really do think it's an elephant!"

I felt pretty pleased with myself as shifted into third without much of a hiccup. It felt good. The speed was right. Though ungainly, the caravan cooperated with me. And the road, though bumpy, was not too bad for a forest road. I remembered Daddy rattling us up forest roads to trailheads as if every joint of his little car were about to fly to pieces. That was a long time ago.

Beside me, Shem was quickly falling asleep.

"Hey! Tell me where to go!"

"Just stop when you see a . . ." A snore escaped him. I slapped his arm.

"A what! Wake up!"

"A camp. Thirty, forty people. You'll know it when you . . ." He was out.

As I drove, the shadowy forms of trees took on definite shapes and color began to seep into the forest. The road slipped away under my wheels. All I heard was the rumble of the motor and the shushing of leaves against the sides of the caravan. I felt grateful to Shem for falling asleep. The silence was refreshing as a cool drink.

After a while, the road began to climb. We were heading into switchbacks, but there was a good shoulder. No sudden drops, at least not too close to my wheels. Those used to terrify me when Daddy drove us out here.

We emerged from the trees, and I could see the thin edge of the sun peering around the mountain's hulking peak. It brightened the sea of fog that lay in the hollows and sparkled the dew on the hemlocks.

Shem had brought us all the way south to Mount Avo—Grandmother Mountain—the sleeping volcano that, on a clear day, you can see even from Oestia, looming over the city like the shoulder of God. I'd forgotten how it felt to be this close to it. As I drove, I caught glimpses of the long glaciers running down from its peak and the blue shadows in its valleys. A shivery mix of elation and fear bubbled up inside me. I remembered that strange combination of terror and joy that the nearness of such grandeur had always brought when I was a child.

But this time, I felt something else as well.

It was hope. For this was where Anchara Pulchra was camped, the mara chan of the Kereskedo tribe. The woman who could help me.

He was right, Shem, when he said gasoline was more valuable than gold!

The road plunged downhill again and we were back among the trees. But by now the light was stronger, and the mist clung only in scraps.

A moment later, I caught sight of a boy carrying kindling. I slowed, easing the car into a lower gear, so I could watch where he went. He was picking his way along a faint path downhill. My eyes followed and I saw the bumper of a caravan half concealed in a hollow. Hanging from its side mirror was a brass owl—the protective symbol of the Kereskedo tribe: Don't try to trick us, it says. We can see in the dark. A long blue magpie feather was woven defiantly through the amulet.

I pulled into a turnout and brought the car to rest. Sounds like the hammers of disgruntled trolls pounded and knocked under the hood, then sighed into silence.

I held Shem's keys close and tight for a moment before dropping them reluctantly into his jacket pocket. This was as purifying as the smell of a baby's head or the galloping hoof of a beautiful horse: my foot on the gas, the dirt road slipping away under my wheels. I wished I could just let the road fall away behind me for days and weeks together, for, despite my flickering hope, I felt suddenly unready to bring my suit to another like Nico Brassi.

There was nothing for it. I nudged Shem awake.

"Is this Anchara Pulchra's camp, do you think?"

He blinked, looked about, and nodded.

I stepped out of the car onto the moist and muddy surface of the forest road. Morning had just broken. The sun was still a hot, new-struck penny in the sky, but the camp was already astir. The Yulang never sleep, I thought. At Nico Brassi's the men were probably only now stumbling off to bed, while here the women and children were up before the sun.

The boy I'd seen by the road raced up to us. He stared rudely, then reeled downhill, calling, "Avo Anchara! Travelers! Zimbali!"

Shem had gotten out of the car just in time to hear this. I saw him flinch as the boy named his tribe.

Before I could wonder at this, he grabbed my arm. "What do you bring?"

"What?"

"A gift." He frowned. "Come on, Jalla—what's your name, anyway?"

"Serena."

"Serena?" His mouth quirked. "Good name. Though maybe not for you. Well, your serene highness, surely you know there has to be a gift?"

"Of course I know that!" I spluttered. But in truth, I *had* forgotten. What kind of ignorant, Gorgio-bred girl would he think I was? I felt angry at him for finding me out.

"Well? What will you give the mara chan?"

"Give her? Don't be ridiculous! What have I got to give?" I was still in my slippers—no coat, no pack, no wallet. He could see I had nothing! "Don't you have anything in the caravan you could let me have?" I'd certainly heard things crashing about in the back every time we plunged into a pothole or hove up against the root of a tree.

"Nothing I can spare. And you're the one asking for help, Jalla. Not me."

I stared at him in disbelief. What was he expecting me to do? Offer my fingernail clippings? Chop off my hair? Pull out a tooth? How could he be so tightfisted?

I stomped back to the car and yanked open the door. Under the

74

glove compartment, where I had shoved it last night, was Shem's violin. I pulled it out and waved it at him.

"How about this? You can spare it. There's a pawn ticket for it right in your pocket! Besides, you can't even play it properly! It's worthless to you."

He drew in a soft hiss of breath. "Even you know such a gift has no value."

He didn't say it sharply, but his words cut because I knew they were true. He'd told me the night before that the instrument meant nothing to him. To give a present to someone only because you didn't care about it yourself—that was worse than miserly. It showed meanness of spirit. And no trait was held in more contempt than being mean-spirited.

"No Yulang would give such a gift," he added, and this time he couldn't keep the scorn out of his voice.

"I know that," I muttered. But I didn't know it the way Shem did, as taken for granted as the blood running in his veins. And because of that, I would always be foreign, even among my own mother's people.

I turned to put the violin back in the car.

But my hand clung stubbornly to the handle of the case, and I couldn't let it go. Real was real. I had to give something. Anchara Pulchra was my thin straw of hope. I couldn't go to her empty-handed and hex my chances before I'd even asked. If it shamed me to give the worthless, so be it. As long as I got her help.

Shem had gotten sick of waiting for me and was already halfway down to the camp. I hurried after him, sensing it wouldn't do to arrive trailing after him. The people here didn't know me. Why start off with the impression that I had to walk a pace behind?

These people didn't know me.

I stopped in my tracks.

They didn't know I was ma'hane.

My heart skipped a thump, and then I was rushing through stripped huckleberry bushes in my haste to catch up with Shem.

Down in the hollow there were tents spangled with dew, laundry lines stretching from tree to tree, and nine or ten caravans, all parked a little distance from each other under giant cedars and hemlocks. Orange-, yellow-, and rose-tinted slabs of fungus stuck out of the tree trunks. No one here would be foolish enough to eat any of these, even if they weren't poisonous; Yulang food laws declare them out of bounds, because they grow in the air rather than on the ground, as proper mushrooms should. There, I thought. I *do* know something. I tried to take heart from this shred of knowledge.

Only the boy who'd spied us on top of the hillock, an old woman, and a few shadowy girls were in evidence. I pulled my shoulders back and smoothed my rumpled hair. *They don't know me. I must look my best.*

But even as I thought this, I stumbled over a tree root and my slipper somersaulted away. My foot squelched in the damp mossy dirt. The boy who'd announced our coming gave a hoarse caw of laughter.

"Here's a real traveler come to you, Grandma," he mocked. "Ready to cross the Big Mountain in her soft bedroom slips."

The old woman cackled as I hopped after my slipper. She was squat as the huge iron pot on the hook over the fire. The hook hung from an iron pole planted in the ground. Though many caravans now had kitchens, I remembered that cooking on the iron was considered the best way to prevent pollution, and traditional Yulang bands still stuck to it.

The boy prodded the fire with a long stick. A haze of damp cedar smoke eddied in the air. The scent bit pungently and my stomach clutched with hunger. What were they cooking? Would they offer me some?

"Our city cousins think little of mountain wear," the old lady observed. Her eyes—one bigger than the other—examined me under brows so black they looked like greasepaint. The map of wrinkles on her face scrunched in amusement.

One of the girls, wearing the long skirt and headscarf of a married woman, swung up to the fire. She was lugging a heavy kettle full of stream water. "The garb's easy to explain." She giggled. "Hopped in their car right after the wedding night, I'll bet. Too dazzled to change into walking boots."

My mouth fell open. If the men had been around, a young wife like her would never have spoken so. But her words brought only a ribald laugh from the old woman and a light cuff on the ears.

I snuck a horrified glance at Shem.

To my annoyance, he'd ignored the innuendo and was bowing to the old woman. She waved a hand in regal acknowledgment and looked expectantly at me.

It had been a long time since I'd been at a Yulang camp. And then I'd come invited, welcome and beloved, as all Yulang children are. Now I came citified, unwed at marriage age, with a muddy slipper in my hand, a filthy sock on my foot, and nothing to offer but trouble.

"Respect, Avo," I began.

The old woman stiffened and drew herself upright. "What do you want?"

No smile and wave for me. Even so, despite her unfriendly tone, the story of Zara and the Cruelty man was as ready to spill as wine from a bottle. I nearly launched into it right then and there.

I opened my mouth—and fortunately, remembered what I should do instead.

"I've brought you a gift," I said.

The old woman's face remained impassive, but she folded her fleshy arms, waiting to see what I produced.

I glanced nervously at Shem as I approached her. His eyes registered the violin case in my hand with unmistakable disgust. I supposed he hadn't noticed that I'd picked it up again.

I sighed. Even without Shem's withering look, I realized that I couldn't give such a gift. It just wasn't in me.

I set the violin on the ground and left it there.

One of the matriarch's eyes shot a look at it, while the other eye wandered slowly behind. I licked my lips nervously. What now? I had to do something. But what else did I have to give? My brain felt gummy. If only Mother were here! I thought with longing. She'd tell me! No etiquette of the traveling tribes was secret to her!

Then, from wherever I'd left it when I was rattled awake, the dream I'd been sent that morning poured back into my mind. *The perfect gift . . . because you can give the charms away one by one.* I drew a sharp breath and my hands flew to my collar.

Brushing my hair aside, I felt for the thin golden chain and twisted it until I touched its clasp. With some difficulty I unhooked it with my ragged fingernails.

Holding the chain taut, I laid it on the log by the fire, taking care that it not slip into the cracks in the bark. My eyes flew from one charm to the next. The Yulang have deep associations with each animal—associations that I only partly remembered. To pick the wrong one would be worse than giving nothing at all! It would be an affront.

And Anchara Pulchra would have to be satisfied with her gift if I was to have hope of her help. I'd have to choose carefully.

I felt the old woman's eyes on me and hoped that I hadn't betrayed my uncertainty.

Which charm? The cat was Zara's favorite, and I would never part with it. The snake, a certain insult. The howling dog with his bristling chest was so exuberant that I could hardly give him to this ancient, menacing woman. Nor could I give the rabbit, a harmless, fleet—not to mention delicious—beastie. I could hardly see anyone catching and skinning Anchara Pulchra. Nothing of the soft-haired, twitching sacrifice about her! The scavenging eagle? The shy dove? I was starting to feel frantic. No. None of them was right.

There was only one I thought might do, but it could easily be as offensive as the snake.

The old woman shifted impatiently.

No help for it now. I would have to take my chances.

I unclasped the hook, dropped the golden charm into my palm, and held it out to the mara chan. Squinting, Anchara Pulchra leaned forward and examined the eight pincer arms of the golden spider picking its way across a fine-spun web.

Her frown plunged her lips into deep black gullies.

I held my breath, silently cursing myself. A spider! Good thinking, Serena! Why didn't you choose a cockroach while you were at it? What unbelievable ignorance have you displayed now?

The old woman raised her head and looked me straight in the eye. I braced myself for instant denunciation, outright dismissal.

Instead, the matriarch burst out laughing.

I let my breath out. A touch flickered against my elbow, and I turned to see a surprised grin on Shem's face.

Anchara Pulchra held out her hand. With the other, she walloped my upper arm.

"I'm the old spider spinning out the threads, am I? Is that what you've heard? You're a bold girl, I'll give you that."

Limp with relief, I dropped the spider into her palm.

The old lady's smile disappeared. "Next to a gift of love, a gift that reveals true thoughts . . . It pleases me to know what people think." Her eyes met mine. "I accept this gift."

She leaned over and patted the log. I picked up my necklace and fastened it securely around my neck before sitting down across from her.

"Now, tell me what you've come for. Quick, before the menfolk are up." She shot a sidelong glance at a young woman who was mashing tea in an aluminum pot. The girl met her gaze and the two of them burst out laughing. I understood by this that the men would not rise for hours. Shem shifted uneasily from foot to foot.

Anchara jabbed a stubby finger at him. "Sit, bridegroom. Her troubles are yours now." She laughed again, mockingly. I stiffened. The old woman glanced at me, and I could see she was enjoying my discomfort.

Shem was oblivious. He just sat down beside me, quite matter-of-factly. How could he! Bridegroom indeed!

For my part, I shrank away from him. What had made Anchara presume such a relation between us? It made me feel as if I had just trod barefoot on a worm. It must have been that stupid girl's joke! How could Anchara believe that nonsense? I couldn't speak a word for shame.

But Shem, at least, should have.

I glanced at him slantwise. Even this inept boy must have seen that words were needed! Such a mistake couldn't be let stand.

But his face betrayed no awareness whatsoever. I could have slapped him.

Suddenly, I remembered how enamored of him Janet had been. Was Anchara's mistake just the sort he expected people to make? Did everyone assume that if he was with a girl, she must be madly in love with him? I studied him a moment, feeling irritated and resentful. There was no denying he was handsome. His skin was dark, his lashes and brows darker still, and his mouth was generous and expressive. Like many of his tribe, he wore a small gold hoop in one ear, which shone beneath his cropped, curly hair. I bet he had gotten a lot of mileage out of his looks, not to mention that grin of his, which seemed to put you in league with him, whether you wanted to be or not.

All this only made Anchara's presumption more embarrassing. For I could see, just a little, how these things could make you forget the wretched violin playing, the rotten driving, and the suspicion that there really was nothing he could do properly at all. Not even correct Anchara—the dolt!

"What's your name, then?" the old woman rapped out.

I turned my attention to her, even more flustered now that she'd seen me lost in thought over my companion. "Serena Wallace," I said, with all the dignity I could muster.

"Wallace?" The old woman looked at Shem with a baffled expression. "Why would you be named Wallace?"

Shem shrugged and held up his hands. "I'm not. It's not my name."

Now I flat-out glared at him. What he said was true. Wallace was not his name. And this truth only served to cement the lie that we were bride and groom, flesh and blood. So Shem, who had been so delicate about truth when it was not his to tell, was not above a light trick or two!

"Whose name is it, then?"

"My father's, of course," I said.

Anchara nodded. "Half Gorgio. That explains it. I hold no evil thoughts on that account, Jalla. But what was your mother's name? That's what matters."

"Silvani."

Anchara's face slammed shut like a book. *"Ma'hane,* then, through your sister."

I stared. How could she know that? Perhaps I should say it was some other Silvani family she was thinking of.

The old woman read my thoughts. "Why pretend otherwise? You're outcast. What was your sister's name again? Ash, Elm, something . . ."

"Willow," I said sourly.

"And who sent you to me? I can see you're not just passing through."

"Nico Brassi."

A snort. "Ah! Nico. I must thank him. He sends me all his trash."

I jumped to my feet. "I'm *not* trash!"

"The *ma'hane* verdict says otherwise." She looked down at the spider in her hand. "Still, your gift speaks for you. A little. Sit down. You may tell me why you came, impure or no."

I sat back on the log, trying to swallow my indignation. To no avail. When I spoke, my voice was trembling with it. "My niece has been taken by the Gorgios."

"And?"

"And I want to know how to get her back."

Anchara cocked an uncharitable eye upon me. "Wisdom to the worthy. Which you surely are not. What is it you need?"

I forgot I was a humble petitioner. "What do you think I need? I need help, of course! I need to know what to do! I need someone to speak for me."

I stopped and looked at her unsympathetic face.

She thought I had given them a reason to take Zara. I could see it clearly in her mismatched eyes. Just like Nico Brassi. My misfortunes were my own fault. She wouldn't help me!

"But that's not what you want to hear, is it, Avo? I've tried for help from Nico Brassi, and now from you, and I can see my mistake. I'm crazy even to ask. Why do I need the Gorgios to wipe their snot on me, when you Yulang are tripping over each other to do it? What I really need is the *ma'hane* verdict wiped away! As long as I'm outcast, you've no more interest in helping me than helping a stray dog!"

A sharp kick on my ankle brought me up short. I knew it was Shem, but I was fuming too much to wonder why.

Anchara Pulchra's face was hard as stale bread.

"You're wrong," she said coldly. "I would always help a stray dog."

My anger was so big in my chest I thought I would burst.

"But—"

Shem kicked me harder.

"But nothing. *Ma'hane* is *ma'hane*," the old woman continued. "Even your words show your nature! I cannot wipe *ma'hane* clean. It cannot mix with those who are untouched any more than one washes underclothes in a tub for dishes. It needs an extraordinary person doing an extraordinary thing to overturn the tribunal's verdict." She gave me a withering glance. "And that is not you, Jalla. Be satisfied."

She turned her head pointedly away.

"Goodbye."

What will you give me, oh darling, my son,
What will you give me, my darling young one?

—Kereskedo song

Anchara gathered herself together, pulling her mug of hot tea in toward her belly. It was a sign that she would offer no hospitality to me.

My skin prickled, numb with shock. What had I done? I'd known Anchara was a person to approach with etiquette and every show of respect. A minute before, she had been ready to listen. Now she would not even share a spot of hot water. I'd thrown away my chance for the sake of a few angry words. Though surely she'd deserved them, I thought rebelliously. But for this, I was going to leave empty-handed?

"Go!"

I tried to rise but couldn't.

Anchara smashed her cup down. The tea splattered. To my horror, she grabbed the fringes of her shawl and began to shake them at me. This was how old women threatened pollution. In a moment it would be the skirt flapping and she'd be casting the taint upon me. It would have been less humiliating if she had just hit me with a rock.

"Begone! I'm finished with you! You're not welcome here!"

Miserably, I rose to my feet. Perhaps Nico Brassi was right. My family brought our troubles on ourselves. Me as much as Willow.

I turned and trudged stupidly back toward the road. My slippers made sucking noises in the mud—a fit accompaniment to my ignoble retreat.

No one had ever threatened to cast pollution upon me before. I didn't know a single person that had ever happened to. What was wrong with me? Was I really so bad?

I looked over my shoulder to make sure Anchara had stopped. With great relief, I saw that she'd sunk down again on her stump, muttering.

Shem was watching me thoughtfully. My ankle was sore where he'd kicked it, but I hadn't the spirit to be annoyed. He'd been trying to warn me, of course. Warn me that my big mouth was chewing up my chances, as it always did. Amazing, that even someone I'd known less than twelve hours could see that, but I seemed unable to keep it in mind. He'd brought me all this way to help me and all I'd done was embarrass him. For this I felt a tiny glimmer of guilt.

But I reminded myself that Shem really had no troubles compared with mine. He could easily tell Anchara's band I was a hitchhiker and, despite what they thought, he didn't really know me. That would be the end of it and good luck to him.

I set my foot on the forest road and strained my eyes to see where it went. Nothing but endless stands of cedar and spruce, thickening and darkening into the far distance. A pang jangled my stomach. I couldn't even remember the last time I had eaten. How was I going to make my way through the forest without food, without even boots on my feet? Where was I going, anyway?

Miserably, I turned around again.

I didn't mean to. Anyone with any self-respect would have marched off without a backward glance. Why couldn't I?

Anchara looked enraged. In a second she really would curse me. But Shem was still watching me calmly, with his chin cupped in his hand. I couldn't read anything in his expression.

My eyes caught his. Three true things, I thought. He'd asked, I'd told him, and he'd brought me here. Our bargain was finished. It was useless to look for more help.

But all of a sudden, he stood up and walked over to where I stood. With a businesslike gesture, he took me by the arm and led me back to the fire, where Anchara still sat, watching me with a hostile gaze.

"If she goes, I must go. But I haven't given my gift yet, Avo Anchara." I could only stare.

The old woman peered at Shem distrustfully. "Well?"

Shem let go of my arm. He took off his jacket and his vest and folded them neatly and laid them on a wooden crate by the fire. Like most Zimbali men, he wore suspenders over a white shirt. Tied fast to one suspender was a small leather bag.

Anchara watched closely as he untied the bag, pulled its drawstring loose, and poured its contents into his hand. I caught the gleam of gold and heard its heavy chink. I, too, was watching him narrowly. He hadn't said anything about a hidden bag of gold last night when he'd turned out his pockets and demonstrated himself to be poor but honest!

But I hadn't time to wonder at that. For when he opened his hand, even I knew enough to be shocked.

He held out a strand of heavy gold coins stamped with the head of an ancient emperor—real wealth to any who knew. They were all strung together on a wire that could be twisted and untwisted at will but broken only by extraordinary force. It was Kereskedo braid gold, meant to be woven into a woman's hair and never given away except on her deathbed. And then only to her daughters. Mother wore such coins. I'd often helped her weave them through her braids after she'd washed her hair. They were the reason I would not let myself believe her dead. Because if she had died, her tribe would be honor bound to return the braid gold to me and Willow.

How had Shem come by the gold? If a woman has no daughters, a son might inherit. But he would give them immediately to his bride. They belonged properly only to women.

But to give them away as a gift? And for one of the Zimbali tribe to possess them at all?

The old woman raised a bristly eyebrow.

She lowered her mug of tea onto the log without looking at it, perching it at an angle that tempted fate. Then she cupped her hands and Shem dropped the gold into her wide palms. The coins clinked against each other as they fell.

Shem yanked my arm, and I took this to mean I should sit down beside him. I did so, warily, fearing Anchara would snarl at me to get moving. But the wise woman was too interested in the coins to care.

"If this is stolen," she whispered, "I'll send a curse to dog your steps."

"It's not stolen."

"Then how does the musician tribe come by it?"

"My grandmother was Kereskedo. She bore only sons. My father gave it to my mother, who left it to me when she died. I was their only child. They both died when I was small." He said this dispassionately, as if it were only a matter of record. Perhaps that was what it was to lose your parents young. I had already passed through the arch of my twelfth year when my father arrived home in an army coffin, and I could still feel the hole it had torn in my heart.

The woman glanced at me. "Then why does *she* not wear them?"

"She is *ma'hane*." Shem answered so quickly I suspected he was warding off any objection of mine. Such as "Why would I? I only met him last night!" Though he had no need to worry. I would have to be really stupid to call attention to myself that way.

"Then why stand by her?" Anchara peered at him shrewdly. "You must fear the taint yourself, Jal, my lad?"

Shem drew breath but answered without hesitation. "There are ways to avoid pollution, Avo. But a bargain is a bargain, and I have made a bargain with this girl. The mara chan of the Kereskedo must know that we honor our bargains. Even we Zimbalis. I—" He bit his lip, and I saw how fast he must be thinking. "I hope for the day things may change," he concluded with a shrug, as if consigning his future to the hands of fate. I watched him in amazement. He had transformed himself into the kind of man the Yulang sympathize with most—one who has suffered misfortune but bears his affliction bravely. In this case, the man who marries badly and makes the best of it.

He *was* clever.

But what was it all for? His expression reminded me of those of the old men who played chess in Plaza Ridizio, determined no one should guess their next move. Once again, he'd spoken nothing but the simple truth, and it only served to strengthen a lie. We had a bargain, true enough: I'd spared his family business, and he felt he had to pay what he owed me. But that wasn't the bargain he'd conveyed to Anchara!

Why was he doing this? What use was it to him, pretending we were wed?

Whyever it was, Anchara seemed satisfied with his explanation. The young man had the misfortune of marrying an outcast. Of course he would not entrust his family treasures to her.

"And what is it that is worthy of such a gift?"

"Listen to the girl's story, Mara Chan. Perhaps you'll change your mind and help her."

I couldn't believe it. Kereskedo gold to overcome Anchara Pulchra's bad opinion of me? Was he insane?

"Why are you doing this?" I burst out.

A thin smile spread across the old woman's face, showing a sliver of teeth. "There's your thanks, Jal. Would you really give such a gift for this ungrateful girl?" She looked long at him, then shook her head. "No, you want something more. Am I right?"

Shem spread his hands, palms up, and bowed. It was a gesture of respect to elders, but he did it as if he was sharing a joke with her, as well as acknowledging the truth in her accusation.

Anchara gave a bemused laugh. "I like the way you bargain. I like to be surprised." She turned to me as if I'd just become visible again. "All right. I'll listen. But mind your mouth."

I did. As dispassionately as Shem, I told her what had happened to me and my family.

When I finished, Anchara Pulchra sniffed. "How old are you, Jalla?"

"Sixteen. Just."

"Old enough to be wed, but not old enough to know your elbow from a matchstick. Here, girl, shall I tell you your greatest stupidity?"

I knew I didn't have a choice. I nodded.

"Biting that Cruelty man and leading him on that mad chase. Fool! Do you even know if he lives?"

The fear I'd kept at bay came hot and close, breathing down my neck.

"No, but, Avo, that was an accident, when he fell down the stairs. *I* didn't do that!"

Anchara's mouth pulled down like a flounder's. "And since when does that matter?" She sucked her lips with yellowed teeth. "If you hadn't run, you'd be in a cell and no mistake about that. Still, if he's not dead, there might not be a charge—"

"Can't we find out?"

The old woman fixed me with her larger eye. "*We?* If *I* chose, *I* could find out." She let this sink in. Then: "If you are lucky—if!—and the man is not dead, then your problem is easily solved."

"How?"

"The Cruelty took the little one, you say." She looked at me scornfully. "They count on your ignorance. Anyone of legal age in your family can declare they are willing to raise the baby, and the Cruelty must allow it. That's law. Of course, to the Gorgio you are not of age yet. Not competent to care for the child. But your mother . . ."

"She's left us. I don't know where she is!"

"True. I recall something of the sort. Don't you have an aunt?"

I shook my head.

"A grandmother?"

I thought of my father's mother in her Gorgio mansion.

"*No.*"

Anchara's voice took on a slightly kinder note. "Do you even know if your mother is alive?"

"Of course she is!" Even to my own ear, my voice twanged like an untuned guitar string.

The mara chan looked at me heavily. "Well, if she really is alive, as you say, I can find her. Any of the Kereskedo tribe I can find."

I forgot everything but the mad happiness that gushed into my heart. This was better than I'd dared hope! Anchara must have been the person I was looking for these long years. The one person who could find Mother out in the great unfriendly world!

If—the thought rose unbidden—if Mother wanted to be found.

I pushed away that evil suspicion, as I had many times before.

It was so simple! Once I had reunited with Mother, we could get Zara back. Of course we could. I turned to Shem, forgetting all my distrust, and beamed at him.

He looked surprised, but a smile broke through his impassive expression. A true smile, too.

I leaned toward the old woman and seized her hand in mine. Hers was strong and heavy as a kitchen weight, cut and creased a hundred ways. I kissed the knuckle, as I'd seen my mother do to Yulang elders.

"Thank you, Avo Anchara! You don't know what this means to me! How soon can you find her?"

Anchara Pulchra yanked her hand away. "You need sharper ears, Jalla. I said 'I can,' not 'I will.' You are still *ma'hane*. And angry. And wrong-headed. And if your man had not spoken for you, you would be miles away in the mud by now. It will take time and trouble to find Galeah Silvani. And I shall only go to that trouble if you work for me first."

"Work for you!"

"As I said."

The sun was well up in the east. Somewhere, Zara was awake, in the hands of strangers. In a nursery or an orphanage, where children expect no words of kindness or arms to nestle in, and where no one will come when they cry. The pain of it winched the breath tightly in my lungs.

"But I need to get to Zara right away!"

"So? You refuse?" The old woman looked from me to Shem and slapped her palms together. "Then the bargain is off."

"But I can't wait! The Cruelty may have given her to a Gorgio family by then. Who knows what they'll do?"

"I am growing weary of you, girl. Did you think I would wave a branch and shake my skirts and the baby would be returned? You are *ma'hane!* Why can you not understand such a simple thing?" She spat. "Pah! Set your mind to my service, or leave now!"

"Take it, Serena." Shem sounded exasperated. "Last night you had nothing. Now you have the help of the mara chan herself."

I was barely able to swallow my indignation. But I kept silent. For once, Shem had spoken the unalloyed truth.

"Work doesn't frighten you, does it?" he added. I heard scorn in his voice.

I shook my head. "What must I do?"

The boy who sat by the fire, tending the embers with a stick, looked up at me, smirking. "Hauling boulders, *Ma'hane*. That's the price for the mara chan's help. For dirt like you, that is."

"Boulders?"

The old woman reached over and smacked the boy's ear hard. "Shut your mouth! Baby tyrant, are you?" He whimpered with pain.

Then she turned to me. "Not boulders, girl. I'm no slaveholder. Collecting gems from the streams and the caverns. Nothing to break the back of a healthy girl like you. But important for us. We must have them to sell at the harvest market in Eurus Major." I looked at her in surprise. Eurus Major was the eastern capital of the province—two hundred miles inland. "The Gorgio prospectors are laying claims and waving papers to keep us off the best land," Anchara continued. "And what they don't have by law, they take with bribes. We must work hard and work clever to grab what's ours. And all the gathering must be complete astride the time."

"Gathering what?"

"Agate and thunder eggs. Tiger's-eyes, rose quartz, obsidian on the volcano, carnelian, and onyx—like that. To be tumbled and set as quickly as we can. Jasper, too. Anything that will sell." She gave me a shrewd look. "Why that moon-calf face, girl? Are you ashamed to do this?"

"I thought—I thought you were traders. Don't you travel like the others and buy what you sell?"

"We've already sold all we bought during the collecting season. It will not be enough to feed our people through the winter. So we turn our hand to what we have the gift for. Stone setting. Gold working. Now, before the harvest markets end."

I supposed I had known that not everything the Kereskedo sold had actually been bought. I'd heard Gorgios complain of it—how the Yulang poach fish from the lakes, timber from the forests, and gems from the earth. Stealing. Scavenging. Hiding their finds away. Even Anchara admitted that Gorgio prospectors had permission papers and we didn't. It was as my teachers said—no respect for the laws.

A dull heat began to glow in my face: despite all my years at the Lyceum Romanae, I was fated to be a Magpie indeed. Catch-as-catch-can ... The taunts of Janet's friends had proved true.

But if I was to have the mara chan's help finding Zara ...

I swallowed the bitter thought and tried to meet the old woman's eyes.

"I'll work for you, Avo Anchara. Tell me what I must do to gain your help."

The old crone looked at me thoughtfully, watery eyes glittering. "Find me something of worth, outcast. That's all I ask. Something rich to see our folk through the cold winter. Surely you recognize the gems that will bring us a good price, daughter of Kereskedo traders? Surely Galeah would have instructed you?"

"If only!" I burst out bitterly. But then I caught Shem's warning eye.

"I'll do as you ask, Mara Chan."

But if Anchara's help was to hang on my knowledge of this or that sparkling rock, I was in trouble. The names of the gemstones she had rattled off like well-loved incantations were nothing but names to me.

I recognized none.

8

Father, have you brought me gold?
Or have you paid my fee?
Or have you come to see me hang
On the gallows tree?
                                    —Paria song

I awoke to a harsh shriek and half sprang out of bed, thinking Zara was crying to be let out of her crib. But there was no night-light glowing in a wall socket. No Willow. No pile of rumpled skirts and baby clothes.

The shriek was only the call of a crow piercing the raucous bird chorus that announced first light. A murder of crows, I thought blurrily, remembering Janet's word games. But then I ceased to notice the cawing, becoming aware of another, less easily explained sound: soft breathing, from somewhere nearby.

I bolted upright.

It was Shem, of course, stretched out on the rag rug on the floor of his caravan, with a heavy wool blanket thrown over him and his head pillowed on his arm.

Nearly two weeks had gone by and I still had not become accustomed to the situation. I must have been dead tired last night if I was in such a muddle as to have forgotten it.

Clutching my blanket to me, I slid open the window and yanked in my clothes from the drying rack attached to its frame. They were still damp. Without leaving the shelter of the blankets I managed to wriggle into my sweater, trousers, and stale socks.

Shivering, I threw off the covers, tiptoed around Shem, and opened the caravan door. The steps were like ice under my feet. Fortunately, Anchara's son, Rass, had kitted me out with a good pair of heavy work boots. I opened the trunk of the car, where I'd thrown them the evening before, and gratefully slipped my feet into them. In a thick cardboard box beside them was my equipment for the mountain: pail, shovel, sieve, flashlight, rock hammer, and chisel.

Downhill from Shem's caravan, I could see a girl setting split logs to the kindling in the near darkness. As always, Anchara sat by the fire, ceaselessly twisting fine silver into settings for precious stones. More than ever, I was reminded of an old spider knotting and spinning her webs.

The fire would be kept ablaze all morning, and as the dawn crept in, it would draw the women of the camp to it, heavy-footed and yawning, to start the day's work. Each morning I watched them and envied their companionship while I ate my solitary breakfast on a rock by Shem's caravan. Without variation, it comprised a bowl of oat porridge, coaxed into sticky life over the thin blue flame of the camp stove, which Shem left out for me. Even though he didn't—or wouldn't?—share my meals, he left the bag of oatmeal for me every day, underneath the waterproof tarp, along with the camp stove, his ax, and a few logs. I was never sure if he wanted me to use the firewood or not, so I never lit a fire. Often he also left bread and cheese, dates, and apples, which I would pack up for the mountains.

It seemed generous, but I knew it was also a clear hint not to make free with the pantry in the caravan. As he'd told Anchara, there were ways to avoid pollution. I supposed I shouldn't have been surprised that in saying so, he had actually told the truth. Ever since we'd settled here, he'd kept his distance, never rising in the mornings until I was nearly on the road.

The people in Anchara's camp, too, kept clear of me. I had seen a girl make the sign for warding off evil after she'd caught my glance. A little boy had once clambered up to my rock, wriggling like a puppy, reminding me marvelously and horribly of Zara. His mother had charged after him, letting loose a string of Yulang admonitions. "Ya! Shula-ya! Keep away! Don't touch! It's dangerous!" The same words my mother had used once when I was little and tried to pull a toy out of the fire.

Pollution like mine was catching. I could not approach Anchara's people's fire or share their food. I couldn't even fetch water from the stream by the camp, for fear I would be driven off like a raccoon. Instead, I dipped into the water barrel Shem had filled the day before.

As I drank the icy water, Anchara's son, Rass, came and squatted by my side. Rass directed the everyday work of Anchara's clan—the prospectors in the mountains, the gold- and silversmiths in the camp, and, undoubtedly, the traders in the markets. Of all the clan, he was the only person who ever spoke to me.

Today he was carrying a pile of folded clothes, which I eyed curiously.

"You're going up high today," he told me. "You'll need this."

He placed the pile on the rock between us. I glanced uncertainly at him and, at his nod, unfolded the clothing with eager hands. It proved to be a dull green jacket of heavy, lined corduroy.

"Thank you. That's kind—"

Rass snorted. "Good business, Jalla. You're no use to us dead of exposure."

I studied him curiously as I slid my arms into the jacket's sleeves and huddled into its warmth. Why didn't he fear pollution, as the others did? He was a man in his middle years, black of beard and lumpy of feature, tall and strong where his mother was stumpy. His cheek had been ripped open in a fight with the White Shirts—three of them to one of him, I had overheard one of the men telling Shem. The scar that remained ran in a jagged seam down the side of his face.

No, I doubted Rass was much afraid of anything—though I wouldn't lay money that he didn't fear Anchara. Everyone else seemed to.

"I'm sending you to Hammerhead Ridge," he told me. "East along the forest road. The trailhead is at the mile forty-two marker or thereabouts. Lots of skunk cabbage in the lower reaches of the stream—you can't miss that. We had some luck up at four thousand feet. You might go even higher, if you've an itch to. My nephew, Hendry, found some good rose quartz there, and a bit of carnelian that was worth keeping."

After many days of hard work, I finally knew what he was talking about. I'd begun to recognize the look of different gems. Enough to know I was now bringing in a modest amount of agate, and some dull green jasper. But nothing of great value.

Nothing that would prove my worth to Anchara, or win her help.

"You're the only one I'm sending up the mountain today, Jalla. I'll need all the hands I can muster to work the metal and facet the stones before we leave for Eurus." He frowned. "We won't do well this winter on what I see in my workshop."

"I'm sorry to hear it."

"Well, then. Find us some real treasure before the Gorgios snatch it all."

"Will I run into Gorgio prospectors?" About four days before, the men from Anchara's camp had gotten into a fight with a gang of Gorgios who were mining the same area. I didn't relish the idea of encountering them.

Rass stood. "Don't concern yourself, Jalla. Even a Gorgio won't lift a hand to a girl like you."

Wouldn't hit a girl? I wondered. Or wouldn't touch me because I was *ma'hane?* Either way, I wasn't reassured.

But there was no point wasting time in worry. The trailhead was a good five miles from our camp and light was already breaking through the canopy.

Hurriedly I organized my equipment. Just when I had succeeded in getting my pack strapped on and everything in place, the door of the caravan creaked open and Shem stuck out his head.

"Take a ride today, Serena. At least to the trailhead. I'll unhook the car."

I shook my head and set off, without so much as glancing in his direction.

"You'll wear yourself out before the day's even started!" he shouted. Still I didn't turn around.

I would take nothing more from Shem. Nothing. No matter how lonely I got.

After all, I'd had his help, and he'd helped me so well and so thoroughly that I was now sharing his sleeping quarters.

Who in their right mind adds to such a debt?

I walked along quickly in the direction of the rising sun, remembering the Gorgio boys who crashed at our apartment after Willow's parties. I had to be on my guard just to get up and go to the bathroom at night. One time, one of them cornered me, shoved me up against the kitchen counter, and stuck his big meaty hand inside my shirt. I landed him a crack on the head with Mother's rolling pin. It was hard not to hit him again once he'd stumbled backward, moaning and cursing! But if I had hit him a second time, I would have certainly killed him. And that knowledge was all that had prevented me.

No. I didn't like to share sleeping quarters with boys.

But now, since everyone assumed Shem and I were married, here I was, forced to do it again. Why hadn't he set Anchara straight by now? It only added to my mistrust of him. Though I had to admit that Shem hadn't taken advantage of the situation. He'd never laid a finger on me. Perhaps that was one benefit of being *ma'hane,* which also means "untouchable." He didn't speak to me in the caravan, or even meet my eyes when he came in to sleep after a day in Rass's workshop.

Still, I flinched when I heard him turn over in the night, and sleep scurried from me. When it finally came, it was uneasy and full of nightmares. Such nightmares! I wished with all my heart I could tell someone about the pictures that haunted those dreams! And then I cursed Shem, for I might have told him, if I hadn't been so sure that he was using me somehow. And because of that, I was left with the nightmares and loneliness weighing in my gullet like a lump of porridge.

I could escape my loneliness only when I was alone, roaming in the mountains, searching for shiny objects like the solitary, sharp-eyed Magpie I had become. And maybe it wasn't so bad, this scavenging in the wild, since it released me from the sentence of solitude. Only when I was alone was I not an outcast, not shunned as if the very air I breathed were infected.

I stretched my arms wide and turned my head up to the sun as I crested a hill and the camp slipped away behind me. Another dry day in October. You couldn't buy this kind of luck. If I had to serve Anchara, I thanked Mother Lillith I could do it in the mountains. I'd always loved the mountain world of moist cedar and blue spruce and clear cold waters, from way back, when my family still followed the long roads.

"We'll go there soon," Mother had promised the very last night I saw her. "Up to Lookout Pass. I'll bake a honey cake and pack white peaches. We'll hike to the lake."

But that night I'd woken to angry voices downstairs. And when I came home from school the next day, she was gone. The photos of us she had displayed on her dresser were missing. Scratches on Grandmother's floor were all that remained of her dowry chest, where she stored her few treasures.

From that time until Shem brought me to Anchara's camp, I had never set foot on a mountain trail.

It was midmorning when I reached the stream Rass had directed me to. I untied my equipment and set to work. I heaved sievefuls of dirt and sand from the streambed, shaking them side to side, squinting at the stones that were left when I'd sifted off the gravel. Once in a long while, I found something worth popping into my backpack.

The wet sand was heavy. When my back ached too much to keep going, I put down the sieve, pulled on a pair of rubber gloves, and waded into the water.

A glimpse of green by the bank caught my eye. I pushed aside a curtain of ferns. Careful not to stir up the silt, I plucked a greenish pebble out of the streambed. But the green was only algae. Underneath, the rock was gray as cement. Cocking my wrist, I winged it back into the water and waded on.

After a time, my hands became so icy I couldn't feel them. I yanked off my gloves. Rivulets of water poured from the fingers. I smacked the gloves against a tree and rubbed my hands together hard enough, it seemed, to spark fire. I blew on them noisily and—yes, being alone for many days had made me peculiar—berated them aloud for not warming up faster.

A branch shook in a sudden breeze. Under its rattle, I thought I heard something strange. I lifted my head and listened.

Then I stopped dead.

Someone had spoken my name. My name.

I prayed I hadn't really heard it. There is nothing frightening in being alone. I'd been rejoicing in it as I left camp. But to think you're alone and suddenly discover that you aren't . . .

I stood still, straining my ears. For a few moments, only the rustle of little animals in the undergrowth disturbed the perfect silence. I sighed. My imagination after all. Always too active . . .

"Serena."

It was a man's voice, faint as the small wind turning the branches at the tops of the trees. I could hardly make it out. Was it Shem? Rass? I hoped so! That would be all right.

But somehow I knew it was neither of them.

Terror splashed through my veins, icier and more absolute than the chill of the stream. Someone was behind me in the forest. Had he followed me? I'd heard no footfall, no crunching of the fallen spruce needles. Perhaps because he was so far away? I shivered. Something told me that wasn't the reason.

Then, a tiny bit louder, I heard it again.

And suddenly, my heart filled and flooded with joy. I recognized the voice!

"Dad? Is that you?"

I whirled around, searching for a sign of him, but there was nothing behind me except tree trunks and the spreading licorice fern I'd chewed earlier to soothe my ragged throat. Softly, I stepped away from the stream, following the voice back into the trees. A spirit is a fragile thing, as likely to take flight as a butterfly. I had to tread lightly.

"Serena! Jalla!"

And suddenly the voice was no longer in the trees but back at the bank of the stream, downhill from where I'd been working.

I whirled about, peered downstream, and froze.

Perhaps twenty feet away, forepaws planted in the streambed, stood a bear. I watched as it turned its massive head from side to side. It must have heard my voice.

Gulping sharp, shallow breaths, I pressed myself behind the nearest tree trunk.

The bear continued to search up and down the bank. Then, after a while, satisfied that no one was there, it plunged its muzzle into the water and began lapping up great mouthfuls.

My heart rattled like a dry pea in a pantry tin.

A moment later, amid snapping twigs, rustling leaves, and little grunting noises, a cub tumbled out of the undergrowth and joined its mother at the stream.

I remembered a little of what my parents had taught me about bears when we had gone to the mountains. Bear bells, I remembered, and bear bags. But not what to do if you found yourself within biting range of one. I couldn't remember whether I was supposed to stay still or run or climb a tree or play dead. I couldn't even tell if the bears I saw were black bears or grizzlies—black, probably, from the smooth coat—but what difference did it make? All I knew for certain was that no bear was so likely to attack as a mother with her cub.

Frozen, I watched the cub plunge into the stream. She rolled over, splashing and wallowing. Playfully, she charged up the bank at her mother and nudged her with her snout. The mother pushed her away. The cub charged again, provoking a powerful shove from the mother. The little bear tottered into the water with a splash. Disciplined, she dragged herself to shore with her shoulders drooping, shaking the water from her fur in a pinwheel of silver droplets.

A blue jay dropped a jagged blade of chatter through the branches right above my head. The mother bear raised her snout and sniffed the air.

This time surely she would see me.

I couldn't move. My eyes shut of their own volition. My muscles tensed, my ears strained for the rustle of the bears' movements. The inside of my mouth was as dry as a salt flat. I prayed for my limbs to grow bark, my fingers to stretch and bud with branches and leaves, my roots to sink into the ground, and all human scent, all human fear to petrify into hard wood.

The rustle of the bears' movements whirled about my ears like a windstorm.

I opened my eyes.

To my weak-limbed relief, I saw the mother bear's broad bottom hulking back into the trees on the other side of the stream. With a final look at the sparkling water, the cub turned and followed.

Even after I heard the last crackle of a twig under their paws, I could not move. I memorized the pattern of ferns, the great stands and snags, the exact melon-gold light of the hazy afternoon. I felt as lonely as Mother Lillith, the solitary wanderer from whom the Yulang claim descent, who was cast out of the Garden long before Eve. How could I be an outcast, when the whole Yulang race stems from such stock?

But the outcasts cast out, too, or I would not be alone in these woods. No, if I were not *ma'hane,* I would be prospecting with the others with a good pistol among us to protect us from wild beasts.

After many minutes, I forced myself to walk back to the stream. There I stuffed the equipment into my pack, tying my sieve on with trembling fingers. If running didn't make such a huge clatter, I would have sprinted all the way out to the forest road.

The problem was that to get back to the road, I'd have to follow the stream. And the bears couldn't be far from the water yet. So I cut into the trees, thinking to make my way through the bush, hiking parallel to the stream. My legs were shaking so much that I had to pick up a tall, stout stick to steady myself.

Mother once told me about the Yulang tribes across the great ocean, in the old lands of Romana, who train bears to dance for their livelihood. Surely that was only possible in the tame stretches of the old lands! Not in our roaring wilderness. A bear in our mountains was more likely to make *me* dance.

After I had walked a quarter of an hour, I began to breathe more deeply.

It occurred to me that I was being a coward.

Instead of running away, I should have been remembering Zara and how a few gems of real worth could enlist old Anchara's help! I forced myself to stop and nerved myself to head back to the stream.

Then, out of the corner of my eye, I saw something dark and low to the ground.

The cub?

My heart pounded. But it was only the mouth of a small cave, concealed behind a tangle of blackberry vines.

A sunbeam slanted through the lacework of shadows.

And there, in the shimmering light, I saw my father. He was leaning against the side of the cave, grinning at me. The light struck the gold bracelet on his arm that had sealed his betrothal to my mother. He wore the shapeless Yulang felt hat Mother had given him, as well. Beneath its dipping brim, his sky blue eyes smiled at me. His face was as summer-freckled as it often had been in life.

Ever since he'd died, I'd caught fleeting glimpses of him, as I had on the carousel at Plaza Ridizio. And each time I saw him, he looked younger.

Now I realized it was simply that I was aging and he was not. The clocks were stopped in the land of the dead. Perhaps they even went backward. It was a mystery beyond my comprehension. But I realized with a start that my father looked not ten years older than Shem had that morning, when he'd offered me a ride to the trailhead.

I sat down on a boulder, drinking him in with my eyes. I was so glad to see him and there was so much to say that no words could make their way out of my throat.

"Are you afraid?"

If my father had been alive, he'd have leaned over and taken my hands in his to reassure me. The thought of that gesture, and what separated us now, brought hot tears to my eyes.

"Yes." My voice caught. "But not of you."

His quick smile flashed. "No. You've never been a fool, Reenie, and only fools fear the dead." He rocked back on his heels. "Now that all's said and done, the only thing I ever should have feared was that tank of gasoline and Private Moran's cigarette. . . . Don't, Serena. No crying. I want to tell you something about fear."

"All right." I batted back my tears and tried to keep him fixed and solid in my gaze.

He nodded, looking as he had when I was little and he had dusted me off from some tumble or other. "You shouldn't fear anything, Reenie, in this world or any other. Except losing your honor."

I looked at him in puzzlement. "What do you mean? Not—like Willow did?"

"No. I'm not talking about Willow having her baby. Or what you're afraid that Zimbali boy might do to you, or that old witch calling you *ma'hane* . . . or those Yulang folk afraid to touch your hand or catch a look from your eyes. . . . None of that can take away your honor. Not even the words of that blowhard Brassi." He looked at me intently. "You know that, don't you, sweetheart?"

I hung my head, feeling the humiliation of all the things he had just listed. I couldn't bear that my father—even dead and in the spirit world—could see it all so clearly.

"Reenie, listen to me. You have nothing to feel ashamed of. Honor is a straight line between what you do and what you believe. That's all it is. No one else can touch it. If you can stick to that, then there's nothing to fear."

It was the longest and most serious speech I'd ever heard from my father. I wanted to hold his words like new-baked bread and warm my soul with them. I wanted to believe that honor was mine, no matter how worthless others thought me or how cowardly I seemed to myself.

But I didn't believe it. I was despised. I was cowardly. And my fears were so real.

My dad shook his head. "Which is the worst?"

"Which what?"

"Which fear?"

I stared down at my hands in a patch of sunlight, then flicked my gaze back to him. "Mother," I whispered. "Is she with you, Dad? Is she in the land of the dead?"

A loud snap behind me made me jump. Then a noise—a rustle of movement in the underbrush. I turned to look.

Nothing showed itself, but shadows were thickening among the branches, marking how the sun was slipping over the mountain.

When I turned back, my father was gone.

My heart pinched with disappointment. But I held tight to a glimpse I'd had, a flickering sliver of sight. Before I'd looked away, I thought I'd seen my dad slightly, just slightly, shake his head.

Crack open the door, dig under the stone.
In the land of the dead, you're never alone.

—Zimbali ballad

The noises were coming closer. Leaves shook and shivered together. Twigs snapped and feet crunched the undergrowth.

An animal was stalking me.

I couldn't see the beast, squint though I might into the shimmering light between the trees. But I heard it, right enough, crashing through tangled branches. My heart was thudding nearly as loudly. Not much time had passed since I'd seen the bears by the stream. The sounds I heard could easily be the mother bear, following my scent.

Following my scent? Think, Serena. What kind of bear stalks humans? Bears were more likely to stalk ... *blueberries.* Or fish, if they were feeling really bloodthirsty. They wouldn't be stalking me! What an idiot I was!

Then I paused. Grizzlies might stalk. I'd read about grizzly attacks. And mountain lions. There were mountain lions all over this range. Signs at the trailheads told people to carry sticks, even on the shortest hike, in case a mountain lion attacked.

Another crash sent me scrambling to the cave mouth. I wedged myself in behind the blackberry brambles. But the autumn-thinned vines provided little cover.

Behind me, the cave mouth yawned.

Without a second thought, I crept into the darkness.

But even as I entered the cramped, cool space and felt moss in my hair and smelled the scent of wet clay in my nostrils, I knew I'd made a mistake. What was I? Crazy? Hiding from a bear *in a cave?*

This place was probably the bear's winter home. Mama Bear could have littered her cub right here. There was probably a sign in bear language on the door: MAMA BEAR'S CAVE: TRESPASSERS WILL BE EATEN.

Unless it was a mountain lion's lair. Then there would be splintered bones and blood on the walls.

Shut up! I told myself. Don't stay here mithering, girl. Up one, up all and run!

I crouched down, legs bent in a runner's squat, nerving myself to go. But the shuffling outside the cave held me frozen.

Oh, Daddy, I thought, no matter what you say, fear is real! And there's more to fear in this world than losing your blasted honor!

I turned away from the cave opening and inched myself deeper into the darkness, clutching Rass's warm corduroy jacket around me. The walls closed in as I went farther and the cave narrowed to a tunnel. The air became cold and heavy. I kept moving, but panic churned in my chest. Close, tight spaces, earth pressing in around me . . . Maybe this was a mistake.

But I was too frightened to stop. Instead, I pushed on, farther into the earth, farther along the narrow tunnel, over rock and along soft, caved-in dirt, stooping so as not to hit my head. The pale light from the cave mouth receded.

Darkness muffled me like a shroud.

I gulped for air. But then, to my infinite relief, the tunnel opened out, and it was as if my lungs were expanding, too. I felt my chest rise and fall. Thank goodness it hadn't dead-ended! Now I wouldn't have to retrace my steps. Perhaps there was another way out. If I found it, I could emerge miles away from the bear. . . .

But if I was wrong, my reasoning brain said coldly, I would hit a wall. Then, when the animal made its way in, I wouldn't be able to escape.

The thought sent me scurrying even faster. I knew I should stop and find my flashlight, but I couldn't force myself to slow down. My brain said one thing, but my feet just said walk.

I scrambled along, listening for animal noises, and brushing my palm against the cold, cold rock to keep my bearings in this black tunnel. My breath rasped in my ears and bounced off the walls.

A step. Another step.

Then the ground fell away under my feet.

A piercing emptiness surged from my stomach to my chest. I clutched for a handhold, but my fingers closed around nothing. Pebbles and dirt were cascading down around me.

Jagged rocks smashed into my legs and hands as I landed. Pain shot through my shin. I could feel hot blood seeping through my trouser leg.

"Mother Lillith!" I shouted. And clamped my hand over my mouth. I'd come into this stupid cave trying to hide. And now, like an idiot, I'd called out my whereabouts to any predator that might be lurking: Here I am! Come and get me! I groaned.

But then my brain chinked like a cash register swallowing a coin.

Was I mistaken, or had I heard my voice echo?

I had to test it. Quietly, I spoke the first words that came into my head.

"Dad? Are you there?"

A shiver ran down my spine as the echo boomed back. The reverberations seemed to tunnel into the depths of the earth. Perhaps my words even reached into the vast realm of the dead that extends through the underground passages of Mount Avo, as it extends under every piece of earth you put your shoe on. So Mother's people say, anyway.

More loudly, I called out, "Dad?"

My father had helped me once today. He had warned me of the bears. Perhaps if I called on his help here in the land of the dead, he would lead me to safety. . . .

No! I called on reason. The echo told me the tunnel must open up into a cave, and the cave must be a large one. And if it was, there was a good chance of another way out.

There was some sort of misty light here, and in its dim glow I rolled up my trouser leg and examined the bloody mess on my shin. Of course I didn't have any bandages. But I remembered the bandana in my pocket and tied it around the gash. I was carefully rolling down my trouser leg when I stopped short, struck with a realization.

I could see.

Why could I see? *Where* was the light coming from?

I turned my head, searching for the source of the light. In the faint glimmer, I saw how the floor of the tunnel sloped downward, slippery with a loose scree of pebbles and trickling water, and then turned sharply round a bend. The light pulsed from beyond that turn, pale as a moth, flickering fitfully.

I shivered. If this was an entrance to the kingdom of death, then surely that ghostly light streamed from the portal that separated the worlds. There are stories of those who cross that threshold, though the wise do their best to keep it sealed. Yulang families host ceremonial dinners a month after every funeral. Elaborate food is prepared, songs sung, libations poured, all to persuade the spirit of the departed to remain in its proper place. At the end of the feast, the guests troop to the nearest shore—be it lake, river, or ocean—bury the coins for the boatman, and sing their last farewell. Then the spirit is satisfied, and the boatman ferries him or her across the waters of death. And the door between life and death remains shut.

But we had no such dinner for my father. The guests were invited. The hall was rented. Mother had even started cooking when my grandmother cornered her. As Willow and I watched, the old woman smashed plate after plate of Mother's wedding china. She'd break every dish in the house, she declared, rather than let her perform her bar-

baric ceremony. *An insult to my dead son! Haven't you dragged him down enough?*

The funeral feast was never held. There was nothing for us. No comfort for Mother. No coins for Daddy. Nothing.

That was why I could still see my father. For him, the door must still have been ajar. Perhaps I had now come to the place where it swung wide.

I expected to find myself shaking, but my hands were steady. After all, there was another possibility. The light could come from a cave mouth! I pulled the flashlight out of my pack and switched it on.

All there was to see jumped out at me. I nearly smacked my own head when I saw that there were toeholds in the vertical wall over which I'd fallen. I could have climbed down if I'd had the wit to stop and turn on my flashlight! Holding my leg gingerly, I limped down the uneven incline, wishing I hadn't thrown my walking stick into the clearing when I'd dived into the cave.

But when I rounded the bend, no second cave mouth opened to the surface. Nor did a supernatural gateway gape before me.

Instead, a small lantern rested in a hollowed-out niche, its artificial light already starting to dim.

I caught my breath. A lantern! Someone else must be here with me. Perhaps it was some of Anchara's band? For a moment, I felt hopeful. The men never went without lanterns. Not that they would welcome me, but there was safety in numbers. . . .

But I remembered that Rass hadn't sent anyone out today besides me.

That meant this light could only belong to Anchara's rivals: the Gorgio prospectors.

I whirled my flashlight in a full circle around my body like a sword. The shadows seemed full of fingers ready to grab my shoulders and pull me down. I dug into my pack, pulled out my rock pick, and held it in my stronger hand, poised and at the ready. Feeling only slightly safer, I pushed on.

The ceiling of the cave rose higher as I descended. Soon, my flashlight could not penetrate its shadows except to expose jagged teeth of stalactites. The walls of the cave swung out, and I found myself in a vast, echoing cavern. Tunnels funneled off into pitch darkness to right and left; sudden drops made me sway with dizziness.

I remembered once sailing on the Sound with Daddy in one of his friends' boats. There'd been a snorkel and a pair of goggles, and I'd begged to try them. I dived in. But when I opened my eyes and peered through the bleary lenses, there was no sight of the bottom. I had hung suspended over an infinite drop, hardly able to tread water, feeling as if the whole world had fallen away and there was nowhere to anchor myself, nowhere solid in the whole watery universe. I had never been so frightened.

And here I was again, with the hugeness of the unknown world opening out around me. I wanted to rise to the top and rip off my goggles as I had in the water that day. But there was no surfacing here.

Instead, I plunged deeper. The slope became rough and choppy. Spurs of rock stuck out from the walls, forming arches and columns— a fantastic underground architecture. Thin rock ridges dropped off into nothingness. Pools of water glittered with glowing mineral hues.

Time had taken on a syrupy, dreamlike quality. Perhaps there was no portal to the land of death. Perhaps I had simply crossed into that land without realizing it. For there, the Yulang say, a traveler may remain an hour and return to the world of the living to find that ten years have slipped away.

A drop of freezing water splatted down on me. The cold jolted my brain. I was letting good daylight slip away outside. I needed to be on guard for the Gorgios, who would not take kindly to a stranger in their underground haunts. I needed either to find a way out, and soon, or to start retracing my steps.

High above, I heard the whir of papery wings and knew that bats must be stirring. My steps on the crumbling rock scritched and echoed. I could hear water dripping from the stalactites, sharp and precise as it hit the rock floor.

And then something different—a soft plash. Water dripping into water. I trained my flashlight downward.

A lake stretched out below me.

There was hardly an inch of flat cave bed by the shores of that lake. Into the softer rock someone had driven a post. And tied to the post, slumbering on the water, was a sturdy canoe.

I caught my breath. The boatman, I thought. My hands were like ice. Had I stumbled upon his craft?

But with my thinking brain, I knew the boat belonged to the Gorgio gem hunters, not to any supernatural being. And there must have been several of them—to carry a canoe all the way down here!

Slowly, I trained my flashlight along the edges of the lake. Although I didn't know what I was looking for, I suddenly had the strongest feeling that something was hidden here. Something that would make people lug a canoe down that dark and difficult tunnel.

But all I saw, far off, on the other side of the lake, was another post like the one on this side, for tying up the craft once you'd come across.

I tugged the bow of the canoe up onto the shore and climbed in, careful not to soak my boots. The rope was fresh and slippery, and easy to untie. I pushed off, clenching the flashlight firmly between my knees. As I paddled, I tried not to think of the boatman. But I couldn't help wondering what would happen to me if I was stealing the boat for the transport of dead souls. Whose anger would be worse: that of the ghosts forced to linger hopelessly on the shore, or that of the flesh-and-blood relatives, unable to lay their dead to rest?

There was no reason to fear the dead, I reminded myself. But if people with warm blood in their veins were there in the dark with me, and I was paddling their canoe, then I had something to worry about!

I began whistling low, to settle my nerves. My dad had had a way of whistling between his teeth when he took us out in the canoe on Lake Zephyr in the rain forest. My whistle echoed back now, and it was as if my father were keeping me company, telling me not to be afraid on the dark water.

I swallowed my whistle abruptly. No need to advertise my whereabouts. Fearfully, I stopped paddling for a moment. But I could not stop simply because I might be discovered, I realized. I had to follow this road to the end.

I grounded the canoe, got out, and tied it to the second post.

The shore sloped upward and then leveled off, slippery under my feet. It stretched much farther than the shore from which I'd come. As I walked on, I discovered giant boulders lying next to each other, just touching, like peaches in a fruit bowl. Pyramids of rock and rubble stood nearby. They seemed weird—unnatural—to me. Too symmetrical. More like slag heaps than natural rock formations.

I climbed over a boulder and peered behind it. Hidden in its shadows were tools—picks and shovels and screens, a dirt-encrusted wheelbarrow.

It was a stash of miners' gear.

A feathering of excitement ran down my neck. I rounded the jutting rocks and stumbled over the miners' refuse, shooting my flashlight beam down at the ground and up along the rock face.

Then I stopped short. I'd been lucky so far, but what if someone was hiding here, watching me poke around? They had a secret to protect. That much was clear. Why else conceal the gear when it was already hidden so deep in the recesses of the earth? The secret must be valuable indeed if they would go to such trouble! I wondered what they would do to someone who discovered it.

The urge swept through me to jump back in the canoe and retrace my steps. Rass's assurance that the Gorgios wouldn't raise their hands to me was hollow comfort, as far from help as I was now. I remembered the knife wound one of Anchara's prospectors carried back to camp after his run-in with them.

Before I'd even made a conscious decision, my feet were walking back to the canoe.

But I stopped halfway. The canoe had been moored on the other side of the lake, I told myself. The Gorgios must have left it there when they finished on this side. No one would be over here! And you can't leave without looking. . . .

I took a deep breath, gathering every scrap of courage I possessed—it did seem to lie in scraps at this point—and turned back.

The far wall of the cave stretched twenty or so feet beyond the pile of equipment. I approached it, slowly examining the rock face under the small beam of my flashlight. The wall was pocked with crevices, and here and there small crystals flashed.

But I saw nothing spectacular, nothing to make the Gorgios go to such lengths to secure the area.

Disappointed, I went back to the pile of mining gear and set off in the other direction along the rock face.

I pried and peered, but unearthed not a glimmer of gemstones, not a streak of metal. I strained my ears for sounds of approaching feet, searching fast and clumsily. Oh! I was taking too long! They would return and find me here, and then what?

Noises in the cave made me jump. By now, the cold had penetrated even Rass's warm jacket, and I was shivering. But somehow I couldn't stop looking. Whatever the Gorgios were so anxious to conceal lay within arm's reach, only muffled in darkness. . . . Think of it as a birthday treasure hunt, I told myself weakly. Look high and low, the way you and Willow did when Mother hid candies around the house. How will you ever be a proper Yulang collector if you can't stick with a search? How will you ever find anything to bring to Anchara?

And so, bullying and coaxing myself, I looked further. And further. I was about to give up when I spied the fissure in the cave wall.

It was so deep that it was almost like the entrance to another cave, but so narrow that there was barely enough room for a person to stand inside it. And even at fifteen paces, I could see what all the secrecy was about.

The fissure was crusted with amethysts.

They glittered like a purple waterfall frozen in midgush, imprisoned in the gray stone of the cave. The floor was littered with shards, which must have fallen away from the miners' picks as they hauled out the bigger chunks. Some of the gems glowed a deep, rich purple, like the petals of a violet. Others were nearly transparent, stained pink as a pale dawn. They shimmered under my flashlight beam like a mosaic. How rich the miners must have thought themselves, to leave so much of their treasure scattered on the floor!

For a moment, I could only stare.

Then I dropped my backpack and went straight to the wall with my pick at the ready.

But why? Why waste time excavating my own gems and risk the return of the Gorgios? The pick's noise would echo from here to the tunnel, broadcasting the fact that I was poaching on their territory—surely they would see it that way! I couldn't risk it. I grabbed my pack and loosened its ties, shoving the pick into a long side pocket.

Then I bent down, lay the open mouth of the pack near the scattered pile of gems, and began sweeping the amethysts in, not pausing to separate them from the rubble and dust left by the miners' tools. The jewels sparkled and tumbled under my hands.

As I stuffed them into my pack, I thought of the look that would be on Anchara Pulchra's face when I returned to camp.

And I laughed to myself, very, very quietly.

Prove to me the sun does shine,
Prove to me the darkness,
Prove the water isn't wine,
Prove the mountain's starkness.

—Jersain riddle song

The forest was dark, a vast whispering wilderness, when I emerged from the same cave mouth I'd entered hours before. For all my wanderings underground, I had found no other exit. It was sweating work, climbing the long way back with my injured leg and the heavy pack hanging from my shoulders, especially clawing my way up the sheer drop where I'd fallen. But I delighted in the weight of the amethysts and nearly sang with joy when I crawled out through the low aperture into the open air.

I could not see the moon through the branches of the trees. Their leaves had become a sort of knitting, pulled tight, tucking a close-woven blanket over the forest. Beneath it, the dark was thick and full of sounds.

By the cave mouth, I saw the heavy walking stick I'd thrown to the ground when I scrambled to hide myself. I picked it up, switched off my flickering flashlight, and closed my eyes to listen.

The forest babbled in whispers, like the half-heard intimations of dreams. The wind skipped from tree to tree, touched a bough here, rattled a pinecone there, like a child playing tag. Owls hooted, questing and mournful. Screeching, chittering noises came from bats stretching their wings after a long day's rest.

And underneath it all, low and unceasing, I heard what I'd been listening for—the bubbling, rushing song of the stream. It was ahead of me to the right, on lower ground. Switching on the flashlight, I made my way toward the sound of the waters.

Though I'd gained some mastery of my fears, I still had to spend a good minute or two calming my heart and staring down a silvery twig in my path that might have been a snake. When I raised my walking stick and poked at it, the twig helpfully remained a twig, and I was able to pass.

Then, at last, I saw the stream. It was wearing its nighttime garb, black and shiny as the obsidian Rass's men had taken from the volcano. The rest of the way down the mountain, I stuck by its side. I felt I was walking next to the closest friend I had, a friend who would laugh and gossip to me, keep me company in the dark, and rejoice with me in my secret—my wonderful secret—that hidden in my bag was the treasure hoard with which I could buy Zara's freedom.

Joyfully, I quickened my steps, ignoring the noise I made. The forest now seemed quite loud to my sharpened ears, full of chirping, knocking, whooping, cackling things, and I was just another of them.

After a while, my feet hit a trail and I parted ways with the stream. In a few yards I would be heading down the forest road. I switched off the flashlight to save the battery, hoping the moon would light my way now that I was coming out from the shadow of the trees.

Instead, as I set foot on the forest road, two balls of fire burst to life in front of me. I flung my arm across my eyes.

They were the headlights of a car, not the flames of hell. But this only made me more terrified. As my dad said, only fools fear the supernatural. Humans were the ones to beware of. And humans drove cars.

I heard the car's door creak, but my eyes were too blinkered to distinguish the person who jumped out. Terror pumped through my veins. It was as though an engine had been switched on inside of me.

With a surge of speed, I dashed back toward the forest, blind and trip-ping in panic.

Through the pounding of blood in my ears, I heard my name.

But I couldn't force my legs to stop. The flight coursing through me was more powerful than reason.

The voice called again.

Panting, I looked back.

It was Shem. He caught up to me and grabbed me hard by the shoulders. But the flight was still in me and I twisted in his grip, though I knew I should be thankful it was only him.

He took in my disheveled state with dismay. "What happened to you, Jalla? I thought you were gone for good. Is that blood on your leg?"

"I'm fine." I shrugged off his hands roughly.

Then I remembered. The triumph of what I had to tell was in my mouth like honey, but it came out sharp as bitterroot. "Fine, and richer than you'll ever be, fiddler."

"What?" Shem bent down to look at my trouser leg. "It's blood, all right. And dirt everywhere else. You look like you fell down a hole."

"I did. And look what I found down there."

I pulled my sack off my shoulders, untied it, and plunged my hand into the cold jumble of rock and dust at its bottom. When I opened my fist and Shem saw the stones sparkling in my palm, I could have danced at the stupefaction on his face. My head was light with hunger and exhaustion.

But even more dizzying was the thought that hit me afresh—that now I really had something to bargain with. I had fulfilled my part of the deal with Anchara. Surely she would not make me wait any longer to find my mother!

Shem pulled my outstretched hand into the glaring headlights to examine the stones more closely. But when he made as if to pick one up, I clenched my fingers into a fist.

"No one touches these except Anchara Pulchra. Understand? If you've been sent to fetch me, you can take me back to the camp. But if you're going to try anything, be assured, my legs can carry me just as well."

"I wasn't sent. I've been up the stream chasing your track half the day." I noticed a raw red scrape across his face from his jaw to his eye. He rubbed it ruefully. "Nearly had my eye out for my pains."

A horrible thought came to me. "That isn't from the bear, is it?"

"What bear?"

"A mother bear and her cub. That's how I ended up in the cave. I was getting away from them. I thought maybe you'd . . ."

"Fought them bare-fisted?" He eyed me mockingly and burst out laughing. "We're not really married, friend. I'm not going to fight bears to get at you!"

"Hmmph."

He folded his arms. "So that's where you were. Underground. It's funny—I'd as much as decided that you'd fallen through a crack in the earth. You really are a surprising girl. . . ."

"There's no need to make such a meal out of it. Why were you looking for me?" I asked sourly.

"To warn you."

"Warn me about what?"

Suddenly, I remembered how Shem had handled Anchara. He wasn't the fool he sometimes seemed. I was suspicious of this warning of his. Perhaps he hadn't been looking for me at all. He was acting concerned about me for a share of the amethysts.

"What nonsense is this? Take me back to Anchara's camp if that's what you've been sent to do."

"I *wasn't* sent. What do you use your ears for? I told you that already. And I can't take you back to camp."

"Why not?"

"Beause there is no camp anymore."

"What?"

Now that I wasn't moving, the cold bit into my limbs. I was far too weary for games. And though I had spoken little to Shem these last many days, I'd never stopped suspecting that he was playing some elaborate game with me. Tired as I was, I knew I needed my wits about me to deal with him.

"Take me back there. I want to see with my own eyes."

"Don't be stupid, Serena! It isn't safe. Anchara's folk are gone. And we should be, too. We're hours behind them already."

"I don't believe you!"

Shem looked offended. "I told you back at Nico Brassi's. I don't hold with lies, Serena. I tell the truth."

"Ha! As it conveniences you!"

He stared at me. Angrily, I stared right back. If he has the smallest drop of shame, I can stare him down, I thought.

It took only a few seconds.

"You mean about us? About . . ." Shem made a gesture of slipping a ring on his finger. He looked sheepish. "That wasn't an outright lie. I never actually said you were my wife."

"Oh, and a huge difference that makes! A lazy man's lie. Couldn't be bothered to tell it yourself!"

"Did you want me to tell Anchara the truth, Jalla?" He gave me a sharp look. "You know she let you stay on sufferance because of that lie. I let it stand because I wanted to help you."

"You wanted to help yourself. You said so!"

"Also true. What do you expect? But if you knew why . . . I wanted to talk to you about it, but you haven't let me."

"Is that a surprise?" I spoke through my teeth. "A convenient slip of the tongue and you share the sleeping quarters of a Kereskedo girl!"

He looked at his boots. "Not even you would say I've betrayed any trust there. Truly, Serena. Have you thought I would—"

"It's not what you've done!" I spluttered. "It's what you can do! And anytime you like! It's a dishonor to me. If my father were alive . . ."

The words my father had spoken in the forest made me pause.

"Take me back to the camp," I said flatly.

"I told you, there is no camp! The Forest Service gave us an hour to pack our gear and go!"

I narrowed my eyes. "You've just seen the gems. Now you tell me there's no camp to go back to. Which leaves me alone with you and the amethysts. I said, take me back!"

"Look, Serena. You're crazy, you know that? It was under pain of arrest. Don't you know anything about life on the road? You don't go back and take a chance like that!"

"I've taken more chances than that today. Take me back and show me or I'll never trust your word again!"

Shem opened his mouth and then shut it tight. He seemed to be fighting down some strong impulse.

"All right," he said. "But I'll give you some soap and a towel first. And some clean clothes. You're a mess and that leg is caked with blood. Go and wash at the stream. We won't have a chance for a while."

At the expression on my face, he sighed and added, with wry emphasis, "I'll go back to the caravan and look for some bandages for that leg of yours."

Well, he had spoken the truth, after all.

There was nothing left of the camp but a patch of blackened ground where the campfire had burned. The pile of leaves and branches where the children had been playing shuffled softly in the light wind. Muddy hollows showed where water had been dumped, and the imprints of tire treads sketched the position of caravans.

"Satisfied?" Shem sounded unusually short-tempered.

I spun about slowly in a bemused circle, trying to take it in.

"Get back in the car, now that you've seen it," he said. "We can't stay here."

But I didn't move. I just stared dumbly at where the night before the camp had bustled, preparing an evening meal I could not share: the daughters-in-law squatting down, assaulting vegetables at a staccato pace with knives and peelers, the men trickling in from a day in the mountains, rolling wagers and telling stories, grabbing their kids by the scruff of the neck and dispensing rough but enthusiastic affection.

With hardly a mark on the landscape, Anchara's people were gone, and with them, my hope of finding Mother.

"Where are they?" I asked numbly.

"Over the mountains, by now. They took the road to Lookout Pass. ... Look, Serena. I'm serious. We have to get out of here."

I marched up to him and seized the lapels of his jacket in my fists. "No, *you* look, Shem. I'm not losing my chances because they've taken it into their heads to flit away like the untrustworthy good-for-nothings they are! We're finding them. Right?"

Shem lifted his head suddenly, staring out into the dark wilderness. Absentmindedly, he pulled his lapels out of my hands.

"Shh!" He listened for a moment, then frowned and shook his head.

His voice prickled with annoyance. "I'll help you find them. All right, Serena? I've business with them, too. Though I don't know exactly where they're going once they're over the mountains. We'll need to find the tidings." The reflected glare from the headlights made his eyes glitter. "I'll do that for you, right? But you need to give a little, too. You can't go on being so . . . Look, I'll help you wrap up your deal with Anchara. And then I've got a bargain to discuss with you."

I shot him a mistrustful look. "We need to make a bargain before you'll take me to Anchara?"

"No. I didn't say that. That wouldn't be fair dealing."

"What bargain do you want to strike, then?"

"There'll be time for that later. We have to go now. And you need to rest. I don't make deals with people too tired to think."

"I can think," I muttered. But it wasn't true. Exhaustion had fallen on me like a hundredweight of earth from the maw of a dump truck.

Shem went and opened the door to the back of the caravan. I flinched and shifted away from him. But he'd only gone in to light the lantern for me. A moment later, he came out again.

"Go on," he said. "I'll get us out of here."

"You'll drive?" I said doubtfully. My memory of his driving was still vivid.

Suddenly, his head went up and I could see the whites of his eyes. He was listening again.

Then I heard it, too: the high-pitched wail of a siren, as out of place on the mountain as a coyote on a city street.

Shem grabbed me by the arm of my jacket. "Go on! Get inside!"

He pushed me up the steps and into the back of the caravan. I stumbled and knocked my knee against the bedframe. I heard the door shut behind me and the hacking of the car's ignition as we jolted to a start.

The rig bashed up and down as Shem turned it out onto the forest road.

I held tight to the bedpost. Behind us, the siren grew louder, shrilling as the police or the Forest Service, or whoever it was, drew closer.

The lantern on the scrubbed pine table fell over as Shem jounced the caravan around potholes, trying to build up speed. I snatched it from the floor and switched off its light. My breath came fast and shallow, even though I was motionless, stiffly bracing myself to keep from tumbling over. But my tired muscles could not hold me long against the wild bouncing of the caravan. At last, I climbed onto the bed and lay belly down, trying to slow the hiccupping of my heart.

What would happen when they caught us? Why had they turned the Kereskedo band out of the forest in the first place? It wasn't illegal to camp here. My family had camped on the mountain many a time. There had to be some other reason.

The memory of the musty-smelling man from the Cruelty sprang out at me like a goblin.

He's fallen! the Paria boy had yelled.

With a twist in my gut, I suddenly wondered if it was me the Forest Service was looking for.

Had the Cruelty man died? Did the police really believe I'd killed him? Was that what Mrs. Palmer had told them?

But how could they find me way out here? Who would have told them where I was? I suddenly felt weak. Could it have been Brassi himself? Was this the way he would keep the peace with the Gorgios?

Then another thought hit me, even more sickening.

If they caught me, Shem was in trouble. He'd helped me escape from Oestia, so he was an accessory to whatever I had done.

We all feared wrangles with the Cruelty, but I knew—everyone knew—it was the boys they came down on hardest. The Gorgio jails were crammed with our young men. I'd seen one of the Paria boys after the police had taken him in for questioning. Cuts and bruises on his arms. His face mottled the color of an eggplant from lip to temple.

I didn't trust Shem. I wasn't sure I even liked him. But I would never put him—or any Yulang boy—into the hands of the Cruelty men.

That would be real dishonor.

I closed my eyes tight and burrowed my head into the pillow to think. Words, words. I tried to flood my mind with words to exonerate Shem if we were caught. I tried to build a case. It shouldn't have been hard since he really was innocent. The trick was to argue this without admitting my own guilt. . . .

But when I tried to think of the words I would use, my thoughts jammed and jarred.

Outside, the siren had stopped.

Shem still drove as if the car's exhaust pipe were on fire. The cop could still be in pursuit, but silently now, realizing that we weren't going to stop for his siren.

We drove on and on—for hours, it seemed—until finally our speed slackened. Rather than flying over potholes and skidding around hazards in the road, we settled into a regular, rolling ride.

All my fearsome thoughts began to blur and run like sidewalk chalk in a rain shower.

My knuckles loosened and my heart began to beat time with the lurch of the caravan.

At last, sleep curled up to me, velvet and welcome as a well-loved cat.

One for sorrow,
Two for joy.
—The Magpie Counting Song

I knew in every sinew and joint that the danger had passed.

A sense of peace flooded my limbs like the first flush of red wine, despite the ache in my back and the throb of pain in my shin. My mind was drugged with the first true rest I'd had in days. First light was creeping through the green shutters. I realized that the caravan was no longer moving. The fears of the night before had dissipated.

When I looked over the edge of the bed, Shem was nowhere to be seen, but my backpack was lying on the floor. Hurriedly, I pulled it up, untied its strings, and reached inside. With great satisfaction, I felt the rough edges of the amethysts and, when I peered in, caught their glint in the pale morning light. Now all I had to do was find Anchara, a task that seemed ridiculously easy after a good, deep sleep.

It must have been the freedom of finding myself alone, for once I'd tied the backpack together again, I had no desire to rise. Instead, I sat up in bed with the warm blanket gathered round me, examining the interior of the caravan, which I had only caught glimpses of after slinking in at night and instantly dimming the lamp to undress.

Now, alone in the light of day, I could appreciate its neatness and ingenuity. Certainly not Shem's work. But he had never claimed it was. He'd only bought the caravan from his uncles the day we left the city.

Everything that could be done to multiply space had been done, turning one square foot into the equivalent of ten. The bed, where I sat, had three large drawers built in beneath it. The first drawer, I knew, contained Shem's clothes and the sheets and blankets and towels. The second was locked, and rattled when shaken, as though crammed full of small, heavy objects like wrenches or kitchen weights. The third was nearly empty. I opened it and shoved my backpack with the amethysts securely inside it. All it had held before were my slippers. I didn't have anything else to store. The rest of my clothes were constantly on me and constantly damp, since I scrubbed them ferociously before I went to sleep each night.

The night before, though, I hadn't been able to wash my clothes. I'd left them on the floor and was still wearing the shirt and overly long trousers Shem had loaned me when I took off my bloody dungarees and mud-caked sweater. I groaned to think of putting them on again. I would have to do laundry, and soon.

Fortunately, the stout posts that anchored the bed to the wall were fitted with wooden clothes racks. They could be detached and hung out the window when the caravan was parked, so that clothes could dry. I decided to stick one out and get busy.

But then I saw something as puzzling as it was welcome. The window was already propped open and a drying pole extended. I poked out my head.

Waving like flags in the wind were my sweater, shirt, and jeans. They'd been scrubbed, wrung dry, and hung out while I slept. I wrinkled my forehead. What happened here? Had Shem washed my clothes for me?

No. Of course not.

He must have caught up with Anchara's clan. One of the women might have cleaned the clothes out of generosity. Though, no—that didn't make sense, either. Even the kindest woman wouldn't touch the clothing of an outcast. And it went without saying that no Yulang man would risk pollution by cleansing a woman's garment, *ma'hane* or not.

What if she was on her blood? He'd sooner step on a live wire. No, Shem certainly wouldn't have done it.

Well, I'd find out soon enough who my benefactor was. I pulled the drying rack in and scrambled into my clothes. My shirt and trousers were stiff with frost—the dew must have frozen on them. But they were clean, and the blood that had soaked through from the gash on my shin was hardly visible.

I pulled on my socks and crammed my feet into the boots I'd left by the bed the night before. But when I stood up, my head swam, and my eyes filled with blackness. I had to sit down again with my head cradled in my hands, waiting for sight to return.

Hunger had made me dizzy. That was the problem. My stomach ached with it.

I got up slowly and made my way over to the pantry. It seemed a shabby way to repay Shem's kindness—putting my hands upon his food. I was *ma'hane,* and that meant that my hands carried pollution. But I had to eat.

I hesitated. Perhaps I should find Shem and ask him to get the food out for me. After all, he'd been careful to separate the food he left for me from the food he ate when we were back at Anchara's camp. It was only right....

Black sparks were dancing before my eyes. I closed them and examined my conscience.

I knew I was *ma'hane,* all right, by the rule of the court. And I knew that the really degenerate, the really evil, transmit their malign influence like a sickly wind. I could understand not allowing someone like that to touch your food, or take your hand.

But I remembered, too, what my father had told me in the forest. *I still had my honor.* He had told me so. Weren't his eyes clearer than the eyes of the Kereskedo court?

No. I couldn't believe I would infect Shem by taking a piece of his bread.

Carefully, I creaked open the door of the pantry and searched the shelves. They were stocked with the most durable foodstuffs: yellowish grains and sticky raisins; cans of beans, dried dates and cranberries, and cereals; evaporated milk, coffee, sugar, and the tea that everyone in Anchara's camp drank by the gallon.

My hands were shaking as I seized a handful of dried fruit and wolfed it down. I grabbed another handful of cereal and closed the door.

I sank down to eat on the stool that stood beside the small workbench in the center of the caravan. The table was of a beautiful pale maple, smooth and clean enough to prepare food on in inclement weather. Above it hung pots of herbs nesting in wire nets, very green and healthy and well tended. Maps were stuffed in the cubbyholes in its thick legs. No books here, of course, though there might have been room for them. Shem, I guessed, like most Yulang, did not read, or at least no more than he could when he left school at nine or ten. My mother had not read much, either. Enough for street signs and labels for the mushrooms she sold at market. But she'd given in to Daddy's insistence that Willow and I learn. She had even let us take a newspaper, because I had inherited my father's passion for the news of the day. I had to know when the Yulang picketed a police station or when Roman Stanno gave a speech. How I'd missed my paper in these long days on the road!

What would Shem and the others think if they knew how much I loved reading? Or how much joy I got piecing together the translations in my Romanae class? Romanae, which no one had spoken outside a court of law these last six hundred years, at least?

I knew very well what they'd say: Crazy! What for? To read the lies of the Gorgios? To talk to dead people? The girl's *ma'hane*. See where all that book craziness gets you?

I got up quickly, scraping my shoulder against one of the empty racks in the wall. Strange, those four pairs of empty racks, one small bar up high and a larger bar about a foot and a half below, each of differing heights. Strange because they were used for absolutely nothing in a place where space was used to its limit. There were many other racks on the wall, but they held things like brooms and dustpans, saws and wrenches. In fact, there was hardly a slat of wall free, except up by the roof and down at ankle level. And these, in true Yulang fashion, were encrusted with triangular mirrors and medallions, Mother Lillith's feet and owl eyes, harps and zithers.

The empty racks were a puzzle.

I shrugged. They weren't a puzzle I needed to solve right now. What I needed was to know whether we had found Anchara.

I opened the door and stepped outside. My feet crunched a thin crust of snow. We were parked in a little lay-by on the side of an empty highway, far up the side of a mountain. Across the road was a small weather-beaten grocery store. Two ancient gas pumps sat out front, looking like defective refrigerators someone was trying to get rid of. There were no other cars or caravans to be seen.

Shem was asleep in the driver's seat, huddled under his coat, with his knees on the steering wheel. There were dark rings under his eyes, and the scrape on his face stood out, red and puckered.

I stared at him, reminded unwillingly of the Paria boy with the marks of the policemen's fists on his face. It was a few moments before I could turn away.

My breath made wisps of steam in the air, little bits of my soul venturing out before me to test the day. The air was so crisp with pine that I could almost taste it. Off to the side of the caravan I could see a thin line of evergreens just barely hiding the drop. We were at Lookout Pass. With a shiver I remembered the siren and wondered why Shem hadn't driven farther—or at least concealed the caravan better.

But perhaps it was all right. There was no one around. Not even the little grocery store showed signs of life.

I wandered into the trees. The cold and solitude of the brink of morning exhilarated me. I stopped next to a great blue-needled spruce, with the frost glittering along the cracks in its bark. Down below, the valley slumbered in the shadow of the mountains. Their peaks broke the sky, white and glistening with glaciers. Streaks of sunrise edged them with palest gold.

In the valley, wooden lodges dotted the shore of a clear blue lake. They were holiday retreats, with boat launches and decks and water slides. I wondered which one Willow's friend Alex owned. Had Willow really come here for a weekend of pleasure after the Cruelty took Zara away? I didn't want to believe it, but I knew Willow. She was always one to take advantage of what she could get.

The thought gave a harsh metallic taste to the pure cold air. It would not help to think of Willow and Alex, I told myself. I could only think ahead one step at a time. I could think of finding Anchara and showing her the amethysts. But if I went on from there, the road would seem too long and I would sink under my imagining.

An OPEN sign flickered on in the little store. As I walked back to the caravan, I saw that Shem had woken up. He was leaning on the hood of the car, staring across at the store thoughtfully. A faint smile crooked his lips as he caught sight of me.

"I'm puzzling how to get a tank of gas without paper money. Any ideas, Kereskedo trader?"

"Not the amethysts, if that's what you're thinking."

"Trade your gems?" He looked genuinely disgusted. "You're addled if you think I'd ever make such a stupid bargain! The Gorgios really must have had the raising of you. You don't understand the game at all, do you?"

I was ready to fling an insult back when I remembered my freshly washed clothes hanging from the window. No one but Shem could have done that. He might scorn my half-breed ignorance, but I couldn't deny that he had washed my clothes.

So, with some effort, I kept my temper. "Maybe, maybe not. What game are you talking about?"

"Bargaining, Kereskedo girl," he mocked. "Didn't you know it's a game? There's a strategy to it. And secrets, too."

"Such as?"

"Such as: the Gorgios are the real thieves, not us, whatever they tell you. We only try to beat them at the game." He stretched and yawned. "Oh, yes—another secret: never cheat them. Give them what they want. But if you want to survive, make it less valuable than they think, and get something you really need in exchange. You're no true Kereskedo if you can't make them believe they're the ones cheating you."

I stared. "How do you know what's true Kereskedo? And if you're so good at bargaining, what made you fling that braid gold at Anchara? That's an inheritance right there, or didn't you know that? You'll never get anything from her worth half as much."

He looked at me without a shred of expression. "So you say."

Clearly, the subject was closed. He pulled the keys out of his jacket pocket and gave them to me. "Come on. Let's try our luck here. And you drive the rest of the way, trader. I'm spent."

I steered the car across the road and parked it by the gas pump. Both of us got out. As we approached the little store, Shem dropped back, frowning at the uneven pavement in the parking lot.

"Go on," he said. "I'll be in in a minute."

More craziness, I thought.

Chimes jingled as I opened the door. They were little white ceramic doves that looked as if they should be helping a saint ascend to heaven. A shellacked wooden plaque next to them read WELCOME.

The shelves were stocked with food and camping goods, fishing rods and hooks, and expensive wine, which I guessed was for the holiday makers in the valley.

The woman behind the counter glanced up from lacquering her nails. "Can I help you?"

She had beautiful wavy hair gathered into a bun. Her face was Persian-cat pretty, with a small smoochy mouth. But the effect was ruined by her eyebrows. The hairs had been plucked right out and replaced with arched crescents of brown pencil. The skin around them puckered, as though smarting from its harsh treatment. She noticed me staring at them.

"Can I *help* you?"

I had no money. I was a cheat, a fraud. She could see it in my face!

"I—um—need a fill-up." My voice all but squeaked.

Shem was right. I didn't know how to play the game. I was going to blow everything. Where in the world was he, anyway?

The woman's eyes were sharp and appraising under those tortured brows. They traveled along my uncombed hair and hard-worn clothes. "You coming to work on the apple harvest?"

It was a fair guess. It was the right time of year, and the Paria pick if all else fails, though most would prefer any other kind of work. Working for wages is considered the lowest way to earn your living.

"No," I replied. "Just traveling."

There was a shrewd look in the lady's eyes, as though she knew something I didn't. Something it wasn't safe not to know. I felt disconcerted. Not just because the lady gave me a creepy feeling, but because

I felt dishonest. Could I actually start pumping, knowing full well I had nothing to pay her with?

Just then Shem sauntered in and lifted his hat to the shop lady.

"Looks like you've got some pretty bad paving out there," he said. "The chains folks put on their tires must rip it right up."

The woman carefully replaced the brush in her bottle of pink nail polish. Her expression was noncommittal.

Shem ran a hand through his hair and continued. "Come a hard freeze, you might get some of those ruts breaking apart, get some real cracks. You thought of getting a new seal put on before the snow gets heavier, missus?"

What he said sounded like good common sense. Anyone could see the lady's parking lot was pretty chewed up. "I could put a good seal down for you. One-, two-hour job, before the traffic," he offered. "Nothing fancy, but it's my business and I'm pretty good at it. Got a few references from these parts, too."

I realized, suddenly, that Shem sounded like another person. His words were different. His voice had acquired a faint mountain twang and his tone was just offhand enough to sound sincere. As if it made no difference to him whether she accepted his offer, but she'd be losing out if she didn't. I admitted myself reluctantly impressed. We were going to get that tank of gas, even off this sour glamour-puss.

In the silence, a clock clicked like someone's spine cracking.

"He with you?" the lady asked me.

"That's right."

"Then both of you get the hell out of here."

My stomach flip-flopped.

But Shem only smiled disarmingly. "Hey, lady, there's no call to use language like that. I'm not trying anything on you. You aren't interested, fine. We'll just get our gas and be on our way."

"You're not getting any gas here." One of the woman's pink-polished hands slid under the counter. "I don't need any trouble from you people, you hear? Now get out before I call the police."

"You can't refuse to sell us gas!" I exploded, forgetting that we had nothing to pay with anyway. "That's against the law!"

The woman's face went red beneath her penciled brows. "It's against the law to kill cops, too, but that didn't stop you people, did it?" She was trembling with fury. "This is the last time I'll say it. Get moving. I can have an officer in here in less than five minutes."

"Are you crazy?" I yelled. "We didn't kill any cops...."

But Shem had grabbed my wrist tight and was pulling me out the door.

"We'll be going, then." His eyes were narrow, the pupils tiny slits. But he tipped his hat again as we left, as if he were responding to applause in a fashionable jazz club.

As the little doves jingled and danced our departure, I saw the lady finally locate what she'd been searching for under the counter. I'd guessed it would be a telephone, but I was wrong. It was a pistol. She laid it on the counter and snapped it open. I didn't wait for her to start loading the bullets. Now I was the one pulling Shem into a run.

"What cops?" I was shaking as I scrambled into the driver's seat. "What cops does she think we killed?"

That man from the Cruelty! He *had* died falling down the stairs of our apartment building, and they were calling it murder. What else could it be? The thought sucked the breath out of my body.

Shem slammed his door. "There was a jailbreak yesterday. A guard was killed. The Forest Service people told us. Everyone's saying it was two Yulang guys who did it. That's why they evicted us."

I looked around frantically, not even registering my relief. "Where are the keys? Shem, give me the keys! Didn't you see? She's got a gun in there. Hurry up!"

"You've got the keys! I gave them to you!"

I rammed the rearview mirror into place with one hand; the other I plunged deeper into my pocket. Shem was right. I had them. But they slipped out of my hand as I pulled them out and jangled to the floor by the clutch.

I glanced in the rearview mirror and bent down to pick them up. She comes out with the gun, I'll run her over, I thought.

I retrieved the keys and stuck one in the ignition. The engine turned over. But to my horror, I couldn't remember what came next. I jammed my foot down on the clutch and my hand hovered over the gearshift. It fought with me as I maneuvered the stick into first. Now what? Gas. I lowered my foot onto the gas pedal, remembering how little we had. The car lurched forward and puttered to a halt.

"Mother Lillith! Are we totally out of gas?"

"There's enough gas," Shem snapped. "You just stalled it. Do it right this time!"

"I don't know what I did wrong!"

"You didn't give it enough gas."

Gritting my teeth, I ran through the whole ritual again, this time jumping on the gas pedal.

We shot out onto the highway. But we still had to reach the pass. It would be a rising road for a while yet, and I'd have to pump more gas into the line. Quickly I dropped my eyes to the dashboard. The gas needle twitched on the edge of empty.

"Shem! We'll run out!"

"No, we won't. Not going downhill. Just get us to the pass and then we can coast."

I tried to pick up speed. But the incline was too steep. The caravan pulled against me, dragging the car back. I thought that if I could just get into a higher gear, we would be all right. But when I pushed the gear stick into third, a stuttering sound chugged out from beneath the hood.

"Drop back to second!"

"But we have to go faster!"

"Well, we can't! And you're going to burn through the transmission if you keep doing that!!"

I downshifted, and the hideous noise subsided. But it felt as if the whole weight of the sky was pushing against me. I was practically standing on the gas pedal when we reached the top of the pass.

The downhill didn't look as steep as I'd expected. I relaxed as we rounded the first bend in the road. Pine trees rushed close and then receded. Snow-crusted borders shrugged away from our wheels.

But then the acceleration juddered through my legs. The road was slipping away fast and smooth as sand running through my fingers. Too fast. The next loop swung us out. I had to drag on the steering wheel to keep us on the asphalt. Another curve was coming. I half closed my eyes, sure I couldn't control the bulk of the caravan around another bend.

"What are you doing? Ride the brake!"

I crashed my right foot down onto the brake. The car began to spin. We were heading for the trees and the drop beyond.

"Blood and bones, Serena! What are you doing? Turn the wheel!"

I pulled my foot up and heaved on the steering wheel.

The car obeyed. I moved my foot back to the brake and pushed again, this time lightly.

Gradually, we slowed. I kept depressing the brake gently, feeding more control into my hands. Soon I began to sense the right pressure to place on the pedal.

A few moments later we were coasting down the incline. I had no more fear that the car would shoot away, ignoring the signals from my hands and feet.

I had been hunched forward, practically wrapped around the steering wheel. Now I eased myself back, spreading the tension in my back out across my shoulders.

Through the window, the fresh scent of the air caught me again, wonderful and clear.

"You're doing good." Shem's voice startled me. I'd been concentrating so hard, I'd almost forgotten he was there. He grinned at me and drew his hand across his brow in a pantomime of relief.

I couldn't help it. Before I remembered that I shouldn't, I blazed a big warm smile back at him. For half a moment, I couldn't remember why I didn't trust him. All I knew was that I was on a mountain, driving into the heart of a sparkling autumn morning, and I was glad he was with me.

Half an hour later, we hit the valley floor. The acceleration slowed and I had to push more of our remaining gas into the line.

Specks of habitation began to appear: a diner here, a souvenir shop there. A few houses. But I could tell that in a moment or two we'd be back in empty territory. I could see the peaks of the range stretching out before us for miles and miles.

"There's another gas station, Serena. We have to try again."

I slowed the car and pulled off the road.

"This time just pump it," Shem said. "I'll work the deal from there. If we can't bargain, you just climb back in the car and gun the engine."

I nodded. As he was getting out, an idea struck me. I didn't want any more threats or guns.

"Shem." I grabbed the brim of his hat and pulled it off his head. "Too Yulang."

"And you think getting rid of the hat takes care of that? Think again, Jalla."

This shop was sloppier than the one at the pass. Some shelves were heaped with items. Others were nearly empty, with a lone box of bandages or a packet of lady razors on them. There was a calendar on the wall, with pictures of skaters on an ice rink, dated five years back.

The proprietor wasn't in evidence, until I noticed a pair of shoes crisscrossed on the counter. An aroma of coffee rose from somewhere below the shoes. Peeping over, I saw an old man scrunched down in a swivel chair with his feet propped up, a travel mug of coffee balanced on his stomach, and a battered old paperback in his hands. The title was *Bears in the North Andera Range*.

"Excuse me," I said. "Can we pump a tank of gas?"

"Anything's possible if you know how." He didn't look up from his book. "Help yourself."

As the gallons glugged into the tank, I reflected that the storeowner was so wrapped up in his book that we could probably drive off without any trouble. But I couldn't bring myself to say this out loud. I hoped Shem would suggest it. He didn't, and that made me feel even more dishonest.

The man ambled out before we'd pulled the pump out of the gas tank. He was barely an inch taller than me, and wore pointy silver glasses and a small, well-trimmed mustache. I caught a whiff of pipe tobacco and menthol rub off him.

"You live in there?" He jerked his thumb at the caravan.

So much for thinking Shem's hat was the only thing marking us.

"Yes," Shem said guardedly.

"Can I take a look inside? I always wanted to see one of them things."

Shem shrugged and opened the caravan door, and the old man disappeared inside, hoisting one leg with his hands. It looked as if his knee might be too stiff to bend. Shem went in after him and I leaned against the door, watching them curiously.

The old man inspected the interior, shoving his face up to things. He must have been ferociously nearsighted. "Good carpentry. Your work?"

"My uncle's."

The man ran his hand along the edge of a cupboard. "Nice smooth joints. Everything in its place, eh?" He came to the empty handles on the wall. "Except here. What're these for?"

For answer, Shem picked up his violin case, which had been shoved under the workbench. He unclasped two of the handles, slid the fiddle in, and snapped the handles shut.

"Very neat," the old man approved. "There must've been some other instruments once, as well?"

Shem just nodded.

"Smart way to make sure they're not damaged in transit. You should use it, even for that lonely fiddle."

"Not worth the trouble."

I thought the old man would go then, but he wasn't done. "No water? Plumbing?"

Shem twisted his lip and shook his head. How would a Gorgio know how polluting it is to have plumbing in one's sleeping quarters?

The man whistled. "You folks live rough. Mind you, it'll be even rougher for you now. Do you listen to the radio?"

"Not lately."

The old man gave us a keen glance. "You listen. That's all I got to say. It's ugly news, but maybe knowing it will keep you safe. Hear what I'm saying, Jal?"

I blinked. The old man knew something of the Yulang if he knew to say "jal."

"What have you heard?" I asked.

"Only that no one's going to leave you in peace since those jail-breaks. One of you does something, folks think you all do it. I'd steer clear of the small towns until this wind against you dies down."

He came and stood in the doorway. I put out my arm to steady him as he eased himself down. He smiled at me once he was safely on the ground and patted my hand. Shem followed.

"Seventeen forty-nine on the pump," the man said.

Shem and I looked at each other.

"You need your parking lot paved?" Shem asked halfheartedly.

"Paved?" The old man looked at the asphalt with all the moss growing through its cracks. "Can't say it's occurred to me."

I could tell Shem didn't want to play the game with this old man. "Any carpentry you need? Rub the rust out of an old car? Bang out some dents? Clean up your store?"

The old man chuckled. "Why'd I want any of that? The state of the store never deterred anyone. My car ain't rusty. What are you getting at?"

Shem opened his mouth again, but I stopped him with a touch on his arm.

"The lady at the top of the mountain chased us from her gas pump with a pistol. We aren't out to cheat anyone, but we have to move on and we don't have any paper money. What Shem's trying to do is give you something in fair trade." As I said it, I realized it was true. Shem hadn't been trying to cheat anyone. Not really.

The old man scratched his head. "Chased you with a pistol, did she? That little waxwork up there?" He gave a snort. "Well, as to the trade, I don't want what you got on offer, nor any Yulang gold, neither. And from what I can see, you've got the gas. Besides, it's Friday. I'll make up the difference when the rich folks come in for their weekends. You better get your wheels on the road."

We stared after him as he shuffled back to his store.

Shem looked at me and shrugged. Then he climbed back into the car.

But I couldn't leave it like that. There had to be something we could do for him.

Suddenly, I remembered my necklace. I fiddled with the clasp at my neck and ran after him. "Wait! Grandfather!"

Shyly I held out the golden owl with its head cocked to one side, its wise eyes half lidded. I would not feel right with myself until he took it. And from what I'd seen of him, I was afraid he wouldn't.

"What's this trinket for?" To my relief, the old storeowner took the owl delicately out of my hand and examined it with delight.

"For being a friend to us," I said.

A tiding of magpies that flaps to the south,
A murder of crows that drives them back north.

—Gorgio hunting song

Shem was driving as we descended the last spur of the great mountain range. I'd taken us through most of it, but navigating mountain passes and sharp ravines was taxing, so I had grudgingly let him take the wheel. He was actually very good at telling me what to do when I was driving. But it didn't seem to improve his abilities much. When he teetered the caravan along the edges of plunging chasms, I could only grab for the door handle, squeeze my eyes shut, and try not to gasp in terror, for that made him swerve. I let out a great breath when we finally entered flat terrain.

It was unnerving how utterly the land changed within spitting distance of the familiar peaks. The evergreens thinned and trailed off. Evening was drawing in, but the sunlight was still intense. Even when I closed my eyes, it pried under my eyelids like an interrogator's flashlight. I felt a stab of homesickness for the familiar misty light I knew so well back on the coast.

My parents had refused to travel east of the mountains when we were trading, even though I knew many Kereskedo caravan routes cut through these passes on their way inland. I had never understood why Mother, especially, was so set against it.

So even though I knew from geography class that the land out here beyond the eastern slopes turned to arid sage steppe, I'd never seen it with my own eyes. Accustomed as I was to the lush, rain-soaked coast, this reddish ground looked wrong and artificial to me. But not as artificial as the patches of green orchards we passed, with the big silver irrigation pipes spewing out the water that never fell from the sky.

I didn't like it. The brown hills dotted with gray-green sagebrush were ugly to me. They reminded me of the flanks of a balding poodle I'd seen once in Plaza Ridizio, with its curls all matted in sparse clumps and great expanses of raw, unhealthy flesh showing through.

Though the sun was brighter than on the coast, it was much colder here. We passed isolated fruit stands still crammed with apples after a day's selling. Girls in fingerless gloves were packing the fruit in crates for the night, stopping now and then to blow on their fingertips.

Then, rising up ahead of us, I saw an empty field crowned with a huge dead tree, black enough to have been blasted by lightning.

Shem glanced at the tree and, without bothering to signal, swerved the caravan over onto the shoulder.

"Take a look, Serena. Is there anything on the branches?"

I squinted at the black branches etched against the glowing blue sky.

"There's a ribbon or something on that lower limb."

Shem ground the car to a halt. "Jump out and see if you can read it."

Puzzled by his words but willing to stretch my legs, I got out. What I'd seen was a bright rag cut in a familiar shape: a flat oblong, neatly prepared for the quilting the old women had been working on in Anchara's camp. There was no writing on it that I could see.

Shem called after me, "It's the tiding they've left for us. What does it say?"

"Say? It doesn't say anything."

"Can't you read the tidings, Jalla? I thought you'd traveled."

"Long ago, I said! And I can't read quilting."

"Then it's time to try," he said, with annoying equanimity.

I plucked up the fabric between my fingers, examining it with growing frustration. Of course I realized it was some sort of code, but I wasn't sure what it communicated. Yet another thing I didn't know! Sullenly, I dropped the rag and shook my head.

"No? I'll help you, then." Shem pointed at the branch where the tiding was tied. "How many times is it knotted around the branch?"

"Once."

"So it took them one travel day to reach here from the camp. See how simple it is? They're still a day ahead of us." He shaded his eyes and squinted into the distance. "No sign that they camped here, though. And no wonder. This place isn't good for us. What side of the tree is it tied on?"

"The right, of course. Can't you see for yourself?"

"Not 'right,' city girl," he retorted cheerfully. "What cardinal direction?"

"East," I said sourly.

"Northeast or southeast?"

"East, Shem!"

"You're sure about that?"

"No!" I snapped. "And you know I'm not. But I don't see why you have to grill me about it, either."

"Because you're traveling now, Jalla. How do you think you'll learn anything on the road if you can't read the tidings? They've gone northeast, not due east, Serena," he said patiently. "Look at the sun if you're not sure. We'll have to take the next turn, and strike off that direction. Do you get it now?"

"I suppose so," I said, somewhat mollified by the change in his tone.

"Good. Next time you'll be able to spot the tidings yourself."

I wasn't so sure about that. But Shem had a point about needing to know the Yulang travel codes if we were going to find Anchara.

I unwound the quilter's strip from the tree, thinking that whatever old lady had donated it would be glad to have it back. The Yulang are generous but thrifty to an obsession.

I was just about to put it in my pocket when Shem said, "No—don't do that. Leave it. There may be others coming. From what the old man said, I wouldn't be surprised if a lot of our folk are on the move. Far more than should be, now that it's marketing season, and the collecting's at an end."

Collecting season. I hadn't heard that phrase for years, not since my mother named the seasons of our lives for all those doings that were so distinctly hers. Jam making, mushroom gathering, guest season, bargaining time . . . Shem's words brought it back to me. Collecting season ran all the way through spring and summer—the good travel weather. That was when the caravans went on the road—as my family had, up and down the coast and out to the islands, for those few brief years. Those happy years.

I clutched at the memory. There was some sort of all-night party to mark the start of the collecting season, I remembered now. And a garland of earliest spring flowers—crocuses and daffodils and those purple starflowers—thrown in the water. An offering, Mother said, to the spirits that charm strong feet and sharp eyes—and safe journeys.

"The celebration! What's the name of that celebration in the spring before the caravans go on the road?"

Shem looked at me in surprise. "I don't remember what the Kereskedo call it. The one the musicians have before spring travel is Vernalium."

"That's it!" I said, delighted to find the memory drifting to me, like the loose petals of garlands on the waves. "We had it at my grandfather's caravan, up on Whale Isle—I was seven or eight. I remember, my dad had his banjo—and there was a bonfire . . ."

Shem leaned his arms out the open window, laughing at my excitement. "There has to be a bonfire, Jalla. It goes all night. Rotten luck if you let it go out."

I went closer to the car, with the scrap of fabric in my hand. "My father loved those big gatherings. The men called him Yulang-re. You know? It means a Gorgio who fits in with the Yulang, like he'd been born one."

"Then why did your family go off the road? Didn't you say you haven't traveled for a long time?"

I leaned against the driver's side door. "Daddy fit in with the Yulang as long as they were playing music and telling stories. He didn't do so well as a trader. People used to say that he never saw a good bargain but he let it get away."

Speaking of my father brought a stab of loneliness, like a stiletto blade. Gone. All gone. Daddy. Mother. Willow. Zara . . .

Quickly, I changed the subject. "It's marketing season already? I thought that started later—with the cold weather."

"Near enough. Can't you feel the chill in the air? Anchara's tribe will head to the harvest market in Eurus Major soon, remember?" He looked up into the sky. "Speaking of Anchara, we should get moving. It's late, and we don't want to stay here. That's for sure. Hang the tiding on the branch, Jalla. Make sure you position it right."

I went back to the tree and knotted the strip of fabric where I'd found it. Now that he'd mentioned Anchara, I, too, was eager to get moving. Every moment we lingered was a moment we fell behind. The tiding was a good find, but it wouldn't help us at all without speed.

And we would have left then, too, except that once I'd made the tiding fast, I chanced to look out across the field and my eyes caught hold of something.

I strained to get a closer look, but the thing I'd seen moved rapidly. It was a flash of white amid the trees in the neighboring orchard. Faster and faster, it streaked behind the trunks and apple-laden branches.

Then it burst into the empty field behind me, and the speeding blur resolved itself into a white horse and rider. The animal was pearly with sweat, glowing and ghostly. Its hooves beat out a rhythm beneath its stride. I gazed at it, mesmerized, forgetting my hurry.

What was it that held me? I wasn't sure. There was something so lovely and haunting about the horse that I couldn't tear my eyes away. It was as if a creature from the most rare, longed-for reaches of my dreams had just come thundering out of the realm of sleep for my delight. And my wonder.

At first glance the rider, clad all in white, was another such creature: an ancient rider bearing a message along the royal road from Romana to some far-flung outpost of the empire. I actually thought I saw a roll of old parchment in his hand, like the ones I'd seen in pictures in my history books.

But on second glance, something clicked in my brain. Nothing that would give the rider a name, but enough to know he was no dream.

He was something much closer to a nightmare.

The spell dissolved. I realized that the rider was only a young Gorgio, with his hair clipped close to his head. And yet, this realization didn't have enough power to make him ordinary, or less ominous.

His eyes were wide and ecstatic. His lips were moving and sounds of triumph poured from his throat, whoops and yodels and hollers. He was so fair that the wind had lashed red splotches onto his cheeks and the color showed clear even at the distance between us. His white trousers were tight enough around his calves to be leggings, and his shirt was long and cinched at the waist like the tunic of an ancient fighter in the Colosseum.

No wonder he'd seemed a creature of a dream. The Yulang say that all time past is buried in the human brain; that each of us carries the history of the world inside of us, if only we can find the key to unlock it. This horse and rider seemed to gallop out of an age long past, embedded in my mind. Straight out of the womb of Mother Romana herself.

The boy pulled his horse into a sharp turn and I saw the sign on his tunic. It was the sign of the trident. The Trident Gladiators fought wild beasts in the bloody Colosseum of old Romana, I thought. One would fall: man or beast.

It was the same trident I'd seen before, chalked on the walls of the Parias' enclave, always after the White Shirts marched. The White Shirts—

"Get in the car, Serena!" Shem's voice was low. "Gently. Don't do anything to call attention to yourself."

The horse wheeled about. It was too late. The rider had seen me.

"Do you hear me, girl? Get in the car!"

But I was transfixed.

"Come on, Serena!" I heard Shem fling the car door open.

The rider's eyes were like those of a rabid dog I'd seen once in the alley behind our apartment building. He must have been half a playing field away, but even at that distance I could feel his gaze tunnel in on me, sighting me as a hunter sights his quarry. The thing in his hand was not a parchment but a gun.

As I stared, he gouged his heels into the horse's flanks.

Shem grabbed my arm and dragged me back to the car, slamming the door so hard the window shook.

He pulled out onto the highway with gears asqueal.

When I looked back, the boy was riding his horse in circles, pulling the animal onto its back legs, and shooting his gun insanely into the air.

"What does it mean?" My hands were shaking. The pistol had been drawn for me.

Shem kept his eyes fixed on the road. The speedometer needle trembled at seventy.

"Shem! Tell me! You can talk while you're driving, just this once!"

He didn't answer.

When he finally spoke, I could hear the anger in his voice. "You know," he said slowly, "it can be dangerous to be as ignorant as you are."

"Ignorant!"

"The White Riders are abroad with the trident on their backs for all to see. What does that mean to you, Serena? Why did you stand there and stare? Were you waiting for him to come and shoot you?"

"I—I don't know." It was true what Shem said. I'd just stood there like a fool. "I've seen the White Shirts marching in our neighborhood before. I know they're trouble. But the Trident Riders—I didn't even believe they were real. And he looked so crazy. Like a picture of a gladiator from my history book."

"From your history book?" He could hardly contain his scorn. "Do you think this is ancient history? Do you?"

"I—"

"Listen, Jalla, it doesn't matter if you've seen something like him in your book! How does that Gorgio learning help if you don't know what any Yulang child of two could tell you? What he means to us is death. *Death.* Have you got that?"

I swallowed hard and nodded. I had read stories about the Trident Riders in the papers. I just never thought I would see one in the flesh.

Shem glanced sideways at me. "You see another like him and you don't hesitate. Right?"

"Right," I muttered.

I drew my knees up to my chin and wrapped my arms around them. I felt clammy. It was as if I'd just seen Death on that white horse, instead of a boy my own age.

"The Trident Riders have a compound near here," Shem explained more gently. "This is their territory. I only stopped because of the tiding. I didn't expect to run into one of them. All we can do now is drive as fast as we can and hope we don't need to stop again."

13

If ever I return, pretty Peggy-o,
If ever I return, all your cities I will burn,
Destroying all the ladies in the county-o.
　　　　　　　—Gorgio marching song

Night was falling when we came to the town. It was a smallish place, but spread out. There were cheap canteens and auto-parts stores along the highway leading into it. Down a broad cross street I caught a glimpse of a school, with its flag snapping on the flagpole, and felt a wave of longing. Despite Shem's words about my Gorgio learning, I yearned to be reading books again, hearing the stories of ancient Romana from our teacher. Before I ran away, we'd even begun to learn about the Lex Romanica, the ancient law that still rules us today. I loved when I got to understand some point of justice and then—there in the newspapers—I would read about the great Yulang advocate, Roman Stanno, using that exact point on the floor of Parliament to drive the Gorgios crazy! How far away that life seemed now.

On the block across from the school stood a fire station and a town hall with pretentious pillars. But the rest of the streets were scrubby, red and empty. Lights winked on in the houses as we passed by. Cars were parked in driveways. But only a few straggling figures showed that people actually lived here.

Soon the town dribbled away and we were driving through large orchards again. In the gathering gloom, I could see ladders leaning against trees. Whole swaths of fields had been picked clean, but farther down the road, I saw branches bending under their weight of apples.

This fruit must have been grown for the upscale market in places like Oestia and the glittering cities far to the east, for each apple was wrapped in a net bag to protect it from bruising, so it would look perfect and unblemished for the picky city buyers.

It was through these heavy branches that I saw the first ripples. The air thickened, and there was something in it that tickled and rasped at my throat.

I squinted through the uncertain glow of twilight and realized that the ripple I'd seen was smoke. A trail of it rose above the treetops, high, thin, and ominous, like a black bar of music unraveling in the sky.

When we passed the next field, where the trees had been chopped down and their trunks bulldozed, we saw the first flames snapping. They came from a slapdash cluster of shacks, which sat beside the bulldozed field. The shacks weren't much more than a jumble of clapboard and aluminum, with sheets of plastic for insulation in the windows and chicken coops tacked on beside. Close by, a collection of dented cars and patched-up Yulang caravans were parked in a dirt lot. It was the kind of place I'd read about in the papers. Migrant workers' housing. About a year back, there'd been a battle between the orchard owners and the workers over improving the living conditions. Scanning the pitiful settlement, it was easy to see who had won.

Shem slowed the car, and we both stared. One shack was already nearly consumed. Its black frame shimmered like a silhouette inside the raging flames. People were teeming in the open area between it and a second building, which was also ablaze. In a nearby yard, a gaggle of scrawny chickens ran in frantic circles, squawking inside their makeshift enclosure. A woman was trying to chase them out and away from the encroaching flames. As we watched, she laid her hands about the ruffled neck of the rooster.

Across the trampled grass, men and women were running with

pitchers and washbasins and flinging water at the bristling walls of the shacks. The fire cracked and danced. It seemed to be laughing at their efforts.

I'd seen the fire station in town, but there were no fire engines here. What made them so slow? I wondered.

Our car crawled by the settlement, and for a long syrupy moment it felt as if the two of us would stare, passive as cows, until the burning houses slipped away behind us and were gone.

Then, on the unpainted boards of one of the shacks, we saw the trident jeering in bone-white spray paint.

The moment snapped. There was no screen between us and the fire. It was as real as the singed smell seeping into the car. The men and women had faces. The children were screaming.

Shem pulled the caravan off the road into the dirt lot with the others. As he parked, I caught a glimpse of a woman leaning against a car not far from us.

"I can't believe it," I whispered.

"Believe it." Shem shut off the engine. He meant the fire.

"No, that girl standing over there—do you see? I know her!"

Without waiting for his response, I flung my door open and sprang out into the choking air.

"Lemon!"

Lemon Bardoff turned at the sound of my voice.

To my astonishment, I saw that she was holding a little Yulang girl of maybe four or five in her arms. Her simple goldish brown Jersain tunic was smudged with soot. Her pale skin was bright in the flames, and her face went stiff with shock as she took me in.

Then she reached out her hand to me, and I rushed to her side. "Not you, too!" she cried. "Were you and Willow forced out as well?"

I took Lemon's hand, feeling the strength in her fingers from years of playing her violin. "What do you mean?"

"Don't you know?" She squeezed my hand and pulled me closer to her and the child. "People in the Paria quarter were turned out of their homes after the jailbreak. I heard on the radio . . ."

"What?" My thoughts flew to Willow, alone in our apartment. "Slow down. Who forced them out, Lemon?"

"The White Shirts! They marched—two or three times, I think. There were hundreds of them. They broke into people's houses—Paria houses. The Kereskedo and the others were better protected."

"But Willow? You had no news of Willow?" My hands felt like lumps of ice.

Lemon gave me a pitying look. "No. But you mustn't assume the worst. Not every street was hit. Those who could hid in other parts of the city. Doesn't Willow have a lot of Gorgio friends?"

"Yes . . ."

"Well, then! Even Willow would have had the sense to go to them. For the sake of the baby, if nothing else. It's only logic, Serena. And the police *did* get the streets under control. Eventually."

Swallowing hard, I nodded. Willow would have gone to Alex. Of course. That would be ample protection. And—I couldn't believe I ever would think this way—I was almost thankful that Zara was in the hands of the Gorgios. She would be safe—at least from the White Shirts.

"And thank goodness you're safe!" Lemon continued. "Now we can thank God for one blessing at least. Perhaps if we remind him, he'll find a blessing to spare these poor wretches, as well."

I looked around at the panic and confusion that seemed to grow as the fire spread. "What's happened here?"

A grizzled old man knocked into me, sloshing water from the saucepan he was holding. " 'What's happened,' Jalla? You can see what's happened! The Trident Riders set fire to our homes!"

"Shall I go for the fire engines, grandfather? Our car is right here. . . ."

The man just glared at me, spat a thick glob of spit, and rushed off. I looked questioningly at Lemon, who was gently stroking the frightened child in her arms. Her green eyes were filled with anger. "They already went for the fire engines, Serena. The station door was bolted."

"That's ridiculous!" A gust of hot air scorched my back, and Lemon and I scrambled away from it. "Fire houses are always open. I've never heard of one being closed. What sort of town is this?"

"Do you really want to know?" Lemon asked bitterly. "Then listen. The townspeople didn't set this fire. The Riders did that. But it's the townspeople who are going to let it burn."

A bright spurt of flame shot from a nearby shack. Curses and shouts erupted. "Damn their lungs!" "That's our place!" "Bastards!"

I looked around in disbelief. "These people need fire hoses! They can't put this out by throwing little pans of water on it!"

Lemon put a finger to her lips and nodded toward the child.

"Who is she?"

"Rochelle. She's one of the apple pickers' children. Her mother, Estraella, was a servant in our house. Do you remember her, Serena?"

"I do. Where is she?"

"My father's taken her to the hospital." I realized that Lemon was speaking more to the girl than to me. "Rochelle's mama breathed in some bad smoke, but she'll be better soon."

Rochelle burrowed herself deeper into Lemon's side. I looked at her curiously, remembering the baby whose bassinet was sometimes beside the music store's counter. The baby's mother had been widowed, and stranded in the city, far from her people. I remembered now. She'd been working for the Bardoffs to save money so she could return to her clan.

"What hospital has she gone to? The one in the town?"

"No! They won't treat Yulang there. Da's driving her all the way to the nearest city. I promised I'd stay with Rochelle until they return."

I stood up and looked about with my hands on my hips. A third shack had now caught, and the wind was slapping the flames toward the cluster of buildings closer to the car lot.

People were streaming out of their houses with sheets they'd pulled from their beds. They laid the sheets on the ground and carried out clothing and pots and pans and cans of food, which they threw on top. Then they tied the sheets up in great bundles and stuffed them into their cars and caravans, tripping over each other in their rush. Little kids were trailing after the anxious grownups, crying.

I saw Shem approach one of the women with the enamel basin he used for washing dishes. He asked her something and the woman pointed to a row of water barrels leaning against the wall of an out-house in the field behind the shacks. Through the gusts of stinging smoke, I could see the others filling their containers at those barrels.

As I'd expected, they were all Paria tribespeople. I could see that now, by the men's flat caps and the women's bright headscarves. They ran from the water barrels to the shacks, faces streaming with sweat as they labored to smother the flames. But the fire ran quicker than they. It tore through the flimsy walls and devoured the window frames with hungry smacks, licking from floor to ceiling.

As I watched Shem heading for the water barrels, I thought I had better help, too, fruitless as it seemed. There must be something else in the caravan I could use to haul water.

I turned and bashed my injured leg against something hard.

"Ow!" It felt as if I'd been hit with a crowbar. I grabbed my bandaged shin, cursing a river. But when I looked to see what I'd run into, I was struck dumb.

It was a disconnected irrigation pipe, propped up on its legs. Where did it come from? I squinted into the gathering gloom and saw silver links of piping extending through the uprooted orchard next to the settlement. Probably one of the Paria had hauled this over, hoping to use it to put out the fire, but had given up, since it was too far from the rest of the pipes to be any use.

All these fields with thousands of gallons of water pumped in every day to grow the farmers' crops, and the fire department couldn't direct any of it to the pickers' burning houses? It didn't seem right. Wouldn't a good long fire hose be all they needed to hook up to those pipes over there? Surely, even if the fire department didn't come, they could still spare a hose.

Someone had to talk to the Gorgios.

I went limping into the thick of the crowd, shouting Shem's name. He heard me and turned.

"Give me the keys to the car!"

He put his pail down, dug into his jacket pocket, and threw the key chain at me. It flashed through my mind that he didn't even ask me what I wanted them for.

The fire was so bright, I nearly forgot to switch on the headlights as I pulled the car out of the lot. Careful not to hit any of the other vehicles—or the women who were still packing up their family belongings—I pulled the caravan into a U-turn and sped the three or four miles back to town.

By the clock on the town hall tower, I saw that it was barely six-thirty. But it might have been midnight for the closed-down look of the place. The streetlights were on, but everyone had gone home. I pulled the caravan to the side of the road and ran to the fire station.

The building was dark. Its huge garage was shut, and the engine slumbered inside like a dragon sleeping off a snack of princess. The season's last roses bloomed in its well-tended garden. Did the firefighters have so little to do, they'd become avid gardeners?

I knocked on the big garage door. When no one answered, I bent double and tried to pull the glass door up by its handle. But it stuck fast. I couldn't get in that way. So I circled back around the building.

As I'd hoped, there was a back door. Through the lace curtain covering the glass pane, I could see that a light was on, here and on the second floor, as well.

I rang the bell impatiently.

No one answered.

From above I heard a muffled, uninterested woof. A fire station dog. Would it have been left there all night by itself? Weren't the firefighters supposed to be there, too?

I rang again.

Still no one came.

"Hello?" I called. "Is anybody there?"

Even here, I could smell the burning. What if there really was no one at the fire station? Without help, the pickers' homes would all be burned to ash.

"Hey! Open up!" I shouted. "There's a fire in the orchards! We need help!"

I looked up. A window on the second floor was opened a crack. A thin line of smoke snaked out, lazy and unhurried. Surely there couldn't be a fire in the fire station? Was that why no one answered? Had the Trident Riders got this place, too?

But I realized how ridiculous that was. A familiar scent tickled my nostrils. It was applewood tobacco. The old women in Anchara's camp were addicted to it. Someone was upstairs smoking a pipe.

"What are you doing up there? Come down!"

I began pounding and banging on the door with my fist. Frenzied barking answered me. The fire station dog must have been straining at its leash, dying to get at me. But there was no human response. Whoever was smoking the pipe was just sitting up there, maybe playing solitaire or listening to music on the radio. Doing a puzzle.

He wasn't coming down, at any rate. Not to answer me. Not to put out the fire.

How foolish I was. The Parias had tried this already. Why did I think I could get help when they could not?

The answer surfaced nearly without thought. It was because I had something they didn't. Because I knew how to talk to the Gorgios.

The second I thought this, my grandmother's commanding tones burst from my lips. "Come out this instant! Whoever's up there, you're shirking your duty! I'll report this to your chief! Come down before I have you prosecuted for criminal negligence! Do you hear?"

He heard, all right. I don't think anyone within five blocks could have *not* heard me. But even the blood of the Gorgio dowager that threaded its way through my veins wasn't strong enough to rouse the firefighter. Grandmother's arrogance was no help. I let her sink away and became myself again, raging and slamming against the bolted door. I smacked it with my palms and hammered with my fists. I threw my whole body against it.

Then I tripped over something.

I looked down and saw a rough chunk of concrete that was probably used for propping the door open. The muscles in my back pulled taut as I lifted it. But that was the hard part.

Heaving it through the pane of glass in the back door was easy.

The glass shattered. I looked through the hole I'd made and saw the shards lying in a sparkling circle around the block of concrete, like ice that would melt away at the first touch of day. I put my hand through the jagged remains of the window and undid the bolt.

Upstairs the window banged open. Ha! Finally, I'd got his attention!

"What's going on down there?" a man's angry voice called.

But I had already let myself in. Quickly, I crossed a galley kitchen and opened the first of two doors. It was a coat closet. A big lumberjack coat hung inside. The second door opened into the garage.

Once out in the garage, I slammed the door shut behind me. There was a dead bolt under the knob and I shot it to. Steps thudded on the stairs. I fumbled and found a light switch.

I drew a shaky breath, hardly able to believe what I was doing. This wasn't what I'd intended when I screeched out of the Yulang camp.

But whoever was smoking his pipe upstairs wasn't going to help. And here was the fire engine, with its shiny pipes and long black hoses that could attach to the irrigation pipes and let the water out. What else could I do? Surely it would be a greater crime to leave the engine here than to take it. Gathering my courage, I hopped up on the running board and opened the driver's door.

The cab was much bigger than I'd imagined. My feet couldn't reach the accelerator. I jiggled the handle under the seat and it shot forward almost into the dashboard.

I could hear a heavy fist hammering on the door to the garage. I shut out the racket as well as I could, knowing I could get out of this unhurt only if I focused on the task at hand.

Of course, there were no keys in the ignition! I thought of the Paria boys back in the city who could jump a car with a coat hanger. Why hadn't I asked them to teach me their trade?

The man was banging on the door and yelling, "Get out of there! I'll have the law on you!"

I wanted to laugh at him, and hurl insults. But I didn't waste my time. As long as he was there, I was safe. Although, if he had a brain in his head, he'd run back upstairs and slide down the fire pole, right into the garage. If I could just start this thing before that blazingly obvious step occurred to him . . .

Mother Lillith must have been looking out for me, for as I scanned the garage, I saw a row of keys neatly hanging on hooks by the door. I rushed over and swooped all of them up.

I couldn't hear the firefighter yelling at me anymore. He'd soon get in another way.

I got back in the truck and tried one key after another. On the third try, I found the one that started the ignition. Leaving the engine running, I leapt out again and grasped the heavy handle on the garage door, heaving it up so I could drive the truck through.

As it rolled back over my head, I found myself face to face with the fireman. He had a bristly beard and biceps as big as my waist, and his face was as red as the fire engine.

"What the hell do you think you're doing?" he was shouting. "You Magpies can't keep your fingers off anything, can you? Nothing's sacred! Not even government property!"

A look of surprise slid over his face as he took me in. Whatever he'd expected, it wasn't me.

I knew that if I ran back to the truck, he'd catch me in a second. There wasn't much chance for me in a fight. My tussle with the man from the Cruelty had shown me that. I wasn't about to mess with that Evil Eye stuff again, either.

Instead, I edged slowly backward, my eyes fixed upon the big man in front of me.

But he wasn't going to let me get away like that. For every step I took, he took another, and came closer. "Tell me what you're doing here, Magpie, or you'll tell the police."

"I'm doing your job for you."

"You're not doing *my* job," he said automatically. Then his hands fell to his side. "You're from the camp?"

"That's right. I'm from the camp. So get out of my way, unless you want to help us."

"Help you? I'm not going to help you break the law."

"No?" My voice was sharp as a kitchen knife. "Fine. But don't stop us from helping ourselves."

"You can't steal that engine!"

"What do you mean, steal it? Is this your private fire engine? I thought you said it was government property. Doesn't the government pay you to put out fires with it? Even in Yulang houses?"

The man's face mottled like half-cooked meat.

"What are you using it for right now?" I pressed. "Do you think you could spare it for an hour or two?"

He shifted uneasily. "You can't just take it."

"Oh, for goodness' sake, I'll bring it back! What do you think I'm going to do? Go joyriding?"

"Nah, I don't think that, girl." Was he weakening? I didn't know if I had the patience to keep pushing him with my words. The burning shacks blazed in front of my eyes. How many were alight now while he stood here, barring my way?

"Look," the man said, "if it was up to me, I'd help you."

"Wonderful!" I snapped. "That'll buy you a seat at the table in paradise. Now get out of my way."

"I can't, girl. The chief told us to let it burn. We're not to do anything unless it spreads to the orchards."

In a second I'd rush at him, claw his face, kick his kneecaps. . . . But then I remembered where that had got me with the Cruelty man.

"Some fire chief! He decides who to let burn and who to save!"

The man looked away. "I've got a wife and four kids. The chief tells us to let it burn, we let it burn. If we go against him, we lose our jobs. I've got my children to think of. . . ."

"Don't you think there are children in those shacks you've let burn?" This time my voice rushed out at him like a lion. "What would you do to someone who stood by while your house burned with your kids inside?"

Without waiting for a response, I turned and ran back to the truck. He could get out of my way or get run over. I didn't care. He could bash my head in, but I wasn't going to stand here arguing with him any longer.

Before I could grab the door handle, his hands clamped down on my shoulders.

I whirled and launched my fist straight at his face.

He caught me by the wrist and swore.

"Don't try that with me, girlie! You're not getting in that engine!"

He shoved me aside and I nearly reeled onto the cement. When I regained my balance, I saw him open the driver's door.

"Oh, yes I am!" I shouted, charging after him. "You'll have to run me over if you think different!"

"You don't know how to work the hoses, do you, stupid girl? Now shut up and stop fighting me or I really will hurt you!"

But I was scrambling up after him, striking out blindly with my one free hand. He held up a gigantic arm to ward me off.

"For God's sake!" he spluttered. "Get in the other side. We can't both fit here. And stop trying to hit me." He jerked his head at the passenger's side.

It took me a moment to realize what he meant.

Then I dropped back onto the floor of the garage.

"You take the engine. I'll drive my car," I said. "It's just outside."

14

Nothing falls from the sky by accident.

—Jersain saying

I drove with my eyes shifting to the rearview mirror every few seconds, hardly daring to believe the firefighter would follow me the whole way.

I'd been gone only twenty minutes or half an hour. But the time had made a difference.

The mothers and children who had been dragging their belongings out of the shacks were nowhere to be seen. Out in the distance, a dance of lanterns and flashlights showed that at least some of them had run to a neighboring field for safety. The others, who were still fighting the fire, wove and stumbled on tired legs, their faces masks of exhaustion.

The flames were dying down in the first two shacks. But others were ablaze now. The water barrels must have been drained. I saw two middle-aged women trying vainly to fill them under the outdoor spigot. It amazed me that these people just kept on, even with their water low, knowing that their efforts made little difference.

No one looked up as I swung the caravan onto the shoulder of the road. The fire engine was right behind me. But since the fireman had not turned on his siren, no one noticed him, either.

I jumped out of the car. "Shem! Where are you?" I shouted.

It was difficult to find him in the smoke and confusion. But finally, I spotted him arguing with the old man I'd spoken to earlier. Shem was pointing at the irrigation pipes in the neighboring field—he must have had the same idea I did—and the old man was expostulating and slicing his hands through the air like axes. I yelled as loudly as I could.

But my shout was crushed by the snap of the flames and the clamor of people bellowing orders at each other, so I had to run right up to him and grab him by the sleeve.

"Look! I've brought the fire engine!"

Shem glanced from me to the huge engine. His mouth fell open and in the glaring firelight a look of astonishment swept over his face. His eyes flickered over me, as if he would say something, but no words came. Instead, he turned and grabbed the old man's arm and yelled into his ear. The old man registered the fire truck and, without another word, ran off toward it, with Shem at his heels.

Everyone turned to see where he was going.

Sharp honks came from the fire engine's horn. The Gorgio leaned out of his window. "Move your goddamn caravan, girlie! You're blocking my way!"

Feeling stupid, I rushed back and jumped into the car. As I pulled the caravan forward, the fire truck shot into the space I'd left. I parked and waited to see what I should do.

When the firefighter jumped out of the cab, he was immediately mobbed by the Paria. Some of them were already climbing up the sides of the truck, trying to unspool the hoses.

"Get off," the fireman shouted, "unless you know how to operate fire hoses, which I doubt!"

The Yulang do not take orders well, though they like to give them. People stopped climbing, but no one got down until the old man who'd been talking to Shem called out, "You heard the man! Get down!"

The boys—it was mostly boys—dropped like cicadas off a summer tree, though they still crowded close.

"What I need," the Gorgio yelled, "is someone to guide me back across the field to those irrigation pipes. And I don't want to break my axle on any of those trunks there. Who can direct me?"

"I'll direct," the old man replied, "and the rest of you clear out so the man doesn't run you down with his big wheels!"

From the authority in his voice, I knew that he must be the bora chan among this group of ragged Parias. His small band of traveling laborers were even poorer than my Paria neighbors back in the city, but like any other clan, they had their leader.

The old man turned to Shem and said, "You win, Jal. Run over there." He pointed at the uprooted orchard. "Help the man hook it up when he gets the truck positioned."

The Gorgio backed the engine slowly through an opening between the shacks and as far into the abandoned orchard as he could, with the bora chan walking by the side of the truck, gesturing and shouting instructions. Finally, the truck stopped. The crowd of boys who had run after it, disregarding the old man's warning, swarmed around and began unrolling the long hoses and running them across the fields. Shem hooked them up to the shining metal pipes while the Gorgio got some Paria women to unroll extra hoses. He attached them to the ones Shem had hooked up to the irrigation pipes. When he judged they were long enough, he organized runners, who carried the hoses toward the fire.

A strong wind stirred the trees in the orchard and blew the flames from the shacks higher. I watched the sparks rushing into the air, my heart pounding, yearning with every bone in my body for the water to finally come gushing out of the hose.

The firefighter shouted, "Let it go!" to Shem. With the sound of a cymbal crash, the water pounded out, flooding the roof of a flaming shack.

Suddenly, I realized that I should get the caravan out of the dirt lot. The other cars had been driven farther up the road already, so that flying embers wouldn't land on them and ignite their gas tanks. Surely I owed it to Shem to protect his caravan. So I got back in and pulled it about a quarter of a mile farther along the soft shoulder, parking it on the western edge of the bulldozed orchard.

As I was walking back through the uprooted field, something strange happened. Strange but beautiful.

I heard noises at my back and turned to see small bright lights floating toward me like a flurry of fireflies. The glimmering emerged from the dark shapes of the apple trees in the adjoining orchard. My eyes made out shadowy human forms behind the lights. As they streamed toward me, I realized that it was the mothers and children of the Paria enclave rushing in from the neighboring fields, carrying lanterns and flashlights. They had caught sight of the fire truck and were running back to their clan.

With their long hair streaming behind them, the mothers ran, shouting songs and uttering cries like bridesmaids chasing the newly-weds at a wedding and pelting them with flowers. Children raced after them, shoving and laughing. To my great surprise, a fat old woman caught me in her arms and gave me a smacking kiss on my cheek as she stumped along. The others touched me lightly as they ran past me, a palm on my arm, on my cheek or my forehead, as the Yulang touch a baby or a wise woman for blessing.

Puzzled, but buoyed by their high spirits, I turned and ran with them back to the burning shacks.

As the mothers and children poured into the crowd, a pulse of energy swept through it. I pushed my way through, trying to reach Shem. He was as much a stranger as I was here, and I thought I should stick with him and help him out. But he wasn't by the irrigation pipes anymore. I had to give up searching for him, anyway, since, like everyone else, I just needed to do whatever had to be done from moment to moment.

The fireman was showing people where the masks were, and a few people got them on and seized axes from the truck. Meanwhile, he shoved a mask over his own face and ran toward a newly burning shack. I watched as he smashed a window with a blow of his ax. A tongue of fire licked out at him. I gasped as he jumped clear. It was hard to believe that this was the same man who, half an hour before, had been content to smoke his pipe while the Yulang shacks burned.

A scream cut through the air. I turned and saw a boy running in circles, his sleeve ablaze, the fire traveling up his arm. The next second, a woman had knocked him to the ground and smothered the fire with a towel. I hurried to find a cloth to wet and lay on his singed flesh.

The firefighter rallied the others and they struggled on.

When I rose from the boy's side, leaving him in his mother's care, I heard my name and turned.

It was Shem. His face was streaked with soot and his shirt was dripping wet from the hoses, but he was grinning and his eyes were shining.

"Not bad, Jalla," he said, jerking his thumb at the fire truck. "I was right when I said you were a surprising girl."

I dropped my eyes to hide the broad smile that had broken out on my face. I didn't want Shem to think I was too pleased with myself. But he'd made me realize that I was.

When I looked up, he'd already run off again and in another moment a girl came up to me to ask for my help. A moment later, I was dragging a big mattress along the highway with four other women, and helping to shove it into a burned-out family's caravan.

It took hours of wearying effort, but at last we quenched the fires the Trident Riders had lit. Six homes had been destroyed. But with the help of the fireman and his equipment, the Paria had managed to save the rest.

A gibbous moon had climbed toward midnight by the time I brought the caravan back to the dirt lot for the night.

The only fire left was a campfire the Paria had built of split and splintered planks that had once been a dwelling. The wood was already warped and charred when I helped some of the women drag it to the clearing between the shacks and the outhouse. The night was cold, and the people whose homes had been destroyed needed a place to sit and rest, and food to eat.

The families who had not been burned out brought their pots and plates and cups to the fire, along with meat and vegetables and grains. The gifts were generous, for I was sure their kitchens were none too well stocked. An old woman planted a large iron hook in the ground and hung a pot over the fire.

She looked at me. "You, Jalla. You brought the water truck. You are the hostess of this feast. We eat what you make with your own hand."

Foggily, I half remembered some reason why I shouldn't cook for all these people. But I couldn't quite catch it. Besides, there didn't seem to be any questioning the old woman's tone.

And even though she had to show me how much barley to add to the water and when to add the meat and vegetables, no one corrected my fumbling efforts or laid a hand on the cast-iron pot. The stew I managed to make was thin and flavorless, but no one passed a word of judgment. And as far as I could see, everyone was fed.

The excitement that had greeted the arrival of the fire truck had evaporated. The flames were gone, and all that remained were these poor, exhausted apple pickers: six families without a place to lay their heads, the rest only now beginning to realize what the fire meant to them.

After the meal, the homeless families piled into their trucks and sped off east—no, northeast, I remembered—along the road Shem and I had been following. Dust wafted away beneath their wheels like small, melancholy ghosts. Perhaps there would be work for them in other, less troubled fields.

The Gorgio fireman had never stopped working. When everyone was eating, I caught a glimpse of him filling the Parias' water barrels with a hose attached to the irrigation lines. I ladled up a bowl of stew and carried it over to where he stood.

"You haven't taken anything, Uncle. Please eat."

The man rested the hose inside the barrel and took the chipped bowl from me without a word, holding it in his big, blackened hands.

He looked up and his eyes flashed into mine. The irises of his eyes were a robin's-egg blue and the whites as bloodshot as if sparks from the fire had landed in them. Suddenly, I felt I could sift through his mind the way I might leaf through the pages of a book. And what I read there was fear: Fear that his fire chief would strip him of his badge and he would have to struggle to feed his kids. Fear that the Trident Riders would hear he'd helped us, and his house would be the next to burn. And worst of all, fear that his friends would shun him for what he had done tonight.

"You're worried about how your neighbors will treat you," I told him. "But not all of them will turn from you." Not all! I knew that now. There must be other Gorgios like him, who would help his family as he'd helped us.

"No?" His face was hard and weary.

"No. There will be people who'll stand by you. I'm sure of it."

"Maybe," he grunted.

He knew as well as I did that he would suffer for what he'd done tonight. I watched him spoon the stew into his mouth, feeling an overwhelming pity.

My mind jumped to the amethysts buried in my sack in the caravan.

"Please. Let me at least pay you for your pains. Wait here."

"I *am* paid," the man interrupted. "Like you said before, girlie. I'm paid to put out fires."

"But you might not be much longer!"

He ignored me and ate hungrily. Then he handed the bowl back to me and shifted the hose into another bucket. I watched him, feeling helpless.

Remembering what I had given the man at the gas station, I slowly pulled my necklace out of my collar, aware—and ashamed—of how little I was giving. But it would have been more shameful to leave one who had served so many without a gift. I glanced at the charms on the golden chain and unhooked the dog, with its jaws open in a brave howl.

"Uncle?"

He turned back to me and I held out the golden charm to him.

"Give this to your wife when you get home."

With a look of surprise and suspicion, the man took it from me.

"Why?" He turned the charm over in his hand, examining it.

Because I know what you risked, I wanted to say.

But other words spilled out instead. "Because my father was a Gorgio, too. And he was brave and good, like you. But he died in a fire...."

Suddenly, the tears were streaming uncontrollably down my face. I turned away, stumbling toward the darkened fields. Loss and loneliness had smashed into me, as wide and endless as the clear black sky above. I felt that I could have put my head back and howled like the dog from my chain. But I didn't. Underneath that aching emptiness, I could feel something glowing, warm and golden—a gift from the firefighter ten times more precious than the gift I'd given him.

I collided with someone and nearly fell.

"Ho! Watch out, girl!" Shem's arm quickly steadied me. I didn't jerk my elbow out of his grasp as he bent down and peered into my face.

"What's this? Tears?" He gave me a quizzical look. "Now, that's something I thought I'd never see."

"Oh, shut up." I swiped my tears away roughly with the back of my hand, but they kept coming. It was horrible. I tried to pretend they weren't there. I spoke in the most collected voice I could muster. "I've been talking to the firefighter. Can anything be done to thank him?"

"I'll mention it to the bora chan." His eyes were resting on me with unwonted gentleness. "Serena, Jalla, go and rest, will you? You've hardly been still since I met you."

"How can I rest? There are still the dishes—"

"There are many here to do that, Jalla. Didn't your mother ever tell you not even the mountains stand forever?"

I choked out a laugh through my tears. "How did you know that? She used to say it when I stayed up late, studying for a test or something."

"Mine did, too." His smile was ironic. "But never because I was studying! Now go and rest!"

He let go of my arm, and I had the strangest feeling, warm and painful at the same time. Against all reason, I wanted his hand clasping my arm still. I wanted more words to pass between us, binding us, as words sometimes—sometimes—can. Even though they more often divide.

What was wrong with me? It was only Shem, after all.

I was bone weary. That was the explanation. Nothing a good night's sleep wouldn't cure me of.

I didn't go and rest, however. Instead, I dropped down beside Lemon where she sat by the fire. The little girl, Rochelle, leaned on her knee, doggedly fighting sleep, eyes darting here and there in search of her mother.

Lemon turned her friendly gaze on me. "Who would believe you'd only just stumbled onto the scene, Serena? You seem to have everything well in hand."

"Me? What do you mean?"

"I mean what I say." Lemon gave her bubbling laugh. "What brings you out on the road like this, O queen of your own caravan?"

I smiled despite myself. "You know that caravan's not mine!"

"Whose is it, then? That boy you were with?"

"That's right. His name's Shem Vadesh."

"Vadesh? What a familiar name! I wonder where I've heard it before." She frowned and shook her head. "Maybe I know someone else in the family. Not your friend, at any rate."

"*Friend* might be stretching it," I said automatically. "He's just given me a ride."

"A ride where? Why are you on the road, Serena-lo?"

It felt good to hear the old Jersain endearment from Lemon! "It's a long story. The Cruelty's taken Zara off Willow—"

"No!"

"Yes. And I'll need to find Mother in order to get her back. That's why I'm traveling. What about you? Was it the Tax Service drove you out?"

Lemon nodded. "We had to sell the shop to pay them and get Da out of debtors' prison. And all we have now is a fiddle, a cello, and my old viola da gamba from all our vast inventory! We've cash in hand, anyway." She looked at me wryly. "That, at least, travels well."

"But what will you live on, Lemon?"

"We're trying to gather commissions. But we need a workshop so Da and I can carve the instruments to fill our orders. If we'd had the wit to buy a caravan like yours, we could have used it as a workshop and a place to store inventory. As it is, all we've got is the car." She shrugged. "Serves us right for getting too comfortable in the city. Then when they kick us out, we find we're not prepared for travel. I think we Jersains fool ourselves more than you Yulang do."

"But how did you end up in this place?"

"We ran into a Kereskedo band camping here last night. They invited us to share the site in exchange for some music. And when we found Estraella here with the pickers, she asked us to stay."

I sat upright. "Was it Anchara Pulchra's band?"

Lemon nodded, surprised.

"Do you know where they've gone?"

"Heading to Eurus Major, they said, for the market."

I smiled at her. "You've saved us some guessing! We thought they would be heading that way, but we didn't know they were aiming to get there so soon. Is it a big market, Lemon?"

"Very big. Eurus is nothing compared to Oestia, but it's the center for all the inland trade routes. Father and I are heading that way as well. Are you seeking Anchara's people, Serena?"

"Yes." I thought anxiously of the amethysts, burning their purple fire in the drawer back in Shem's caravan. If only we could move faster! Suddenly, I couldn't wait to get them out of my hands.

The little girl clutched Lemon's arm. "Where's Mama? You said she'd come back!"

Lemon gathered the child to her side and rocked her. "Soon. She'll be back soon. I promise."

This was rash of Lemon, I thought. Promising a child a thing like that.

Rochelle's eyes were large. "But I need Mama to put me to bed!"

Beyond the rim of the firelight stood the black husk of her mother's shack. Inside, the bed her mama laid her in every night was charred and sodden. I saw Lemon's eyes flicker over the ruin and return to the girl's face.

"I'll stay with you," she promised. "Until your mama comes back. She's my old friend, sweetheart."

Rochelle would not be comforted. "Where will I sleep?"

"You'll sleep in Serena's caravan," I said, touching the top of her head as gently as if she were Zara. "Would you like that? There's a soft bed and a red blanket. I'll wake you when your mama comes."

Rochelle looked at me mistrustfully, but with a trace of curiosity.

"Do you want to see?" I asked. "Lemon can come with you."

The little girl was enchanted by the caravan's neatness, the crowded order of it all. She touched the woven blanket once and then again with the tips of her fingers, as if stroking a silky cat. I could tell she had nothing so fine in her possession.

"Does that bed look nice?" I asked, knowing, with pleasure, that to Rochelle it looked as snug and comforting as the bed of a fairy godmother. She smiled shyly at me.

What would it be, I wondered, to really be the mistress of a caravan like this? To have a refuge to give to whoever needed it, and the means of escape? Not to have to depend on chance and the whims of strangers? I could understand why Shem had pawned and scraped to get the money to buy it.

Lemon sat beside Rochelle on the bed. It was no surprise to me when she carefully extracted Shem's violin from its neglected place on the wall rack. In all the time I had known her, I had rarely seen her without an instrument in her hands.

"Will you sleep here, Rochelle?" she asked.

The little girl nodded and looked at Lemon worshipfully. "After lullabies?"

I laughed. She had obviously heard Lemon play before.

"Out by the fire, then," Lemon told her. "The music would beat against the walls in here, trying to fly out. The notes would get cranky. Will that suit you, sweetheart?"

Rochelle nodded.

When Rochelle and Lemon had gone, the thought hit me that I'd left the caravan alone and unguarded for many hours that night. Swiftly I crouched down and yanked the backpack out of the drawer under the bed. I undid the buckles and the drawstring and held up the lantern to examine the contents. Beneath the gear, I still caught the glimmer of the gemstones, and when I lifted the pack to fasten it again, the weight pulled reassuringly.

Relieved, I stuffed it back into its hiding place and followed Lemon out into the night.

An' thou wert my own thing . . .
—Kereskedo song

A scattering of the apple pickers sat by the fire, clustered in tense groups.

"I'm not leaving without my pay and that's that," one man was saying. I'd seen him earlier, with his wife and four or five children.

"But I'm telling you, the Trident Riders will be back," a frail old man cut in.

A gray-haired woman sitting by his side threw her arms up in exasperation. "Here or away, it makes no difference. They'll follow us. They're like mosquitoes. They need us for our blood."

"In the cities we'd be safe!"

"And what can we do in the cities?" the first man objected. "We're not Kereskedo traders or Zimbali musicians. I'm sick of fighting Gorgio workers for a chance to unload at the docks. The crop is here to be picked. And a cold winter coming, they say."

"We'll stay here and make the growers put out protection for us," the grizzled old bora chan declared.

A burst of sarcasm and disbelief greeted this suggestion. No one believed the Gorgios would protect them. Not after this night.

I saw Shem sitting on the edge of this group, holding a mug of tea in his hands. I beckoned to Lemon and Rochelle to follow me, and we sat down beside him.

"My friend knows where Anchara is," I whispered.

"I thought you were going to sleep," he grumbled, then managed a weary smile. "That's good news, anyway. Where?"

"Near Eurus Major," Lemon said.

"So they're going straight to the eastern capital." He turned to Lemon. "Thanks for letting us know, Miss ..."

"My name is Lemon Bardoff. I'm an old friend of Serena's."

Shem raised his hat to her and introduced himself. Why hadn't he observed that nicety with me when first we met? I wondered. Because I was *ma'hane*, I thought bitterly. Why else?

I swallowed my annoyance. "Lemon and her father are the finest instrument makers in Oestia," I told Shem. "But they've been forced to sell their store. Do you know it? Bardoff's?"

"The instrument shop in Plaza Ridizio?"

I nodded.

"Who doesn't know it? Panno swears by their work. But wait a minute—" He turned and looked keenly at Lemon. "The night we left Oestia ... There were cops in Plaza Ridizio. At two in the morning. That was your place, wasn't it? The place they were raiding?"

Lemon's lips thinned. "That's right," she said shortly.

Shem caught her expression and looked away. "I'm sorry for your misfortune."

"Thanks," Lemon muttered. For a moment the fury stood in her face, as clear as it had that night we'd seen her shrieking after the Cruelty. Then she glanced down at Rochelle, and gathered the girl to her side. It seemed to help her collect herself. When she turned back to Shem, her voice was calm and courteous once more. "Serena says you're heading to the eastern market. My father and I are going there, too. Perhaps we could travel together?"

"You're both welcome."

"The Bardoffs have nowhere to practice their craft," I cut in, feeling Lemon might not ask this herself. "Couldn't they use your workbench, Shem? And maybe store their instruments in those hooks on your walls?"

Crimson flared in Lemon's pale cheeks, but she bit her lip and said, "My father and I would gladly pay for the space."

Shem looked startled but not displeased. "Then we should easily come to an agreement. After all, we still need money for gas, don't we, Serena?" He looked at Lemon and gave half a bow. "But why are you traveling at all, miss? Your people settle, or so I've heard."

Lemon's mouth crooked. I could tell Shem's Yulang formality amused her. Jersain men treat their women in a more direct way. I've heard many Yulang complain that the Jersains are too blunt, that they lack chivalry.

"We Jersains are like flies in the pantry," Lemon replied. "Settled until they swat us away. But that only makes our people better brothers on the road." She held Shem's violin out to him courteously. "I borrowed your violin to play lullabies for Rochelle, but of course, that's presumptuous when we have a Zimbali musician here already. Will you play the first piece?"

Lemon had easily identified his tribe, as the Jersain often do. Even in the firelight, I could see the color that swept across Shem's face.

"No, thanks," he said.

"Come, I insist! I really didn't mean to steal your fiddle!"

Shem looked at his feet. I could feel his discomfort like an itch on my own skin. Every rule of hospitality demanded he be polite. But I knew nothing in the world would induce him to pick up that violin. I felt annoyed at Lemon. Couldn't she see how he felt?

"Thank you, but I won't play."

"A Zimbali musician who refuses to play? That's modesty indeed! How do you make a living?"

"Not from my music," Shem said shortly.

Lemon's teasing dropped away. "How, then?" She sounded puzzled.

"I—I don't make it at all right now," he admitted. "But I have plans."

My skin prickled with quick mistrust. I gave Shem a hard look. He pushed the violin back into Lemon's hands. "Please. As our guest. You play first."

Lemon shrugged, giving me a bemused smile. Then she tuned the strings and positioned her bow. After a silence she pulled the first thread of melody out of the darkness.

I drew my knees up to my chest and rested my chin on them, listening. As always when Lemon played, familiar chords sounded new, filled with unexpected shading and color. The Yulang say that heaven is full of unheard music; I've always thought that Lemon was one of the few who could reach up and pluck it down from the spheres.

I had heard Lemon play many times, but never with the piercing melancholy of the lullabies she played that night by the gold and black of the fire. It was as if she wove the child's simple sleep song into the night sky on a warp of musical notes. Even the Parias left off their worried bickering to listen.

But I could not relax. Instead, I found myself watching Shem under carefully lowered lids, pulling things apart and laying them out as clearly as I could. The feeling I'd had earlier when we collided still lingered. There had been an aura of care in his voice when he'd spoken to me that I longed to hear again. For whatever weak reasons of my own that might be.

But what he had said about his plans reminded me to be wary.

He'd chosen to have me with him for purposes of his own. He'd said as much, and I knew he hadn't forgotten it. I was the one who had let down my guard—so much so that I had dumped the amethysts in his caravan and left them there unprotected! Yes, they were still where I'd put them, but for how long?

What had made me so foolishly trusting? Ever since Shem had come looking for me in the forest, I had assumed that where I would go, he would go. But I'd forgotten to ask what he was going *for*. To escape his uncles and the shame of his family? Surely. But there was something more. He had plans. Why did those plans hinge on helping me? Why was it important that I be in his debt? These questions still stood unanswered.

I determined to find out that very night.

My eyes lit on the little girl at Lemon's knee. For a moment, her head was in shadow, and it could have been Zara sitting there, grown into a big girl of three or four. What if I couldn't see Zara again until she was Rochelle's age? The thought sucked the breath from my lungs. Would she forget me by then? Could she forget her own Serena?

Lemon put down her bow. The night air was still tainted with the smell of smoke and charred wood. Even so, I drew it deep into my lungs, trying to calm and drive out the fears that had beset me.

Without a word, I took the violin from Lemon and placed it lightly on my shoulder. A melody had laid hold of me. It was a nursery rhyme Mother had taught us long before on an evening when Daddy had gone seeking a loan from his rich relatives. I remembered how Mother had gathered us onto our broken-down couch while we waited for his return and the rain needled against the windows of our caravan. And she'd sung us this tune.

At first I had to search for the notes. Then in a great rush of memory, the melody flowed into my head and I played through a verse, unaccompanied.

A woman's voice drifted over the fire, taking up the song.

The hairs on the back of my neck prickled.

It was as if I'd called my mother out of the thin air into which she'd vanished and here was her voice again, summoned out of that long-ago rainy afternoon.

But the moment passed, and I knew the voice was not my mother's deep contralto, but a reedy soprano, thin and penetrating and sharp as old cheese. I looked across the fire and saw a woman with a rough, wind-chapped face. There was a gash across her nose, and her hair streamed long and tangled from beneath her modest headscarf. She groped for the words of the first stanza but then fixed on the rhyme I remembered Mother crooning.

> "Run, bonny horse, like a bird on the wing,
> Over the land and sky,
> Always we travel, no masters nor kings
> Heed how our wrongs do cry."

The melody was sweet and sad, its repetitions like switchbacks on an endless road. The sort of song that brings a tear to the eye and resignation to the heart. I remembered how it had moved me as a child. But now, I suddenly realized, it dissatisfied me.

I put greater force in my arm and doubled the tempo. I didn't want to play a dirge! If this song was a journey, it had to go somewhere.

The singer followed my lead. She picked up the timing and gradually her voice ceased mourning and began demanding, though the lyrics remained the same.

> "Ever we journey, burning our roads,
> Never left to rest,
> Hunted and hindered, carrying loads
> Down the long years that pass."

She sang these words, but there were lyrics beneath the lyrics, smoldering like the fires that had burned her people's homes. Together she and I made the music spark, building its power as the Yulang build their blazing bonfires. But like the bonfire, the power was harnessed within bounds of harmony. We were singing our fury at all these never-ending battles, all these long injustices. Our music spoke this to all the other Yulang around the fire. Yet at the same time, we offered them beauty, for who was more deserving of the gift?

Rochelle's eyes were closed when the woman's voice fell silent and I stilled my strings. Shem was watching me steadily. I could not read his look, but as I met it, I dropped my eyes hastily. It was as if too much light shone into them.

"Your playing has improved, Serena," Lemon said quietly. "Now I can hear the love in it."

I looked at her in surprise. I'd thought it was anger I'd poured into the notes.

Silence held the circle another moment. The notes still lingered within me, leaving my heart big in my chest. I wondered if the others had felt the music fill them, as I had.

Lemon shifted Rochelle's knees over one of her elbows and slid the child's head gently into the crook of her arm. Quietly, she lifted her and carried her over to the caravan.

"I told her the little girl could sleep in there," I whispered to Shem. He raised an eyebrow—Who are you to rent out space in my caravan? But before I could explain, he got up and went to open the door for them.

Then the bora chan's voice broke the stillness. "A petition," he said. "We must prepare a petition."

"What for? What kind of petition?" The others sounded leery.

"A petition to the mayor for justice. And for protection."

"He'll ignore it," the frail old man said.

"They'll say the town owes us no protection since we're here only for the harvest."

A beetle-browed man interrupted. "What really matters is that the orchard owners will oppose it. They'll think it has to come out of their pockets. They're probably right, too."

"So?" It was the woman who had sung with me. "If they want our hands picking their apples, they should at least ensure we aren't burnt to death in our own beds! You talk of justice, but you're afraid of the harsh words of a few farmers? We'll have more than words to worry about if we don't get some police out here!"

A few of the men looked abashed. The old bora chan leapt on her words, his hand chopping the air as I'd seen it do earlier when he was arguing with Shem.

"You hear what Lal says? We must petition the mayor at dawn's light. Until they promise our safety, we don't pick a single apple, you see? I'll wait on the steps of town hall all night with the paper in my hands."

A man with a heavy shaving shadow shook his head. "A paper? And who will write on this paper?"

"I can write!" The bora chan's voice was fierce.

"You write your name well enough, Bora Chan," Lal said gently. "But I think you may not have the skill to write a law paper that the Gorgios will read. Your voice is strong. Why not just speak our demands?"

The shadowed man looked even gloomier. "Gorgios don't hear a man's voice. It's all got to be crowded together in black scribble-scrabble, and even then just Gorgio words aren't good enough for them. You'll need their law language, too. We need a man like Roman Stanno, with his silver tongue."

"He's Kereskedo," the old woman said bitterly. "When have you seen a Kereskedo so much as loosen a button from his vest if he thought it might help us?"

I bit my lip, remembering the scorn I'd heaped on the Parias in our neighborhood back in Oestia. I knew I wore no distinguishing clothes, and my hair was not braided, but I wondered if I had any trick of speech or behavior that had let them guess I was one of the haughty Kereskedo.

"Stanno's different," Lal insisted. "He sees beyond tribe."

"But he's not here, now, is he?"

They didn't need Stanno, I thought. The Gorgio law language was Romanae. All they needed was a translator.

Shem dropped down beside me, settling into the circle with the patched knee of his trouser leg just touching mine, the way no Yulang man sits except with his wife. I glanced at him suspiciously. But when I thought to shift my leg, I found that a stillness had taken hold of my body and I let us rest that way. I had something to propose to this circle of Parias, and I felt better able to say it with Shem so obviously at my side, his touch—in an odd way—strengthening me. I leaned forward.

"Perhaps a Gorgio could help us," Lal was suggesting. "One who knows the language of the law."

"A Gorgio!" the man with the bristly face said scornfully.

"There was a Gorgio helped us tonight," a young girl said softly.

I had opened my mouth a few times, but no words came out. I didn't want to interrupt them, not being one of their tribe. But the grizzled bora chan noticed me. "Would you tell us something, Jalla? Don't be shy. You're here as one of us now."

"I—I write the Gorgio law language." My hands were practically shaking. "I could write your petition if you tell me what you want to say...."

The old man stared at me. His mouth opened in astonishment and then relaxed into a tissue of laugh lines. Laughter spread from face to face around the campfire. I looked about in bewilderment and saw that only two people were not laughing: Shem and Lal. The rough-faced woman regarded me encouragingly. Shem looked affronted.

I understood. The Paria were laughing not because their troubles were over but because my words were absurd. I had never had so many

186

people laugh at me in my life. Not even Janet's friends back at the Gorgio school. Or at least not so I could hear them. I wrapped my arms tight about myself and hung my head, wishing I had kept my mouth shut.

"Of course you write the law language. Perhaps you bang the gavel in the court as well!"

"Maybe she serves in Parliament! The first Yulang representative from the orchards! They've been longing to hear from us!"

Shem touched my arm and whispered in my ear, "They don't know any different, Serena."

He was right, of course. They just looked at me and saw one of their own girls. A young girl who knew something as exalted as Romanae, the language of law and government, *would* be incredible to them.

The grizzled old man held up his hand. "No more teasing now. This girl brought us help and we should treat her with respect." He turned his kindly face on me. "We don't mean to laugh, Jalla. Perhaps you know a word or two. But what we need is someone with real fluency. A young wife has enough on her hands without struggling with the law language. No matter how brave she is," he added.

I was so annoyed that my words tangled as they tried to jump off my tongue. "I'm not—"

"It's true what she says!" Shem interrupted—very quickly. "Her father was a Gorgio. She went to one of their schools. Test her yourself, Bora Chan. I give you my word of honor, she can do what she says."

Lemon's voice came from above my head. "Serena? Even my father does not know the language of Mother Romana as she does."

The bora chan looked at me and his eyes were bright as an inquisitive bird's. "I know it, too, for speaking purposes. All right, Jalla, tell me what I mean when I say: *Legea e rege. Legea domnes, te populum. Deasupra legii nemo praesedet.*

It sounded so different from the way my Romanae teacher would have pronounced it that I was puzzled. But then I heard the echo of her genteel voice vibrating under the old man's creaking tones.

"It means the law is king. The law reigns over the people. Above the law let no man sit. But I think it's *legea e regina,* Bora Chan. Law is feminine, so you say the law is queen, not king."

The last wisp of laughter disappeared into the air.

"*Is* that what it means, Grandfather?" Lal's eyes were bright, and I saw a quirk at the corner of her lips.

"Yes. And those Gorgios claim they believe it, too." The old man got up and went to snatch a stick from the pile of kindling just beyond our circle. As soon as he handed it to me, I leapt to my feet and began scratching the letters into the stamped-down dirt before he'd even had a chance to ask. When the sentences showed clear in the firelight, I read through them once, made a quick correction, and tossed the stick aside triumphantly.

Everyone got up and clustered round, peering at what I'd written.

"It looks like the letters I've seen carved on the courthouse," the bora chan acknowledged. "But how would any of us know if it's right?"

"Of course it's right!" Shem snapped.

The bora chan bowed. "It is an honest question. I mean no offense to you."

"Offense to *him?*" I spluttered. No one but Shem registered my annoyance. And his eyes darted away from mine.

The bora chan turned to Lemon. "We hear Jersain women have skill in letters...."

Lemon returned his slight bow of the head. "I don't know Romanae as Serena does. Only enough to tell you that the words she has written are the words of your mouth."

The old man came to me and enveloped my hands in his. I felt, as when Shem sat close beside me, a flood of strength. Despite the mockery I had just endured, I was honored, and I knew that was the old man's intention. He turned to face his tribe.

"Jalla Serena will help me tonight. And tomorrow we'll demand justice of the Gorgios."

Lal came to my side. She kissed my cheeks once, twice, three times, as the Parias do. And it seemed to be a signal to all to take their children back to their shacks and trucks and go to sleep for the night, in expectation of the great day tomorrow.

Soon only Shem, the bora chan, and I remained. The old man turned to Shem. "Can she help me in my house? I have a table to work on there and my wife is within."

He was asking Shem's permission! This was one step too far, I thought. Especially after begging Shem's forgiveness for insulting me! I turned to him in great indignation. But Shem looked right past me as he nodded agreement to the old man's request.

"It's just here." The bora chan pointed.

When the old man had gone, I turned to Shem, planting my feet firmly and digging my knuckles into my hips. "Now," I said. "Right now, Shem Vadesh. You tell me what this is all about. Why do you go around pretending we're married?"

"I—"

"Anchara's not with us anymore, did you notice? So why keep up the pretense? What are you trying to do?"

"It's—"

"And please don't tell me you're trying to save my modesty since we're traveling together, because I won't believe it! No one bothers with the modesty of an outcast!"

"Are you finished?" Shem inquired.

I was so angry, I was out of breath. I just nodded.

"Okay, then. You're right, Serena. I'm not doing it to save your modesty." He bent down to pick up the stick I had written with, and crouched by the fire, shooting me an embarrassed look. "Sorry about that."

"Why, then?"

He was silent, needlessly shuffling the logs in the fire.

"Shem! Answer me!"

He looked up at me from under his hat brim. "Listen, Serena." He paused, and seemed to take another tack. "You're a smart girl. You know that if you can't make do with what you're born into, you seek to change it. You of all people know that. You were born to have a sister who would shame your family . . ."

"She didn't shame *me!*"

"I'm only saying what we both know is true," he said in a conciliatory tone. "You don't need to yell—"

"She didn't shame me!" I yelled louder. "Only I can do that! And don't I know it!"

"Oh, come on! Stop jumping all over me! You'll have to curb that tongue of yours someday, Serena love!"

I drew my breath in a sharp hiss. "Don't call me that! How *dare* you call me that?"

I could hardly forbear smacking his nose off his face.

"Pull your claws in, girl, just this once! It wasn't your doing that made you outcast. Everything you do is for changing that. *I* can see that, clear as day. Try to hear what I'm saying."

"Well? What *are* you saying?" I squatted down beside him. "And stop messing with that stick. You're only putting the fire out."

Shem dropped the stick abruptly and looked straight at me. "All right. Listen, then. I want to change my tribe. I want to travel and do business, as your people do. I'm no good as a musician. What is there for me with the Zimbalis? Only failure. I want to become a Kereskedo merchant."

I stared at him. "You can't change your tribe! It's like a donkey trying to become a horse!"

"No. You're wrong."

"According to the Kereskedo it is," I said, thinking of the rebuffs I'd had at Nico Brassi's and Anchara's hands. "They're very strict. You're born one thing; you stick with it. You only set yourself up for disappointment when you try to change that."

"Whose thoughts are you spouting? *You* don't think that way, Serena. Why should I?" He seemed annoyed. "Look at it honestly. You're *ma'hane*. You have no tribe. You do realize that, don't you? Outcasts have no clan—no tribe. They belong nowhere! Yet with my own ears I heard you tell Anchara that you want the *ma'hane* wiped clean. You want to be Kereskedo again. Where's the difference between us?"

I blinked. That was exactly what I wanted.

"No difference," I whispered.

"You see?"

On the other hand, I thought, how was Shem going to become Kereskedo? Kereskedo traders had skills. They spoke languages, made calculations, valued goods, negotiated with Gorgios, and played the bargaining game. But even if he mastered these—and I had my doubts—the Kereskedo jealously guarded entry to their tribe. I knew how rigid their rules were.

"I don't think you should waste your time, Shem. It can't be done."

"It can. Anchara told me. Why do you think I went to her? If a man accomplishes some great business venture, wins some big gamble, then it can be done." He picked up the stick again and shoved a log over with it, carefully avoiding my eyes. "As long as he also marries into the tribe."

I sprang up and took a great step back and away from him. My legs felt weak as water. "So—that's why—" Then the anger came roaring through. "You can't use me that way, Shem Vadesh!"

"Use you?" He scrambled to his feet, dropping the stick. "I don't see it that way."

"Oh? And how do you see it?"

"I see it as an honorable marriage. Why not? Don't you think that would wipe the *ma'hane* clean? You wouldn't be an outcast anymore. How often do you think that happens? And once you're Kereskedo—"

"Don't pretend it's for my sake!" I exclaimed. I couldn't believe he had the face to stand there and propose such a thing. "Anchara thinks we're married already and her clan still treats me like dirt! You can't fool me with your clever talk! I'm not all Gorgio, you know!"

"Serena, do you honestly think Anchara's stupid enough to believe we're wed? That was just a first-sight mistake."

"What?" The heat flared in my cheeks. "What *does* she believe, then?"

"She believes in the braid gold I gave her."

I was dumbstruck. How far ahead *had* he been thinking?

"Look, Serena. It just— The idea came to me when Anchara made that mistake. But I didn't have the courage to tell you right then. I figured you would smack me." A trace of a smile appeared. "I'm impressed you haven't smacked me yet. Thank you, by the way." The smile was gone. "But I'm not joking, Serena. I need you to marry me. Seriously. Otherwise, I won't have a chance."

For a second I stood there with my mouth hanging open like a trout, feeling fury and hurt and an idiotic pleasure all churning inside fit to make me sick.

Now that he'd suggested it, I did want to hit him.

Then, without a word, I turned on my heel and ran to the home of the bora chan. At least I knew what awaited me there: Romanae verbs, passionless and predictable.

I'd never had a more welcome translation assignment.

16

Send us holly for today
Anise for tomorrow,
Send us mayflowers fine and gay
And send us rue for sorrow . . .

—Yulang dirge

Sister! Wake up!" Willow was shaking me, her long pale fingers curled around my shoulders. On the fourth finger of her hand an amethyst ring blazed. I knew two contradictory things at once, as one does in dreams. I knew that Alex had given her the ring and that Willow was safely engaged to a rich Gorgio. And I knew that the amethyst was one I had found in the cave.

Willow had stolen it from me.

I sat up in bed, awash in the familiar resentment and rueful love that my sister awoke in me. Willow knelt beside me, wearing the gorgeous emerald green dress Alex had given her.

"Shake off your sleep!" she cried. "There's news!"

"You're engaged to him," I said dully.

Her smile was brilliant. "Of course. I told you love solves everything. Why did you run off, you silly girl? We can protect you now. Come back."

I drew back from her, gathering my blanket tighter around my body.

"No."

Willow gave me a puzzled look. "Come on, Serena. You're always the tripping stone to your own happiness. Don't you know that by now?

Come back to us. With your brains, there's no telling what you could do in Alex's world. Why do you struggle so much? Look at you!" She glanced around the shadowy caravan, her lip curling. "With these miserable people! Even among the Yulang they're the lowest of the low."

"They have troubles, Willow."

"So?" Willow's eyes narrowed. "'Their trouble is not our trouble. Why waste your strength on them?' Who was it who told me *that?*"

"I was talking about some foolish Gorgio boy you were fretting over."

"You were talking about everyone, Serena."

I glared at her. "What about Zara? Are you and Alex protecting her? Now that you've the power to protect everyone?"

Willow's beautiful face went rigid.

"Who is Zara?" she whispered hoarsely.

I awoke, cold and sweating in the clammy morning air.

Lemon lay on the floor, in Shem's accustomed place. He had slept outside by the fire. Next to me, Rochelle still lay curled up like a puppy, her little body radiating warmth.

The night had passed, yet still she was here with us.

I brought my feet down silently onto the cold floor, careful not to disturb the pile of blankets under which Lemon slumbered. Her mouth was partly open, making her look oddly defenseless. Her black hair, with its shock of white streaks, was tumbled and clinging to her face.

I'd always admired Lemon. She had a well of anger as deep and full as my own, but she turned hers into cool observations and devastating wit. I'd seen her take the skin off a customer who asked her to shoo me from her shop. She was sophisticated, talented, and goodhearted. I used to look at her and think enviously that Jersain women could do anything. Yet here she was, the marvelous Lemon, penniless and asleep on the floor of a Yulang caravan.

I felt a wave of tenderness such as I never expected to feel toward her. Suddenly, I wondered if the white streaks in her hair were marks of anxiety rather than a striking accident of nature. And whether she was sad that, at twenty-five, she was still unmarried.

I need you to marry me, Serena.

Was Shem completely mad?

No. Not mad at all. He knew exactly what he wanted. That we'd known each other less than a month wouldn't faze him at all. I'd lay beetles to buttons that even the daughter of Nico Brassi had never set eyes on her bridegroom before the wedding day. It was common as spitting.

I'd simply lived among the Gorgios too long to take it for granted, besides having Willow as a sister, lapping up her sappy Gorgio romances. Marriage was a business arrangement among the Yulang as often as not. Mother and Daddy had been an exception in more ways than one. And I knew that for all the supposed romance of Gorgio marriage, far more of them broke up than the cold-blooded Yulang ones. Affection grows after the ceremony, the Yulang say.

So why was I offended?

Because *this* was why he'd been so generous with his time and his help. It was an excellent Kereskedo bargain. A bit of his help with present difficulties in exchange for the rest of my life. Maybe he really did deserve to enter the tribe!

With renewed fury, I snatched my clothes from under the pillows. Then I remembered to move gently so I wouldn't wake Rochelle.

Seeing her lying there brought Zara again to my mind.

And it gave me pause. What if Shem hadn't helped me? What of my little niece, then? He'd gotten me out of Oestia, and away from the Cruelty. He'd given Anchara priceless braid gold to make her listen to me, when I'd managed only to get myself sent away. And now he was taking me back to Anchara so I could find Mother. I hadn't even had to ask.

Why, then, did it hurt to find he wanted something in return?

If I said no to Shem, would he leave me here with the Parias and their burned-out shacks?

Well, I wasn't going to marry him just for a ride to Eurus Major! I'd walk if it came to that. Ever since we had gone to Anchara's camp and his debt to me was settled, I'd felt my own debt growing. For a long time I'd suspected that he was marking what I owed on a balance sheet somewhere. Now I knew I was right.

Silently, I slipped my shirt over my head and pulled on my trousers. There'd been no chance to wash. My clothes smelled charred and smoky. Soot had settled in the lines of my knuckles and the whorls on my fingertips. A bracelet of speckled black encircled my wrists. Under my clothes my skin felt sticky.

A memory of the honey-colored marble tub at my Gorgio grandmother's house assaulted my senses: the hot water gushing from the chrome taps, the scented bath oils she sometimes forgot to lock away. *Hurry, Serena! She's left out the eau de violet! Splash it in and I'll paint your nails while you bathe. Then it's my turn!* Willow's conspiratorial giggle tickled my ear as I stepped out of the caravan.

At a wooden table outside, the bora chan sat talking with Shem and Ren Bardoff. Lemon's father must have returned deep in the night. The three of them sat with their heads together and their shoulders hunched.

I was glad that they were too occupied to notice me. In the bora chan's pocket was the petition I'd labored over the night before. I remembered how he'd looked at me as my pen sped and I debated whether a noun took the dative or accusative, as if I were some strange creature, half girl, half beast, come from the other world to sit at his kitchen table. He'd had the grace to look embarrassed when my eye caught his. And when I left, he'd placed two fingers on my forehead and given me his blessing that the light would shine on my road and all my ventures would bear fruit.

Still, I knew he thought me a freak of nature.

The sight of Shem so soon after the night before irritated but also pained me, like a splinter under the skin. And Mr. Bardoff? A warning struck within me like a muffled bell.

Mr. Bardoff had returned. But where was Rochelle's mother?

"Leave them to set the world to rights," a voice whispered in my ear. Lal was standing next to me in a red apron, holding a jug of cooking oil. "Come break your fast at my stove, Jalla."

I smiled, on the verge of acceptance. And then I remembered what had slipped my mind last night, when I cooked supper for the entire camp.

"I'm *ma'hane*," I blurted out. "I can't break bread in your house."

"*Ma'hane?*" Lal drew back, regarding me curiously. I flushed, knowing she wondered what terrible thing I had done. She was forthright enough to ask, as well.

But instead she snorted. "*Ma'hane!* Don't you know that my whole tribe is *ma'hane* among the Yulang? Unclean? Unmarriageable? And every one of us Yulang, even the high-nosed Kereskedo, are *ma'hane* among the Gorgios. And the Gorgios, who knows, they may be *ma'hane* among the angels of God. I see no blot on you."

Lal's hard features at that moment were the loveliest I had ever seen. I wanted to snatch up her hand and hold it but wasn't sure if it was the proper thing to do. Then I remembered that a Kereskedo would never willingly touch the hand of a Paria—it was true what Lal had said. So I clasped her hand with a grateful smile and followed her to her house.

The house was cramped, jerry-built by the apple growers to rent out to whatever laborers came along. In the muddy alley between it and the house next door, Lal's sons crouched moodily, chewing the ends of cigarettes. They would not work today unless the bora chan gave the word, and I could see that the leisure made them uneasy.

Children ran in and out the door, half clad, as if it were the height of summer instead of the last fine days of October. One of Lal's daughters-in-law scooped them up by the necks, one by one, and carted them into the back of the house to dress. The other daughters-in-law crouched in the tiny yard over plastic tubs full of bubbles, scrubbing clothes as if they were washing away the stains of a sinful soul, and not the grime of the apple orchards.

Every day the wash, I thought. Bales of it! And the food. And the kids. And picking in the fields, as likely as not. What a life!

I followed Lal indoors. The house smelled of bleach and tinned tomatoes. The kitchen and the sitting room were all one, cramped but scrubbed and tidy. Lal lifted a thermos from the counter and poured me a cup of throat-stripping Yulang coffee and began scooping corn-cake batter onto a griddle slung over the electric burners. She was an island of calm in the hurricane of her household. She followed my eyes out the open door to her sweating daughters-in-law.

"You and your man," she said, dropping her voice to a whisper. "You're not wed, are you?"

I choked on a mouthful of coffee. It was true what Shem said! Nobody was fooled. "I'm— We're—" But why lie? I thought. It would be playing Shem's game for him. "How did you know?"

Lal threw back her head and laughed. "*How?* You sleep late, Jalla. No wife does that. I saw your man washing his own clothes at the pump this morning! That would be your job if all were to rights."

Mother Lillith, I thought. A lifetime of scrubbing Shem's shirts for him!

Though, of course, I'd washed Zara's and Willow's laundry time and time again. Cooked the dinners, cleaned the dishes, done the shopping.

The work came with being part of a family. But Willow and Zara *were* my family. Shem? What was he? A trickster! A con man! I thought of how he'd tried to cheat the woman on the mountainside out of a tank of gas. (I shoved the image of her little pistol into a darker place in my mind. I wasn't in the mood to complicate things.) He was what the Gorgios meant when they called us Magpie. Conning me into a lifetime of labor for him!

I shook my head, trying to shake my ugly thoughts out of my brain. What nonsense, anyway! I didn't need to worry about Shem's shirts. No one was going to force me to marry him.

The shirt I'd worn searching for the amethysts, cleaned and carefully hung on the drying rack, suddenly floated into my mind. But I dismissed it. All part of the plan, no doubt, that little kindness.

"You'd better hurry up and tie the knot, Jalla," the Paria woman advised, throwing a spoonful of sugar into her cup. "Before you have to. You follow me?"

"It's not like that!" I cried in horror. "It's not what you think. We're not— We don't—"

It was hopeless to even try to say the words. Instead, I hid my face in my hands. My cheeks were so hot, they burned my palms. From between my fingers, I peered at Lal. She raised an eyebrow at my outburst and then went back to flipping the cakes. At least, I thought, she probably believes me.

In the silence one of the girls sloshed into the house, her long skirts leaving snakes of water on the floor. She grabbed a box of detergent and stomped out again. Lal tipped the corn cakes onto a plate, passed a pot of blueberry jam, and plumped down in a seat across from me.

"Ah, stop glenching, girl, and eat your food." She grinned, showing a mouthful of brown teeth, and drew a pipe out of her apron pocket. With a deft hand she scooped fragrant tobacco leaves into the pipe and lit them. None of the young girls would be caught dead with tobacco on their lips. It was a sign of looseness. But I'd hardly met an older Yulang woman who did not smoke.

"I'll tell you a confidence, deary," Lal went on, drawing on the stem of her pipe. "And tell no one I've said it: I'm glad you're not married. Mother Lillith witness me, every woman should wed. No tribeswoman will tell you different. But a Yulang girl with Gorgio learning in her? You'd not waste that!"

I stared. It was the sort of thing my grandmother used to say. But she'd said it to hammer home how lucky we were that she acknowledged us. She'd even talked of sending me to university. But only so I wouldn't be a disgrace to her family. A good education would groom the Yulang out of me. That was my grandmother's thought.

From Lal, I knew, the sentiment had something else behind it.

"What do you mean?" I said cautiously. "People have told me that before. That I could get a good job if I'm lucky, or even pass as a Gorgio. But I'd never be able to pass, you know. People take one look at me and they know I'm Yulang."

"A good job?" Lal said "job" as if it were a word in another language. "You mean work for a boss, like a Gorgio? Why would you need to do that? You're Kereskedo, aren't you? I've seen Gorgios knocking down the doors of Kereskedo merchants for a loan. There's nothing special in that. But you have a heart beating behind your ribs, and all that learning in your head. Think of the good you can do."

"The good!" Lal didn't know me. She didn't know I'd maimed a man with my Evil Eye—maybe killed him—or that the Gorgios wanted to put me in jail. I'd decided that I wasn't evil enough to be justly called *ma'hane*. But I wouldn't claim I was the opposite. "What good could *I* do?"

Lal shrugged. "More good than washing one man's laundry, anyway.

You helped us, Jalla, that's all I know. Perhaps you're one of those who can shake down justice from the tree of life. There are some people like that."

I chewed thoughtfully on my corn cake. Lal's words made me feel a sort of light inside me. As if I'd been trapped in a dark room and had suddenly discovered I could break the lock. And when I threw the door open, there were vistas and sunlit trees and roads rising to a distant horizon. I could use my Gorgio learning to aid the Yulang. Lal's people I would help with no question. And as for Nico Brassi—he could whistle for my help. That would show him what I thought of his *ma'hane!*

These thoughts had the oddest effect: they made me feel more charitable toward Shem. I no longer wanted to flay the skin off his back. It was strange, but my anger was gone. He'd helped me, fine. But I had other possibilities, beyond those of other Yulang women. Far beyond some marriage of convenience.

"Can you answer a question, Avo Lal?"

"Of course."

The question made me sound like an outsider, but I had to know. "Why can you and the older women smoke? And talk back to anyone you like? When the girls out there just work like slaves?"

Lal laughed. "How do you think, smart one? A woman works like a camel, carrying everything on her back. The more she works, the more she knows. She is arguing with the police over her campsite, cursing the Cruelty, teaching the children, keeping the Gorgios from robbing her blind. And eventually she sees that the men can't do a thing without her. Then who's going to tell her to keep quiet and stick her head in a laundry pail?"

Maybe so, I thought. But that wasn't enough for me. I hadn't even given Shem an answer last night, had I? Well, I'd better make sure he knew the answer was no.

I sighed, suddenly depressed. Below the peppery smell of the coffee and the oily, savory scent of the corn cakes, I caught a whiff of my own stale sweat.

"Can I ask another question?"

"If it's as good as the last." Lal flung a crust out the open door, where it was caught by a bony mutt.

"Is there somewhere I could wash myself? Could I use your bathroom?"

"No plumbing here, love. But there's the shower stall uphill from the latrine. Here. You're my guest this morning. I don't care if you've got finer in that grand caravan of yours. I'm honored to share." Lal stood up, and I saw that she was sitting on a dowry chest, like the one Mother used to have. Piles of clean linen were stacked inside. She pulled out a snowy white towel—no doubt tortured into whiteness by the daughters-in-law—and threw it over my shoulder. From a small rack she took a cake of soap and handed it to me.

"Real pressed rose petals. Guaranteed to pull your true love straight to your side." She winked at me. "At least that's what we tell the Gorgios who buy it."

When I was finally in the shower, I could see why the Gorgios believed her. The soap was transparent pink and had rose petals floating within, as if frozen in a winter pond. And the scent it gave off as I slid it over my shoulders was at once fresh and swooning. The water sluicing over my head from the rusty showerhead was warmer than I'd expected, and the stall cleaner, despite being shared by so many women. The daughters-in-law had doubtless been at work here as well. I knew others would soon be waiting for a shower, but I could not wrench myself out of the world of water and steam.

My body was strange to me after weeks of huddling to undress in the dark and furtively washing at a pump. The razor stubble on my legs had sprouted into a soft tangle of hairs, less disgusting-looking than I would have believed. The sooty bracelets around my wrists dissolved into bluish rivulets and were gone. I dug my fingernails into the soap and worked at the little soap crescents until the dirt rode away on them.

By the time I was working the soap into my scalp to banish the rank smell of my hair, I felt so wonderful I stretched my arms up over my head as if to grab the sun down from the sky. For once I could see the fullness of my breasts and the curves of my waist without my usual dismay. I wasn't sure why, for my breasts had been always the bane of my existence. They'd budded early and grown on my chest like unwelcome cantaloupes. I'd always known they were a byword among the Gorgio boys at school, and the subject of a lot of bad and derisive poetry in the boys' john. I could never listen to Mother's reassurances or wear the traditional tight-fitting vests favored by Kereskedo women. After Mother left, and as Willow's belly grew, I took to wearing baggy sweaters all the time. After fending off a few drunken fumbles from Willow's Gorgio friends, I'd acquired the habit of folding my arms in front of my chest.

But now I had a rebellious thought of my own. Couldn't there be something graceful about the way my hips balanced my breasts? Not cheap, or vulgar? Not a subject for smutty jokes or nasty grabs? Was it possible that someone could look on me and find me desirable and that would be all right?

What did Shem see when he looked at me? Anything beyond a free ticket into the Kereskedo tribe?

Quickly I jammed off the spigot and wrapped Lal's towel around me, tight as a bandage.

A mad honking burst out all around the shower building. I jumped, wrung out my wet hair, and scrambled into my clothes. The honking became louder.

When I stepped outside, I found the whole camp in commotion.

The girls had left their washtubs, the women their stoves, and the men their early morning idleness to pile into their trucks and trailers and cars. The drivers swung out onto the shoulder of the road and lined up one behind another. They were not honking to get other cars out of their way but all together, like a flock of geese taking flight.

And rising from beneath the sound of the horns was a noise that raised the hairs on the back of my neck. At first I thought it was loons—unnatural loons lifting their voices in the morning light. But it wasn't.

It was the wailing sound my mother had made at Daddy's funeral.

The keening throbbed from the throats of women standing on the flatbeds of the trucks.

With my wet hair spreading a cold stain across my back, I raced back to Lal's house. But when I burst through the door, I found the household gone. Lal must have been adding her wails to the other women's. Who was this mourning for?

I laid Lal's precious soap on top of the neatly folded towel and steeled myself to step back into the chaos. With the din pounding in my ears, I ran to Shem's caravan.

An ancient sedan was parked beside it with its trunk open. In it lay the body of a cello, carefully wrapped in canvas. Seeing it made me shudder. It reminded me of the linen they'd wrapped Daddy's body in before we buried him.

I looked up and saw Lemon's father approaching me. Ren Bardoff's step was heavy, as if his polished shoes had lead weights in them. He glanced at me without surprise. His eyes were as kindly as ever behind his spectacles, his beard as neatly trimmed, his Jersain skullcap as scholarly-looking. But no greeting sprang to his lips. He only smiled at me sadly. Then he pulled the cello out of the trunk and carried it, with difficulty, up the steps and into the caravan.

I just stood there, with the wailing in my ears.

Shem stepped out of the caravan a moment after Mr. Bardoff entered.

"What's happened?" I whispered, hardly wanting to know.

For answer, he put his hands on my shoulders and turned me toward the line of trucks and cars on the side of the road. "Look there."

The old bora chan was carrying a bundle wrapped in Shem's red blanket from truck to truck. As he stopped by each vehicle, people brought their faces down to lay kisses upon whoever was wrapped in the blanket, once, twice, three times. Men took off their hats and bowed their heads; old women laid their hands upon the blanket, while the younger women threw their heads back and screamed, "Aieee! Aieee!"

I knew then.

I knew before I even caught a glimpse of the small face peering out of the blanket.

It was Rochelle. She was awake, but her eyes were gluey with shock.

"Where is everyone going?" I whispered.

"To bring the body back," Shem answered.

With a shudder I turned to him. But he didn't meet my eyes. His face was pinched as he watched the progress of the little girl through the crowd. I followed his gaze, straining for a glimpse of Rochelle's face. The bora chan turned and I could see her clearly.

Under the barrage of kisses and blessings and shouts, Rochelle moved not a muscle.

"The Trident Riders will dance tonight," Shem added bitterly.

I closed my eyes. A shot of silver exploded behind my lids, like a flashbulb from an old camera. The picture that formed in my dark mind was cold and underexposed as a film negative—a world of barren fields and stripped, empty trees. I saw the white horse tearing clods from the earth with its hooves. I saw the rider's cruel, laughing mouth and his finger on the trigger, speeding the bullet into the air.

My mother sank to her knees by the gaping hole in the ground as the pallbearers lowered my father's body in. I saw her lift her face to the heavens and howl. *Like a dog,* my grandmother said in disgust. *Like an animal.*

Like any other Yulang woman, grieving a death that came too soon.

Was that our fate? To howl like animals at our losses?

My heart felt as though it, too, had been wrapped in canvas and was suffocating in my chest. I couldn't bear to see what I was seeing, whether my eyes were open or shut.

Shem was shaking me by the arm. Unwillingly, I opened my eyes. Nothing had changed.

"Serena?" He stooped down and peered into my face. "Do you hear me? Hey? What are you mumbling, girl?"

I didn't know I'd been mumbling. But I tried to tell him. I tried to tell him what it had felt like to be twelve years old and have the Gorgios send your father home in a box, and now to see Rochelle with her mother returning the same way. But I couldn't speak of that, for there was an even more despairing thought beneath that thought.

"What good are petitions?" I burst out. "What good are amethysts? Why should we collect scraps of paper and purple rocks? What good are Romanae words and Gorgio learning? What good does it do us? The Trident Riders will keep laughing. Children will be stolen and parents will be killed—there's not a thing we can do to change it."

"You can't take it like that, Serena." He gave my shoulder a rough shake. "Snap out of it."

But I was unable to stop. "I'll never get Zara back! I mean, look at us! Look at these miserable people." Those were Willow's words. "We're powerless. Completely powerless."

Shem bent down and whispered in my ear. "Then we have to take some power for ourselves. What do you think we're trying to do, you and I? Hey?"

I stared. "You and I?"

I hadn't expected that.

"And you will get Zara back," he added. "I'll help you."

"For your price," I said bleakly.

"No. That's not tied to any other bargain. The other matter—" He glanced over my head. "The bora chan is coming. Pull yourself together. Here." He fished a twisted bandana out of his coat pocket. "Dry your eyes."

"I'm *not* crying!"

"I agree. But dry your eyes anyway. Whoever's those tears are, they'll upset the little girl."

I pulled myself up straighter and tried to shake off the despair I felt. When Daddy died, that was what scared me the most: the despair on my mother's face. The expression that would come when she thought I was not looking, up until the very day she left.

Others might have shown that look to Rochelle. But I wouldn't, though I thought that looking on her might break me into pieces. I managed to give her a small smile as the bora chan approached, and Shem removed his hat. As I'd seen her tribe do, I brought my lips to her forehead and her cheeks.

Lemon came out of the caravan with her father and took Rochelle in her arms, rocking her as if she were a baby.

"Estraella worked long and well for us before this child was born," Ren Bardoff said to the bora chan. "I held Rochelle when she was named in your camp. Our offer still stands."

"You'll care for her until this trouble passes?"

"As long as you wish."

The bora chan gripped the old Jersain's wrist. "And when we tell you to bring her to us, you will? You will remember that she is ours?"

Lemon looked up. "She'll always know who her people are. And we'll be traveling with Serena. She and her friend can keep Rochelle to the Yulang ways. All we can do is care for her."

"Thank you."

Tenderly, Lemon carried the girl up the steps into the caravan.

The bora chan turned to me. "There will be trouble now, Jalla." He waved his arm at the procession lining the road. "We'll deliver your petition once we've fetched Estraella home. We'll hold her wake on the mayor's steps. And if he won't give us justice, we'll stay there till we get it. The Gorgios won't like it. It's good our friends can look after Rochelle. This will be no place for a child who's just lost her mother."

I could see the truth in that. But it would be hard for Rochelle, to lose her mother first, and then all her extended family, too.

"I welcome her, Bora Chan. But must we take her so far off? We could stay and look after her until the trouble's passed."

Shem raised an eyebrow. I knew what he was thinking. I had been in such burning haste to find Anchara, and now I was offering to wait.

"You have your own losses to redeem, Jalla. Shem told me." He gave me a fleeting look of compassion and turned away. "Good fortune go with you."

I watched as he hurried along the roadside to his truck, which was parked at the front of the procession. Engines turned over. The caravans and trucks skidded out in full U-turns, pebbles spraying from their wheels. Soon dust devils swirled and hovered over the whole stretch of road.

Before I could swallow them, the words were out of my mouth. "Why should I travel any farther? My losses will never be redeemed."

"All losses are redeemed," Shem said, impatiently cramming his hat back on his head. "That's the Kereskedo code. Must I teach you every-thing about your own tribe?"

"That means business losses," I said sullenly. "All business losses are redeemed. So what?"

"Not everything is about business, Serena."

"What do you mean?"

"I mean get in the car." He grabbed my elbow and started steering me toward the passenger-side door.

"No!" I said quickly.

"No what? You can't mope here forever. What nonsense is this now?"

"It's not nonsense. Not when it comes to your driving," I said. "I won't sit in the passenger seat, thank you very much. I'll drive."

Shaking his head in exasperation, Shem threw me the keys.

Promises march ahead; doubts creep behind.

—Jersain saying

It was near midday, much farther along the road, when I climbed out of the car to investigate a clicking sound coming from our left front tire.

As I bent to look at it, I could hear hoarse sobs coming through the cracked window of the caravan. Rochelle. I hadn't been able to hear her while I'd been driving. Had she been crying like this the whole way?

"Mama! I want Mama!" she wept.

Lemon murmured indistinctly, trying to soothe her.

Shem had come out of the car to examine the wheel with me. I saw him register Rochelle's wails. I met his eyes and shook my head. Though I pretended to look for the problem in the wheel, I couldn't focus on anything. All I could hear was the little girl's cries. I couldn't bear them. I could hardly bear to think, for in my thoughts I found Zara, lonely and abandoned, crying for me and Willow just as Rochelle was crying for her mother. I could only blink back tears and examine the tire with my jaw clenched so tightly I thought I would crack a tooth.

Then, abruptly, Rochelle quieted. I heard Lemon singing her a snatch of a lullaby.

"It's only a rock," Shem was saying.

The tire came back into focus. I unclenched my jaw and tried to breathe deeper to loosen the tightness in my chest as I watched Shem work the stone out of the tire tread with his pocketknife. He looked up at me, but I turned away. Without a word, I climbed back into the driver's seat.

My heart was low as I restarted the engine.

But after a time, the ride across the cut and stubbled fields and out into the canyons and coulees did something to soothe my despair.

The feeling I'd had the first time I ever drove the caravan came back to me. The longer I drove, the more the ribbon of asphalt unwinding under the wheels became a kind of hope in itself. Or at least a promise of change. And although I knew that this road might lead only to loss, I fortified myself with the possibility that my mother was among the living and that at the end of this journey I might find her.

We ate our midday meal on the edge of a great dried-up waterfall. I had no inclination for words and only stared out at the beauty of the harsh, dry landscape, taking now and then a bite of an apple or the flatbread Lemon had packed for us. Shem was preoccupied, twisting bits of wire into intricate shapes, as he had all the time we'd been driving. Lemon looked drained, and Rochelle didn't even leave the shelter of the caravan to come out and eat.

When Mr. Bardoff pulled up in his old sedan, he began collecting flat stones, which he piled one atop the other at the side of the road. The Jersains do this in remembrance of the dead.

We drove on. The great Serpentine River, which twists and curves all the way from the inland ranges to the coast, finally cut across our road and we had to head to the boat landing to wait for a ferry to take us across.

Once I'd parked, I got out and wandered down to the rocky riverside to stretch my legs. There was no longer any noise from the caravan. The ferry was all the way at the far shore, loading farm trucks heavy with wheat and corn. I felt relieved that there was a little time before I would have to drive again, and that Rochelle was quiet. I hoped she might be asleep.

The sun struck out through the clouds and lay warm on my back— an unexpected gift on this bleak afternoon.

I crouched beside the river, watching bright green frogs jump from rock to rock and pollywogs shiver in the water. For a moment, I was able to put the unhappiness of the day out of my mind.

I cupped my hands around a frog and lifted it up in my palm. Not caring for me a bit, it pushed off with its long legs, executed a graceful arc, and plopped into the shallows. I laughed and tried to follow its progress as it swam away from me, but gave up when my eyes caught on an extremely bizarre creature.

"Look at this!" I called out, for I'd heard Shem's boots in the sand behind me. "This one's just turning into a frog—do you see? It's still half pollywog. Have you ever seen anything like it before?"

"As often as I've seen my uncle shave his beard," Shem said absently. He was wandering up and down the length of the fence between the parking strip and the shore, peering closely at the fence posts.

"That's not very informative." I dipped my hands back in the water, trying to scoop up another frog. "That could be every day or not at all."

I saw he still wasn't really listening and, taken with a sudden desire to tease him, added, "How about as often as you shave yours? Once a week, is it?"

He left off his searching.

"What kind of remark is that?" He ran his hand over his chin, pretending to scowl. "Does my beard seem insufficient to you?"

"Bit sparse," I said airily, trying not to laugh.

"I didn't realize you took such note of it!"

"I don't!" In a sudden foul temper, I picked up a rock and threw it into the water as hard as I could, horrified to realize I was acting like Willow....

"Here it is! Ha!" Shem cried, ignoring my bad humor. He was unwinding another quilting square from the bleached and splintered fence—just in time, too, as the ferry was now midstream and quickly approaching.

"I thought I was supposed to find the next one."

"Too busy thinking about frogs and beards, Jalla. You need to concentrate."

As he untied the fabric, a flat black rock dropped into his palm.

"A bit obvious!" He turned to me. "They'll be at Plateau Rock. It makes sense. They've camped there before."

"How do you know?"

"I used to come to the eastern market with my uncles. Half the traveling tribes in the city drive out here every October—musicians, smiths, traders—you knew that, didn't you?"

"I knew there was something this time of year...."

"Who's aboard?" yelled the ferryman.

Shem wrapped the rock in the cloth, and tied it to the fence post.

As we ran back to the caravan, I stopped by the Bardoffs' black sedan and leaned in the window to nudge Ren Bardoff awake. The old man had fallen asleep on his steering wheel in the warm afternoon sunshine.

That night, we camped on the other side of the river.

Before I lay down to sleep, I dumped out Rass's backpack and carefully wrapped the amethysts in a sturdy cloth I'd borrowed from Lemon, making sure to empty out all the dirt and sand before I repacked it. I didn't expect Rass would appreciate having it returned in such a shambles.

We reached Plateau Rock by the middle of the next morning.

Anchara's camp was up on high, level land, way upstream from a Gorgio campsite. Plateau Rock itself was an enormous flat boulder by the banks of a tributary of the Serpentine, and the caravans of Anchara's clan were clustered around it. From here you could see the outskirts of Eurus Major.

As before, we parked the caravan at a distance from the others.

While Lemon and I dragged out coolers and camp stoves and gathered kindling for the evening fire, Shem went to Anchara's campsite and found it nearly deserted. Most of her people were out selling at the market, which had opened that morning.

Once he'd got directions from the men left to guard the caravans, he and Lemon and I drove the Bardoffs' car into the city. The grand old sedan, with Lemon at the wheel, glided smoothly along the road. It was like flying compared to the straining, bumping progress of our caravan.

We drove into Eurus Major along broad, sun-baked streets. I'd imagined elegant boulevards and squares like Plaza Ridizio. But Eurus had a slapdash, frontier feel to it. Scaffolding was everywhere. Peddlers and beggars crowded the alleys and overpasses. The buildings were layer cakes of cement and their adornments were sale signs. Hired security guards lounged casually outside trading emporiums under banners reading FIREARMS *MUST* BE CHECKED AT THE DOOR. A furious flow of people and cars and jeepneys pulsed through the crowded streets.

The market was set up in a fairground south of town. We drove out there and parked at a small train station nearby, where cargo was being loaded to journey inland. We were lucky to get a spot, too, with so many cars honking and cutting each other off, trying to park. Once Lemon had eased the sedan into the cramped space, we set off along a footpath that led across the overgrown fields to the outlying tents.

The mournful lowing of cattle in the stockades carried over the open wastes as we approached, and we heard the auctioneer's voice ringing out as he banged his gavel and sealed their fate.

We joined the throng of people flowing into the market to buy or sell or gawk. Nervously, I tightened the straps of Rass's pack, securing the precious amethysts against my back. Lemon, Shem, and I drew closer together as the crowd thickened around us, and we finally had to stretch out single file amid the press of bodies.

We pushed on past knots of people bidding on farm machinery, past tables stacked with smoked pigs' heads, haunches of ham, and enormous wheels of cheese. The vendors shouted at the top of their lungs, waving fingers in the air to settle their prices. The pushing and shoving and noise made me edgy. How would we find Anchara in this mayhem?

Lemon fell behind in the crush. I tried to stop for her. But if I waited too long, I would lose sight of Shem. All I could do was to keep looking back to make sure she was following.

Suddenly, someone in the crowd grabbed my bottom and pinched hard. I screamed and whirled about with my hand raised to smack. But in the sea of faces, I couldn't fix on who had done it. I stood there, balked of my prey, seething with anger and frustration.

Lemon caught up with me and grabbed my wrist. "It was that bald oaf." She pointed and I saw a squat man with a sloppy gait ambling off down a side aisle. Feeling my eyes on him, he turned. He didn't see me, but I saw him. He was smirking.

"Oh!" I snaked my hand out of Lemon's grip. "I'll go unscrew his head for him!"

"I know how you feel. But you're not going to waste your time chasing him, are you?" Lemon said reasonably. "You have more important business to take care of."

I tried to swallow my rage, but it was hard. Concentrate, I thought. All that matters is Anchara and the gemstones. I glared at the bald man for a moment, then turned away, nodding mutely at Lemon's words.

"Come on, then," she said, grabbing my hand. "We've nearly lost Shem."

With difficulty, I took a breath and put the fury out of my mind.

We struggled on through the crowd, trying to catch glimpses of Shem's now rather dusty hat, which was all we could see of him. I knew we were heading in the right direction when we left the farm stalls behind and saw tables laden with rich fabrics, laces, silks, and hooked rugs of the sort that take years to make.

Then, to my delight, I recognized a big man with a pale scar stitched across his cheek. I saw him walk up to Shem and grab his shoulder in friendly greeting.

"It's Rass!" I exclaimed.

"Who?"

"The mara chan's son. Look, he's pointing. He must be directing Shem to her stall—"

The next moment, Rass was gone and Shem turned about, searching for us. We waved and he pointed down a side passage. It was the gem sellers' area. Here, as throughout the market, the stalls were only tables with tarps hung overhead in case of rain, and the aisles were beaten-down grass that smelled heavy and rank from trampling. But even so, this section of the market glittered. I couldn't believe the number of vendors. Thick-necked guards loomed by the sides of display tables. We pushed our way past fantastic racks of emeralds and sapphires, torques and tiaras, bracelets and amulets. One table sold nothing but rings that hung like golden fruit on sculpted trees. Betrothed couples hovered around them like hummingbirds.

Finally, we caught sight of Anchara.

I was stunned to see how shabby her stall was next to those of the Gorgio merchants.

Amid all this glitter, Anchara herself was shrunken: a wizened Yulang crone crouching beside her wares, smoking her smelly pipe. With shock and disappointment I took in this woman who had seemed so powerful in the forest, and whose words were the difference between hope and despair for me. Compared to the Gorgio traders, she was nothing.

I could not rush forward and flaunt the amethysts under her nose, as I'd dreamed of doing. I suddenly had no desire to mock her or laugh at how she'd underestimated me.

Instead, I stood quite still and waited while two teenage girls fingered the hammered silver bracelets she displayed atop a swath of green velvet. Money changed hands and the girls slipped the bracelets on their wrists. Anchara shoved the coins into her pockets and the bills securely into her bra.

None of the wealthier buyers were here. The polished tiger's-eyes, bloodstone, and carnelian on Anchara's table were dull compared with the sparkling gems the Gorgio dealers had brought from mines across the seas. And even if she'd had diamonds and rubies to sell, I realized, Anchara would never acquire the fortunes of the Gorgio dealers who stood nearby in their sleekly cut suits. She was the head of a Yulang clan, as well as serving as mara chan to the entire tribe. Her gains went to the care and feeding of fifty souls. In this company, the great and wise Anchara Pulchra was nothing but a poor woman trying to eke out a living for herself and her kin.

The disappointment I felt was shot through with a small glimmer of pity. Lal's words came back to me: in the world of the Gorgio we are all *ma'hane*, even the high-nosed Kereskedo. Even the awesome Anchara.

We waited until the Gorgio girls had left to approach her.

Shem greeted her first. "Respect, Mara Chan."

Anchara's eyes brightened as Shem bowed and kissed the knuckles of her hands.

"It was well with you, then, boy?" I was surprised to hear concern in her voice. "I worried when you refused to leave with us."

"It was well, Mara Chan. The road has been kind to us," Shem assured her.

Not true, I thought. But certainly the best thing to say.

Shem introduced Lemon, who bowed her greeting before taking leave to find a musician who had stored some instruments for her. Once their pleasantries were over, I stepped forward.

"Respect, Avo Anchara," I mumbled, fearing she might not acknowledge me.

But to my surprise, Anchara's old face broke into a smile. "I'm glad you were not caught by the forest police, Jalla. Though I urged the boy not to wait for you."

Her expression of pleasure was typically double edged! I thought. No matter.

I looked her in the eye. "I found something of value, Mara Chan. Something to barter for your help. Shall I show you?"

Anchara inclined her head slightly.

Seeing this as encouragement, I took the bag off my back, opened it, and pulled out the cloth in which I'd wrapped the amethysts. I set the bundle in front of Anchara and carefully unknotted it, working slowly, lest any of the stones spill on the ground.

I'd feared that the brilliance of the nearby Gorgio jewels would dim my gems' sparkle. But as I pulled the cloth flat, the amethysts shone upon it as bright as ever. Next to Anchara's jaspers and agates, they burned like sunset on the waters. Out of the corner of my eye, I saw the shrewd, appraising look in Shem's eyes as he got his first look at them in broad daylight. Calculating their value, or mine? I wondered.

Anchara's expression was easier to read. A smile escaped her and grew broad and sweet and wondering, like the smile of a child watching a magic trick. I glanced at her dull stones and was glad in my heart I had not flung my gems in her face.

"Rass!" she shouted. "Come here, Bor!"

I followed her gaze and saw Rass making his way down the gem sellers' aisle, returning from whatever errand he'd been on. As he approached the stall, he stamped out a cigarette and gave us a slow, ironic smile, which I took as a commentary on his mother's imperious summons.

"Look what the girl's brought us!"

Half interested, Rass glanced where she pointed.

His eyes widened, and he bent closer. With his precise silversmith's hands, he picked up a stone and held it in a shaft of light that slanted in under the tarp. "You found *this,* Jalla?"

I nodded.

Rass's grin raveled up the scar on his cheek. "Something worth keeping, I told you. I'd no idea you were listening so carefully! A find like this is a sign of fortune's favor. Perhaps you merit it, after all."

I looked at him in startled pleasure. These were the kindest words any of Anchara's band had ever spoken to me.

"Perhaps. Perhaps not," Anchara croaked, as if just remembering her usual bad temper.

Rass ignored her. "Where did you find these?"

"In a cave near Hammerhead Ridge. Not far from the stream you had me prospecting."

Rass whistled. "There are Gorgio miners in the caves thereabouts. That's why I sent you to the stream. They generally don't stake out running water. Was this one of their claims?"

I had shoved this thought out of my mind long before, I realized. "Yes," I admitted uncomfortably. "It must have been. There were tools and—other things...."

Rass grinned wolfishly. "Ha! Took it right from under their noses, did you? Good girl."

But I wasn't so delighted when he put it that way. "Have I stolen it?"

"Would you run and give it back, Jalla?" Anchara's look was withering. "Stolen, you say? Nonsense! Those Gorgios weren't there any more legally than we were."

"But—what would the law say?"

"There's law and then there's justice," Rass said. "Do you think those Gorgios were driven out of the mountains as we were? The Forest Service allows them to prospect because it gets rich on their bribes. It's just bad luck for them that you found their strike. And good luck for us, Jalla, that the market has yet some days to run."

"Can you polish and set them before morning, Rass?" his mother demanded.

"Of course not. Not without the help of every hand in camp. And not with our hand tumblers." Rass looked worried. "I'll need to make bargains with the Gorgios. Without electric tumblers we'll have no hope at all of having them polished. And even with them, a day is a miserably short time. As to cutting ..."

"I'll help you get the tumblers," Shem offered.

"Well," Rass said doubtfully, "if we can get them quick, and without paying too much ..."

"I'll get them. Just tell me who to deal with." Shem turned to Anchara. "How much do you expect to get for Serena's haul?"

The old woman's face became guarded. "I don't know. How many stones have we got here? A good many. But without time to polish or cut properly ... Five hundred, at the most."

"Double it. I'll get you double the price. And maybe half again."

Rass gave a bark of laughter. "A thousand? You must be joking."

"And half again," Shem said. "Twelve fifty—if you'll give me the selling of them."

"And in return?" Anchara shot back.

"A tenth of the profit. That's fair. And ..."

"And?"

"And a word with Nico Brassi. To consider whether I'm fit to become a Kereskedo merchant."

Anchara glared at him with her hands on her hips, resembling nothing so much as a squat, two-handled earthenware jug. She looked tough and sneering, but I knew—*I knew*—she would come to terms. Shem had been very clever. She could not deny he was offering much and asking little. For his part, Shem looked as nonchalant and confident as when he'd been bargaining with the grocery lady atop Lookout Pass.

Before she started loading her ammo, that is.

"It's a lot to ask, Zimbali," the old woman snapped. "Why should I grant any of it?"

But Shem only grinned. "Because I can wring more gold out of those little stones than anyone in your band, Kereskedo or not."

"And what gives you this marvelous ability?"

"I tell the truth in a bargain."

"Hah!" Anchara gave him a cynical look. I was sorely tempted to say something as well, but I pressed my lips together. I didn't want to put myself on Anchara's side.

"You can laugh," Shem told her. "But the truth makes you stronger than any living liar. I promise I can do what I say."

"With what security?"

"If I haven't made good by the end of tomorrow, you can pull me off the stall. No money owed. No promise to keep."

"I can do that anyhow. Why else should I make this bargain with you?"

Shem was silent. Then he pointed at Anchara's long gray hair. Woven into her thick braid was the strand of golden coins he'd given to convince her to help me.

"I've given you a token already, for Serena's sake. Do you remember asking me what I wanted for myself?"

Anchara's eyebrows shot together. "Yes, I remember. Frightening, the memory you young people have." A cunning light entered her eye. "But you speak of Serena. You don't claim the favor in return for your wife's feat in finding these gems?"

She was baiting him now. What Shem had told me was true: if Lal had guessed after one morning, Anchara must have known the truth the minute she laid eyes on us.

Shem shot me an uneasy glance. He was worried I would betray him. As well he should be! I thought indignantly. After all, I hadn't sought those amethysts for his benefit, yet here he was, reaping a profit from them!

Still, I held my tongue.

Perhaps he did deserve some percentage of my find, I thought. He wasn't getting any other return on his help, since I wasn't going to marry him. Ten percent, just as he said. That would be fair.

Besides, I enjoyed seeing him stand up to Anchara. I had never seen anyone do that before, and I didn't want to spoil it for him.

Meeting his eyes, I shrugged. Play it any way you like, I thought. I won't interfere.

He let go a breath. "I don't have any claim on Serena's find. That was her neck and her risk. I've no part of the amethysts. She did that so you would help her find her mother."

"You'll still help me find her, Avo?" I broke in. If Anchara was giving Shem such a hard time, perhaps she'd find some reason not to help me, either.

"I'll help you," she said, then muttered, "if you'll call it help when the last comes to the last."

Her words brought a chill. But before I could question, her attention was back with Shem. "All right, Jal. You have a bargain. But only because you didn't presume on the girl's accomplishment."

Shem grinned. But Anchara shook a thick finger in his face. "There's just one thing."

"What?"

"A twentieth of the profits. Five percent."

Shem's smile disappeared. "Nine. It's robbery to go lower."

"Six."

"Eight. You're a cruel, wicked old woman."

I yelped with laughter.

"Seven," Anchara said implacably.

"Seven and a half."

"A dog with its teeth in a bone!" Anchara narrowed her eyes. "All right! Seven and a half. And the wax from my ears, if you'll haggle for it!"

They shook hands, Kereskedo style, by the wrist. Anchara's laugh crackled like a bad phone connection. "Seven and a half! You're mad, boy! Who do you think will do that figuring?"

"I will. Serena understands any scribble written, but numbers are like songs to me. I'll figure to the last penny and you'll never come short."

Anchara shrugged extravagantly and said to Rass, "What he promises, let him do."

Shem smacked his hands and rubbed his palms together. He'd played the first round and won. When he turned to me with an irrepressible smile, I couldn't help smiling back. It was good to see him get his first chance. Maybe he would even succeed in raising this fortune for Anchara. He had self-assurance, if nothing else, and my mother had always said that went a long way in trade. Then perhaps he'd forget the crazy idea that he had to marry me to get what he wanted. It would be one less thing for me to worry about, anyway.

"I'll need a favor, Serena," he said cheerfully.

My smile dropped away. "What favor would that be?"

"Your necklace, Jalla. Will you trust it to me for one night? I promise I'll return it."

My hand flew protectively to the necklace. "You'll take good care of it?"

"I swear. On my poor uncle's head."

"If you break your word, I get Panno's head? Terrific! Can I have it on a skewer?"

I thought I'd needled him, but his eyes were bright with laughter. In the afternoon light, I could see the gold flecks in them. There was a song I'd always loved about eyes with gold in them, like Shem's. . . .Oh, what twaddle was I thinking now? I turned red and quickly looked away, hoping he wouldn't notice.

"I'll work with Rass tonight," Shem was telling Anchara, "and any-one else you can spare. I'll need a stall. Where's the market manager? I'll fix it with him." He spun around to face me again. "What about it, Serena? Just for the night, I promise. Will you trust me with your prized possession?"

"My only possession," I said ruefully. "All right, then. But it isn't complete, you know. I've given some of the charms away."

"More than just the one you gave to Anchara? I didn't know that. Who did you give them to?"

Somehow, I didn't relish answering him in front of the others. It felt private, for some reason. "To—to the old man who gave us the free tank of gas. And the Gorgio firefighter. And . . . Rochelle. Before we left her just now, I put one in her hands. The monkey. I thought— I hoped someday she might take some pleasure in it."

Shem looked at me thoughtfully. I felt embarrassed. Unlocking the clasp with clumsy hands, I handed the necklace over to him.

He dropped it into his jacket pocket.

"Come, Jal," Rass said. "I'll take you to the market agent."

Shem bowed to Anchara. He took a step to follow Rass, then stopped, turned back to me, and grabbed my hand. I watched in confusion as he raised my hand to his lips and quickly kissed the knuckle. Without meeting my eyes, he turned and walked away.

The Kereskedo call it the kiss of honor. Agitated, I watched Shem's back as he disappeared into the crowd.

"Just remember that you can wash it sometime," Anchara jibed. Following her gaze, I found that I was holding on to my hand as if it were a gift I'd just been given. Hastily, I dropped it.

Anchara cackled. "Don't worry, Jalla. Kisses like that don't come off with soap or water."

No, I thought. Maybe not.

With difficulty, I put it out of my mind.

Ask her, I told myself. Ask Anchara before she remembers you're *ma'hane* and stops talking to you.

I leveled my gaze on the old woman's face. "Avo Anchara, you have the amethysts. Now can you tell me how to find my mother?"

The wise woman sighed and her face fell into folds of age. "Not far, if you can reach her."

"Of course I can reach her! Give me directions and I'll be off."

"That's not what I meant. Come here, girl. Close, so I can look in your face."

I forced myself to kneel down at her side. She put her hands on my shoulders and scrutinized me. "You've learned some patience," she observed. "You've seen there are other people in this world with troubles, eh? Or you'd never have let Shem have his say before you claimed your reward. Shem, I'm calling him, you see, not 'your man.' Though you've a kinder eye for him than you did." She sighed again. "Perhaps wisdom comes to us all. Even you, Jalla Serena. So now I'll give you some of mine: You need patience, girl. Patience to swim the ocean and walk the desert and patience even beyond that."

"Patience?" I squawked. I'd already been patient!

Anchara frowned, regarding me with a critical eye. Suddenly, she turned her heavy hand palm up. "Listen, what I have right now I'll tell you. About the Cruelty officer—the man you left on the stairs. Nico Brassi managed to make peace between the tribe and the Gorgios. Fortunately for us—for *us*, Jalla—the man didn't die."

225

I gasped and pressed my hand to my heart.

"Have you thought on it, Jalla?" Anchara continued. "What that act of yours could have cost many people? Look what the prison break cost us."

I bit my lip and looked down at my muddy boots, feeling I had escaped a terrible fate.

"I've thought on it, Mara Chan."

"You keep thinking, girl. Just keep thinking every time you want to open that mouth of yours in anger, or swing that fist. Do you see what I say? Before you barge back into the Gorgio world to snatch your little niece, you need patience and you need wisdom. The former I can't give you. The latter—"

"I need my mother, Avo! That's what I need! You told me yourself."

"You'll need more than her. What do you know of Gorgio laws, Gorgio courts? Without that knowledge, you could be in the right and still fail."

I said nothing. Her argument had the ring of truth. Still, I felt suspicious. Why did she keep dodging the topic of my mother? Was she going back on her word?

I forced myself to stay calm. "But—where will I get this knowledge?"

"That is where you have luck, Jalla. I hope Rass is right and you deserve the good fortune that I am about to shower upon you! I know a man well versed in the Gorgio laws. I want you to speak to him before I take you to your mother."

"No!" I cried out before I could control myself. "Please, Anchara! I've come such a long way. I've worked hard. Surely you can just tell me where to find her!"

"You come to me for wisdom, girl," the old woman snapped. "Trust me to give it to you! Before you see your mother, I want you to visit this man. He's expecting you. And he isn't the sort of person who you make wait. Listen to me, Serena. He will make a great difference in your life. Will you do what I say, or no?"

Lemon had returned and was waiting quietly at my side, with a new violin in her hands. I turned and caught her sympathetic eye. It was torture to agree to Anchara's conditions when I longed only for my mother.

But a small voice told me that Anchara knew things I did not. If this man could help to bring my family together, then I would do as the mara chan said, no matter how I felt.

"All right," I said. "Tell me what to do, Grandmother. I'll give you no argument."

18

Five for silver,
Six for gold.
—The Magpie Counting Song

Shem left for the market with Rass before Lemon and I had even finished cooking our eggs and peppers the next morning. He gave an absentminded wave as he passed us, walked into our clothesline, and got tangled in the wash. That reduced me to helpless laughter and I found I didn't even mind the dirt on the blankets Lemon and I had washed. I strongly suspected that Shem had worked all night, and that accounted for his clumsiness. I hoped that in his exhaustion he wouldn't misplace the amethysts. Or my necklace.

I, on the other hand, had slept for blissful hours and awakened with one refrain in my head: soon, my mother's arms would be around me. Anchara had promised it. Soon we would be a family again. We could bring Zara home. . . .

I didn't mind anything today. It was no longer lonely to sit on the edge of camp eating my breakfast. Lemon cared nothing for the Kereskedo court's verdict, nor did her father. Nor, I thought with surprise, perhaps did Shem, anymore. It took the sting out of being near Anchara's people and knowing that, in their company, I was once again an outcast.

But perhaps it was a blessing to have to stay apart from the bustle of the camp, at least for Rochelle's sake, since the little girl still shied away from human contact. The night before, when Lemon had taken her to wash in the river, the children of the camp had come to ask her to play, and I'd seen her wrap herself around Lemon's leg, trying to hide from them. Better for her to come to terms with things in our little group, where no one would push her too hard.

The weather had turned. There was still crimson and gold on the maples. Their leaves shook and turned side to side in the wind. The sky was of that astonishing pure blue that cold weather brings. I felt fortunate that Rass had been too distracted by the amethysts to ask for his jacket back!

As Lemon and I drank our coffee, I was surprised to see a woman from Anchara's camp walking toward us. In her hand was a dripping honeycomb, which she offered to us. I recognized her as Rass's wife, a girl with a long, serious face, a chipped tooth, and a sweet smile. We accepted her gift with warm thanks. She said it was less than nothing. A lucky find, that was all.

But I knew it was more than that. None of Anchara's band had ever approached me at mealtimes, much less given a gift of food.

Something had changed. I had felt it the day before in the way Rass and Anchara spoke to me. Could it have been because I had found the amethysts? Or because the Cruelty man had lived? I was still *ma'hane*—no tribunal had reversed that decision. What had happened?

Once we'd washed up, Lemon slipped into the caravan, retrieved the instruments, and packed them into her father's car. At the market she would play them to demonstrate their excellent qualities. It would be a day of hard work. But Lemon said when you love what you do, a hardworking day is a day of pleasure.

Rochelle was still sleeping when we left. Ren Bardoff sat at the workbench, concentrating on his carving. He would bring Rochelle to the market later, when he came to help Lemon at the stall. I hoped it might be good for the sad little girl—a distraction, if nothing else.

Lemon sang as we drove, one of the Jersain riddle songs, which aren't riddles so much as nonsense, at least to outsiders' ears. I knew she heard jokes and references in them that I could only guess at.

> *"I am a lock without a key.*
> *Who is there who can open me?*
> *I am a wall without a gate.*
> *Who can walk through stone and slate?"*

I listened to her husky alto with pleasure, enjoying the sun on my arm and the brightness in the sky. Even the cement caverns of the city seemed friendly and bright. Nothing could look ugly to me this day.

Lugging the instruments through the market and bashing my tender shin with the cello did nothing to dampen my spirits. Shem had promised to find the Bardoffs a stall. Of course, he'd neglected to tell us where *he* would be, so we had to drag the instruments up and down the market trying to locate him. Still, even this bit of sloppy planning couldn't ruffle me.

But when we finally found him in a row of herbal medicine stands, my heart sank.

I'd truly hoped Shem would be a success. Perhaps as a merchant he would find his true calling, I'd thought. But what harebrained idea had led him to set up business here among the healers? Gems aren't medicine! Only quacks pretend such nonsense. And selling the amethysts as cures for the gout—or whatever he planned to do—was the surest way to make my hard-won gems look worthless!

Obviously, I'd been too hopeful. Shem was feckless. He couldn't drive. He couldn't play music. Most probably, he couldn't trade, either. He would lose money the way a broken clock loses time.

Of course, I reminded myself, it was nothing to me what price the amethysts fetched. I was getting my heart's desire regardless of Shem's folly. Even so, I wanted to grab him by the collar and shake him.

"You look like you've swallowed a mouse," Lemon whispered. "Try to contain your joy, would you, Serena?"

Shem turned and noticed us. "I think of you and you appear. Have you started to read my mind?"

"No. You can still surprise me." I couldn't curb this little jab.

Lemon was examining the empty table next to his. "Is this ours?"

"There weren't any free over by the other musicians. Can you make do with it?"

It was a good thing he was busy breaking rolls of coins into a battered cigar box, so he couldn't see the expression on my face.

But Lemon was gracious. "Of course. Put the cello down there, Serena. I'll unpack the cases. My friend should deliver the rest in a little bit. Thanks for getting us the table, Shem. It's a big help."

"Well, perhaps we can help each other as the day goes on. Can you help me, too, Serena? I need a scribe for the sign over there. I *can* write," he added dryly, "in case you wondered. But I thought you could do the fancy script. Do you see what I've done so far?"

He'd done something interesting, I'd grant him that. I didn't know whether it would sell gems. But as an art project it was first-rate.

He'd shoved together Anchara's two little card tables and balanced an upright wooden pallet on top of them. A green velvet cloth was fitted onto the pallet and nailed down at the corners, to make a background for his display. Mounted on the pallet—one in each corner— were models of four of the animals from my necklace: the hawk, the rooster, the eagle, and the dove, all wrought with silver wire. Shem's work, I was sure, since I'd seen him messing about with those wires all along our journey. In the center, he'd rigged up a great wooden wheel. With white paint he'd quartered it, so that each quarter seemed to belong to a bird in one of the corners. A pointer like the hand of a clock radiated from its center. The amethysts, displayed on the table below, had been tumbled, cut, and set in bird pendants copied from the charms on my necklace, like those on the pallet above.

So that was what he had borrowed it for.

The workmanship of Rass's smiths was nothing to the skill that had fashioned my charms, but it was passable. I supposed Shem hoped the pendants would draw attention away from the fact that the amethysts were only roughly faceted and polished because the men had had to work in such haste.

It was clever, I admitted grudgingly, though hardly enough to ensure huge profits.

"What do you think?"

I studied the display. There had to be something to this beyond camouflaging hasty workmanship. "What's the wheel for? Spin the dial and get a prize?"

"Sort of."

"Shem . . . you're not turning this into a fun fair, are you? Please tell me people aren't going to spin the dial and win a necklace."

"Only if you think I'm crazy."

"And that means yes, does it?"

Shem shot me a look. "It means no. I'm not giving away the amethysts, Serena. I'm just making it more interesting for people to buy them."

"Of course!" I smacked my hand to my forehead. "Why didn't I see it? Just give one of those Gorgio ladies the thrill of spinning the wheel and boom! She'll pay any price!"

"You overestimate the Gorgio ladies," Shem said mildly, though I could see a spark of annoyance. "That's your trouble, Serena. If you'd reined in your tongue a moment, I could have explained it to you. But with that attitude, you'll just have to wait to find out."

He pointedly went back to counting the coins.

"I'm sorry. I didn't mean to be . . ." I sought for the right word. "Snotty," I said in a small voice.

He ignored me and pulled a sheet of paper out of a box under the table. On it he began to trace lines, like those in an accounting ledger.

I didn't want him to be mad at me. But I felt exasperated. The day before, it had seemed as though he was really going to succeed—for once. But now, he just made me want to wring my hands until my fingers dropped off. Why did I want to hang about with someone who couldn't do anything right? If I had any sense, I'd leave him to it. But somehow I couldn't just abandon him to his folly.

He put aside the accounting sheet and pulled a gleaming white signboard out from under the table. With no grudging expression, he produced a green marker from his coat pocket and handed it to me.

"Am I right? Can you write fancy calligraphy?"

"Yes."

"All right. Then just write down what I say. This needs to be in big letters—maybe three-quarters of the paper. It's our shop sign."

"Okay. What does it say?"

"Shem's Psychic Gems."

"What?"

"Psychic. Don't ask me how to spell it. That's your department."

I threw the marker on the ground.

"Oh, Shem!" I groaned. I could relieve my feelings only by grabbing a big hunk of my hair and yanking it.

"What? You sound like a squeaky door. What's wrong now?"

"What's wrong? *Psychic* gems? That's complete garbage and you know it! You think a Gorgio is going to pay more for these rocks because you tell her they can magically dissolve her gallstones or bring her the winning lottery number? They don't believe that kind of nonsense!"

"Who are you kidding, Serena?" He rounded on me. "They believe it like it was the headline in yesterday's paper! That's your Gorgio side talking. You must really believe what they say: they're great rational intellects and we're primitive and superstitious. Think about it a minute. Who do you see lining up at the Yulang fortunetellers? Not us. We wouldn't be caught dead. But the Gorgios? That's different. They go crazy for it. It's the only reason they haven't driven us out of the province altogether—we're the gateway to the spirits, aren't we? Their ticket to all that's exotic and mysterious. Or didn't you realize that?"

In fairness, I had to admit he had a point. The palm reader who worked on our street back in Oestia made a better living than her husband ever did at the docks. And now that Shem mentioned it, I *had* noticed that the people waiting outside her door were all Gorgios. Yet I'd seen it and not seen it at the same time. Maybe because the teachers at school drilled into our heads how superior the Gorgio intellect was. Perhaps their words had carried more weight than what my own eyes told me. . . .

"It's true," I admitted. "But that's fortunetelling. It's traditional. They expect it from us."

"They expect all sorts of psychic powers from us."

"What about speaking the truth? You told Anchara that's what you'd do!"

"How am I not telling the truth? I say I'm selling valuable amethysts, and I am."

"What about the psychic powers?"

He shrugged. "How do I know? What gives a thing power? The badge the Cruelty wears is just a thing, but it has the power to make any Yulang kid scared. And what about those charms on your necklace, Serena? You give them away for more than their prettiness, don't you? No matter how rational you try to be, you treat them like amulets. You believe they have some sort of power."

My tongue was ready to launch another barb, but I kept it in check. What he said was true, at least partway. And I really did want his idea to work, whether I agreed with it or not.

Shem saw me deliberating and grinned. "I'm right, aren't I?"

"Maybe," I admitted. "But it's not such nonsense as you think...."

"I never said it was."

"I mean, the power isn't in the charm." I paused, trying to sort out my thoughts. "It's— I think it's in the person I give it to. Like the fire-fighter. I gave him the dog, not because the dog is brave, but because *he* is.... And the monkey to Rochelle because I'm hoping she'll laugh and goof around again someday...."

"I'd be curious to see what you'd give me, Jalla."

Something about the way he said this made me pretend to be very concerned with a splinter in my palm all of a sudden. "You never know your luck. But you might not like what I picked!"

"I'd take my chances." His voice was light again, but I felt a quiver in my belly, as if I'd swallowed one of those pollywogs we'd seen by the ferry landing.

"Now, don't give me any more trouble," he added. "I'll go get Lemon in on the plan. But do one more thing for me."

"What?"

"Look at the birds I've chosen and write down what their powers are. Just as if you were giving them away to someone. All right? The market opens in ten minutes, so think fast." He winked. "You're getting a little better at that."

"Wait!" I cried. "What about the amethysts? What powers are they supposed to have, these psychic gems of yours?"

"Don't you know?" he mocked. "Amethysts cool anger. Look at yourself. See how biddable you've become since you found them!"

I sneered horribly, but he'd already turned his back.

Without my realizing it, he had made me his assistant. He quickly enlisted Lemon's help as well. When the market opened, Lemon lured customers into our stall with gay tunes on her fiddle and melancholy airs on her viola da gamba. Knots of people gathered to listen. She would draw off those who had come to commission her to make instruments. The rest stayed to be entertained by Shem's inventions.

And his inventions seemed endless. He would pull someone from the crowd and dare them to submit to a blindfold before spinning the "mystic wheel," as he called the flimsy dial he'd hammered together. It would reveal secrets they kept even from themselves, he told them. Disbelief was nothing to him. He heckled the hecklers without fear. When the dial landed on a bird, he'd ask the blindfolded one which bird they thought they'd hit. If he or she guessed correctly, the crowd would murmur (and I had to agree with what he said about Gorgio credulity). If the customer guessed incorrectly, Shem would declare this guess significant and nimbly show how the bird actually revealed his or her true nature.

At first he stuck close to what I'd written: the eagle for tyranny, the dove for peace. . . . But with every customer his inventions grew. And they got better. Soon I was as spellbound as the rest, though I knew I had to keep an ear cocked for when he'd need help.

"The eagle in the third quadrant. You swoop quickly when opportunity gleams. Often you win the prize. But sometimes there is disappointment. True? And now more often than not, am I right? You fear your powers are fading?"

And the brawny builder who had come swaggering up to be blindfolded would nod regretfully.

That was my cue to pick up a chain or a pendant and ask for silence.

"Gaze into the amethyst," I'd direct. "Lay the gem on your heart. . . ."

If she could, Lemon would break off her own business and play a few otherworldly chords.

"Can you feel the calming power of the gems?" I would murmur. "Can you see how your troubles break apart so the strength of the eagle can shine through?"

And we would sell. And sell. Whether people believed or not, they were caught up in our performance. Shem had magicked the jewels with imagination. Every hour, the prices nosed up.

After an hour or two we knew we were on to something. After three or four hours, we were struggling not to burst out laughing every time we caught each other's eyes—the success was making us flat-out giddy.

It was past midday when Lemon picked out a melody to draw new customers in. I was halfway through a great yawn when she broke off and tapped me with her bow.

"Over there. You see?" She pointed with her bow at a man in the back of the crowd gathering around our stall. "That man with the bald skull. Do you recognize him?"

Blood boiled into my head. "He's the one who grabbed me!" I leapt forward in fury.

"Wait! What are you going to do?"

I stopped.

It was hard not to rush over and break his nose. As unnatural as stopping a swell on the sea. But I remembered how I'd funneled my anger into music back in Lal's camp, and a notion took hold of me.

I put a hand on Lemon's wrist. "Play 'Traveling Tinker.' Quick, before the crowd breaks up."

Lemon raised an eyebrow. But she tucked her fiddle under her chin and started drawing out the dance melody. People who'd been drifting away from her stall came back to hear the tune.

I nodded my head in time to the beats and began singing out new words for the old song.

"Oh, there was a sweet young Yulang girl
A-going to the fair,
Along came an oaf and pinches her—
An oaf who had no hair."

I stared pointedly at Bald-Head as I sang, and the crowd immediately caught on.

"'Oh, but I can't get my own woman,' he said,
'I've got to grab who I can.
Oh, I can't get my own woman,' he cried,
'So I'll pinch and I'll prod with my hands. . . .'"

I'll never know how the words came to me. But they flowed like water. The man shifted nervously on his feet, trying to ignore the stares and giggles as heads turned toward him. At first he was befuddled. I supposed a bit of girl grabbing was so much his habit that he didn't even remember the previous day's incident. But by the time I sang the second stanza, awareness flashed into his face, and he looked foolishly over his shoulder, as if trying to locate the offender in the crowd.

"'My hair retreated long away,
My haunches shrink to my side,
My belly swells and wobbles,
And wrinkles cover my hide.

"'Oh, what's a young girl's dignity
Compared to my wants and needs?
Oh, I can't get my own woman, me boys,
I'll have to grab who I please!'"

Women hooted. Bald-Head practically knocked people over trying to push his way out of the crowd. He wouldn't be back, I noted with satisfaction, and tacked this coda onto the song.

> *"Let this be a lesson, girls,*
> *And pay strict attention to it:*
> *Vengeance with your fist's never so good*
> *As vengeance you claim with your wit!"*

There was a burst of laughter and a smattering of applause. I bowed and broke up laughing.

Shem gave me an inquiring look. "Good enough, Serena. But are you sure I shouldn't break his arm?"

Mighty words, and you use them well, I thought, but what's behind them? I stared at him, amused and curious. "You'd never do such a thing!"

"Of course I would."

I cocked my head. "How did your nose get broken? Defending some girl's honor?"

To my surprise, he actually blushed. "I fell off a stage. When I was playing my violin."

"You what?"

"Panno nearly killed me."

I hooted. "What an oaf you are, Shem!" I took his chin in my hand and turned his head to examine the crooked nose. "You must have driven your uncles crazy!"

He snatched my hand away and twined his fingers through mine before I knew what he was about. "I like driving people crazy. Haven't you noticed?"

"Yes, I've noticed—"

I tried to slide my fingers away, but he caught them and held on, teasingly.

"And if you ever want me to defend your honor, Jalla," he continued, "just say the word."

"Oh—" I cursed the color shooting up my neck and struggled even harder to extricate my fingers from his.

"I mean it."

He let go of my hand.

"Um—well, thanks," I mumbled. "But— What I mean is— I think I managed pretty well by myself, don't you?"

"You did, at that."

Hastily, I turned away, hoping that Shem hadn't noticed how easily he could twine me up in knots.

After we'd been selling another hour or two, I realized we had a companion. It was a little ginger cat—not a kitten, but so ragged and thin that it could easily be mistaken for one. He had a bold eye and a cocky set of the head. His tail had a kink and he held it high, like a weather vane.

When Rass came with iced buns for us, I shared mine with the little animal. After that, the cat stuck beside me, slinking against my legs and meowing in a polite but persistent way. He'd decided I must have other delicacies concealed in my pockets, and was not going to give up until he found them. This one, I could see, was a survivor.

Ren Bardoff and Rochelle arrived soon after. Lemon's father was wearing the embroidered skullcap and caftan that marked him as a Jersain craftsman. He carried the bag with his carving tools, for people always liked to watch him work. Rochelle trudged beside him. She held his hand trustingly, but her expression was shuttered.

While he conferred with Lemon, writing out timetables for commissions and double-checking the terms, Rochelle sat down on a low stool, listlessly watching the crowds go by.

My injured shin had started to throb from so much standing, so I left Shem to manage the stall and sat down near Rochelle on an upturned crate. As soon as I'd got settled, the scrawny cat leapt into my lap. I was about to shove him off when a thought struck me.

"Rochelle, look at this cat. Have you ever seen a sorrier specimen? What do you think made him such a scarecrow?"

Rochelle glanced at the skinny little tom. Then she quickly looked away, giving her head a little shake.

"I think he's a runaway." I stroked the tawny fur and examined a bald spot by the cat's ear, where a cut had healed. "Maybe the open road wasn't all he'd thought it was cracked up to be. He looks as if he's been in a few spats and missed a few dinners, doesn't he?"

Rochelle looked again. This time her gaze rested on the little animal. She nodded solemnly.

"I've nothing to give him," I continued. "Could you find him something to eat?"

She didn't move. I began to feel my maneuver was too transparent. But it didn't stop me. "See how hungry he is?"

The cat brought his head up energetically under my hand and let out an inquiring *reow?* He leapt to the ground by Rochelle and wreathed about her ankles plaintively.

Rochelle reached into a little bag that hung around her shoulder. I recognized it as an old pocketbook of Lemon's. Her fingers slowly managed to push open the latch and flip back its leather top. She hesitated, in that way little kids do when it comes to sharing food. But with another look at the cat, she pulled out a packet of paper and began to unfold it with great care.

The cat sang with joy when the contents of the paper proved to be a tuna sandwich. I sympathized. My stomach echoed with emptiness as I smelled the vinegar and olive oil, tomatoes, anchovies, and tuna that Ren Bardoff had lovingly prepared for her.

In an instant the cat reached its paws up to Rochelle's chest, out of its head with delight. In some alarm, Rochelle lifted the sandwich over her head. I snatched the animal off her and plumped it down firmly at her feet.

"Mind your manners. Maybe she'll share."

Gingerly, Rochelle pulled off a little morsel of bread and tuna and held it out to the cat, who approached it in as gentlemanly a manner as one might expect, and slurped it down.

A thin burble of laughter escaped Rochelle's lips. "His tongue tickles."

"You're his hero. Just don't let the little monster eat it all up."

Rochelle nodded and protectively took a bite herself. Then she ripped off another bit for the cat. I watched them for a moment, smiling.

"Serena?"

I started, sprang to my feet. Too fast. Blackness bloomed in front of my eyes. I quickly sat back down on the crate.

In the blackness, Zara's face peered at me, eerily unlike the face I remembered. The real Zara had lively eyes and a wide, happy mouth. One of her front teeth had come in earlier than its stumpy companion, which gave her a sweet snaggletoothed look. But now I saw her eyes hollow as a skull's, her mouth pinched, her cheeks thin. Carrying the same burden of grief and fear as Rochelle, but without the power to reason it away ... without even some fool like me to distract her with a hungry cat ...

"Serena? Are you all right, girl?"

The market came pouring back: the purple amethysts on the table, Lemon holding out her violin to a customer, Rochelle stroking the frantically happy cat, Shem crouching down beside me. I was back in the world without Zara.

"You look like you're about to flatten a few mice." Shem was watching me with some concern. "Poor working conditions?"

"It's that slave driver boss of mine," I joked weakly.

"Seriously, are you dizzy?"

I nodded. Dizzy, yes. But more than that. For a moment, that terrible sadness of losing Zara had frozen me to the bone.

"You need food. Let's go see what there is. I've got a few coins."

"Oh, I'll mind the stall. Just bring something back for me."

"No. I want your company. Rass will look after the table."

Holding fast to my elbow, he steered me past the market stalls and out to the grasslands where the food stalls were set up. The sunlight was so bright that tiny sparks blinkered my vision and I feared the blackness would fill my eyes again. But it didn't.

The grass in the meadow had been tramped flat by the crowds. We bypassed the vans lined up along the dirt paths, which were selling food from their kitchens. They were Gorgio trucks and the food could easily be tainted. Worse, the vans probably had toilets in them. Even the possibility made them off-limits. I was surprised to see how much I had started to think this way. We needed to find a Yulang food stall. But unfortunately, the Yulang places were all the way on the other side of the market.

Though faint with hunger, I willingly followed Shem until we found a vendor who suited Yulang standards of cleanliness: a wide-hipped Jersain woman who was flipping yam cakes on an outdoor griddle.

With the spicy cakes and cups of mint tea in our hands, we dropped down thankfully on the little hillock facing the alley of vendors. It was past lunchtime, but the hill was crowded. A tangle of little boys were pelting each other with grapes, deaf to their mothers' scolding. An old man hunched himself around a folded pita as if it were a confidential missive from the foreign ministry. A pair of Gorgio lovers shared a sugared fry-bread, pulling it apart with their fingers and nuzzling in public the way the Gorgio do.

Shem and I ate in companionable silence for a moment. The food did me good. I was glad he had dragged me out here. The cold, bright air seemed to drive away my sadness. After all, why should I feel sad? Anchara was putting everything in place for me, wasn't she? Once we'd packed up for the day, I knew she'd come to me. Maybe she'd even bring the man she'd told me to talk to. . . .

"Serena—"

"Yes?"

Shem was hunched forward, arms around his knees.

"There's something I've got to tell you." He sounded nervous.

It was so out of character that I found myself looking around warily. What would make him anxious? Was it the Cruelty?

"What is it, Shem?"

His words gave me no clue. "Do you remember I told Anchara I'd earn double what she predicted? More than double?"

I nodded.

"We've done that already, with two days left to sell."

"Ha!" I yelped in triumph. "That's wonderful! I can't believe it!"

But he didn't return my smile.

"What's wrong with you, Jal?" I looked at him in puzzlement. "Why do you look that way? Aren't you happy?"

He put down his tea mug and set about pulling blades of grass out of the ground, as methodically as if he were being paid to do it.

"No," he said. "I mean, yes—of course I'm happy."

"That's funny. You sound miserable."

He gave me a peculiar look. "I'm not miserable. But I have to know—" He stopped short, searching for the words. "Tell me what you think now. About me, I mean."

"Oh, forget what I said this morning, Shem! I'm sorry I gave you such a hard time. You were right. That psychic stuff was a great idea."

"That's not what I'm talking about, Serena."

"Oh." I drew Rass's jacket closer around me, picked up my mug, and stared into the green circle of tea, as if expecting a frog to jump out of it. From the tone of his voice I knew exactly what Shem was talking about, and I didn't want to look at him if I could help it.

"I mean, have you changed your mind? About what I asked you?"

"About marrying you?" I glanced up at him and quickly looked away. "That was so crazy, Shem."

I wasn't mad anymore. I was calm. I told myself I was calm. I didn't care.

I just didn't know why my hands felt so clammy.

Shem cocked his head to one side and smiled tentatively at me. His voice was coaxing and persuasive. "It doesn't have to be crazy."

"No? You don't think so?" I'd meant to sound sarcastic but somehow didn't manage it.

I reminded myself that the day I'd talked with Lal and watched her daughters-in-law slaving away, I'd decided to calmly, even dismissively, turn Shem aside. His offer wasn't to my advantage. I still knew that.

But despite that, I also knew why my hands were clammy and I couldn't meet his eyes.

It was because I wasn't looking at the whole truth. Not even in my thoughts.

Something else had crept into me since that day at the Parias' camp, and it was grinding away inside of me, slow and subterranean, like the movement of the earth's plates, altering the ground beneath my feet so gradually that I hardly knew when the change had come. I felt different than I had before. Much different.

"Give me one reason it isn't crazy, Shem," I said.

What was I doing? Asking him to convince me? Why? Simply because I'd liked him kissing my hand, because he'd made me laugh? Because I liked being with him?

Such things counted for little among the Yulang! I thought scornfully. That wasn't how Shem was looking at it. No need to doubt that! His game was the game of bargaining and advantage. *I* was the one who was Kereskedo. Was once, anyway. I should be weighing pros and cons and sending people packing who offered me less than I was worth.

But instead of weighing advantage and disadvantage, I was only inviting him to tell me why I should accept! What was wrong with me?

"You've seen I can handle a business," he went on. "I know I'd succeed as a merchant, really, Serena. If you give me the chance to enter the tribe." His voice dropped uncertainly. "I've done what I said I could do. Aren't I good enough for you now?"

"Good enough? Don't be silly, Shem! You were good enough the first day I laid eyes on you!" The words were out of my mouth before I could even wonder at them.

"Do you mean that?"

A trace of a surprised smile appeared on his face. He looked like a boy who had caught a trout on his first try, whose kite had lifted on a cloudless day. I couldn't fight the smile that answered his. . . .

But I didn't mean it as an acceptance.

It was just simple truth. Good enough for me? I had been deceiving myself about him from the start. He was everything I wasn't: generous, patient, kind, clear-sighted. The deception he had practiced on me melted out of consideration. I could see it for what it was: a first move that he had been careful to carry out as honorably as he could.

What I'd said wasn't an acceptance.

But somehow I neglected to explain that to him.

I neglected to tell him why I was turning him down—or that I was turning him down at all. I couldn't. The happiness in his eyes stopped me dead.

"Of course I mean it." I laughed for the pure pleasure of saying it. "Of course you're good enough for me."

He took my hand from my lap and held it up in his, palm to palm. It wasn't the teasing way he'd grabbed my fingers earlier but quietly and seriously, as though he were making me a pledge. I sat quite still, looking at him. Suddenly, I wanted always to be here, always sitting on a hill, under a cold autumn sun, the only warmth of the day glowing in the space where Shem's hands touched mine.

All the sourness and pain I'd felt before dissipated like vinegar in water. I could hardly even remember what had brought me here. Only that I didn't want to leave. Without realizing I had done it, I'd pulled our clasped hands toward me, and brought him closer to my side. I didn't meet his eyes, but I knew that if I had, he couldn't have looked more surprised than I was.

But it wasn't as easy as that.

"You see?" whispered Willow. In my mind's eye I saw her, belly swollen to burst the seams of her emerald gown. "Why do you stamp all over happiness as if it were a rag rug? You should be more like me."

"What about Zara?" I hissed at her. "Have you forgotten her? I haven't!"

But that was a lie. For a moment, I had.

"Who . . . ?" Willow's voice trailed off like a lonely loon.

Mother Lillith! I was just like her.

"What is it, Jalla? What's wrong?" We were so close, I could see the tired red lines in his eyes that made the brown bright as polished wood, and the three good-luck coins tucked into his hatband. He took his hand from mine and laid it on my cheek.

I pulled away sharply.

Willow, I thought bitterly. If she would think this is a good thing, there must be something wrong about it, something wrong and foolish and dangerous.

The warnings were as strong as the pulse in my wrist. The sunlight lay hard and brassy upon us. I noticed for the first time that the ground was cold under my knees.

"No," I said.

"No? No to what? To me?"

There was a sad edge to his voice. My heart leapt open to it. But there was Willow's voice, too, the voice of my bad conscience—weren't their voices one and the same?

That was the problem: I'd seen that joy in his face and his hands pressing mine, and suddenly my reason had flown out the window. I turned my head away in shame and disgust. It was my Gorgio side rising up, soft and sentimental and as childish as Willow ever was. . . .

My heart snapped shut like a mussel shell.

"That's right." I folded my arms across my chest. "I'm saying no. I'm not a fool, Shem! You'll get your chance if we marry. You'll become a Kereskedo merchant—maybe even a great trader. But what do I get in return? A lifetime mending your socks?"

He stared. For once, I had shocked him into silence. Even to myself, I sounded like a harpy.

"I'm not the one you want." The words stuck like a bone in my throat. I had to struggle to get them out. "You could find another Kereskedo girl, easy. You don't need me."

That was as far as I could go. I jumped to my feet. But Shem jumped up, too, and caught me by the elbow. His boot knocked over my tea and it splashed on my foot.

"Mending socks? Don't pretend you're turning me down over torn socks, Serena!"

How bitter he sounded! "It's that Gorgio blood of yours, isn't it?" he continued. "You think it makes you better than the rest of us."

I stared. "How can you think that? I put no stock in Gorgio blood! My *father* put no stock in it—" I stopped short, remembering Willow examining her skin, weighing her chances of passing her way into Alex's family.

Shem caught the hesitation. "Oh? Or is it the book learning? Would it be wasted on me, Serena?"

I colored, feeling the pinprick of truth. What Lal had said was stored in my heart. A Yulang girl with the Gorgio learning in her . . . There were possibilities, chances. But as a Yulang wife with six children and housework from rooster crow until the moon was high? What then?

Shem saw the acknowledgment in my face.

"That's it, isn't it?"

"No! It's not that—though the learning . . . it's important. It's not something you can just throw away."

"Throw away!" He half tossed my elbow out of his grip.

"You know what I mean!" I cried, shaking out my arm.

His ears were red. "You're right! I do!"

"You're twisting what I say! It's not that I'm too good, Shem! Try to understand."

"It's what do you get in the bargain, is it? That's the way you Kereskedo do it, after all." His words were cold and businesslike. "Okay. Not that I think I want to pursue this transaction anymore, *thanks anyway*, but just for argument's sake, what are the bargaining points?"

"I don't want to bargain!" I shouted. "That's not what I want!"

It was the kind of outburst that brings silence crashing down like a crate, right onto your head.

Shem just looked at me. We were sizing each other up now, like fighters. It was unnerving. A wave of fear washed over me. What was I afraid of? His words. I was afraid of his words. And with reason.

"That's good," he said. "Because I don't want to bargain with you, either. People will hear of my success here. Thanks for pointing it out. I won't have to marry a girl who's *ma'hane*. What was I thinking? A Kereskedo girl of good family might consider me now. You're right to say I don't need you."

He might as well have punched me in the ribs.

For a moment, all the sounds seemed to have been sucked out of the air. Then the din of the market burst through my eardrums. Crows cawed, diving at garbage, vendors yelled and haggled, lovers giggled, mothers scolded. All the sounds in the world were sharp and ugly, and Shem's words were the ugliest of all.

"Serena? Did you hear what I said?"

I gave him a blank stare. In one second I would start crying. And that was humiliation beyond what I could bear.

I turned abruptly on my heel and fled, my boots crushing their prints into the mudflats at the bottom of the hill and scattering pebbles on the market pathways.

The crowds caged me. I couldn't stand all the backs and legs hedging me in. I jabbed my elbows in people's sides, pushed them out of my way.

"Hey!" someone yelled. "Rude little—"

"Who do you think you're shoving, girlie?"

I ran half the circumference of the market before I found Anchara cracking peanuts and gossiping at the fortuneteller's booth. She stopped midsentence and looked at me in astonishment.

"What's wrong with you, Jalla?" she demanded. "You look like your caravan's caught fire."

"Please, Avo." The tears began to spill as soon as I opened my mouth. "Take me to my mother."

"But I told you. There's a man you must speak to first."

"I need her right now. Please, Mara Chan!" I looked pleadingly into the old woman's eyes. I knew I was acting like a five-year-old, but I couldn't help it. "Please."

Abroad as I went walking, one evening in the spring,
I heard a maid in Bedlam so sweetly for to sing.
Her chains she rattled with her hand, and thus cried she,
"I love my love because I know my love loves me."

—Gorgio song

I stumped along after Anchara on the thin trail leading up the butte. Golden flames of the sunset still blazed around the edges of the rock. But on our side of the rise the shadows had already pooled into darkness.

My mother was up at the top.

If it hadn't been for Anchara's slow, ancient gait, I would have run all the way, ignoring the loose rocks shifting beneath my feet. My heart was thudding. How much time I'd wasted in getting to this place! Why had I lolled around at the market all day when my mother was so close? I should never have listened to Anchara and all her conditions. The moment the amethysts were in her hands, I should have insisted that she take me to Mother. If only I had! Then I could have spared myself all that had just passed between Shem and me....

I drew a black curtain over that memory. If I could just keep from thinking of it, maybe the pain would numb to a dull ache, as the gash I'd gotten in the cave had dulled over the course of our travels, only flaring if I barked the bruise against something. All I wanted was to lay my head in Mother's lap and let her soothe the pain away.

Perhaps she and I could start back to Oestia tomorrow!

It wasn't impossible. Mother had a car and one of those ugly little trailers the poorer Gorgios live in. I'd seen it when Anchara led me off the road and into the scrubby trailer park where she told me my mother now lived. The trailer had been shuttered and locked. The car was the color of rusty water from an old tap. But the state of it didn't bother me. Shem's was almost as dilapidated, and it had survived our journey.

But if Mother had a car, a voice in my head whispered, why hadn't she used it to come back and look after Willow and me?

Up ahead of Anchara, climbing with the steady endurance of long habit, was a woman I suspected could tell me the answer to this question. She was a Gorgio named Desirée, who looked like a female version of a Trident Rider, with her bleached white hair, steely gray eyes, and scorpion tattoo on her neck. She'd appeared as Anchara and I stood outside my mother's trailer trying vainly to get an answer to our knock.

"Is it Galeah you're looking for? Disappeared again, has she?" She'd surveyed us with a dispassionate eye. Her gaze lit on Anchara. "I've seen you before, Grandma."

Anchara regarded her in hostile silence.

"Galeah is my mother," I said. "Do you know where I can find her?"

The woman gave me a sharp look. "She'll be up top, if she isn't in her trailer. You can follow me. I'm taking her dinner anyway." I'd noticed, then, the casserole dish she carried. Through the glass top, I could see a slab of meat loaf and a cluster of bald, overcooked potatoes.

It looked revolting. And it made me feel apprehensive, though I couldn't have said why. It just seemed wrong. My mother was a good cook. She had a hundred subtle seasonings she could crush from fresh herbs or coax from dried roots. She hummed while she cooked, for goodness' sake. Cooking never made *me* feel like bursting into song. Yet here this Gorgio woman was taking her this god-awful food as if it were a foregone conclusion that she would cook Mother's dinner.

Why?

Had Mother been living here since she left us? Had she just arrived? *Why was this woman feeding her?*

I glared at the back of Anchara's head, feeling sure that she knew the answer to that, just as well as Desirée did. But I wouldn't ask her, either. *I* should be the one who knew everything about my mother, not these strangers.

As we climbed, Anchara hobbled along imperiously, looking neither at me nor at the woman who led us. It was in keeping with the way she had behaved ever since I'd begged her to bring me here, speaking little since we left the market and boarded the bus out of town. She'd only said, "All right. I'll take you to your mother before I've a chance to prepare her for your visit. It's a poor idea, but no matter. I will have this promise in return."

"What promise?"

"The man I spoke of. No matter what comes to pass between you and your mother tonight, tomorrow you will speak with this man. And what he has to teach, you will learn."

Of course I said yes.

We climbed until the rising ground cut off abruptly, as if a knife had sliced away the top of the mountain. There was nothing left between us and the stars.

The top of the butte stretched flat as an altar under the sky. The sunset dyed the rock a glowing red. Short scrubby bushes clung to the thin soil. On the western rim a lone tree was stunted sharply to the east by the wind but still held its foliage stubbornly aloft.

Under it a person huddled in a long cloak, half hidden behind the shadow of its trunk. She was stirring the embers of a dying fire with a stick.

I gave a cry and started forward, but Desirée grabbed me by my sleeve. "Wait here. She doesn't like strangers jumping out at her."

"But I'm not a stranger! I'm her daughter—"

"Listen to the woman," Anchara ordered.

I looked at her in surprise. The mara chan's face revealed nothing. Reluctantly, I let the Gorgio woman go on ahead.

I watched as Desirée approached the cloaked figure, squatted down, and laid the casserole on the ground. Out of her pocket she wrested a fork and knife and laid them on top of the dish. Desirée spoke, but I couldn't hear what she said.

She waited.

The hand with the stick stopped stirring the embers.

Desirée raised a hand and passed it slowly in front of my mother's face. If indeed this was my mother. Whoever it was sat cross-legged on the ground, a triangle of darkness. I could make out no profile. It could have been anyone.

Desirée's voice rose in exasperation. "Galeah!"

At that moment I felt the cold wind that blew here unhindered, and it cut through me. I took a step forward, but Anchara laid a hand on my arm and I stopped.

Desirée was walking back toward us, lips tight with annoyance. "See if you have better luck with her." She started down the path. "I'm going home. Bring my casserole dish when you come back, will you?" Her voice drifted back like dust on the desert wind.

All the colors in the sky were crushed thin along the horizon under the weight of the gathering dark. My mother's shape was silhouetted there on the edge of the drop. It looked as if she were perched on the very edge of the world. I had the shaky feeling that I had to yank her back before she tipped over into the void.

Slowly, I crossed the butte to where she sat.

Her back was to me. Her black hair lay braided over her shoulders, and the braid gold still gleamed in the plaits—the gold I'd feared would be returned to me by a stranger. The shawl she had wrapped around her was the same deep crimson as Shem's blanket. She gathered it tightly, as if it were all the shelter she had in the world.

As softly as I could, I put a hand on her shoulder.

"Mama?"

She scrambled to her feet. Her eyes flashed, wide and fearful as a startled horse's. She scuttled away from me so quickly that I sprang forward in alarm.

"The edge! Mama! Be careful!"

Her gaze swept over me. The hollows in her cheeks and under her eyes stood out like smudges of dirt. It had been three years since I'd seen her, but she'd aged at least ten. Her expression was measuring, distrustful. She moved as if expecting harm.

I fell back. Did she fear me? Was it possible—did she not know who I was?

No. I saw her name me to herself. Serena. My youngest. She knew who I was.

She just didn't believe in me.

Sharply, she jerked her head away and looked at Anchara. The old woman had walked to my side and stood perfectly still, her stout walking stick in her hand. She returned my mother's look impassively.

So this is what Anchara already knew, I thought bitterly. This is what she knew but would not tell me.

"I'll have you this time," Mother's voice croaked, so full of hatred that I shuddered. My mother had always been the gentlest of people! So gentle that I had never heard her return an insult. Not even when they were heaped upon her by my grandmother.

"Has it been you, old witch?" she demanded of Anchara. "Are you the one tormenting me with the ghosts of my children? It's good you've come. We'll have it out this time, we two!"

I stared at her in dismay. "Mother? What are you thinking? I'm not a ghost! I'm real! You don't have to have it out with anyone."

Mother looked at me blankly. I stretched out my hand, reasoning with her. "I promise, I'm not night and darkness. I'm flesh and bone, I swear it, and as real as the day you left us! Take my hand—prove it to yourself."

But Mother's gaze drifted away from me. Her face twisted as she turned to Anchara. "You'll not make such a fool of me again, Anna Wallace!"

My fingers turned to ice. It was my grandmother to whom she spoke. My grandmother! Whom no one on earth could mistake for Anchara Pulchra!

No one in their right mind, that was.

I struggled to say something, but only a choking sound came out.

Anchara cut me off. "You're mistaken, Galeah. I'm not the woman you name. Don't you hear your daughter's words? She's come through danger and heartache to find you. You should welcome her. If you are mad, be so no longer. She has need of you."

For an instant, Anchara's words seemed to penetrate. I saw my mother peer out of the madwoman's eyes. I let my breath go. But too soon.

Mother raised her stick over her head and flew at Anchara with a long, wailing cry. Quick as thought, she slashed the stick down. If it had been a sword, she would have split Anchara in two. But the old woman had raised her own, stronger walking stick in defense, and Mother's snapped against it like the brittle twig it was.

In a fury she flung away the remaining piece of the stick and cursed Anchara in language so ugly, it made me sick to hear it. My mother, who never raised her voice to anyone in anger. Who never even spoke bitterly, even of Daddy's cruel family. Whose spirit I had watched Grandmother Wallace crush every day of that endless year we spent in her house after Daddy died.

Here she was, unleashing all the fury she should have spent long ago. And spending it so wrongly, not on Anna Wallace, but on Anchara, the mara chan of the Kereskedo tribe, who had searched her out for me and found her in this desolate place.

My stomach dropped. Why had I not known my mother felt like this? So angry? Why hadn't I stood up to Grandmother for her?

"You witch! Still not gone?" She leapt at Anchara again, hands raised.

But this time I leapt, too, right between Mother and the old woman.

Her hands clamped down on my collarbone. Her fingers dug into my neck. Before I could stop her, she was shaking me hard, rocking my head back and forth like a doll caught in a child's fight.

I caught her hands and forced them away from my throat. She tried to shake me off, but I held firm.

"It's me! Mother, believe me! It's Serena."

Her wrists felt as fine-boned as the legs of the little cat I'd handed to Rochelle. But her movements were quick and fierce. She struggled to wrench herself out of my grasp. She got one arm free, but I grabbed it and pinned it back against her. I would *not* let her be so close and not acknowledge me.

I brought my face up to hers.

Taking a chance, I lifted my hands from her wrists and took hold of her jaw, gently but firmly, so she was forced to look into my eyes. It was the way I'd seen Willow grip Zara's face in the midst of a tantrum. I held Mother's eyes with mine, enunciating every word. "Mother, look at me! Recognize me! I'm Serena. Serena."

There was a milkiness in her eyes when I saw them up close. I kept talking, hardly knowing what I said. I wished with all my heart that my words were threads, and that if I used them skillfully and carefully, I could lash her to reality.

"I'm your real daughter. Not an apparition. Not a ghost."

She was a stranger, and I couldn't bear it.

"Shall I prove it? What ghost would know the place on Whale Isle where you showed me all the mushrooms? Or the lake at Lookout Pass where Willow buried the box you'd given her, and couldn't find it again?" I thought I discerned a light in Mother's eyes, like a star shrouded in mist. I pressed on. "Would a ghost know that you always sewed bells on your skirts, but I never let you do that to mine? Or that you stuffed cotton in your ears when I flew into a rage? You were the only one who could calm my anger. Let me calm yours now. I'm Serena. See? I still wear the necklace you gave me. Do you remember? When you told me our talent is in giving?"

Her eyes connected with mine.

I dropped my hands from her jaw and ventured a small, hopeful smile. "See? I treasure it, still."

I put my hands to my throat, thinking to place the necklace in her hands.

And found nothing.

I stifled a groan. Shem had the necklace now! The whole thing. Why hadn't I thought to get it back from him?

Mother saw my unadorned neck, and her eyes went flat. See? I could almost hear her thinking, this girl means to trick me. This is not Serena.

"But I am!" I said. "Necklace or no necklace. I'll tell you true, Mama. I gave the necklace to a boy yesterday. Not piece by piece, but the whole thing. Didn't you tell me you gave away a gift from your own father once when you met—" I stopped short, troubled by what I'd said. But I had no time to fret about it.

An invisible husk dropped away from my mother. For a moment her face was no longer twisted by rage or shadowed with defeat. I caught a glimpse of Mother as she had been. Just a glimpse. I wanted to catch it in my hand, like a bright stone in a river. But I made no sudden moves. If her spirit was timidly peering from the shadows, I didn't want to scare it back with quick words or embraces. A spirit is a fragile thing. I held my breath, watching and waiting.

She reached out her hand and laid it on my cheek. "A golden bracelet," she murmured. "I gave your father a bracelet of golden links."

"It's on his wrist still," I told her, seeing the glint of gold as Daddy leaned on the rock at the mouth of the cave.

"Are you sure?"

"As sure as the sun plunges into the western sea."

"I'd give every tooth in my jaw to believe that," she said fiercely.

"I know it's true."

"How?"

"I've seen him."

My mother nodded. She looked straight at me, and her eyes lightened. "Serena?"

I sighed deeply. "Yes, Mama?"

"You were never one for visions." She pushed a long strand of hair out of her eyes. "Take care or you'll go as peculiar as me."

I couldn't laugh, though I knew she meant me to. She was herself— but perhaps only for the moment.

Anchara stepped forward. "Galeah, who do you think I am?"

Mother pressed her hands over her eyes. "I thought . . . But I was wrong. Your pardon, Avo."

Anchara's eyes narrowed. "Whom did you mistake me for? Who do you believe torments you?"

"Anna Wallace. My husband's mother. I never spoke up when I ate her bread, yet here I curse her nightly for what she did to me."

"And what did she do to you?" Anchara asked.

Mother turned to me. "Don't you know, Serena?"

"She was never kind. But—"

Mother's eyes darted away from me. She looked instead at Anchara. "She took my children."

"Ah," the old woman breathed.

"What do you mean, she took us?" I forgot to be careful of what I said. "She didn't take us! You left us!"

My mother winced. "She had me declared unfit, Serena. The Cruelty gave her guardianship over you and Willow."

"But why? How could that be?" My grandmother had never mentioned such a thing.

"How could it not be, if Anna wished it?"

I remembered how Grandmother had smashed the wedding china while Mother huddled in a corner, moaning. No. There had never been any question who would win in any contest of strength between them.

"I want to know how it happened."

Mother settled again by the embers of her fire. Anchara and I sat beside her, waiting for her to speak. Her words came, slow and quiet. "After your father died, I went into the gray world. I think it was between the land of the living and the land of the dead. I did things that . . ." She bit her lip. Then she pulled herself up straight. "When I'm clear, I know. . . . I never left you and Willow of my own free will. Anna told them my grieving made me a danger to you."

"She had to be our guardian because you were sad you'd lost Daddy? How could that be?" I said this with great indignation—so great I almost believed it myself.

But I knew it was a lie.

I remembered coming home from school to find Mother curled up in an empty bathtub, or standing in the nearby park in her black widow-weeds, drenched with rain, talking to herself. . . .

Much as I detested my grandmother and what she'd done, it was a lie to say mother's behavior had been nothing more than grieving.

Anchara was watching me keenly, crouched down by the small fire.

Mother's face suddenly gathered in on itself. To my horror, she began rocking back and forth.

"It was true! What she said! I wasn't fit to care for you. Not only Yulang, and poor and widowed, but mad to boot!"

"Not mad." I tried to sound firm.

But if not mad, what? I thought.

"She'd threaten. But then she'd promise—" She looked at me, eyes so big the whites gleamed. "Wonderful things, Serena! Dowries and rich husbands. The university for you, of course. Did it happen, darling? Tell me it happened."

Wildly I looked to Anchara for guidance. She met my gaze with her face hard as iron. *Choose your words,* her expression warned.

"No university yet," I said slowly. "I'm still at the Lyceum, Mother. At least I was until—" I paused. "Until I left to come and find you."

"And Willow? Sweet Willow?"

Before I could decide what to tell her about Willow, Mother began wringing her hands. "I told her no. No, I told her, you can't have them. I just need time. I'm their mother, after all! But then she sent the sly one—the one with the serpent's tongue and the red lipstick. . . ."

I reached over and put my hand on her shoulder. If only she would stop rocking like an old woman! "Who?" I asked. "Who had a serpent's tongue?"

"Sticky perfume she wore, and skirts straight like fence slats. The social worker. Pretending to be my friend. And all the while prying and spying. Anna paid her well to get rid of me."

My head swam. It had the ring of truth, but there was something about the way she said it—*prying and spying*—that made me doubt. Was this part of her delusion as well? Maybe. But, by Lillith's feet, it sounded like the sort of thing that happened to us! Had she been tricked out of her rights or not? Was she paranoid and crazy or did all of us, all Yulang people, have a good reason to be crazy in just this way?

"I don't know why I did it! She held my pen. She helped me sign. And then Anna took the papers to the Cruelty. It was done and couldn't be undone. She gave me money and told me to leave town."

I stared into my mother's wild, tearstained face. "And you just left? Just because she told you to?" I knew that I must try very hard not to upset her. But I couldn't stifle this.

She was such a sad, wretched figure, all wrapped in her blanket like the beggar women I had seen in alleyways of the city, telling me this story that was my story, and Willow's. And now Zara's, too. How could I have not known it?

"I didn't know how to fight her!" Mother wailed. "Who would help me? She had the Cruelty on her side, and the police, she said."

"But it makes no sense!" I cried. "Grandmother never wanted us! Why would she want to get us away from you? She kicked us out the moment she found out—I mean, as soon as Willow turned eighteen."

Mother looked stricken. She closed her eyes. "I could have made my hand into a fist, just once! I kept my anger in check all those years, Serena. Now it eats at me like a worm in the gut. Tell me at least—did she give you anything she promised?"

"It doesn't matter! We never wanted anything of hers! We wanted you. We could have stuffed Grandmother and all her Gorgio promises into a hole and filled it with sand. It was you we needed!"

"And I need you," Mother said softly. "See how I fare without you?"

I could hear her old self again.

Perhaps all she needed was to know that she was still our mother—that no papers in the world, no lapses of judgment, no sickness of the mind, could take that away.

"We still need you, Mother," I said. "Willow has a daughter, now, too, and the Cruelty have taken her away. We need you to help us. If you tell them you'll care for the baby, we can get her back."

Mother stared at me. "A granddaughter?" A smile flitted across her face.

"Her name is Zara."

Mother's smile vanished. "But, Serena, how can I help? The Cruelty won't even let me care for my own children." She raised her face to mine. "Look at me. I can hardly help myself, daughter. How can I help you?"

What makes you go abroad,
Fighting for strangers,
When you could be safe at home,
Free from all dangers?

—Gorgio song

Mother did not lapse into delusions all that long night. But I saw how true it was that she could not help us.

We spent the night in her trailer. It was not in the dreadful state I'd feared it might be. Yet there was much that revealed a spirit living in uneasy truce with itself.

The first thing I'd seen when we opened its door was a shattered pitcher on the worktable. Hastily, I'd thrown out the pieces, reminded of the blue moon cup I'd smashed the night the Cruelty came for Zara. It shook me to see that my mother could be just as destructive as I was.

But fortunately, the pitcher was the only thing that was broken. For the rest, the place was merely untidy, with heaps of dirty laundry strewn about the floor. Many people lived so.

But not my mother.

She had never fussed over housekeeping in the exacting way my grandmother did. But she had always been a natural creator of harmony. Our home had been full of little things she'd collected at flea markets or traded for at gatherings. She loved good-luck charms and storyboards and dried herbs and flowers in painted vases. Our walls had always been full of pictures.

Here, her walls were bare.

Still, I could take some comfort in the smell of the trailer. There were herbs drying in upside-down bunches hung from the kitchen ceiling. A delicate scent of lemon thyme caught me at odd moments, and occasionally a whiff of anise or mint. The dried mushrooms on the kitchen counter, carefully dehydrated and laid out as she always used to do, affected me the same way. They seemed sprigs of hope.

But I could not put too much faith in such signs. They might be touchstones for the future, but I could not let them deceive me into believing that my mother was well or whole.

When she finally sank into sleep, I sat by her bed, holding her hand, for fear the tormenting spirits that afflicted her might claim her in her dreams. I didn't know if a strong hand could pull her back from nightmares, but it was all I had.

Anchara slept upright in the only armchair in Mother's trailer, as if sitting in judgment on lesser mortals, even in her slumbers.

As for me, sleep never touched my lids.

I kept the shutters open wide. The night was long and cold but clear. Above the wash lines and trailer tops I could see the constellations brighten as night climbed to its full. I even fancied I could see them turning on heaven's wheel.

And as I watched, the idea struck me that our family revolved the same way as those far-off constellations, each of us bound to the others no matter how far we were scattered, so long as we had a hub, a center of gravity to keep us from flying apart. I'd set off on this journey hoping that Mother could be that hub. Zara, Willow, and I would be the spokes of the wheel. Mother would save us from the lonely emptiness of space and bind us together as a family once more.

But instead, I'd found her floating, lost and untethered, in a dark, mean universe.

Who, then, could bind us?

Not Willow. My sister had floated all her life, believing that the wide reaches of space were veils of sugarplum pink, and that without effort all of us would drift to a safe haven. She had let go of us as heedlessly as a child lets go of a balloon—amazed that it cannot come back on its own.

And Zara, poor baby, was floating as well, adrift wherever our failures had condemned her.

So there was only me.

I saw it as clearly as I saw the half-moon patterns on my mother's quilt. I was the hub. There was no one else.

I had come all this long way seeking help, but in the end all I had was my own help to give. It wasn't what I'd hoped for, but I knew it was true, as clearly as I knew that my head was heavy and my feet were turning to ice on the floor of the unheated trailer.

I thought with longing of the cheerful breakfast I'd shared with Lemon, when it seemed my troubles were coming to an end. Could it really have been only the day before? I wondered what Lemon and her father would think had happened to me. Would Rochelle miss me with her in the bed that night? And Shem—

Had he really decided he didn't need me after all?

I shied from the thought as from the touch of burning metal. Perhaps he didn't need me to succeed in his plans anymore. But I suddenly wondered if I needed him. As that night rolled into dawn, I imagined a listener to all my anguished thoughts. And he was that listener. Or he would have been, if it all hadn't gone wrong.

I buried my head in my arms. All I could do was wait for the morning and know that my thoughts were just that—mine, and no one else's to share.

Soon there came the first dilution of black into midnight blue. A rooster crowed from a nearby farm and the chattering of birdsong burst from the trees as, somewhere behind Mother's trailer, the sun rose. When the light streaming through the window was bright enough to flutter my mother's eyelids, I was beside her, watching her as she had watched me when I was a child and wracked with sickness or bad dreams. My hand, half numb with pins and needles, still clung to hers.

Fear flashed in her eyes when she opened them and saw me. I was afraid she would again take me for a ghost, but I held steady.

I saw memory come flooding back. A smile warmed her lips.

She turned her head, saw Anchara, and jolted upright. "Do you realize who she is, Serena?"

"I know who she is," I said, hoping Mother really did this time, as well.

"The mara chan in this slovenly trailer! I could die of shame!"

"But she's still sleeping," I whispered. "Let me put it to rights before she wakes."

My mother laid a shaky hand on my arm. "Yes, yes ..." Her eyes were big, as if she was overcome with the thought of this task. Such a little thing, I thought, and it's too much for her.

"But, Mother ..." I ventured.

"Yes?"

"I'm hungry. Will you cook me an egg?" I watched her nervously. Perhaps if the Gorgio woman was cooking for her, even an egg was beyond her powers?

"An egg?" She pulled my face toward her and planted a kiss on my cheek. "An egg. What a good idea. A tea-soaked egg for my darling. Will the mara chan eat one, too?"

I glanced at the old woman asleep in the armchair. Mother didn't know there was any reason for Anchara not to share our food. I hoped, by all the blessings of Mother Lillith, that I could keep that from her. She couldn't learn how far we had fallen in her absence. It would undo her. Surely Anchara would see that? Not that I'd ever noticed that the old woman had a shred of sensitivity. Still, I thought anxiously, if the mara chan had deigned to sleep in the same trailer with us, surely she wouldn't refuse our food?

"Yes," I said, more firmly than I felt. "I'm sure she will."

"And then what must we do, daughter?"

The trusting note in her voice struck me to the heart.

"I'll take you to our camp," I said. That was the important thing—to get her out of this depressing place. "But first I've got to find a man Avo Anchara knows, who understands Gorgio law. I think he'll help us. Once I've spoken with him . . ." I faltered. What then? What could he tell me, except what I already knew: that Mother couldn't take custody of Zara and my search had ended in failure?

But I forced a smile onto my lips. "Perhaps we could sell those dried mushrooms of yours at the big market. After that I'll take you back home."

"Home?"

"To Willow. And Zara." I tried to sound as if I believed it. "No matter what happens, I promise you'll see your granddaughter."

Anchara didn't refuse the egg Mother prepared.

And when the mara chan told me who it was she wanted me to meet, I nearly swallowed my own egg, shell and all.

It seemed incredible that such a man could be found simply by going to his office and ringing the bell. But Anchara had the address, and an excellent set of directions. And she had told him I was coming.

I found his office in a bustling part of town. It was on the ground floor of a town house, hidden away in a maze of alleyways. The door stood ajar, painted with the Kereskedo emblems of the scales and coins.

Outside the office a workman was loading a truck. His sleeves were rolled up. Perspiration beaded his brow and he was whistling in a ragged, out-of-breath way. The truck was parked illegally, taking up the entire alley, with two of its wheels on the curb. I wondered that the great lawyer hadn't told him to get that dirty rig out of there.

"Excuse me," I said to the workman. "I'm looking for Roman Stanno."

"You've found him," the man grunted, heaving a crate into the back of the truck.

It took a moment for this to register in my brain.

This sweating workman? How could this be the famous Roman Stanno?

But as I struggled to make this piece of information fit, I realized that the man was much as he had looked in his photographs in the newspaper: short, barrel-chested, and bowlegged. I had heard that he had once been a longshoreman, and it was easy to imagine when I saw his heavy arms and his hands like pork knuckles. His face was broad, and his lips long, thin, and humorous as a frog's. His hair was just beginning to weather to gray.

He was not dressed as a Gorgio, though his position in the law guild would have led me to expect it. His trousers were conservative enough, but over his fine cotton shirt he wore a spectacular Kereskedo vest, embroidered with mountain flowers in gold and violet and tangerine.

He gave me a glance and wiped a heavy arm across his forehead. I knew I should explain why I was here, but I was too awed. So I stood there gawping and he was the one who spoke first.

"Are you the one Avo Anchara said she would send?"

I nodded.

"Well, I've been waiting, girl. A favor is a favor, but it's been two days since the mara chan honored my humble abode—Mother Lillith send her long life and a sweeter disposition! What took you so long?" He frowned slightly. "I'd hoped to leave this afternoon, but this loading is taking longer than I'd expected. Listen, Jalla, I'll forgive your tardiness in exchange for a pair of strong arms to help me. How do I know you have strong arms?" He winked. "All Yulang women have strong arms. It comes of carrying their menfolk through life."

Too nervous to laugh, I followed him up the steps and into the disarray of his office without a word.

Big wooden crates crowded the room, some with tops neatly nailed shut, some uncovered. I squatted down to lift one and nearly toppled under the weight. But once I had it waist high, I managed to stagger out the door and down the steps with it. That crate was sealed. But the next I carried was open and full of tinned soup and vegetables, rice and pasta, jars of baby food, and soap. A third was crammed with blankets and linen. Others held tents, kerosene lanterns, and camp stoves.

"What's it all for?" I ventured to ask when I'd returned from my tenth load. Forgetting my awe of the great lawyer, I crumpled, hot and sweaty, into the wide leather chair in front of his desk.

Stanno looked taken aback. "Don't you know? Anchara said you understood the situation."

Of course, Anchara had told me nothing. I shook my head, annoyed but not surprised. It was typical of the mara chan to leave me looking like a fool. She certainly liked to keep her secrets. And to spin her little webs. No wonder she'd laughed so heartily when I'd given her the golden spider.

"Open the file on top of the desk," Stanno instructed. "The one on the very top. Read what you find."

I stood up and examined the mound of disorganized papers on the lawyer's desk. A leather-bound folder lay on top of the rest. I opened it. A copy of the petition I'd written for the Paria bora chan five days be-

271

fore—could it have been only five days!—stared out at me, smudged and spotted from a fax transmission.

My eyes flew questioningly to Stanno's face. The lawyer's lips drew into a sliver of a smile. "Beautiful Romanae. Not a declension amiss. Aside from the urgency of the situation, I'm delighted to find a tribeswoman as gifted in the language as I. It can be lonely to have a talent that your companions don't appreciate."

"But why do you have the petition?" I frowned down at my own hurried handwriting.

Stanno's smile disappeared. "See what lies beneath."

I picked up the fax and saw a newspaper article, neatly highlighted in orange ink. It was dated three days before. "Evictions of Migrant Workers Follow Arrests for Breach of Peace," I read. "An encampment of forty to fifty Yulang migrant workers was turned out of their temporary dwellings following a demonstration that quickly turned into what observers described as a riot. The Yulang maintain that the town was culpable in not protecting them from an alleged attack that they claim left one woman dead. . . ."

I read the whole article through twice, my heart sinking.

This was all my petition had done for the wretched Parias.

Now instead of a few houses destroyed by fire, a few families displaced, not one of them had a roof over their heads! No work. No money. No food. My eyes flew back to the headline of the article. Arrests for breach of the peace! Some were sitting in jail even as I read this.

Attacked by the Trident Riders first, then thrown in prison for protesting the attack!

I couldn't believe it.

"The Yulang *claim* a woman is dead! What kind of reporting is that?" I said angrily. "A woman is dead or she is not dead! Yulang or no!

And this woman is dead as stone. She leaves a four-year-old orphan. Couldn't the writer trouble to find that out?"

Roman Stanno regarded me without expression. "No. He would not trouble to. We Yulang lie, you know. Unreliable sources. You might recall, Jalla, that that was the reason our testimony was considered worthless in court—at least until recently."

I poked my finger at the article. "And here, Stanno-Chan. An 'alleged attack'! What was alleged about it? Even if the Gorgios averted their eyes when the Riders fired the houses, no one could miss the Trident graffiti everywhere! They sign their names to their work. I'm sure it's there still."

"The townsfolk say the Yulang put the graffiti there themselves."

My mouth fell open. "Why would they do that?"

"Part of an extortion scheme. We are well known for extortion, you know."

I was so frustrated by what he was telling me, I could feel the tears prickle in my eyes. "Yulang houses may or may not have been burned. A woman may or may not have died. To them it's not so important! But when we transgress—instantly, a protest is a riot! Why not an 'alleged riot'?" I didn't wait for Stanno's explanation. I knew it already. "Because the writer was a Gorgio. And rioting is what they expect from us!"

Stanno laid his ham-fisted hand on my arm. I expected him to tell me to calm down, but he didn't. He gave my arm an approving shake. "That's right, Jalla!"

I looked at him in puzzlement. What was he looking so pleased about?

"That's right!" he said. "You see it clearly and write it clearly, too. Anchara was always a cunning old bird, but I'll lay more trust in her from now on."

Suddenly, I understood. "Is that where you're taking all these sup-plies? To the Paria camp?"

Roman Stanno picked up the leather folder and shook it under my nose. "What do you think, girl? There are big things brewing out there. The Parias are refusing to leave, even now that the Gorgios have evicted them. The boxes you helped me load are donations from all the tribes in Eurus Major. Look how much has poured in!"

"From the tribes? Do you mean—even the Kereskedo? They're giv-ing donations to the Paria?"

Stanno nodded. "Once I thought it might be impossible to trouble the Kereskedo to so much as blow their noses if that would help the untouchables. Even harder than convincing the Gorgios to admit our testimony in law cases. But—" He gazed out the window, as if search-ing for something far away. "But we managed the one—after years of fighting, we managed it." He looked at me and smiled. "So perhaps the Kereskedo can change, too. They've given generously, and more will follow. Anchara had much to do with that—as I imagine she would not have told you."

"What will you do with all this stuff?"

"We'll take it to the Parias. They need somewhere to live and some-thing to eat while their protest continues." His voice kindled. "The days when the Gorgios can answer a plea for justice with arrests are num-bered. I'll get the leaders out of jail. There'll be justice, Jalla, or there will be trouble."

It was an impressive speech. But I couldn't help feeling uneasy. Stanno had a lot of supplies in that truck of his. And the presence of ten men when he spoke like this. But as dazzled as I was by his words, still he was only one man. And for one man to promise justice, up against everything the Gorgios could throw at him . . .

"Is it . . . is it only you going out to the Paria camp?"

Roman Stanno shrugged. "As you see."

"Don't you have anyone else to help you? I was there. I saw what it was like. The Gorgios wouldn't even send the fire engines to douse the fires. They won't be easy people to deal with, no matter who you are...."

"Speaking of who you are," he said mildly, "tell me your name again. I've forgotten."

Did he mean who was I to tell him his business?

"Serena Wallace," I mumbled.

"Ah, yes, I remember. A Gorgio name. I suppose we should have a formal introduction." He bowed deeply. "Roman Stanno, at your service. Advocate, lawyer, and more trouble than vinegar in the eye for the powers that be. I do not say 'to the Gorgios,' you notice. I am part Gorgio myself, you know. My grandfather."

That was kind. He didn't have to tell me that he also had mixed blood.

"You speak of the fire," he added. "Rumor has it that you brought the fire engine."

"It was a Gorgio fireman who did that. And helped put the fire out."

"Yes? I heard it was you."

"I only persuaded the Gorgio." I remembered the man and his family. "You should find out what help he needs. The townspeople will make him pay for what he did, if the Trident Riders don't get him first."

"It's always the case. No good act unpunished. I'll keep an eye out for him. But I hear also, Jalla, that you took in the child whose mother was killed."

"The Bardoffs are looking after her. The bora chan asked them because they knew her mother. It's just that they've been traveling with—" I paused. "With us," I said, and felt sad. It wasn't really "us" anymore, was it? I couldn't imagine that Shem would continue to share my travels. Firmly, I put that thought aside. "Why are you asking me these questions?"

Stanno smiled. "It is information I want. I hear you have trouble with the Cruelty yourself."

"Yes." My throat had closed up and the word came out as a whisper.

"Your niece is in their custody? Unjustly? Am I right?"

I thought of irresponsible Willow and her house full of suitors. I thought of the burn on Zara's foot. These, too, were thoughts I had to shove aside.

"Completely unjustly," I said. "I want to get her back, but the Cruelty won't allow my sister to have her, and my mother is too ill. I'm willing to care for her, but they say I'm underage. Is there any way I could get custody despite that, Stanno-Chan?"

"Under certain conditions, yes. But only then."

My heart jumped like a salmon in the summer run. "But if I can meet the conditions, I can take care of her?"

"It depends. How much will you do to win back the child?"

"Anything! How can you even ask? Do you think I can do it?"

Stanno had an amused glint in his eye. "I'd be afraid to stand in your way. But—"

"But what?"

"You must also have proper representation."

A flame of hope shot up. "Would you represent me, Stanno-Chan?" I couldn't believe I'd asked it, but I couldn't stop myself. "I'd do anything! Please! People say you can talk the scales off a snake. It would be an easy thing for you. Oh, please—"

I sounded like a child begging for candy. But it was because all of a sudden I knew what it was to be on the brink of having your heart's desire. Hope opened my heart as sunlight opens a flower. Anxiety compressed my lungs with pain. It was unbearable.

Stanno looked disconcerted.

I cursed myself. I'd pushed too hard! Now he wouldn't help me at all. Headstrong . . . presumptuous . . . pushy! When would I ever learn?

"I'll put a question to you," the great man said.

Yes, I thought. Whatever it is, yes, yes! Please help me. Please.

I nodded.

"Here is my conundrum," Roman Stanno said. "I have little time. I have a busy practice here in the city. And you ask me to wrest your little sister from the Gorgios."

"My niece," I murmured.

"Your niece. Of course. But there is also a crisis in the Paria camp. Five men and four women are in jail. The others are living rough. Not that that is new to us. But they are at risk. The Trident Riders are angered that they didn't succeed in driving them away—and enraged that the Paria may prosecute." He paused and gave me a piercing look. "Meanwhile, the mara chan asks me to help you. And Anchara is a woman to whom one does not say no. From respect, you see. Always from respect. She, too, would like me to plead your case to the Cruelty."

I stared. *Anchara* had asked this?

"But if I represent you," Stanno said, "I cannot help the Parias. I have little enough time, and as you say, I am only one man."

He paused again, and chewed thoughtfully on his lip. I watched him, hardly able to breathe.

"My question to you is: What shall I do? Shall I drop off these supplies and leave the Parias to fend for themselves in order to make your plea? Or shall I stay in the orchards?"

I felt as though there were a stone in my stomach.

It had started to sink when Stanno began talking, and now it was anchored fast, like wreckage lodged in the ocean floor.

How could I tell him to leave all those Parias to their own devices? I knew well that the people in jail had no one to speak for them. The Gorgios would appoint a poor people's defense counsel for them, who would hardly listen to their case. Some public defenders had been known to sleep through trials! I knew the women of that camp. They had children who needed them. They were unsheltered, at the mercy of the Trident Riders. I shuddered, remembering the pale rider on his pale horse, shooting his pistol in the air, for joy of his hate.

How could I take away from them the man whose eloquence, people said, could charm a grizzly and put courage into a rabbit? I looked down at my feet.

But Zara!

Hot tears sprang into my eyes. She was somewhere alone in the city. Without me, there was no one to come to her aid! How could I throw away this good fortune—the greatest Yulang advocate to plead her case? How could I have come so far only to give up my best chance? I'd promised Mother she would see her grandchild. No matter what, that was a promise I would have to keep.

"What do you say, Serena Wallace?"

I tried to keep the disappointment out of my voice. I would not let Stanno think I blamed him for the good he did.

"Go to the orchards," I said reluctantly. "They need you more." The words hung flat in the air. "But . . ." My mind began to turn. He had said my Romanae was good. And that I could write and speak well.

"Do you think—" My voice sounded very small. "Do you think I could represent myself? Do you think the Gorgios would listen to me if you tell me what I have to do?"

"I have no doubt you could represent yourself, Serena."

"Then you'll tell me the words I need to say?"

"Oh, yes, I can do that," Stanno's long frog mouth suddenly stretched into a broad smile. He looked relieved. And not, I think, relieved that I had freed him of his obligation to Anchara. He stretched his arms out to either side, the way one stretches on waking in the morning.

"Thank you once more, Mother Lillith. And your self-appointed representative on earth, Anchara Pulchra, thank you!" He looked at me with a gleam of amusement in his eye. "You wonder why I thank these two, Jalla?"

I nodded.

"I'll tell you why. Because they've sent me the help I need."

I looked over my shoulder to see if someone had come in.

Stanno gave a booming laugh. "Try looking in the mirror. It's you, Jalla. Anchara sent you to me. I doubted her, though I had seen your petition and heard of your bravery. But I can see now that you are the one. You were right, Serena. I need help. Will you be that help?"

"I don't understand."

"You said I was only one man. That's true. I can't go on fighting alone."

"What? Do you need an assistant of some sort?"

"I need an apprentice. A Yulang advocate to help me in my work. Will that be you?"

"But I'm not a lawyer! I haven't even finished school."

"What do you need with that Gorgio school? What can they teach you that I can't?"

"You need a university paper to enter the law guild—" I felt frightened and excited at the same time.

"Which you shall one day have," Stanno said airily. "Anything else, Jalla Serena?"

"Just—" I felt bewildered. "Just that I came to *you* for help."

I saw the stars wheeling outside my mother's trailer. *We give,* Mother had said. *In love or in hate, we always give.* And she'd pressed the necklace into my hands.

Then her voice was gone. The room was still and Roman Stanno was waiting for my answer.

"All right," I told him. "I'll help you. I'll be your apprentice." Then, with absolute certainty: "I can't think of anything that's more worth doing. But first you must tell me how to bring Zara back to my family."

And he told me.

All my father's ships, a-sailing on the sea,
Could never bring such a sheath and knife to me . . .
— Kereskedo trading song

I carried what Roman Stanno had told me in the safest lockbox in my memory. I carried the papers he gave me in my pocket. Now I had a petition of my own for the return of Zara. The great man himself had helped me write it. Only one line was empty. And it filled me with a sweating uncertainty to know that tonight I would discover if I could write anything on that line or if I must leave it blank. And in leaving it blank, render the petition void.

The number forty-eight blazed in my brain like a talisman.

If the petition could be submitted—if I could find a way to submit it without losing all that I was—then the Cruelty had forty-eight hours to put Zara into my care. By law. By Gorgio law.

I tried not to think about it. Because if I could *not* fill in that one line . . . then I would have to abandon Zara.

Stanno gave me a ride to the edge of Mother's trailer park, promising to speak to me again before he left for the Paria camp the next day.

I walked along the asphalt drive, past the grim-looking trailer homes with their litter of old car parts and mattresses on the stamped-down grass, and the buttes rising behind them. Desirée was dragging an overfed, cantankerous bulldog out for a walk. As I approached her, she raised an eyebrow in recognition.

"Are you taking Galeah away?" she demanded.

"Yes. How did you know?"

"She settled up with me this morning, after the old lady waddled off. I manage this place."

I couldn't read her expression behind the wrap-around sunglasses she wore, but she sure sounded annoyed. I quickly found a reason for this.

"Um—did she—did my mother pay everything she owed you?"

The bulldog was pulling against his leash, whining and growling. Desirée jerked him to her side.

"Uh-huh," she said, after a moment.

I would have bet the feet inside my boots that the Gorgio woman was lying.

But what could I do about it? There was still no money in my pocket. I looked at the ground. "Maybe someday I can set our accounts straight," I mumbled.

"Maybe," she allowed.

Embarrassed, I added, "You've been cooking for her. I wanted to thank you for it."

"That's all right. When she's in one of her moods, I make sure she's eating. That's all." Desirée pulled off her glasses. To my surprise, her gray eyes held a touch of concern. "She's not always like last night. Your mom has stretches when she's fine. She pulls herself together, goes to work..."

"Work?" My mother, as I'd seen her last night, seemed totally unfit for any employment.

"Cleaning at those motels down the road." Desirée gave me a sharp look. "She pays her way, mostly."

My face went slack. Cleaning? My mother cleaning other people's beds and toilets? Work even the poorest Parias would refuse? No court had ever cast Mother out. But she declared herself *ma'hane* by willingly taking on such pollution. Why? Was she punishing herself this way?

With isolation? And filthy work? The thought wrenched like a chicken bone in the gullet.

Desirée looked at me curiously. "She was very private about family. You and your sister. I only knew there was a pretty one and a smart one. Which are you?"

"Can't you tell?"

It was a feeble joke, but Desirée laughed. "Well, the pretty one wouldn't say that. So I'll tell you something, smart one. The other folks who live here ..." She glanced at a woman who had been sitting on her trailer steps about fifty feet away, knitting and watching us sullenly. "They didn't appreciate it when I rented space to a Magpie. People were sure their precious possessions had been spirited away—or were going to be. They wanted me to kick her out. The ones who moaned loudest I'd go and visit. Whatever they thought was missing was right there on the kitchen table or under some pile of junk." Desirée turned and looked at me. "She hasn't suffered anything worse than a little name-calling here. If it were my mother, I'd want to know that."

I could only nod, filled with relief and gratitude, but also with a saturating pity for how alone my mother had been. How vulnerable.

Mother came out of her trailer at that moment. She didn't see us, just stepped down and stood beside her steps in a wrinkled blue dress—no splendid embroidery, no wasp-waisted vest or tiny silver bells sewed to the hem. A bleach stain marred her sleeve. I supposed she'd got it at her cleaning job. Her hands hung limply at her sides.

"Mother—"

She jumped. Then a look of timorous relief crept across her face.

"Serena—are we going to sell the mushrooms?" She sounded anxious. "Because I can't find my crates ... or the display signs ..."

Desirée leaned closer to me and dropped her voice. "The harvest market?"

"I'd thought we could sell there—"

"In that mob? Yesterday I couldn't get her to open her door. She sneaked out to the butte when she thought I wouldn't notice. I don't think taking her into a big crowd is such a good idea."

"What's she whispering to you, Serena?" Mother sidled up to us, looking from me to Desirée suspiciously.

On impulse, I took Mother's hand and stroked it. "The mushrooms will keep. It's late afternoon already. We'd better get moving."

"Moving?" she said in alarm. "Oh, I don't know. It isn't a good day for driving. It might rain."

I looked up into the cold, cloudless sky. Snow, more likely, I thought, in a week or so. But today, rain only in my mother's fearful mind.

"Don't worry, Mama. I'll drive."

"You, darling? Can you drive?"

"Like a trucker!" I assured her.

"But where will we go?"

"Anchara Pulchra's camp. We have friends there. The Bardoffs. You remember?"

Mother nodded.

"They have a little Paria girl with them, too. She lost her mother and they're taking care of her."

"How did she lose her mother?"

"In a fire." Instantly, I wished I hadn't said it.

Mother's eyes filled with ready tears. "Oh, the poor wee'n!"

I felt a flash of anger. At least Rochelle knows what happened to her mother, I thought. You didn't even send word that you were still alive! The words were so sharp and hot on my tongue that I had to bite them back to stop them from jumping into the air between us.

I closed my eyes and took a deep breath.

I couldn't just spit out my feelings like that anymore. I couldn't go to my mother with my hurt or my anger or my need for comfort. I

284

couldn't even tell her of the wonder of my arrangement with Roman Stanno. She needed calm and comfort herself, and a steady hand behind the wheel.

Shem. The realization struck me like a shock from an electrical socket when you pull the plug out too hard. He was the one I wanted to share this with. Suddenly, I wanted to be with him so badly it was like a knife in my ribs.

But then I remembered the papers Stanno had given me.

It would look as if all I cared about was the bargain, the points for my side. . . . It was too late, anyway! How had I managed to tie myself in such a knot?

I put my arm around my mother. She and Desirée had been talking, without my hearing a word they said.

"Thank you. For everything," I said to the Gorgio woman. "It's time to go," I told my mother.

It was just before sundown when we parked my mother's trailer at Plateau Rock. I didn't want to overwhelm her with too many new faces, but it had crossed my mind that coming back to a Yulang camp might help. I wondered what would have become of her if Desirée hadn't looked out for her.

Most of Anchara's people were still out selling. The dirt track— starting to harden with the coming of evening frost—snaked around past their campsite. My heart gladdened at the sight of the caravans, which looked so beautiful, with their painted shutters and amulets, after the ugly Gorgio trailers. Shem's still sat back a distance from the rest. I depressed the brake as we pulled up to it.

But then my courage failed. The last words he'd said to me were still in my ear, and the biting sound of his voice. I pressed more gas into the line and drove across the open field behind the camp.

I parked Mother's trailer within sight but not within earshot of the rest. Better so, I thought. There was a little stream at our back, and a tiny blackened fire pit a few steps from our door. Spreading out beside it was a grandfather chestnut with its conkers already shaken down by the autumn wind, some lying in shining heaps all over the long grass, some still in their spiky green shells.

Mother had no split firewood in her trailer, as Shem had always had in his. What chill evenings she must have endured! I gathered what twigs there were under the chestnut and headed out into the pines to search for more. The cold was rising as the sun sank.

I hadn't slept, and it had been a long, long day. But something about the sharp resiny smell in the air brought back my energy. Words began to gather in my mind: imagined questions, imagined replies. Again and again, I looked to Anchara's camp, willing the cars to start streaming back from the day's selling.

When would he return?

I could find nothing but twigs under the pines. I brought my spindly findings back, somewhat dispirited. I needed real firewood. Tonight, if nothing else, I had to make sure my mother had a proper fire.

Gathering my courage, I set off across the field to Anchara's camp. Only a few women had stayed behind. I walked with my head down, not daring to meet their eyes. It was the first time I had ever ventured where I had been so long shunned.

The fire crackled. The women were cooking the evening meal. It smelled wonderful—sausages from the market, and rice and peppers. I thought of the short-stocked kitchen in mother's trailer and sighed.

To my relief, one of the women in camp was Rass's wife, the long-faced girl with the chipped tooth. I remembered the honeycomb she had brought me the day before and approached her first.

"Mara, please. Could you spare some firewood? I've gone and fetched my mother, but she's ill and we have no wood for tonight."

I felt a cool hand lifting my chin, forcing me to raise my eyes from the ground. The kind, homely face smiled at me. "I'll give it gladly, Jalla. The mara chan told me about your mother."

She went over to the pile of logs and loaded nine or ten into a length of canvas for me. As she transferred them into my arms, she added, "You must never fear to ask me or any of Anchara's people for help, Jalla. Do you hear what I am telling you?"

"I hear it." My face broke into a smile. "Your kindness warms me more than the firewood, Mara." If I hadn't been gripping the canvas with both hands, I would have hugged her.

I carried the logs back to Mother's trailer, split them, piled them by the fire pit, and went inside. The dark was falling, and I needed a lantern, and whatever food there might be, if I was going to start the dinner. The interior of the trailer was shadowy, lit only by candles. The generator had died that afternoon. I hoped that was the only reason for the gloom. Perhaps Mother was resting.

But when I crouched down beside the refrigerator, telling myself that it had only been shut off a little while and that everything was still good, I heard a step behind me. Mother stood there, shadows under her red-rimmed eyes. She looked as if she'd been crying.

Quickly I stood up, ready to hold her and comfort her if the black mood had come upon her again.

But she placed a hand on my shoulder. "No. I'm your mother, Serena, though I've been useless to you in all your trouble. Don't feel you need to do everything for me."

"But I want to."

She shook her head. "Let me cook for you, at least. It's little enough. Let me know that you are off your feet for a few minutes."

I had to accept, even though I thought it would have been better for her to rest. "All right, Mama."

I went back outside, and as I built the fire, I heard Anchara's band return from the market.

As the fire began to lick out from the kindling and catch the dry wood, I sat down beside it and strained my eyes across the twilit fields. Rusty trucks and loud, sputtering cars screeched in, with people jumping out of the backs before they'd even stopped. I could tell by the good-natured shouting and tapping on car horns that they had traded well. It gladdened me that my amethysts and Shem's selling must have made a difference for them. As I watched, I caught sight of Rass exchanging a few words with his wife and swooping up one of his children.

The Bardoffs' old black sedan was the last to pull in. The trunk was riding almost to the ground. Shem got out, long legs first, holding Rochelle asleep in his arms. Her dark head lolled on his shoulder and started to slip off as soon as he was standing upright. When he tried to joggle her into a more comfortable position, her arms flew up in protest and knocked his hat off.

Sweat broke out on my palms. For the thousandth time, I had to call myself an idiot, just to make sure I remembered I was one.

I watched as Lemon got out of the car. Shem said something to her, and she scooped up his hat and walked over to the caravan with him, opening the door so he could carry Rochelle inside.

I'd been watching so intently that I didn't hear my mother's step behind me, or notice when she set the hook over the fire and loaded a big pot onto it. It should have surprised me—and maybe heartened me—that she still kept the pot and hook from when we had traveled long ago. But I was too preoccupied. It was only when she started cooking the onions and the smell reached my nostrils that I became aware of her.

"Is that him?" she asked, so unexpectedly that I drew my breath and spun around.

She'd been watching me. There was a look in her eyes, almost like the look I'd seen there when she learned that I could drive.

"Him, who?"

A ghost of a smile crooked her lips. "The boy you gave the necklace to. The whole necklace, was it?"

I nodded briefly, anxious to dislodge her interest. "Do you need help in the kitchen? Give that to me. . . . There's a plank over here for a table. Did you notice it?"

Mother put a ladle down on the plank. "And shall I see this necklace again?" she pursued.

"I don't expect he'll steal it or anything." Unnerved by her close attention, I bounced up off the stump I'd been sitting on. "I'll go get the soup bowls. Have you got any bread anywhere?"

My mother was laughing softly to herself as I mounted the steps to the trailer.

We ate food of a flavor I hadn't tasted since Daddy died: simmered onions and greens, potatoes basted with rosemary, bacon and golden squash. The last of the season's plums, so deep a purple as to be almost black. Simple though the meal was, I realized it was meant as a homecoming feast.

When we'd scoured the last pot, Mother went into the trailer, seeking her bed. The day and the night before had exhausted her.

Alone, I watched across the sweep of the fields as Anchara's band ate their meals and the dishes were clattered and washed and stacked. I listened to their laughter and heard their songs.

Once and again, I spotted Shem among them all. And each time, unerringly, he felt my eyes and turned, as metal to magnet, squinting into the darkness to where I sat. And then turned away again.

How, I wondered, do most people decide the rest of their lives? Some have no power to decide at all: the Yulang girls given away in marriage at thirteen, mothers twice over by the time they reach my age. Only the very poor among the Gorgios have so little choice. Most Gorgios train themselves for jobs or get the proper schooling, in a logical way. The very rich ones fall into their family businesses. Yulang men and women scramble as fortune buffets them from place to place. Their decisions are made by the day or the hour. But they remain traders, or musicians, or laborers, as their tribe dictates. That much is set for them.

Unless, of course, like Shem, they seek to change the course of the waters upon which they set sail at birth.

I sat there by the fire holding all these differing fates in my hands, like balls to juggle with, knowing that I had been born between one thing and another. I was neither fully Yulang nor fully Gorgio. I had been rich one year and poor another, privileged one and despised another. And so for me, there would be the burden of choice. Though choice was a gift, as well. I realized that.

People began to drag themselves off to bed, unwilling to leave their celebration but knowing that tomorrow was another working day. Children stumbled in nets of their own sleep. Even dogs had trouble lifting themselves from their warm spots by the fire and following their masters to bed.

I saw Shem bow to Anchara and leave the mara chan's fire. Nerving myself to the task, I prepared to follow him.

But there was no need. He was already across the fields, coming toward me. I jumped from my seat, every muscle taut.

The first thing I noticed as he came closer was that he was avoiding my eyes. And the reason wasn't far to seek. He was angry. I could see it from ten paces.

"Where've you been?" he asked coldly as soon as he was within earshot.

Wrong! I wanted to tell him. This isn't how this conversation starts! You aren't supposed to be angry with me still. All the careful words I'd turned over in my mind broke to dust like smashed clay bricks.

"A day and a night and no word—"

"You knew I was looking for my mother, Shem."

"No, you weren't. Not right then you weren't. Not the very moment you stormed away. I didn't even know where you went."

"Just— I went to— Anchara took me. What did you think?"

"I didn't know, Serena!" He threw his hands up in the air. "The night I met you, you'd just run across the whole city in bedroom slippers. If a girl can do that, what crazy thing won't she do? Can you blame me for wondering? For all I knew, you could have hitched a ride back to Oestia." He gave me an angry glance. "Or to the orchards. Do you remember what we ran into in the orchards? Sometimes I think you don't have the wit to keep your head dry in the rain."

"Shem—"

"No. That's all I've got to say. I'm glad you found your mother. Goodbye." He was already walking away across the meadow, a dark figure disappearing into darkness.

In a moment, I was running after him, the long grass whipping around my legs.

"Shem! Wait!"

The strength with which I grabbed his arm surprised us both. I half pulled the worsted jacket off his shoulder.

He turned and looked at me, raising an eyebrow sardonically. Now what? that expression said.

Streamers of cloud were riding across the face of the waning moon on the chill north wind. In the moon's pale light, Shem's face was ashen, and the scar he'd gotten in the woods, searching for me, was darker than it had been for many a day.

I shivered. Away from the fire, the boy I'd waited all day to see had a ghostly look about him. Lillith's blisters! Everyone in my life turned to ghosts, even while they were alive! Willow had appeared to me in dreams and warnings. And Zara. And Mother—even when I was in her living presence, she was like a phantom. Half gone. Half a memory. I couldn't bear for it to be that way with Shem, too.

"Don't go. Not yet." I tugged—not too hard—on his jacket sleeve.

He plucked his jacket out of my hand. Had I done it again? Would I find myself dismissed, as Anchara had dismissed me, for pushing and shoving too hard?

But to my relief, he merely shrugged and followed me reluctantly back to the fireside. Humoring me. He stayed on his feet, several paces from the fire's warmth.

"Shem, sit down. Please. I can't talk if you've got your toe on the starting line, waiting for the gun."

With another even more careless shrug, he walked over to the chestnut tree and sank down on the ground, leaning his back against its trunk. I perched on the stump at the far end of the plank we'd used for a table. The fire was between us, though it had sunk lower by now.

Shem looked up at me, waiting. His expression said "Don't waste my time" as clearly as if he had spoken. But it seemed his anger was spent. Now perhaps I could use all those words I'd saved up throughout the day.

But when I tried to conjure them, it was like searching underground for the amethysts once again, but this time with no lantern and no rock pick. Whatever treasure of winged words I had buried away lay hidden in darkness. I couldn't find it.

"It's about yesterday—" I faltered.

"Yesterday? What about it?"

"When we were talking at the market. About—"

"About what? We talked about a lot of things yesterday."

"Stop it, Shem! You remember what we were talking about!" But I couldn't muster my usual annoyance. The fire just wasn't burning that way anymore. "I wanted to tell you—"

I looked at him in despair. What did I want to say? Only one thing came to mind.

"I just wanted to say . . . I'm sorry," I said haltingly. "I'm sorry if I was insulting, or if I said something to hurt you."

"Oh, is that all?" he said coolly. "Don't worry about it." He planted his hands on the ground and pushed himself to his feet, without sending a look my way. "I've forgotten about it already."

I leapt up and shouted with my whole heart, "That's not true!"

He'd been about to turn away again, but my shout rooted him where he stood.

I don't know where my assurance came from, but I just kept talking. "You know that isn't true, or you wouldn't have been angry when I disappeared. You wouldn't have cared at all. Please stop trying to leave, Shem. Give me a chance to really explain."

He spread his hands in that sarcastic giving-up gesture Kereskedo merchants use with unreasonable customers, and sat down again. "All right. Explain away. I don't expect I can prevent you."

I lowered myself onto the plank table, closer to where he sat, and leaned my elbows on my knees. "Shem, I said those things yesterday because—because I didn't know my own mind. No, that's not true!" I cried. The words were getting away from me again. "I knew my mind, but—maybe not my heart. I was frightened." I looked at his face, much less pale and ghostly now in the firelight but still guarded. "Can I speak to you in all honesty? I know maybe you could laugh at some of what I have to say, but I'm asking you not to. I need to speak with honor, and that means the whole truth."

For the first time, he looked me in the eye. "Speak the truth, then. I don't feel much like laughing."

I didn't allow myself to look down at my feet or off over his shoulder. "I've answered you no twice. This time I say yes. I want us to marry."

For a moment it seemed that the cracking of the dying embers had stopped. The hum of traffic from the highway vanished as if cars had been outlawed.

Shem said softly, "But I haven't asked you a third time. And I'm not going to. So how can you answer when I'm not going to ask?"

It was meant to hurt, and it did. I closed my eyes, drawing a breath. "I didn't expect you would. I'm asking you."

"Why would you do that?"

I opened my eyes and wished I hadn't. The hard look in Shem's face made me feel shriveled and ugly as a grasshopper. I had to force myself to continue talking.

"I told you I've found my mother. I wanted her to be Zara's guardian, so I could get Zara out of the Gorgios' hands. You knew that. But she can't. She's so ill that she can't possibly take custody of a child. Like I told Anchara, I've got no other family who can take her place. And in the Gorgios' eyes I won't be of age for two more years. Unless . . ." It became actually painful to force myself to look at Shem. "Unless I marry.

"That would make me legally competent to be Zara's guardian, regardless of my age," I rushed on. The words were Roman Stanno's. When he had spoken them today, they had given me hope. Now I could hear how flimsy they sounded. Just another rule. Nothing to do with people's lives or feelings. Just a loophole I was asking Shem to help me take advantage of.

Shem's eyes shifted away from mine. I watched him pick up a chestnut and begin tossing it in the air. He fixed his eyes upon its glossy shape as it rose and fell. Even in the glow of the fire, there was a coldness in his face that was like stone.

"Is that all you have to tell me, Serena? Just that you've found your side of the bargain?"

He never took his eyes off the chestnut. His voice held the businesslike tone I had heard when last we parted. A merchant setting up a scale to weigh out advantage and disadvantage.

I hated it.

"No," I said, in a small voice.

I wished with all my heart I could say something that would make Shem more like the boy I'd gotten to know in the last weeks as we traveled together. Less like a merchant weighing the value of the goods on offer. But that would mean dodging what I had to tell him. And even to warm him to me again, I would not do that.

"That's not all. I tell you true, just as I did before: I don't want to be a Yulang wife." It was hard, but it was the truth and I had to say it. "I don't want to rise at dawn to scrub your shirts, or bear a child every year. I don't want to forget I can read and write. If we marry, I'll work as hard as I do in my own family, but I won't live to serve you." He was listening. Weighing. In my mind's eye, I could see my side of the scale rising, and its value sinking, as I took one thing after another off of it.

"Today I met Roman Stanno," I continued. "I'm going be his apprentice. And someday a Yulang advocate in my own right." It sounded so impressive, it made my head spin.

Shem caught the chestnut with a smack in his palm. "Roman Stanno? Is that true?"

I sat up straighter. "Yes."

He inclined his head, the way I'd seen him do at the market, when he was offered a good price for an amethyst. I'd impressed him. But his look also reminded me of the way the old bora chan of the Parias had looked at me when I translated the petition. It was a look that said I was irreparably foreign. A different sort of being. I did not want to see that look from Shem, of all people.

My voice wavered. "If I can do all that and you still think I can be a good wife, I'll marry you."

Shem looked at me, considering. "You really are Kereskedo, aren't you, Serena? I wouldn't have expected it. You've worked out your side of the bargain admirably. But I can't negotiate until you give me all the bargaining points. Do I have them now?"

I could have said yes.

It would have been easier. We were talking business. Perhaps I'd claimed too much for myself in promising to tell the whole truth. All I needed was to make a deal.

But at the thought of the word "deal," something in my heart cracked.

I remembered Daddy telling me to act with honor. And I knew I couldn't just make this bargain and live my life as if that were all there was to it.

To speak all that I felt was like putting my foot on live coals. I would almost rather die than tell Shem the truth, even if truth was what he claimed he valued above all else. But I had to say it, or the deal would be intolerable.

"There's something more." I squared my shoulders. "I need you to marry me or else I can't get Zara. And my heart will break if I can't have her back. But . . ." My throat was dry. I didn't know if the words would consent to leave my mouth.

When they did, they came out weakened, as by a long trudge through the desert. "But I can't marry you just to settle that. I can't marry you at all unless you feel the same way about me that I do about you."

Now my eyes were on the ground. And if my whole body could have followed them into the earth, I would have been very happy.

"But that's a different sort of bargain, Jalla."

My heart sank to still hear him using Kereskedo trade language. But I thought that there was a different note in his voice. Pity? I stiffened my back and waited.

"We are to feel the same way?" Shem continued. "Is that your plan?" I glanced up at him. He leaned back against the trunk of the tree, drawing his legs up against his chest.

"Yes," I whispered miserably.

"And how is that?"

I shook my head and buried my face in my arms. The words were, finally, really gone.

Shem bent forward and tried to peer under my arms, where I'd hidden my face.

"Then you must feel what I feel," he pursued. "Is that possible?" To my surprise, he sounded as if he was about to crack a joke.

"Probably not." I could see disappointment rising like the fixed constellations over my head. Well, I told myself, I would just have to face it. Hope is what turns us into cowards. Not acceptance. I put my arms to my side and raised my eyes to him again.

To my surprise, he was almost smiling. There was a young look about him again. Well, why not, if he was just going to start making jokes?

"For you to feel as I do," he said, "you'd have to think I was the bravest man you'd ever met."

"What?"

"It's a stretch," he conceded.

"Then why do you say it?"

"Because I can swear that you're the bravest girl." He paused, and I realized he wasn't joking at all. "I wish you could feel the same thing about me. You'd also have to think I could do anything I set my hand to." He gave a rueful smile. "And we both know that isn't so . . ."

"And hardly matters!"

"You'd have to think you never knew what to expect on any given day we spend together . . ."

"That's true enough." I almost laughed.

"And good or bad, you'd have to crave that time above time spent with anyone else."

Prickles ran up my arms. I heard those last words with the wonder that only a phrase of Lemon's music had ever brought to me before.

He'd got up from the ground and come to sit down beside me on the rough plank. "And you'd have to feel you'd lose the sight in your right eye and the power in your right hand rather than see me walk away. Can you say that, Serena? Otherwise you don't feel as I do, and the deal is off."

I could feel the rough tweed of his jacket through my sweater, we were sitting so close. I turned to him.

The way he was looking at me brought a lump to my throat.

"Yes," I whispered. "That's exactly how I feel about you."

"Then there's still a token on the wrong side of the transaction." Shem reached into his jacket pocket and pulled out my golden neck-lace. I held out my hand, but he shook his head.

"Let me fasten it on."

He lifted my hair and reached the two ends of the chain about my neck. I could hear the click of the clasp falling into place and the whis-per of his breath in my ear. Then I lifted my face. His skin was warm on my cheek. And the kiss that joined us flooded through me like red wine rushing through clear water, changing it forever.

Then we parted, looking at each other as if only now, for the first time, really seeing.

Shem reached out a finger and touched the necklace, and just the touch of his finger was enough to make the current rush through me again. He held one charm after another between his thumb and forefinger.

"I asked you before which of these you would give me, Serena."

"You'll see," I said, "when they draw the circle for us." And the words, for once, had no shame in them.

Sister, oh, sister, give me your hand,
And I'll make you the lady of all my land.

—Gorgio ballad

Roman Stanno and Mother were our witnesses the next morning as a Gorgio judge bound us in the ways of the law as husband and wife.

The wedding was a quick, formal thing. So quick, it seemed impossible that it really changed anything. We stood at the judge's bench in a stuffy, closed-in office and gave each other all we had in the world, and promised to stand always at each other's side. The words had little substance in their bare Gorgio formality. We had no rings. There was no crown for the bride, no procession of violinists, no path of flowers or cups of wine.

But there was Shem's hand strong and warm in mine.

We left the court with nothing but a state certificate of marriage clutched in my hand. Flimsy as this paper was, I knew its words could be strong as a fist in Zara's cause.

As for our real marriage, Shem and I had agreed we would only be truly wed after a proper Yulang betrothal and wedding ceremony. Until then, we were married in name only.

And we had so much to accomplish before there would be leisure even for the betrothal.

We left for the coast immediately. As we journeyed back to Oestia, I didn't know whether I felt relieved or frustrated by this delay. My heart rolled in seasick ways when Shem's hand brushed my back or I laughingly tangled my fingers in his hair. I'd thought we knew each other, but now it felt as if we had only begun to. It was unnerving. Every shift in my feelings was suddenly so transparent and exposed that I hardly knew if I was deliriously happy or utterly miserable.

It was almost a relief to set myself to the task at hand.

I traveled with my mother, and Shem drove his caravan (somewhat more carefully than before), with Rochelle and Lemon in the back, while Mr. Bardoff followed in his ancient sedan. They had business in Oestia, as well.

We happened upon a Kereskedo camp in the foothills outside the city and were invited to stay, with the Bardoffs and Rochelle as our guests. It was a lucky encounter, since some women in the clan had known Mother from youth. I felt less worried about her, knowing she was with them during the long days that followed.

Once we were settled, Lemon and her father went into Oestia to buy wood and catgut and other supplies from the specialty dealers around Plaza Ridizio. With these materials, they could fill the orders that had been placed at the harvest market, and return to Eurus to deliver the instruments they would carve in Shem's caravan.

It still amazed me: nothing but a workbench in a Yulang caravan for the family who had run the finest music store in Oestia! For what? For the sin of being Jersain? But in my friends' determination, I could see how the Jersain had survived so many centuries in the Gorgios' empire: by working hard, bargaining shrewdly, and being too hard-bitten to give in to despair.

Shem, meanwhile, had a sea of work to wade through, breaking into the jealous enclaves of the Kereskedo traders. I wasn't sure he realized how difficult this would be for an outsider. For one thing, he would have to earn Nico Brassi's acknowledgment that he was worthy to enter the tribe, our Gorgio marriage license notwithstanding. Winning over

Brassi seemed more of an obstacle to me every time I thought of it—given their last encounter. But Shem seemed confident and cheerful—elated, even. And when I put aside the wild card of Brassi's ill temper, I began to feel confident for him, too. I had no doubt that he would succeed if given half a chance.

As for myself, I was not so sure. Success would mean more than merely getting Zara back—and even that had yet to be accomplished.

I'd had much time to think it over while we traveled homeward and I knew the first thing I had to do was find Willow.

I had a job convincing Mother to wait at our camp when I went into Oestia to seek Willow. But I had to. The White Shirts had driven many of the Parias from our old neighborhood. I couldn't risk taking Mother with me and discovering that Willow was no longer there. The comforting routines of her old traveling life had already done her good, but I knew she still wasn't strong enough for disappointment.

I caught a bus into the city, since not even my mother's worthless car would be safe against the theft in our neighborhood. As I watched the city flow by the windows, I was stunned by how homesick I felt. The wrought-iron balconies, the brass lettering on the shop windows, even the pots of dahlias that people placed outside their doorways, braving the November chill, filled me with longing for my city. Everything looked comfortingly normal in the Gorgio neighborhoods, around Plaza Ridizio, and even out on the long boulevards by the Kereskedo enclave.

But it all changed as we traveled farther south and reached the Paria quarter.

The neighborhood was far worse than when I'd left.

Then, I'd fretted about one painted trident on the ball court. Now I saw smashed windows patched with cardboard, gladiator symbols daubed on apartment buildings, and graffiti everywhere, saying things like YULANG OUT! and THIS NEIGHBORHOOD HAS BEEN RECLAIMED. Shops had been looted and the remaining merchandise left behind by the fleeing owners. Up and down the streets, I saw families loading their possessions on the tops of cars and into the backs of trucks.

The wind was rising, blowing a black storm front across the city. I shivered as I climbed the stairs to the old apartment, gathering Mother's plaid shawl around my shoulders (I had returned Rass's jacket when we left Eurus). It was only just past noon, but the sky was darkening fast, and the darkness added to my apprehension as I stopped in front of Willow's door. Thick gray paint—maybe auto paint—was slashed across it at eye level. I could see that it was meant to cover a scribble of graffiti. But the marks shimmered through here and there, indecipherable but visible, like a white scar that never quite leaves the skin even after a wound has healed. My mouth went dry as I stared at it.

The White Shirts had been at my sister's door.

I thought of the boy in the orchard: many like him had marched through these streets. Were they armed, as he had been? Drunk and reeling with the pleasure of their hate, as he was?

I looked down at the narrow streets below and imagined them jammed with angry, twisted faces, clenched fists, and marching feet. I remembered the pounding of my heart and the cold terror as the boy had turned his eyes upon me....

I turned and knocked on the door. Nothing but this flimsy plank of wood had stood between the White Shirts and Willow! I could see scuff marks where their feet had kicked and their fists had hammered.

Did they enter this place? Was Willow here when they did?

In a sweat, I pounded my fist against the door and called my sister's name.

No answer.

My mind raced. If she wasn't here, how would I find her? Would she be with Alex? Would he have protected her if the White Shirts had tried to harm her? And if he had, where did he live? How could I reach him? In a panic I realized that I couldn't remember his family name. If Willow was with him, I wouldn't be able to find her.

On the other hand, what if she had fled the city? Would the tidings tell us her whereabouts, or was she too far out of the Yulang family to warrant travelers' tidings?

I kept knocking, but my imagination had taken my reason hostage, and I was convinced that Willow was gone. More lost to me than even Zara. Why hadn't I spared my sister more thought as I traveled? Why hadn't I come back to check on her? There was no excuse—especially after Lemon had told me what happened!

I pressed my forehead to the door and screamed, "Willow!" at the top of my lungs.

Then, to my unutterable relief, I heard steps approaching.

My mouth was too dry to call out my sister's name a second time. I just prayed it would be she who answered the door, and not a stranger.

"Who's there?"

It was Willow's voice.

"Me," I croaked. I was as much as I could manage.

I don't think she heard over the sound of the locks she was turning and latches she was pulling. I let out a hysterical giggle. Locks—finally, she'd had more locks put on the door! So this was what it had taken to finally make Willow more careful! A full-blown riot!

"Alex?" she was saying. "You're early!"

The door opened a crack and I saw that a strong chain secured it inside.

"I didn't like that fishbone china of your mother's." Willow continued to chatter. I could see a sliver of her face in the thin opening, could hear her undoing the chain.

Then she looked up and saw me.

Silence.

For a moment the door stood motionless. Then the chain juddered as if Willow was fighting with it. I heard it drop and she flung the door wide.

My sister stood before me like a sleepwalker startled awake. Her deep blue eyes were wide and her jaw slack. I stared back, at as much of a loss as she.

Then, with a fierce lunge, she grabbed me by the wrist and pulled me into the apartment.

In an instant I saw that everything had changed. The diaper boxes, beer bottles, and overflowing garbage bags were gone. So was our rattle-heeled furniture. Tidy packing crates rose against the walls, next to smaller boxes wrapped in paper of silver and gold. There was a huge bouquet of cut flowers in a vase on the table.

I looked back from all this order and loveliness to my sister, standing unsteadily before me, wan and . . . unaccountably frightened.

"Willow," I ventured, "I'm back. Aren't you glad to see me?"

To my surprise, Willow's eyes filled with tears. Her shoulders began to shake and she buried her face in her hands.

Gingerly, I put my arms about her. She probably blamed me for what had happened, I thought. The last she'd heard, I had ratted on her to Janet Palmer. What else I had brought upon her, I couldn't imagine.

It struck me for the first time that perhaps she didn't want to see me.

"Oh, Willow! What's wrong?"

She said nothing but pressed her wet face against my shoulder.

"Whatever I've done, Willow, I'm sorry. You're not angry, are you?"

My sister raised her face. "Angry? I'm not angry."

"Then why are you so upset?"

Willow looked at me as if I were crazy or stupid, or both. "I thought you were dead, Serena!" she cried.

"Dead?" I put my hands gently on her cheeks and smiled into her face. "Can't you see that I'm not?"

She nodded tremulously. "But Mrs. Palmer said you'd be arrested when they caught you. And when I went to the police, they wouldn't tell me anything. Alex said you must be hiding somewhere. So I tried to find you. I even went to Grandmother's—"

"To *Grandmother's?*"

Willow's mouth tightened. "You can guess what she said. Then the White Shirts started streaming into the city. They found some girls on the street, some Yulang girls, and they—" She shivered violently and began weeping again.

"But not me, Willow," I said firmly. "The White Shirts didn't find me. I wasn't living on the streets or hiding in the city. I haven't even been on the coast! Though I can tell you for sure, I feel like I've been to the land of the dead and back."

Willow took a very white handkerchief out of the pocket of her dress—a modest green frock, as demure as the little pearl studs in her ears—and dabbed at the skin under her eyes. She drew a shaky breath and managed a ghost of a smile.

"Well, thank God for that."

"But, Willow—did the White Shirts find *you?* When they came through the neighborhood?"

Willow looked at me steadily a moment. "No," she said.

I'd thought not. She didn't have the look of someone who had been attacked or tormented. But it was a huge relief to hear it from her own lips.

"They were gathering for a whole day before the marches began," Willow continued. "People were hiding in their houses, afraid to go out on the streets. It was ridiculous how easy it was for me; I just put on my best clothes and walked by a gang of them who were hanging out on the corner. I made my way to the bus line and then out to Alex's place by the lake. I—" She glanced at me. "I walked right by them. They didn't say a thing. They must have thought I was some Gorgio lady who was down here to—I don't know. Visit a fortuneteller or pawn a watch or something." She looked away from whatever she thought she saw in my eyes. "I *know* other people weren't so lucky, Serena. I know it's only because I can pass. You don't have to tell me."

"I wasn't going to," I said, though of course she had read my thoughts. "I'm just so happy you're safe."

Willow looked harder at me. "I thought of you, Serena. When I was walking past them. I thought about how you would never have made it past that mob."

"Don't think about it," I said firmly. "I wasn't here. And I'm doubly lucky, because I've come back to bring you good news."

"What?"

This was the moment I'd looked forward to. I threw my arms wide, as if the news was too big for me to contain. "I've found Mother."

To my dismay, Willow's face went cold and comfortless as the November rain.

"You know, then," she said flatly.

"Know what, Willow?"

"That she gave us up. Of her own free will. That was the only thing I've ever done for you, Serena. Kept you from knowing what Mother did. And as usual, I didn't succeed," she added bitterly.

I blinked. "What do you know about Mother?"

"Everything, I guess. I heard her fighting with Grandmother the night she left. It scared me, so I sneaked down and watched from the stairway. Mother wasn't making much sense—by the time I saw her, she was mostly crying. But I'll tell you what I *did* see, Serena. I saw Grandmother give her a wad of cash. And once she had it, Mother didn't fight anymore. She didn't argue. She just pocketed the money and she was on her way." Willow frowned and reached out for my hand. "You were so miserable once she'd gone! Many's the time I wanted to tell you not to waste your tears on her. But I never did. I thought it would be worse if you knew."

I just stared.

All Willow's silliness, her daydreams, her self-deception. But underneath it was this secret she'd kept from me. Willow had been protecting me. After all those years when I'd felt I was the caretaker, the one shouldering the burdens . . .

"It wasn't like that, Willow," I said softly.

Willow sneered. "That's what she says now, is it?"

She sank down onto the carpet, resting her back against the wall. Above her head, I could make out the faint outline of the coffee stain I'd left when I'd broken Mother's cup.

I sat down beside her. "Believe me. It wasn't what you thought. She was ill—*is* ill." I looked at Willow's hard face. "Mother didn't think she had a choice, Willow. You have to forgive her."

But Willow only gave her most irritating tinkling laugh and said carelessly, "Forgive her? You're right. Why not? My heart should be light as a feather, and with you returned, to help me plan my wedding." She flashed her left hand under my chin so that a big chunk of diamond tossed its glare in my eyes. "Did I mention we're getting married soon? Alex thinks the sooner I'm out of this dump, the better."

"I mean really forgive, Willow."

"Why should I?" my sister snapped. "*I* had no choice when Zara was taken from me! But Mother did. She threw us away. I *never* would have done that." She choked on the words and went back to turning her hand this way and that, catching the ring in different lights. "Isn't it . . . beautiful?" she asked, in a jerky voice.

I leaned over and caught my sister in my arms—surprising the life out of her, I'll be bound—and hugged her with all the strength I had. And not for the great good fortune of her Gorgio marriage or her heavy ring. But for pity. For love and pity.

"I've come to get Zara back," I whispered.

"Don't you think I've tried, Serena?" She shot an angry look at me. "It can't be done!"

"Of course it can. All losses can be redeemed. That's the Kereskedo code." Who had told me that? Shem. I dropped my eyes to hide the sudden pleasure in my face.

Willow twisted out of my arms. "Oh? And what have the Kereskedo ever done for me, I'd like to know? I've been to the Gorgios' courthouse, Serena. I even went to their orphanages—no one was allowed to tell me where she was!" She turned her head away from me, muffling her words. "They treated me like a criminal."

"Did Alex go with you?" I reached out and took my sister's hand in mine. "They might have been more understanding if you'd gone with a Gorgio."

Willow's voice was faint. "I—I—don't think he wanted to."

The thought that went through my mind never passed my lips.

"*I* want to," I said. "I want to bring Zara back from wherever they've got her, Willow. I can do it, too."

Willow's fingers tightened around mine. "You? You're in less of a position to do it than I am."

"That's not true. I know how to get her back, Willow. Believe me! But—" I held my breath a minute, unsure how to say what I needed to say.

Outside, needles of rain began to slash the windows, darkening the room around us. I let out my breath and continued, "But I would need to take care of her, Willow, from now on. Me and—" I caught myself. I wouldn't tell her about Shem. That was my private joy and I couldn't throw it in her face. Not now, when I had just asked her to give up her daughter.

"Will you let me do this?" I asked softly. "Will it be all right with you for me to become her guardian? If I can get her back?"

Willow turned to me. Lightning flashed into the room and lit her face with painful clarity. My sister looked to me as if she might shatter in a breath of wind.

In the gloom that followed, she drew herself upright and lifted her chin. She held up her hand, which was heavy with the weight of her diamond.

"If you can do this, Serena, I would give you this ring from my finger and half of all I possess."

"Don't be silly," I said automatically. And then, in sheer affection and relief: "You always were silly, Willow."

I would take thee in my arms,
And I'd secure thee from all harms,
So dearly do I love thee.
—Kereskedo lullaby

The courthouse for the Cruelty cases was built of obsidian. In the mountains, I'd seen jagged floes of that volcanic rock catch the sun and shimmer like dark diamonds. But as I walked down the hilly streets toward the court, the obsidian walls rose flat and forbidding before me, a cliff of sheer black glass.

Once through the door and past the security guards, I wandered down glaring corridors. Dust motes sizzled under fluorescent lights, and old plastic benches lined the walls. Whole families clustered around them, Yulang mostly, but shabby-looking Gorgios as well. They argued among themselves, trying to understand the Romanae law forms some member of the family was invariably struggling—and generally failing—to translate. I saw one man give up and cram his form into a trash bin, yelling at his wife that if she was so smart, she should read it herself.

After a few dead ends, I found the Appeals section of the court I'd been seeking and managed to locate the forms I had to fill out. I settled down on an empty square of floor (it was too crowded to find a seat) and read rapidly through the arcane Romanae script. When I'd read it and written my information in the blank spaces, I glanced furtively at the others, feeling as Willow must have when she walked by the White Shirts without being harassed—incredibly lucky and undeservedly so. Besides the fact that I could read the forms and fill them out in good

Romanae in a matter of minutes, I also had the advantage of Stanno's coaching. He'd told me not only what to say but also how to say it.

I folded the papers and placed them inside the petition that Stanno had drawn up for me, which now had Shem's signature on it as well. Then I got up and stood in line to turn it all in to the clerk, feeling somewhat smug and altogether relieved that I'd done exactly what I was supposed to do.

It took me about fifteen minutes to realize that none of that mattered.

The long marble counter I approached wasn't the place to turn in the form after all. Nor was the room on the eighth floor where I was sent next. Nor the window outside the judge's chambers on the second floor.

When I finally got a noncommittal acknowledgment from a clerk on the fifth floor that she did accept forms like mine, she said I couldn't turn it in until my identification and my marriage license had been stamped by a validator. The validators worked in an office across town.

Once I found *them* and showed them my papers, they told me they needed confirmation from the court in Eurus Major that the marriage license was legal. I half desperately offered to bring Shem in to vouch for me, only to be told his word had no merit.

"He could be anybody," the shriveled old clerk pointed out, peering at me through rheumy eyes.

"No, he couldn't!" I muttered rebelliously, but under my breath.

I wasn't going to let my temper get me in trouble. Not at this stage of the game ...

Meekly, I waited for the clerk to put a call through to Eurus. And sat there through his lunch break. And on into late afternoon, waiting for him to get a response.

When the call finally came and my papers were stamped, I went back to the courthouse.

And there I stood in lines. Again.

I gave identification when I was asked for it, explained my business to no fewer than eight different clerks ("Get to the point, girlie! Don't you see all those people behind you?"). I waited, with or without a number, with or without a seat, and with or without any idea of what I was waiting for, for the rest of that day.

When I looked at the clock and saw that all the minutes of my day had been eaten away like this and crumbled into useless bits, I nearly cried with vexation.

Timidly, I approached the nearest clerk's counter.

"When do you think I'll be able to get an answer?" I asked him. "I've been waiting a long time—"

"You and every Yulang with a dirty rag to chew," he grumbled. "What makes you think you're special?"

My triumphal day at court ended with him slamming the plastic window in my face as the five o'clock buzzer sounded.

That evening I arrived at our home fire miserable and no closer to my goal than I'd been at the start of the day. Frustration and anger hung like a mist before my eyes.

"You've brought the storm clouds with you, Serena-lo!" Lemon exclaimed.

Wordlessly, I accepted a bowl of stew from Mother and ate it moodily. The others talked and joked among themselves, and finally drew the story of the day out of me.

"He slammed his window on you?"

"A bad man!" Rochelle crowed. "I'll hit him with my slingshot!" And she demonstrated with the slingshot Shem had made her while the meal had been cooking.

"But what did you do, Serena?" Ren Bardoff asked reasonably.

I thought a minute. What had I done?

"Nothing," I growled.

"Nothing?" Shem stared at me.

"No. What could I do? You have to wait in lines, and fill out papers—"

"Is that so?" He laid his palm across my forehead. "You must be feverish, Jalla."

"Feverish? I'm fine!"

"No. You must be burning up from fever. That's the only explanation. You're not yourself. Anyone can see that."

"I'm *fine,* Shem! What are you going on about?"

"Only that I would give my best pair of boots to see you sitting meek and quiet in any Gorgio waiting room just because some office clerk tells you to! *My* Serena would never be so biddable. There's only one explanation: you're bit with a bug."

"Oh, for goodness' sake!" I stomped away.

But I kept his words in my mind.

The next day when I was told to sit, I stood.

I hovered by the clerks' windows when they tried to dismiss me. I waved my petition under people's noses. I read the Romanae out loud to them and showed them Stanno's signature as my witness. I shoved my marriage license under their noses and pointed at the validator's stamp. I had a journalist friend writing a story about my case, I fibbed. A Gorgio.

"A Gorgio writing about you in the paper, Jalla?" people in the waiting room exclaimed. "What's he writing about?"

"About this court. How it takes children without warrant and sells them to adoption agencies."

"You!" The clerk waved urgently, summoning me to his desk. "Come on. It's your turn. Stop riling people up out there."

"Wait! We want to hear what the girl has to say!"

"Yeah? You'll have to wait. She's coming to the front of the line."

Suddenly, I was being sent from desk to desk as fast as I'd ever wanted. And yet, I think if I hadn't spoken such good Romanae and used Stanno's name so liberally, they would never have believed me enough to worry about what I was saying. They would have kicked me out.

As it was, the clerks looked at me nervously from behind their smudged windows and called in their managers. They twittered together. A few still tried to bully me.

But the upshot was that by noon that day, my petition was received.

And now, as Stanno had promised, the Gorgios had forty-eight hours to release Zara into my custody. They had acknowledged that I was married—at least in their eyes—and therefore legally competent.

And Zara . . .

She had never left the orphanage, I discovered. No Gorgio family had claimed her.

The "facility"—as the clerks called it—was in an industrial suburb north of the city. I drove up streets the wrong way, made U-turns, and ran red lights in my anxiety to get there as fast as possible.

The building was hidden away behind a foul-smelling lumber mill, and I passed it twice before I realized what it was. No sign identified the faceless, slate-colored structure. The parking lot was not even a quarter full. An empty information desk was all that confronted me when I marched through the door. I spun around in confusion, peering down the ill-lit corridors branching off from the reception area. Could the people at the courthouse have made a mistake? Nothing here indicated that this was a place full of children—no bright pictures on the walls, no babble of voices, no candies or toys. And as far as I could see, there were no adults running the place, either, despite the cars in the lot. Perhaps the clerks had sent me to the wrong place.

But just then a janitor rattled by, pushing a cart loaded with big trash bins emitting the unmistakable smell of dirty diapers. She headed down one of the hallways and pushed through a steel door. Children's voices, cheeping like baby birds, rushed into the corridor. Then the door swung shut again, cutting them off.

I shivered. The children were locked away behind steel doors. That was why the building felt so derelict. There was no life here: no color or sound. It was like a jail. Or a hospital? The horrible thought occurred to me: perhaps the children here weren't just orphans, or "wards of the state," but were actually ill!

"Yes? Can I help you?" A querulous voice spoke at my shoulder. I turned to encounter an old man who looked as if he'd just been exhumed from a sarcophagus. His skin was warty and wrinkled as a toad's. He clasped a clipboard to his caved-in chest.

"I—I need to talk to someone in charge."

"I'm the supervisor here. Who are you?"

"Oh." I wet my dry lips. "I've come for my niece. She's—"

"Who *are* you?"

"I'm Zara Wallace's aunt. The—the Protective Services told me I could take her home."

"Papers!" he snapped.

I had to produce every single document I had acquired at the courthouse before the desiccated old man would even consult the list on his clipboard to check if Zara was in the building.

She was.

I nearly knocked over a linen cart as I ran in the direction he pointed. I tripped over my own feet and fell—but jumped up in such a rush that I scarcely felt my knees hit the ground. WARD ONE— NEWBORNS, WARD TWO—OLDER BABIES.

Drawing a deep breath, I pushed through the door marked WARD THREE—TODDLERS and entered a big grayish dormitory. My eyes roved over tangles of wild, unsupervised children who were shrieking and howling, running up and down rows of narrow steel cribs, shaking the bars and banging them with spoons. I saw a girl wielding an adult-sized pair of scissors and snapping at another girl's hair while that girl screamed and swatted at her. A boy was floating bits of paper in a pool of spilled juice. Another very little boy was sitting on the floor crying while other children swirled around him, unnoticing. Still others sat blankly, pulling on hangnails or chewing their hair. Where was Zara in this crowd? My eyes darted from one side of the room to the other.

And then I found her.

The first glimpse nearly tore my heart from my chest. My wild, happy little niece was sitting in the shadows on the far side of the room, staring blankly at the wall.

Her loose blond curls hung over her shoulders, dull and sticky, in a rat's nest of tangles. She wore the sleeper she'd had on the night they'd taken her. It was unbelievably grimy and stained. She didn't turn to look as the door clanged shut behind me. None of the children—and neither of the women who seemed to be in charge of this vast, cheerless nursery—paid her the slightest heed.

Tears gathered in my throat as I gazed at her. I began to make my way to her, past the strangely quiet toddlers lying in their cribs and the knots of howling children. Over by the window, I saw a uniformed girl mechanically changing diapers. The children under her hands lay in stony silence.

Zara had put her feet up on the wall and was banging her heels against it—one-two, one-two, one-two—and making a noise low in her throat like a dog that would growl if it dared.

A woman in a nurse's outfit was making the rounds, shoving pills into children's mouths.

"Stop that banging!" she ordered Zara sharply. "Turn around! It's time for your vitamin!"

Zara paused with one foot in the air and then pounded it down defiantly. One-two, one-two!

I watched her with pride in my heart.

The nurse snatched her arm and yanked her to her feet.

"No!" Zara shouted. "Nonononononononononono!"

"Is that so?" The nurse grabbed her jaw and wrenched it open.

"Get your hands off her!" I shouted, running to Zara's side. "She's in my custody now. If you touch her again, I'll have you up on assault."

The woman glared at me from beneath her white headdress, but she released Zara. "You and who else?"

"Just me. That will be enough." The blood was pounding in my ears, but I kept my voice level.

"Who let you in, Magpie?"

"The court did. And your supervisor."

"Really? And who are you?"

I could see Zara rubbing her jaw and looking at me in alarm.

I swallowed hard and shoved my anger down inside me. Keep it under control, I reminded myself. Don't give this stupid nurse a reason to hold on to her.

"Serena Wall— Serena Vadesh. This girl is my niece. I have legal authority to take her out of your custody."

"Where's your authorization?"

I dug the forms out of my pocket and handed them to her. The nurse examined them intently, holding them up to the thin light coming through the window and moving her lips as she read. I ground my teeth, knowing that she was enjoying this little tiny nugget of power— the power to make me wait as long as she chose.

She took so long over the document that it was in me to ask if she needed help with any of the big words. But I glanced down at Zara's frightened eyes and held my tongue.

It must have been a good ten minutes before the nurse finally handed the papers back to me with a sniff. Without a word, she turned on her heel and stamped away.

I stuffed the papers back in my pocket and knelt beside Zara.

She had turned her face back to the wall, but I leaned forward far enough to see her lovely profile. She was thinner. With a pang, I saw Willow's birdlike fragility in her. Had she grown and lost the baby fat? Or had they filled her up with vitamins and pills and neglected to feed her?

I wanted to pull her into my arms and run out of this baby jail as fast as I could. But that would have frightened her.

"Zara, love." I reached out a finger and gently brushed her arm.

She jerked away.

"It's Reena," I said. "Auntie Reena. I've come to take you home."

Zara's head twitched, but still she didn't turn to me. Hope was too cruel. I knew that. And now so did she.

I didn't touch her again but kept up a gentle flow of talk until she raised her lowered lids and looked me in the face.

Recognition flooded her sky blue eyes. It was not, as I had half feared, that she had forgotten me, for children so young can forget. It was more that, like Mother, she had not allowed herself to believe I was real.

After a minute, she prodded me with her finger. Then, bolder, she stroked my arms and my rumpled hair. She peered into my face. She even pinched my shoulder, testing my reality in the most direct way possible. I submitted to this, keeping as still as I could.

At last, she stood up beside me and fished in my collar for the necklace that Shem had fastened around my neck only a few nights before. I nearly cried with relief when she finally spoke to me.

"Cat," she said.

I felt her twist the small charm in her fingers.

"That's your favorite, isn't it, sweetheart?"

Instead of answering, Zara burst into sobs that shook her from head to toe.

Swiftly, I gathered her into my arms and carried her to the door.

The nurse was standing there waiting, probably to make sure I didn't kidnap a few extra babies as I left. I wished by Mother Lillith I could have!

She gave me a sour look. "That child wasn't a bit of trouble until you came. Never made a peep."

"You made damn sure of that, didn't you?"

"Modern tranquilizers are a wonderful thing," she answered sweetly.

I had to stop myself from smashing the cruel smile right off her face.

I told myself that one sadistic nurse wasn't the reason the Gorgios thought it was fine to dope up children with drugs, provided they had the misfortune of being born Yulang. This stupid woman wasn't the root of the problem. I reminded myself that it was the root we had to yank out of the dirt. And one good smack was not going to do that.

Tempting though it was.

Instead, I marched Zara out of the dormitory, down the long, dim corridor, and out into the fresh November day, where snatches of blue sky glowed between the clouds.

Zara clung to me as if she would never let go. I had to drive with her wrapped around me, like a backpack wrong way round.

Her hair was jumping with lice, and she smelled of some sickening juice that stained the whole front of her sleeper.

Even so, when I stopped at traffic lights, I could still catch the faint whiff of innocence coming off the crown of her head.

I was still carrying her as we approached our family's fire at the Kereskedo camp in the foothills. Rochelle ran forward, all eyes, eager for a look at her new playmate. I settled myself gently by the fire, never letting go of my little burden. Zara twisted in my lap and hid her face against my neck, too shy or frightened to respond to Rochelle's questions.

Lemon and her father came out of the caravan, where they had been busy carving, and Shem pushed aside the box of merchandise he'd dragged back from a wholesale market the day before. Quietly, they all drew near. No one spoke, but Shem bent down and softly kissed my ear.

For some reason, this made me want to cry more than anything.

Mother put down a long swath of fabric she'd been sewing and came over to kneel beside me. She fixed her eyes on Zara like someone who'd stumbled upon a golden fawn in a forest, fearful of startling it, determined to hold the sight in her eyes as long as possible.

I understood her feeling perfectly. I wanted to memorize every line of Zara's body, every shadow on her face, as if it were the only way to hold her fast in the world of the living.

But hold her fast we did.

And so Zara finally joined our band.

Oh, it will not be long, love,
Till our wedding day . . .
—Zimbali song

Shem had reached his understanding with Nico Brassi.

Anchara herself had come back to Oestia to vouch for him. And at her word, I'd also been brought in to the big man's presence, and, before a tribal court, the dictate of *ma'hane* had been formally lifted.

Before we left for the Paria camp, I took Zara to Willow. It was a bittersweet visit. Willow lavished food and freshly laundered clothes on Zara, though she held herself back from any wild expressions of joy. Nor did she lament over what was past, and for this I was keenly grateful; if Willow had indulged all the emotions she must be feeling, she would have distressed Zara and made it impossible to leave. When it was time to go, Willow smiled bravely, though her hug for me was desperately tight, and her voice caught on farewell.

Zara cried a little as we walked down from Willow's apartment to the bus stop, but her tears didn't last long. I think she knew that her home was with me now.

As we rode back to the foothills, she snuggled into my arms and fell asleep, and I leaned my head against the fogged-up window, watching the silver streams of rain shudder along the glass. We would not be coming back to Oestia again soon. But I'd promised Willow that every time we did, I'd bring Zara to see her. I wished with all my heart that I could always bring her back safe and happy. And I wished that the next time we returned, Willow might consent to see Mother, as well.

We were leaving the next day to join our friends at the Paria camp, where Roman Stanno was waiting for me to take up my duties. The Bardoffs and Rochelle would travel with us, on their way to Eurus with the newly made instruments, and so we would be returning with not one but two small children. We had talked much of their safety. No one knew what would happen once Stanno's campaign got under way. I couldn't bear to separate from Zara now that I had finally found her, but I worried that my chosen life might be a dangerous one for her.

It was Willow herself, however, who'd pointed out that the city was no refuge, either, after the recent riots. Wherever we went, there was danger. Lemon and Ren Bardoff would help Mother look after the girls for a brief time while I worked with Stanno. But once they left . . . I knew Mother might still be too fragile to handle the responsibility alone. If so, then Zara would accompany me in my work—many Yu-lang children stayed with their mothers throughout the working day. Perhaps the Paria women would help. And I had it as a glimmer in my mind that if I could find any Gorgios who, like the firefighter, were willing to befriend us, they might be the best security of all.

The bus ground to a halt and I shook Zara awake to walk back to our camp.

It was near dinnertime when we arrived, and I found Shem at the wooden table outside the caravan. He turned and saw me and his face lit up.

"The travelers return," he remarked, rising and pulling me close to his side. "Help me cook the food for our crowd, will you, Serena?" He released me and swung Zara up in his arms, offering her a mint leaf to chew on. "Big supper tonight, so we can leave at dawn."

I nodded and tried to smile, though my heart was like lead.

It had only really hit me in the last few days that Shem could not wait for spring collecting season to start traveling. Unlike the established traders, he had no inventory in reserve. If he went to next year's markets with only what he could collect in the short months of the spring, there'd be little chance of his having enough to sell through the long months of marketing season.

Shem was a Kereskedo trader now. I'd helped him to become one.

And because of that, he would have to leave me.

I knew that the first season was an important one for any caravan. A lot would ride on how well Shem did in the coming year. It was only good sense for him to go off collecting. Once I was settled with the Parias, he would travel with the Bardoffs to do business in Eurus Major. And all through the winter months, he would journey inland, to the small cities and towns where he could be sure his route would not cross those of the great Kereskedo trading families—for territory was much contested among the tribe. It took years of diplomacy, and favors, and bridge building to establish shared terrain.

All through our last days outside Oestia I'd pored over maps with him, helping him plot his route. We both knew that venturing inland was not the best choice in winter, for the weather was fierce east of the mountains. But Shem insisted he didn't want to go back to the coast, because soon all the passes would close and then we would be cut off from each other.

Even so, I doubted I would see him again much before spring.

"But that's nonsense right there," he said, trying to slice a piece of garlic with a not overly sharp knife. "I'll come back as often as I can, blizzard or no. You know that, don't you?"

"All I know is that I will personally kill you, Shem Vadesh, if you drive through a blizzard to see me! You drive badly enough without snow and ice!"

"You'll personally kill me? What fine treatment one gets here! You won't hire someone else to do me in?"

But all the teasing in the world couldn't soothe my feelings. Shem was leaving me, and I couldn't bear it. Months would go by. Anything might happen. Accidents on the road. Other girls. . . . Despite the Gorgio marriage license, we weren't even betrothed, at least not by Yulang standards. Suddenly, I wondered if we ever would be.

"What's wrong, girl?"

I turned away, muttering about the onions making my eyes sting.

"That's not onions." He put down his knife and pulled me around to face him. "Serena, what is it?"

"It's just—" It was still hard for me to say all I felt. "I just wish you weren't going."

"Do you think I want to leave you, Serena?" He looked at me seriously. "Because if you think that, you're wrong. But if you're to help Stanno, you can't come trade in the city. And if I'm to trade, I can't stay in the orchards. That's part of our bargain. There will be times apart."

I shook my head, my eyes hot with threatened tears, even though I knew what he said was true.

"At least for a while, Jalla. But once this winter's trading is done—and once you and Stanno are ready to leave the orchards—then we'll be wed." He caught up my hand and softly kissed my palm. "That's what I'll think of, Serena, while I'm away. Do you agree?"

How could I not?

I blinked away my tears and tried to smile. "But, Shem, we can't be wed at all until there's a circle drawn—"

He grinned and dropped my hand. "Is that so? What strange customs your people have, Serena."

I gave him a light slap and threw him the potato I'd just pulled from the sack under the table.

We left at dawn for the Paria camp.

What with the wind and snow on the pass, it took us twice the time it had taken not a month before. It was deep in the dead of night when we arrived.

As we pulled up to the abandoned orchard that now housed the embattled Paria, I could make out a huddle of dark tents. Winter had truly set in. There was no soft springiness in the ground under my feet when I stepped out of Mother's car to go bid good night to Shem. The earth was hard as an anvil, the fire was out, and no one was awake enough to even boil a pot of tea.

All the exhaustion of the past months hit me at once when I returned to my mother's trailer that night. Mother was already dressing Zara in one of the sleepers Willow had sent with us. Usually, I told Zara and Rochelle a story before bed. But that night, I curled up on the pallet Mother had made for us on the floor and slept like a sleeper in the earth until long after the sun had risen.

When I awoke, I noticed something odd.

Mother had left the blinds shut tight in the trailer windows. That was not our custom. Whoever woke first always pulled the curtains wide. Up one, up all. That was the way of it. But Mother was nowhere to be seen. Zara, who had slept in the crook of my arm ever since I'd taken her from the orphanage, was gone as well, and Rochelle with her. Bemused, I threw on my clothes and stepped outside.

The Paria women were sitting on the ground in a half circle around the trailer door, patiently waiting.

What little gold they had was in their hair and the skirts of their finest dresses were spread around them in swirling circles of color. I stopped short. They turned their faces up to me and I stared back in bewilderment. Lal sat in the middle of them all, smiling.

She lifted her hand, and the women raised their voices together in a long ululation—the throbbing notes that buffet the birds out of the sky and begin the morning of a Yulang feast day. The ancient sound made my skin prickle, and an answering chord thrummed in my heart.

Then Lal rose, came and took my hand, and led me down into the circle of women.

That was when I realized that the feast day they were ushering in was the day of my betrothal. And it was more than shock and happiness that overwhelmed me. It was that in the midst of their trouble, they had set aside this day for us.

There was no ritual bath for Mother and Lal to take me to. But the shower stall had been decked with the last of the dried autumn roses. And when I had washed, they rubbed oil into my skin and perfume behind my ears, and Mother took her heavy golden hoops from her earlobes and stuck them through mine.

Lemon was waiting in Mother's trailer to help me dress. Even though Willow had lavished me with gifts of her old dresses when Zara and I took our leave, I knew I had nothing suitable for such an occasion.

But to my surprise and pleasure, Lemon opened Mother's trunk and lifted out a proper Kereskedo betrothal gown, long and graceful, its red and yellow silk blazing with threads of gold. At first I thought it had been Mother's. But the fabric was crisp and new. I guessed that she had sewn it in the last weeks, hidden away from my sight, while I ran about the city. Lemon insisted on helping me into it, like a lady's maid, smoothing the fabric and ordering me to turn this way and that. Zara and Rochelle sat at our feet, playing peekaboo with shawls and scarves and shrieking with laughter.

Outside, the men had drawn the circle in the ground and filled it with ash from the previous night's fire. Mother took my hand and led me to it, and the women followed us in a procession. Their song changed as they joined the men of the tribe, who came from the other side of the camp, playing zithers and strange percussive instruments that one would never hear in a Kereskedo ceremony: small, easily carried drums and bells that beat out the rhythm of a long journey.

Shem was waiting for me by the edge of the circle, looking unaccustomedly bashful in the crisp white shirt I had refused to spend my life washing. I felt shy, too, behind my long lace veil.

I stopped next to him and he lifted my veil and pushed it over my head so it fell down my back. Our eyes joined in a long look. It was a look that began in shy greeting and deepened until it filled my heart like wine. And I knew it was that look, and nothing else, that bound us in truth.

Then we took each other's hands and stepped into the circle together.

Shem still wears on a chain around his neck the golden horse I gave him there, with the Paria camp gathered round to witness. The horse that travels, as we always shall, that is noble and truthful and beyond any value in coin.

And on my hand I wear the amethyst ring Shem made for me, with a stone I wrested from the earth in a time of anger and despair. It shines on my finger, now and ever, a promise of light in a dark land.